The Beautiful Girls of Piazza Armerina

Alexander Lucie-Smith

The Catania Novels

I The Chemist of Catania
II The Nymph of Syracuse
III The Feast of the Dead
IV The Castle of the Women
V The Gravedigger of Bronte
VI The Good Boys of Sicily
VII The Peace of Palermo
VIII The Beautiful Girls of Piazza Armerina

Chapter One

Provincial Road number fifteen ran, to the left of the Antica Trattoria Norma (named after Bellini's opera, of course), up to the hilltop town of Piazza Armerina, and to the right down to the Roman villa at Casale, the finest villa the Romans had left behind them. To the left, it was a ten-minute walk home to his parents' house, to the right, not so very far to the Roman villa. The trattoria Norma was one of several places that lived off the trade that the villa attracted. You saw people drive down to the villa and drive up again, and when they slowed down and looked at the Norma, your heart fluttered a little; and when they failed to stop, one felt a stab of anger and resentment. Not that Paoluzzu, the manager, felt a great loyalty to the establishment, which was owned by don Nunzio, who had taken him on as a favour to don Calogero di Rienzi, but busy days were better than quiet days. Busy days brought trade, and that made don Nunzio, and the men he employed as accountants, happy; busy days might bring Americans who were generous tippers, or Germans who were less generous, but easy to handle; or the French, who complained about everything, and who were the worst, the most determined not to be pleased, but better than nothing.

The place was empty right now, the floor had been cleaned the tables laid, and, as it was still a few minutes to noon, the restaurant was closed, though the door was open. Paoluzzu stood by the door, surveying Provincial Road number fifteen through the glass, wondering what the day would bring. He was contemplating, as always, his dire financial situation: he had saved up quite a bit of money in Africa, and was working hard here in Piazza Armerina, but he had his parents to support, neither of whom worked, and who had moved to be with him in Piazza Armerina. His car, too, constantly haemorrhaged money; and it was not as if it were a nice car, just as the place he lived with his parents was not particularly nice either. But if his finances were bad, his sex life was non-existent. When he had come back from Africa, where he had been slaving away to save enough to get married, it was only to find that the girl he wanted to marry had changed her mind and found someone else. That someone else, to make things worse, had been his best friend. It had been a profoundly depressing experience, this sense of double betrayal. That was why he had felt he had to leave Catania, and after asking don Calogero, he had gratefully taken up the present job, far from any place where he might bump into her or to him.

This was it – Provincial Road number fifteen – this had been his view for the last six months. The sharpness of his humiliation had still not gone away. Would he be in exile forever? Would he still be looking at the same road, the same cars, and be in the same trattoria in six years' time? In twenty years' time? His heart wilted at the idea.

These thoughts were banished by the sight of a man on foot, approaching the restaurant, and not just any man: a good-looking, well-dressed man, clearly not a foreigner, wearing a perfect pair of shoes and an immaculate suit that fitted him like a second skin, a beautifully pressed shirt and a gorgeous silk tie. The man was not just arresting to look at, he had an air of command, and he approached the door. It was still not twelve, and Paoluzzu liked to remind the presumptuous who turned up early that they were not open; but before this stranger, Paoluzzu hesitated. Indeed, he did what he would normally never do: he held the door open and bade the stranger welcome, for he recognised him, having last seen him two years previously in Africa.

It was the right move. The stranger, who was no other than don Calogero di Rienzi, boss of bosses, was all charm. He smiled at Paoluzzu, and his smile brought a momentary happiness to the young man, of the sort he had not known for many a day. The waiters in the background saw this and ascribed the manager's joy to being the object of the attention of so important, so rich a man (his clothes and shoes proclaimed him such). Or perhaps it was just the prospect of a tip, a generous tip.

'Paoluzzu,' said don Calogero gently.

Paoluzzu was overjoyed that don Calogero remembered his name.

'My friend,' said don Calogero.

Paoluzzu's joy knew no bounds. He just wished there were more people present to witness it. He bent over and kissed don Calogero's hands, and felt his cheeks grow warm.

'They told me you were here,' said don Calogero, 'and I had not forgotten it, and that we got you this job. My wife and children will be joining me soon, so a table for six, please. Perhaps that one over there, in the corner, and while I am waiting, perhaps you could bring me the wine list? Actually, I will leave that to you,' he said, smiling radiantly. 'Bring me something white and, well, suitable for this time of day; then with the food, we will have a bottle of red.'

He took his seat. He had not mentioned prices, but he never needed to ask, so Paoluzzu brought the best bottle of white in the house and the best bottle of red. He explained the virtues of both, and Calogero told him to open them both. He tasted the white and made an appreciative noise, professing himself satisfied. Paoluzzu swelled with pleasure. He was pleased the important guest was pleased; he was even more pleased that he, the manager, always the first to arrive and the last to leave, had had the privilege of serving such an important man.

'Don Calogero,' he murmured. 'The pleasure of having you here in our trattoria, it is… you should have told us you were coming, we could have prepared.'

'I like to surprise my friends,' said Calogero easily. 'It is nice to see you again.' There was no mention of their last meeting, and the circumstances surrounding it, his near-death experience in the thick night of Africa. 'Don Nunzio is well?'

'The last time we saw him, very well, don Calogero,' said Paoluzzu fulsomely. 'I see a lot of him, and his immediate family, the signora, the children… Are you expecting him to join you here, sir?'

'No, this is pleasure, not business,' said Calogero with a smile. 'My three younger sons wanted to go to the Roman villa; it was Francesco's idea that we all come. You remember him, of course, don't you?'

'Yes, sir, he is a cousin of mine, in some way.'

He realised too late that this was not the right thing to say. He was related to the boss's stepson though Francesco's errant biological father, of whom the less said the better.

'I am here quietly with the family,' said Calogero. 'They are still at the villa. I came on ahead. Look, tell don Nunzio you have seen me. Ah!' he exclaimed, looking at the door.

Someone had come in. It was a rather diffident young man, who stood hesitantly by the door, looking for someone, and seeing only don Calogero, realised that this was the person he must have been looking for. He approached the table. Paoluzzu withdrew without a word. Don Calogero waited for the young man to come close, which he did, and gestured him to a seat opposite him. He poured him a glass of mineral water, and a glass of white wine, and pushed both towards him.

He remained silent, waiting for the man to start.

'Thank you, don Calogero, for agreeing to see me, and for setting up the meeting here, not in Messina,' said the man, at last.

'You found the place easily enough?' asked Calogero.

'Yes, sir, I did.'

'No one will know we are here; no one will know we have met. The people here, they won't mention it; no curious passers-by will jump to conclusions. Everyone knows who I am; but no one has any clue about you. You are safe.'

'I am terrified, sir, I admit, it,' said the man. 'I fear every moment may be my last.'

'An honest admission. When I got your message, and when I realised who you were,' said Calogero, 'I thought a meeting here, away from Messina, away from Catania, would feel more natural. If you were to turn up in the Purgatory quarter, asking for me, well, it would start tongues wagging, people thinking. Not that we talk much. My people know the value of silence. I think I know what you are going to ask, and I think it is something that requires a certain, shall we say, discretion…'

'Don Calogero, as you may know, I am the youngest son of the late don Carmelo, whom I believe you knew quite well.'

'Ah, don Carmelo. How we miss him,' said Calogero. 'May he rest in peace. How long has it been? Three years' already?'

'Three years and two months and a bit. The day he died was his birthday, 3rd August 2014. As you know, don Calogero, there were six sons and seven daughters. I am the youngest son, and don Costantino Petrović is the eldest. Both he and I are illegitimate, and don Costantino is decades older than me, born when don Carmelo was a teenager. I was born when he was forty or so. My mother… but let me not bore you. The three legitimate sons died with their father that August day.'

'I remember it,' said Calogero. 'Carry on, Mimmo.'

'I did not know them,' said Mimmo. 'Neither have I ever met don Costantino; I did think of making myself known to him, but I thought it was perhaps not a good idea. I did not want to look greedy, or to be open to misinterpretation.'

Calogero nodded.

'Who is the third surviving son?' he asked.

'He survives no longer,' said Mimmo. 'I did not know him either, so I cannot mourn him. He had a car crash, driving down from Taormina, brake failure, went over the edge. The thing is, sir, that my father was always very good to me, and I miss him. He was kind to me and my mother and my sisters. He would visit us regularly. He would sometimes ask me to drive him places in his car. When I arrived at the age of eighteen, he was generous in paying for me to go to university, here, not in America or on the continent. He was always kind, always generous. He also left me, personally, considerable assets, as he knew I would look after my mother and sisters. I have not been able to realise those assets. The will has been frozen since he died. Don Costantino stands between me and my inheritance, my family's inheritance, like a huge and menacing dog.'

Calogero looked at Mimmo. He was smooth-faced, nervous, rather slight, clearly finding it hard to get to the point.

'What is it you do, Mimmo?' he asked.

'I teach in a secondary school, sir. I teach mathematics. Just recently, sir, I met a girl and, to cut a long story short, fell in love. I know, sir, that you have sympathy for those who fall in love, as my father did. He was a great lover of women, as are you.'

'Mimmo, you pay me too great a compliment. Don Carmelo had thirteen children; I have seven, and two additional ones, if you see what I mean, though I may have more before I stop, I suppose. Who is this young lady?'

'It was a coup de foudre, sir. I am twenty-three and she is nineteen. We want to get married very soon, as soon as possible. We are connected, but when I met her, I did not realise quite who she was, and by the time I had, it was far too late. We were in love, and she was pregnant. Her name, sir, is Maria, and she is don Costantino's daughter.'

Calogero considered and took a sip of wine.

'Does he know?' he asked.

'No, sir.'

'Doesn't that make her your niece?'

'She is the daughter of my half-brother, so that makes her more like a sort of cousin, I think. But her mother is also related to me through my late father, I think Maria's mother is my cousin too. So, but as I say…'

'So, you want me to make your excuses to don Costantino and ask him to, shall we say, overlook this fault and give you his blessing? Is that it?'

'No, sir,' said Mimmo. 'That is not it at all.'

'Spell it out!' commanded don Calogero.

Mimmo took a gulp of white wine and spelt it out. Matters between don Costantino and his wife in Messina had recently taken a turn for the worse. Relations had not been good for a very long time, but what had caused the present deterioration was that don Costantino had fathered another child on his African mistress on one of his recent trips to East Africa. The signora, Anna, his wife, Maria's mother, was furious. Things were further complicated by the fact that Maria's brother, a couple of years older than her, was not, to put it simply, a good boy. He had been arrested several times for drinking and driving, for possession of drugs, for affray, and for assault. All this was most unwelcome publicity, and don Costantino considered his son to be spoilt, and had treated him accordingly. None of the paternal discipline imposed had borne fruit. The signora and Maria took the boy's side. His treatment of his son in Messina, so contrasting to the way he spoiled his family in Africa, gave the signora and her daughter, as well as her son, another cause to hate him. The latest was that don Costantino had told them that he was thinking of bringing his eldest African child, this boy called Bosco, over to Sicily, so he could be brought up here. The signora saw this move as an insult directed at her, the cousin of don Carmelo. Of course, don Costantino was rarely, if ever, at home, but when he was, the screaming and the shouting and the blows were considerable. It upset Maria. She had told him, Mimmo, that he should speak to don Calogero.

Don Calogero nodded and considered.

'Why speak to me?' he asked.

Mimmo looked confused and embarrassed for a moment. Then he screwed up his courage and spoke.

'Sir, my father's world is not my world. Don Costantino's world is not my world. But the signora, well, she knows how these things work. She told me that my half-brother, who went off the road coming down from Taormina, well, that that was no accident. I think I believe her. After all, my three legitimate half-brothers, they were certainly not accidental deaths. I am the only heir left alive apart from Costantino. I constantly look over my shoulder.'

'Oh, you are right to,' said Calogero. 'Go on.'

'Sir, when Trajan Antonescu attacked you in Africa, he spoke first to don Costantino and had his permission to do so. The signora says so.'

'And how does she know that?'

'Her husband told her. In the heat of the moment, in one of their violent quarrels. He said that Antonescu would never have made a move against you unless he had given it, the phrase used was the *nulla osta*, if he had not made it clear that he did not object.'

'Well, well, well,' said Calogero. 'The pieces all fall together at long last. Antonescu caused me much pain. I do not mean physical pain alone, though that was severe. My ankle still hurts me a great deal some days. No, there was the pain of betrayal as well. And there was also the damage to my reputation. The death of that girl and her family in the Philippines was not what I wanted. As for the death of Ginori and his wife and children, that was not what I wanted either. It set us back years. It was the work of Antonescu, clearly, but it has tarnished me, tarnished the Santucci family as well. It gave so many the chance to write about murder and violence and bring my name into it, when, as you know, I am simply a businessman.'

'The signora cannot understand why Antonescu is still alive.'

'Your future mother-in-law is quite a woman. I begin to wonder about your future married life, and to feel almost sorry for don Costantino being married to such a dragon. It is very simple why Antonescu is still alive: because I have left him alive. These endless killings are not good. But no doubt the signora has a more bloodthirsty outlook. As for me, I feel almost sorry for Antonescu. They killed his little boy. So, he became a childkiller himself. So pointless. A lot of people, Mimmo, have offered to go to Africa and bring me back Antonescu's head, but what good would that do? What would be the advantage to me?'

'The signora says people would respect you more,' said Mimmo.

'The signora, no disrespect to her, did not know Antonescu as a child. Nor does she realise how much he suffers now. But we are getting off the topic. My former wife, dottoressa Tancredi, keeps me informed, when we meet, which is often, about the progress of don Carmelo's will. Of course, as expected, he left everything to the boys and nothing to the girls, and he had no idea that he and three of his sons would die together. The whole thing, as you say, has been frozen while the lawyers fight it out. Don Costantino can afford to wait and is in no hurry. The removal of your half-brother who died in Taormina is lucky for him. Your removal would be lucky too. Don Constantino does not have legal possession of anything, but has actual possession of everything, and the moment you make a fuss, well, that would be risky. Clearly the signora and Maria and her brother have lost patience with don Costantino. I mean, we all knew about this African family, but even so, he was unwise to have alienated them.'

Mimmo considered and then spoke.

'The signora said I should speak to you, and you would help,' he said. 'The thing is this, sir. This is not my world. I do not want it to be my world. If I were to inherit everything as the last surviving son, if the courts gave me control of everything, I would sell all the companies, all the properties, to you, for a knockdown price. I would have more money than I have ever had, I would be able to pay off all the daughters, my mother, my sisters, his widow the signora, and still have plenty.'

'The overall value of it is immense,' remarked Calogero. 'It is a very attractive offer. It may be worth in excess of three hundred million euro. And you would accept, what, a hundred million?'

'I am not greedy, don Calogero. A hundred million is more than I can spend in a lifetime.'

'Would it satisfy the signora?' asked Calogero with a smile. 'If we have an agreement for a hundred million, will the signora accept it?'

'Don Calogero, she does not have to know the details. All she will know is that the money will be mine, and she had better not alienate me, given that I shall control the money. Of course, nothing will come through until the courts unfreeze the will. I take it, as it is in your interest that the will be unfrozen so that I sell everything, that the courts would act relatively quickly in this matter?'

'If I want it, it will happen. Dottoressa Tancredi knows all the right people. How do you propose to marry this young lady of yours, this lovely Maria?'

'In church, of course.'

'I meant, given that you are so closely related. You are don Carmelo's son, the will makes that clear, and she is his granddaughter. A little awkward, no?'

Mimmo sighed.

'We have to speak to canon lawyers,' he said sadly.

'I can put you in touch with the ones who arranged my annulment. They have the Cardinal's ear. I like you, Mimmo. Have we an agreement?'

Mimmo paused. It was an important moment.

'We have an agreement,' he said.

They stood. The wine glasses were drained. From the other side of the room, where he could see clearly but not hear anything, Paoluzzu watched Mimmo bend over and kiss don Calogero's hand. The two of them then walked towards the door. At the door, they paused, and don Calogero embraced Mimmo, and said:

'Everything will be fine, trust me. You did right to come to me. Donna Rosa is sensible, and she understands. It will be a good outcome.'

Paoluzzu heard this, and witnessed don Calogero kiss the younger man, pat him on the shoulder, and watch him leave. The young man, he noticed, did not look reassured. Don Calogero stood by the door, watching him go. Then, while he was still there, another young man entered, one a few years younger than Paoluzzu, beautifully shod, beautifully suited, with surprisingly long hair. It was Francesco. He had clearly recognised the man who had just left, as he and don Calogero exchanged meaningful glances, and went to the table together. Then, as promised, his wife entered, with the family, a baby and three other younger boys. The three younger sons were all chatter and excitement. The villa had been so interesting. The mosaics of the girls in bikinis… they pored over the lavishly illustrated guidebook they had bought. Their father should have seen the mosaic of the girls in bikinis. He had seen it before, he told them, but they insisted he could have seen it *again*. Paoluzzu approached, and brought the menus, and retired. Francesco stood when he saw him and shook his hand and smiled. Paoluzzu was pleased by this but left them to study the menus. Calogero looked at his intently.

'So, you saw him,' said Francesco, who was sitting next to him, quietly. 'He looked relieved to have seen you, I thought.'

'Well observed,' said Calogero. 'He did well to approach Nino, and Nino did well to introduce him to you, and you did well to arrange for him to see me. There is that famous quote, what is it now: "If you wait long enough on a riverbank, you will eventually see the bodies of your enemies float past you". Where did Nino meet him?'

'In a nightclub in Catania. He knew who Nino was because the son of don Constantino, the one called Dimitri, told him. Everyone knows who Nino is.'

'I am surprised Mimmo is the sort to go to nightclubs. Though we know that Nino lives in nightclubs.'

'I think Mimmo knew that if he wanted to get hold of you, then finding Nino in a nightclub was the best way,' said Francesco. 'By the way, Nino wants a favour. He made me promise that I would ask you.'

'Well, you have. Everyone wants a favour,' said Calogero. 'You will learn that. Nothing is free. There's no altruism except among the saints. The rest of us…. What is Nino's favour?'

'He said he will tell you himself, if you will allow me to bring him to see you,' said Francesco.

Calogero nodded but said nothing. Then he said: 'This Mimmo seems to be a nice young man who wants to marry the girl of his choice, and… well, we are going to help him.'

'That is nice,' said Francesco.

'Anyway, we had better keep an eye on him. In a few days, after I have sorted out a few things, we will set up a meeting for him. You need to find a nice young woman,' he said, changing the subject.

'Oh, dad, you are embarrassing,' said Francesco, not entirely seriously.

Agata, holding the baby, intervened.

'Stop it,' she said to her husband.

'I only…..' he began, in protest. He turned to his stepson. 'How is Costacurta's sister, what is her name? - Petra?'

'She is older than me. We lived next door to each other. She's very nice. Really nice, but, you know….'

'No, I don't know,' said Calogero.

'We see each other, but….'

'I hope that is all you do,' said Calogero severely. 'What?' he asked, looking at his wife. 'He is eighteen. Yes, yes, I know, he is a good boy, unlike that Nino Santacroce. How old is Nino? No one seems to know.'

'He is younger than me,' said Francesco.

'He is older than me,' said eleven-year-old Renato, from the opposite side of the table, who had been drawing on the paper tablecloth, but showed he was following the conversation.

'So, I would imagine,' observed Calogero, 'I am not sure why you of all people should have anything to do with Nino Santacroce or even know who he is.'

'Nino is nice,' said Renato defensively.

'I am sure he is,' said Calogero dispassionately. 'He has grown up fast, that is all. His father, poor man, should have taken a stronger line with him; but by the time he returned home, his son had been the man of the house far too long and was obviously too wedded to having his own way. I am surprised you know Nino,' he said, addressing Renato.

'Everyone does, Papà,' said the boy. 'We meet in the square, and there he is. I don't think I can remember a time when I did not know Nino, or Marco, for that matter. They are both very nice to me,' he said, with meaning. 'Anyway, you know Nino, Papà, so why shouldn't I?' he added with a touch of defiance in his voice.

Calogero looked at his son with displeasure, and not for the first time. But the boy seemed not to be intimidated. Francesco noticed this and thought he knew what was to come. But the moment was soon lost amidst the return of Paoluzzu, the explanation of the specials that were not on the menu, and then the various choices that they all made for the pasta. Francesco studied the Paoluzzu carefully, noting that his stepfather treated him with consideration, which did not surprise him. Paoluzzu had been a friend in Africa, and he was a friend still. He had not seen him for two years, since that Africa trip. He had heard he had come back, had expected to see him in Catania since his return six months ago. In the interval, he had not changed: still the neatly cut hair, the sort that a boy living in the provinces would have, in an attempt to maximise his charms. He wore a smart, neatly pressed shirt, no doubt the result of his mother's efforts. But he felt suddenly sorry for Paoluzzu, who was his relation, after all, though through his disgraced and forgotten father. He ought to have come to see him before this, as soon as he had known he was back from Africa. Indeed, they were both working-class boys; but one of them was now lucky being the stepson of don Calogero; the other was the manager of the Trattoria Norma.

The food was good, when it came: the conversation descended to an analysis of what they were eating, and how Agata might have done it the same, or better, or differently, or what signora di Rienzi senior, the three boys' grandmother, who was an acknowledged expert in the kitchen, would think. Or Aunt Giuseppina, for that matter, or Aunt Assunta, or Veronica, the faithful attendant of the dottoressa Tancredi. So much food; so many experts! After the pasta, which was served with sardines for the adults, came an abundance of meat and vegetables, the arrival of which was greeted with huge satisfaction. Abundance, the best things that the earth and the sea provided, this was a matter of importance to them all, young and old, and particularly to Agata and Francesco. There had been a time when their food had been meagre. But no more. They had both entered the land of plenty, thanks to Calogero. The two little boys, Sebastiano and Romano, used to nothing less, ate like soldiers who had done a long route march, as did the eldest of the three, Renato. But Renato was observant, and he could see how his stepbrother and his stepmother looked at the food, and he could sense that they, unlike him and his brothers, had not always been rich. But neither had his family, he knew, a few generations back. His grandfather, the original Renato di Rienzi, the Chemist of Catania, whom he had never known, had started as a poor man from Montelepre, he had been told. His grandmother, whom he loved - the Black Widow Spider as they called her - had grown up in poverty, from what he had heard her say, and the family of his late mother, Stefania, had not been rich, or so Aunt Giuseppina had seemed to convey. His sisters, they were different. They, in their school in England, never thought, he was sure, that they were one generation away from poverty, from not having enough to eat. For them, life was not, and had never been, a struggle. But it was, Renato sensed, a struggle they were winning at present, though their fortunes might change.

That fortunes changed, he and Francesco and Agata were only too aware. What had happened to his father in Africa two years ago was a grim reminder of the fragility of life itself. His father, always so strong, so smart, so in charge, so powerful, had come back from Africa a wreck, scarred in his hands and his feet, his ankle broken in several places. If it had not been for Francesco finding him nailed to the floor, going back to the cottage by the beach against his father's orders, then he was sure that his father would have died. He had not thought that then, but the realisation had grown on him in the intervening years. You did not think, at least not at his age, that your father would die, because you did not think your father *could* die. Your father, particularly if your father was Calogero, was immortal. But seeing him in hospital when he came back, seeing him in pain, that awoke in the small boy the realisation that he was not immortal after all, that he could die, that he could be hurt. Sebastiano and Romano did not see it that way, as they were still too young; but he saw it, he saw it clearly now; he was almost twelve; and Francesco saw it clearly as well.

Renato gave every impression of liking his stepbrother Francesco a great deal. Francesco had saved their father's life, and so he was perfectly entitled, as a result, to share in the family life, to call their father 'dad' and be treated like a son, even if he was not a blood relation. After all, if it had not been for him, they would have not had a father at all. Besides, he recognised in Francesco something that he had discovered in himself: a deep and passionate attachment to Calogero. In Francesco, this manifested itself as the desire to do whatever

Calogero wanted, and the desire, moreover, to protect him. Since coming back from Africa, Francesco had spent lots of time at the gun club in Nicolosi. All this was meant to be a secret from the other boys, and it had not occurred to the younger two to ask, but Renato was curious, and as soon as Francesco came to live with them, he discovered that he had a gun, and he made sense of the talk of Nicolosi where his father owned a gun club, and to where, one assumed, Francesco disappeared on his scooter. Moreover, he had found the gun; it was not in the safe in his father's study, but in Francesco's bedroom, usually in the pocket of one of his jackets hanging in the wardrobe, but sometimes in the false bottom of the wardrobe itself, where his stepbrother kept his other secret items. He had examined the gun with caution. He knew that people sometimes shot themselves while examining guns, and he did not want that to happen to him.

Renato loved Calogero with a deep and intense passion, a passion he barely understood; in that he was like Francesco, but his love was mixed with resentment, and the edges of his love had turned bad somehow, and he felt a passionate hatred for his father as well. He loved him, he resented him, and he wanted to hurt him. In this he was like his elder sister Isabella, and like his long-lost mother, who had died when he was a baby; he did not remember her at all, but he communed with her silently sometimes, like a soul in prayer. The woman he regarded as his mother, Anna Maria Tancredi, and who was now divorced from his father, resented Calogero too, he was sure, though she never said so.

As for the gun hidden in the false compartment at the bottom of the wardrobe, that very gun was now sticking in Francesco's back as he leaned against his chair. The feel of it in the waistband of his trousers was reassuring. Ever since they had shot Trajan Antonescu on the church steps and killed his little boy, ever since the family of signor Ginori had been killed at their garage between Montelepre and Monreale, the possession of a gun had seemed a wise precaution. It was nice to have a gun, he was eighteen after all, and it cemented the idea in his mind that he was grown up, that he had arrived at adulthood. He had a gun, he knew how to use it, and he would use it in the defence of his stepfather, in defence of his mother, in defence of little Calogero, and in defence of his three stepbrothers. Of course, the police might suddenly pounce on him, and pat him down, and arrest him for carrying an illegal weapon, but when did they ever do that? And even if they did, he knew that he would not be in trouble with the police for long, given that the police, or at least some of them, were their friends.

No one was frightened of the police, that was for sure; no one ever had been, at least not in the Purgatory quarter of Catania, where the police rarely ventured except to have cups of coffee in the bars owned by don Calogero. The police had one job, to catch criminals, something they were very bad at. But the truth was, he had come to see, that the police did not see the members of the honoured society as their enemies, but rather the lords of misrule in Rome, and the principle that one's enemy's enemy was your friend still held good. The police were really just like themselves, recruited from poor families, men who had no choice but to work for the state, given how few jobs there were. They were men who had drawn the short straw, who would have been far better off working for don Calogero.

The gun, the treasured gun, was untraceable; he had been taken to a man in Librino, a perfectly ordinary looking man, who, out of his dining room, ran an illegal armoury, and whose main skill lay in creating untraceable pistols, usually by adapting stolen guns that were originally made to fire blanks, but which could be turned to a more deadly purpose. Marco, the one they called the Dentist, had taken him. He and the gunsmith of Librino had plainly known each other, and known each other for some time, though their greeting was cool, like that of relative strangers. The gun had been produced, and he had been allowed to try the trigger, which had been adjusted, and a sum of money had changed hands. That was all. Nothing was said, no name asked for (though he was sure the gunsmith knew who he was); everything was veiled in silence.

He had come to understand this in the last year or so: not just the value of silence, but the way silence covered everything, made everything possible; how silence was their world. There were so many things they never talked about. It had come as a surprise to him to hear the signora Assunta, for example, refer to growing up with two brothers, not just one. Who was this other brother, now removed from the scene? How had he died? He did not know, but he did know that it was best not to ask. Here he was, in their midst, the dead brother, unmentioned, forgotten but present.

And what had happened to Cristoforo Antonescu, and whose fault that was, and what had happened to Ginori and his family, and what Antonescu had done to the boss, that too was all undiscussed, unspoken. Well, almost. In the months immediately after his return from Africa, when the boss had been secluded and recovering, people had approached Francesco asking for interviews, asking for messages to be taken to him. He had spoken to his father, who had brushed them all aside. Whatever it was - and Calogero knew what it was, and so did Francesco - the boss did not want to know. All these people were clamouring for action against Antonescu; but the boss had decided, for the moment at least, that no action should be taken.

He did eventually take one message to the boss, when he judged him sufficiently recovered. He passed on the offer of Marco – to go out to Africa and bring back Antonescu's head. Calogero had heard this attentively and then smiled.

'Your friend Marco is young, and perhaps overhasty. What difference does it make if Antonescu lives another ten years? I am in no hurry. It is always good to wait. Besides, Antonescu is a good fighter, and Marco might not find it as easy as he imagines. Thank him for me, but tell him I decline his kind offer. And tell him not to worry. Because he is worried. He thinks every day Antonescu survives, my prestige declines. It is not like that, not quite.'

He had not questioned further. But he knew Marco did think this, and that he regarded Antonescu's survival as detrimental to the boss's prestige, and the prestige of them all. But the boss, he knew, in the months of his recovery, had other things to think of. First of all, the process of recovery itself; then the process of reorganising his life, divorcing his wife, having the marriage annulled, and then marrying Agata, watching the baby being born, organising his baptism, and making sure that everyone knew that Francesco himself had the status of an adopted son. He was thinking of the future, and little Calogero was the future.

Lunch was drawing to a close. Paoluzzu, who had not had much of a chance to speak to don Calogero, now came forward with various bottles of limoncello and amaro. Calogero sensed his desire to talk, and invited him to sit down, and Francesco to vacate the chair next to him; he knew Paoluzzu needed this moment, as did so many others. The boss was kind, he was affable, he acted in a way that would enable Paoluzzu to boast later that he was a friend of don Calogero.

Francesco, who had been holding the baby, little Calogero, got up, and at his mother's instruction, because the baby seemed to be about to cry, took him out of the room, and went to the back of the restaurant, where an open door gave out onto the carpark; the carpark was unpaved, and their own car, which he was allowed to drive, was parked unobtrusively under the trees furthest from the building, where one hardly noticed it. It was a nice car. He liked cars, and as he held the baby, he stood on the steps on the restaurant, contemplating it.

Some time passed and gradually the child became calm and fell asleep in his brother's arms. He returned to the restaurant and placed the precious burden in his mother's arms. By the time he rejoined the table, he saw that Paoluzzu's eyes were upon him. It seemed that don Calogero had liked the wines, both of them, so Paoluzzu was suggesting he give him a case of each. Francesco suggested he help carry both to the car, of which he had the key.

'This is a kind present, just the sort he likes,' said Francesco, as they loaded the two heavy cases into the car.

'I owe don Calogero a great deal, so it is just a little sign of my appreciation,' said Paoluzzu. 'Besides, it really belongs to don Nunzio, and he would want me to do this.'

'Don Calogero is grateful to you, for all the information you sent back when you were in Africa. You know....'

Paoluzzu smiled.

'I was collecting information for him in the quarter when he was a teenager and I could barely walk. You weren't born then, were you? I was at his wedding, as was your mother, and I was at the Romanian's wedding to your cousin Ceccina... Were you there?'

'I must have been, but I do not remember. I would have been quite young then,' said Francesco. 'I was thinking, when I heard you were back, that we would be bound to see each other in Catania,' he added.

They were both standing by the boot of the car.

'That was the idea, that I should come back to Catania,' said Paoluzzu sadly. 'But I decided here was better, and your father arranged it, I approached him through Nino Santacroce. I came back after four years of hard work, expecting her to be waiting for me....'

'I heard,' said Francesco. 'Nino told me the details. Look, if you want me to do you a favour, I will do it.' He drew aside his jacket and indicated the gun. 'That is one way of getting revenge. The other is to find someone else. Sometimes it is best to do both.'

'Are you offering to shoot him or her?' asked Paoluzzu. 'You have grown up a lot in the last two years.'

'The fact that they have made you look and feel bad makes me look and feel bad too, as you are my friend,' said Francesco. 'And we are cousins. Besides, I need target practice.'

'Your friend, Marco, does he shoot people, or just pull out their teeth?'

'So, you have heard about him?'

'I think everyone has. I was at school with him, I seem to remember, not that he ever went to school much. Strange boy. I don't want anyone shot. Just pull his teeth out, his not hers, but don't kill him.'

Francesco nodded.

'Say no more about it. I know who the guy is; he is often in the quarter. After this he won't be. After this, people will realise that insulting you is insulting me too.' He paused. 'Have you got someone new?'

'In a certain sense. Don Nunzio has this daughter, and she has a friend, and she is sort of interested in me, and me in her. She is beautiful and clever and nice, but, oh my goodness, she won't let me come within half a metre of her. She says she likes me, but I am just the manager of a trattoria, aren't I? Piazza Armerina is not a great place, you know. It is the back of beyond. No girls to speak of, unlike Catania. All the young people have left. They have gone to the continent, some even further, to America. Sometimes I feel I am the only young man left here in Piazza. It is all old people… Africa was constricting and boring, but here…. What about you?'

'I am starting at the university. Information technology. But I think I know more than they do. Nino and I have been working on the new website for the Confraternity of the Holy Souls. He is just a kid, but a really clever one. It is excellent, even if I say it myself. People can donate online from wherever they are in the world. It's really cool. Dad hates computers and technology, he lives in the stone age, as you know, but they are the future.'

'What are you talking about?' asked Renato, who had approached unnoticed. He placed his arms around Francesco's waist and looked at Paoluzzu.

'Computers,' said Francesco. 'We were talking about computers and the new website I designed with Nino.'

'I think you were talking about something else,' said Renato, looking at Paoluzzu.

'Is it hard work here?' asked Francesco.

Paoluzzu considered.

'Yes. I mean, this place takes all my time, and when I am not here, I have to think of my parents who are with me, and then I have to think about this girl, and in my free time, I go to the gym. That is my only relaxation so far. You know…'

He made a surreptitious gesture with his hand, indicating solitary activities.

'What about you?' he asked.

'Is it your father who is a relation of mine?' asked Francesco.

'No, my mother is,' answered Paoluzzu, 'But she has not seen or heard of her cousin, you know, your father, for years.'

'Neither have any of us. Nor do we want to. He is not my father any more, he lost that right. No, Catania is fine, but hard work as well. I mean, I spend a lot of time working with Nino, whom you know, or with Marco. And the rest of the time, I am supposed to be at university, but… And then there are girls. One in particular, her name is Petra.'

'How is that?'

'We first met when I was fourteen and a half. It is on and off; currently more on than off, but you never know. It's complicated. She is complicated.'

'Was there ever a woman who was not?' remarked Paoluzzu. 'Will you be coming this way again?'

'Maybe,' said Francesco. 'I would like to. But I doubt it. It is a bit out of the way. We only came for the Roman villa,' he added, though this was not true. The Roman villa was a cover for the meeting with Mimmo. He saw the disappointment in Paoluzzu's face. 'I mean,' he continued, 'not the family. But I might come. Look, if I had a phone, I would give you my number, then if I was passing, we could meet, or when you come to Catania. Write your number down and give it to me. You never know…'

Actually, he did want to see Paoluzzu again, but it did not do to show too much enthusiasm, he felt.

They walked back to the restaurant, with Renato holding Francesco by the hand. Paoluzzu wrote his number on the back of one of the trattoria's cards. The family was now ready to leave. Lunch had been excellent. The compliments were effusive. No bill was presented, naturally enough; one never was when don Calogero visited any restaurant. He shook Paoluzzu's hand, thanked him for the wine, and pressed a banknote into his hand. Francesco shook Paoluzzu's hand as well, and kissed his cheek, as they were relatives, and had known each other a long time, if not well. Seeing this, Renato did the same and felt the momentary but thrilling sensation of rough skin and intoxicating aftershave, along with hard gym-toned muscle under his shirt.

It was a lovely October day, and Calogero suggested that they drive the short distance up to Piazza Armerina to look at the Cathedral which had an unusual bell tower, which none of them had ever seen, and walk around the town. This was met with general and enthusiastic assent; it was not that the Cathedral and its bell tower were particularly interesting or beautiful (though they were); it was rather that for the last two years Calogero had not suggested a walk at all, and this idea, that they should walk, was clearly a sign that he was feeling well, that his ankle was not hurting him, that he was, thank the Lord, healed.

'Don Nunzio will wonder what we are doing here,' said Calogero, as they got out of the car in front of the Cathedral, Renato next to him, and Francesco on his other side. 'He probably knows we are here already. Paoluzzu will have rung him from the trattoria. Or the people at the Roman villa might have told him. Well, we are tourists. And why shouldn't we be?'

'Some people are naturally suspicious,' observed Francesco.

'Oh yes, I am one of them,' said Calogero. 'So, I hope, are you. You'll need it. One cannot afford to be too trusting.' He turned to Renato. 'We need to think about your birthday. What do you want to do?' Without waiting for an answer, he turned back to Francesco. 'Isn't he tall already?' He turned back to Renato. 'You have your grandfather's name, your mother's beauty and you have some of my features as well.'

'Thanks, Papà,' said Renato warily.

His father rarely mentioned his mother, his real mother, Stefania, of whom he had no memory at all. Usually when he spoke of his mother, he meant Anna Maria. But it was clear from the context he meant Stefania, because there was a marked physical difference between Renato and his two brothers, the children of Anna Maria, despite the fact that the age difference was minor. Sebastiano was less than a year younger than Renato, but he and Romano were not children of the Purgatory quarter on both sides. Renato had grown up calling Anna Maria his mother, but now, as he approached maturity, he realised that he was not her son at all. It created a rift, in his mind at least, between himself and his younger brothers. Moreover, he was growing up. They were still little boys, with little boys' interests. And they looked different too. He supposed he looked like his mother Stefania; he had seen photographs of her, and examined them for a resemblance, though not found one.

'Do you like Renato's long hair?' Calogero was asking Francesco.

'Yes, of course I do,' said Francesco, knowing this was what Renato would expect, what Renato would want, feeling Renato's eyes on him. 'It looks good. Besides, we all have long hair.'

'We all' did not include Calogero whose hair was cut short and had been tended by the same barber near the opera house for years. It did include Nino, Francesco and Marco and the two hundred or so men who were associated with the boss of bosses through the various bosses and underbosses who ran Catania in its different quarters. He had allowed this, in that he had not forbidden it. He had forbidden most other things: no tattoos, no beards, no slovenliness, no earrings, smart dress at all times. That was how they recognised each other in the street, that and the long hair. Marco, on certain special occasions, even had a ponytail. The boss barely knew Marco, as everything was through intermediaries. As for those who did not keep these rules, there were punishments. Not like in Africa, where they chucked you out of a plane, but punishments all the same. He frowned. He told Renato to join the others, and the boy obediently went ahead to walk by the side of his stepmother and his brothers.

'You did well to put that man Mimmo in touch with me,' said Calogero to his stepson. 'We had a useful talk, and a profitable one. Once more, we stand to make a huge amount of money, as well as tidying up a little bit of a mess in one corner of our three-cornered island. You can guess what I mean, or at least who I mean.'

'Yes, dad.'

'It will be a tricky job. It will not be immediate, and we have lots of time to plan. But we have inside help. It might be good to use Marco for this; I mean, from what you say, he is very keen, very loyal, very efficient, rather than let us say, calling in Muniddu. If we do that, we let Palermo in on it. We don't want to do that. We want to make gains we do not have to share.'

'Marco certainly is keen to do whatever he can for you, dad.'

'If you mean that business of that man who was refusing to pay up...' he now said. 'I have not forgotten. Yes, I know that it is only a few hundred euro, but if he stops paying, and the rest follow suit... It is a tiny amount, hardly worth quarrelling over, but... You see, it is not the money, it is the idea of tribute, the deference, the respect. This man wants to defy us. Well, he needs to understand the price that must be paid for this treason. As do the rest of them. It could be catching. *Pour encourager les autres...* Tell Marco to see to it. We can trust him, can't we? And you, do you want to help him with that?'

'Sure, dad,' replied Francesco without hesitation.

'Does Petra Costacurta ever talk about her brother?' he now asked, changing the subject.

'Yes. She does not like him. They were close, but…' He hesitated. He did not want to talk of Petra, but he forced himself to go on. 'She was friends with Tonino Grassi, and she blames her brother for that, I mean not explicitly, but now that Tonino is no longer here, she has idealised him in her memory, and she blames Roberto, not in any specific way, but…. Besides, her brother has gone to Palermo, he is rich and successful, and she and the other sisters and the mother think that he has dropped them. They were not even invited to the wedding, and I am not sure if they have even met the signora. They feel that Roberto wants to forget them. He has been generous, given them that nice house in the Furnaces, but it seems that is not enough. He hardly ever comes to see his mother. And he is often free at weekends.'

'Oh, poor Roberto,' said Calogero.

He was indeed free at weekends, as when Anna Maria had the children with her, he was banned from meeting them, under the conditions of the divorce. He did not want Costacurta anywhere near his sons or daughters. To his surprise, Anna Maria had accepted this, though she had stipulated in return that neither Agata nor Francesco were ever to enter her houses, either in Palermo or Donnafugata. The children had somehow understood this, as they never mentioned either Agata or Francesco in either place. Francesco had heard about Donnafugata and was sad at the thought of not being able to see it. He had not met the signora but held her in awe.

'Whatever you hear about Costacurta, remember I want to hear it too,' said Calogero.

'Of course, dad.'

'As for this Petra, she is a girl with a grievance. Not good. Dangerous. When we get back to Catania, speak to Marco about that thing we mentioned, and get it done this week. Oh yes and tell Omar I want to see him; he could be useful to us, and he can bring the family to lunch one day, I am sure your mother would love that. We may well need Omar for what I have in mind. And another thing. I will see Nino Santacroce when we get back to Catania.'

'Yes, dad.'

'I didn't realise you were still with Petra,' said his father.

'Neither did I, dad. It is just the way things worked out the other day. I knew I did not have to tell you because you were bound to find out from either Renato or Marco. Though I could have been spending the night with someone else, I suppose.'

'Renato…' said the boss, thinking of the child now walking ahead of them. 'He seems to worship you. Does he know about Petra? And the others?'

'Yes, dad, but when he asks, I tell him to mind his own business.'

'He....' Calogero considered. He was so dissatisfied with his first-born son. He was beautiful and clever, but he was not as his father had been approaching the age of twelve. He would never get into a fight with another boy, that was sure. He would never break the law either; never steal, never kill, and never, his father feared, sleep with a woman. The other sons, he was more confident of. But Renato, who he loved, well... He was Stefania's son, not that it was her fault, but like his mother, destined, he could feel it, to frustrate his father. 'He needs to get his hair cut. You can take him to the barbers. And take no nonsense from him. If he is cheeky, slap him.'

'Yes, dad,' said Francesco, knowing he would not, and knowing too that Calogero knew he would not.

It was forbidden under the terms of the divorce for Calogero to cane his sons, though this did not apply to Francesco.

'If you make Petra pregnant...' his father now said, returning to another worry, thinking of Mimmo and his girlfriend.

'Dad, it is impossible. I told you. Belt and braces. She takes the pill, and I make sure by, you know... And, dad, you are hardly one to talk, you had Isabella when you were seventeen.'

'Yes, but I am different. The rules don't apply to me. They do to you,' said Calogero with a smile. He frowned. 'Why did he kiss Paoluzzu? He only needed to shake his hand. He is a friend, but not a family member.'

'He did that because he wanted to. He may even have done it just to upset you. Maybe he kissed Paoluzzu because he is so handsome. Paoluzzu spends his life, when not working, in the gym, and it shows.'

Calogero looked displeased. Others did not dare provoke him, but his own son....

'I wish you would speak to him,' said Calogero.

'I do. All the time,' replied Francesco. 'He will grow out of it,' he said, without much conviction.

They walked on. Calogero's ankle was not hurting him. The town was rather pretty, he thought, though the cathedral, apart from the bell tower, was nothing special. He put aside all thoughts of Renato and felt, for a moment, happy; his wife, walking ahead with the baby in her arms, and the younger children, clustered around her, smiled and looked back. And when they reached the square, there was don Nunzio, the local boss, smiling, ready to kiss his hand.

It was Sunday night.

'Where were you yesterday?' asked Petra Costacurta, studying the beads of sweat on Francesco's forehead.

'We all went to Piazza Armerina, to see the Roman villa, and then we went for lunch at this trattoria, then we visited the town and met up with some people – all of us: me, the younger ones, my mother, my dad, all of us.'

'And you could not get out of it?' she asked.

'It would have been hard,' he said, with a touch of shame.

'Well, there is a price for everything,' said Petra seriously. 'Even for this.'

'He wanted me to be there,' said Francesco.

'I don't care what he wants or does not want,' she said.

'Yes, but I have to. He is my father.'

'Stepfather,' she corrected him. 'Perhaps, if he does not like it, you should have thought about that before going to bed with me.'

'I wish it were that simple,' he said. 'I don't think about going to bed with you, I just do it. It's so wonderful. You are irresistible. I am a young man in love, don't you realise? Didn't you feel it?'

'I felt something,' she conceded. 'But if you are so much in love with me, perhaps you can rouse up your courage and tell him to go to hell.'

'No one tells my dad to go to hell.'

'Then maybe I should tell you to go to hell,' she said.

'Don't say that,' he said. 'Please.'

'You need to get a phone,' she said, after a pause. 'Then I will know where you are all the time.'

'I don't want a phone,' he said.

'You mean, he does not want you to have a phone,' she said.

'He and I agree that phones are bad.'

'You agree with him on everything, don't you?' she asked.

'Yes, I suppose so. I love him. He has been good to me and to my mother. He is a really nice, kind man. Not like my biological father. Not like your father. Neither of them hung around, did they? He is nice, he wants me to do well. He is educating me. And you know why we have to keep this secret? It is not you or me, it is your brother Roberto. You can hardly expect my dad to like the man who married his ex-wife, or to be pleased by me going out with his sister.'

She sighed. This was true. Her brother was a problem. She also knew that her brother would be horrified by the thought of her now in bed with Francesco di Rienzi. That was one of the reasons she was in bed with Francesco di Rienzi. She did not like her brother anymore.

'When will your mother be back?' he asked.

'I told you. She is at the evening Mass. It takes at least an hour. Besides, I do not care, and I doubt she will, much. She must have realised you were here the other night, but she did not say anything. And when she does see you, she seems to like you, doesn't she?'

He nodded.

'Nino is in trouble; did I tell you?'

'The very pretty blond boy? What has he done?'

'He has made his girlfriend pregnant.'

'I am surprised he has one. Oh well. That won't happen to me, or if it did, it would not happen for long, if you get my meaning. My brother treated his girlfriend appallingly when she got pregnant. Men! How old is Nino?'

'Younger than me.'

'Who did you see in Piazza Armerina?'

'We saw the manager of the trattoria. I know him, I am related to him, but I had not seen him for some time. Then just the family of some business friend of dad's,' he said evasively.

She recognised the evasion.

'Business friend,' she said. 'We all know what that means.'

He ignored this and looked at the watch he had left on the bedside table. It was time to go. He got out of the narrow bed and began to pick up his clothes. She watched him. She liked him. She liked his hazel eyes, unusual in Sicily. His long hair was attractive. He felt a little guilty leaving her like this; but his bike was outside and might be recognised. And when he got back home for supper, he would have to lie to everyone about where he had been, if they asked, which they would. He was particularly worried about Renato blurting something out. Renato was observant, and though he was careful, he did not trust the boy not to find things out and not to betray him. He was certain that his father knew he had spent the previous Tuesday night with Petra was because of Renato. Once dressed, he sat on the edge of the bed and kissed her. She smiled at him, and then a moment later, he was gone, and she heard the front door of the house close behind him.

It had been a busy week for don Calogero. The parents of Nino Santacroce had come to see him to make excuses for their son's behaviour; to share their distress; to ask don Calogero to intervene. But when he had asked them just what they wished him to do, they were silent, incoherent, grief-stricken. He understood even if they could not explain it. Their son was beyond their control; but he was not beyond don Calogero's control; their son was a problem they could not solve, but they trusted the boss to solve the problem for them.

He told them he would see what he could do. They were grateful for that, they trusted him. He was the one who would make all things right by a judicious use of his power.

Then the parents of the girl in question had come: the policemen and his wife. They too had expressed their discontent at what Nino had done to their daughter, their outrage, their distress, and they indicated, a little to don Calogero's annoyance, that they held him partly responsible. He asked what solution they had in mind. The policeman, who seemed deeply uncomfortable, looked at his wife. She was hard-faced: the couple, she announced, believed that the best solution was for don Calogero to send the boy away. While she said this, her husband looked at the floor.

'Send him away…?' asked Calogero, seeking clarification as to the exact nature of this sending away.

'You have, sir,' said the woman, 'a hotel in Africa. It employs a lot of people from Catania. We know some of them. It is nice there. This boy could make himself useful there.'

'I am sure he could,' he agreed mildly. 'But why would he want to go there, and leave his parents? And indeed, leave your daughter?'

'Because you would tell him to do so, don Calogero, and he would obey,' said the policeman, now speaking. 'People obey you, sir.'

Calogero looked at him with distaste. But he nodded and sent the couple away. He was thoughtful for a long time. Later that evening, when it was almost midnight, he sent Francesco to get Nino. He knew Nino had been waiting for this interview and expected him to be terrified. Presumably the boy had wanted to see him before the two sets of parents. A little before midnight, Nino came to the silent flat and was shown into the boss's study. Francesco came with him.

Nino stood in front of the boss humbly, realising that there was nothing he could say and that silence was best. He felt the eyes of the boss on him. The boss, he knew, was considering. Indeed, he was. He was remembering his own past, and how he had married Stefania at the age of seventeen, when she had been about to give birth to his eldest child, Isabella. He was thinking of Trajan Antonescu, a father at fifteen to the poor little boy, his godson, Cristoforo. He was thinking how much embarrassment and annoyance Nino had caused him, but at the same time thinking of how the two sets of parents had not helped themselves. If Nino had annoyed him, they had annoyed him more.

'Your mother and father do not want a grandchild?' he asked.

'No, boss, they want me to tell Daniela to, you know, get rid of it.'

'And you have refused?'

'Yes, boss.'

'And they were not happy with your refusal?'

'They were not happy, boss.'

'And her parents, the same thing?'

'Yes, boss.'

'And if I told you…?'

Nino looked at the boss.

'If I told you to get rid of it,' said Calogero. 'What would you do?'

'I would refuse to obey you, boss,' said Nino. 'But you won't ask me to do that, I know. You are a good boss.'

There was silence. Francesco, who had said nothing, and who knew that he ought to say nothing, was shocked and angered by Nino's daring. He, the son, was the favourite, and here was Nino presuming that he was the favoured one, the one who could act with impunity.

'That policeman…' said Calogero.

'Boss?' asked Nino.

'He…. he seems not to like you much.'

'I knew him back when,' explained Nino.

'Back when…?'

'Yes, boss. He is a friend of Andreazza.'

'He works for us?'

'Of course. As far as he can. He will be my sponsor when I join the police, not that he knows it yet.'

'He wants me to send you to Africa,' said Calogero.

'As you say, boss, he does not like me. I remind him of the things he would rather forget.'

'Still, he is right to be annoyed with you, and so am I right to be annoyed with you. They expect me to show my displeasure. You have annoyed me.'

'Boss,' said Nino humbly, and at the same time interiorly pleased, knowing he had won.

Calogero looked at Francesco, who understood. Francesco went to the cupboard in the corner where the boss kept the canes.

'And?' said Marco. 'That was it? He just gave him a good smack, and sent him off?'

For once, Marco seemed animated, almost angry.

'No. Afterwards he said that he congratulated him on his forthcoming fatherhood and wedding and sent him off. And he told me that we were not to touch him.'

'Ah, that means he knew we would be angry.'

'Are you angry?' asked Francesco.

'Are you?' asked Marco.

It was a dangerous question. How could one be angry with the boss's decisions? He was the boss. One had to obey. But this was hard to accept. Nino Santacroce, of whom they were both in their own way jealous, had done something neither of them had done or, in fact had any immediate prospect of doing. He had defied the boss and got away with it. Nino was younger, better looking, more confident, richer, somehow more daring than them. He had not got their advantages, but that somehow did not seem to matter.

'Just as well your father said we could not touch him, because if we started, we would not finish until he was dead,' said Marco.

'I thought you liked Nino,' said Francesco.

'Of course I do. Everyone does. So do you. Yeah, I like Nino. But when he makes me look foolish…'

They were sitting in the subterranean changing room of the gym, on the central bench. It was late at night, and they were alone. The gun, Francesco's gun, lay on the bench between them.

'After you use this, then he will be able to deny you nothing,' said Marco, gesturing to the gun. 'Then you will be a man, and that will be that: he will give you all the freedom you need.'

Marco was the nearest thing he had to a best friend, and he knew about Petra Costacurta. Marco was older and he had been deputed by the boss to 'educate' Francesco.

'I am not so sure,' replied Francesco. 'On Saturday we went to Piazza Armerina, and I have to go back there soon. You see, we met up with this don Nunzio by chance – well nothing is by chance. Don Nunzio later phoned my father, his wife phoned my mother, and then, well, what has happened is that when he sent Nino away, he told me that he wanted me to go up to Piazza and make friends with don Nunzio's daughter. She is at Catania University like me; we spoke about that when we met. She is gorgeous, and it seemed she told her mother she liked me, and, well, my father wants it. He says we cannot afford to alienate don Nunzio, who is thrilled by the prospect. Besides this girl, Ida, is from our sort of people, and that would be good for me.'

'But you told him about Petra?'

'I had to. He seemed to know about her anyway. He knows it is on-off; it always has been. He asked me if there was anything going on, if it was serious, and I did not have the guts to say that it was, or at least I think it might be. It is hard to tell. I had more or less promised him, in the past, not to see Petra, all because of her brother. Now, if I have to go up to Piazza every weekend and walk around the town square with Ida and eat ice-cream with her, which will be boring, even if she is beautiful and nice, and if Petra gets to hear of it, which, knowing my luck, she will…. I mean, nothing will come of it, but still. Paoluzzu is in love with Petra's friend, but getting nowhere with her, so perhaps I will see him too. Dad says that Giuseppe Santucci has this wonderful girlfriend whom he is going to marry, the daughter of Muniddu, and how everyone likes that. Well, I suppose I should be grateful he does not want me to marry Beppe Santucci's sister, the one who had the child with Tonino Grassi, or someone equally difficult.'

There was silence between them.

'Dad said I was immoral, with girls, you know, and that I need to be more serious and responsible.'

'He's right,' said Marco.

Francesco considered. He had been fornicating with whoever would have him (and a surprising number of them did have him) since the age of fourteen, since he had been under the boss's protection. He liked it. It was a good experience to have. Marco, of course, was different, much older, and had presumably got over this wild sexual excess of youth. Francesco supposed he would too, in time, and worried that the time was growing close, closer than he would like. He wondered, just for a moment, about Marco, who, according to Nino (who knew everything) has a secret girlfriend in somewhere like Caltagirone, whom he visited once every two or three months. But the sex lives of others were dull compared to one's own, and the thought deserted him.

'Well,' Marco was saying. 'You will go by bike to Piazza? It won't take more than an hour and a half. Oh, you will go up there and make yourself agreeable to her, this Ida, but above all to her mother and her father, and then when they see there is no spark, the thing will die down. Give my regards to Paoluzzu. I remember him, from before he went to Africa. We will do him that favour. He is a nice guy, I am sure. Now, we need to speak about the man from Librino, OK?'

Later that week, don Calogero sent a messenger over to don Giorgio, the priest who had care of the Church of the Holy Souls in Purgatory, carrying an envelope, in which was a letter and a large sum in cash. Don Giorgio took the letter and motioned to the boy who had brought it to wait in case it needed an immediate reply.

It was a polite thank you letter for don Giorgio's recent kindness in officiating at the wedding of Calogero and Agata, and all his help with the paperwork to do with the annulment, which had been done with a dispatch which was unusual in Sicily and unusual too in the universal Church. Don Giorgio frowned; he was not altogether happy at being reminded of the way don Calogero di Rienzi had received an annulment of his marriage to Anna Maria Tancredi so swiftly; but don Calogero had wanted it, Anna Maria Tancredi had wanted it, and above all the Cardinal of Palermo, who had celebrated the original marriage, had wanted it too. Three such powerful people working in conjunction were impossible to resist, and so the desired annulment had been very swift, and so had the subsequent wedding of Calogero and Agata. He would have liked to have made them wait, but had seen early on that that would not have been possible, so he had given in to the pressure, the subtle and unspoken pressure that had made him act swiftly. What don Calogero wanted, he got.

He did not like this state of affairs, but he was used to it. He did not like the way he had allowed himself to grow used to it.

Apart from the money, there was an invitation to lunch any day that week at home with don Calogero and Agata, as well as a mention of a matter on which don Calogero wanted to ask the priest's advice and a favour that he wished to ask for. Don Giorgio looked at the boy who had brought the letter. He told him to take his reply to don Calogero, to the effect he would come that very day at 1pm. He watched the boy trot off with the message. Left alone, he contemplated the money once more. It was generous, but by no means extravagant. It was a carefully calibrated amount, he could see, a reminder that don Calogero controlled the Confraternity that paid don Giorgio and was the man who controlled the money supply; but it wasn't so very much as to look like a bribe.

He wondered what favour don Calogero would ask him; but this thought was dismissed by another, the constant nagging thought that there was a favour that he wanted to ask don Calogero, something he was sure that don Calogero had already guessed. So, they would do each other favours. Favours would be exchanged. This was the Sicilian currency. He sighed. So, it had ever been.

He presented himself at 1pm on the dot. It was Agata who answered the door, not Calogero's mother. He had wondered who would answer the door, and he had also wondered how Agata was getting on with her mother-in-law and her sisters-in-law. But she was charming, from what he could see of her, an unassuming type, the sort that everyone liked. The sisters and mother of don Calogero were, by contract, powerful women. They must be grateful, he reflected, that Calogero's new wife was not a potential rival. She was, he was sure, a nice girl; though a doubt crept into his mind: would a nice girl really marry a man like Calogero?

She greeted him warmly, saying that her husband was in his study. He asked how she was, and how her son was. He had a vague memory of baptising the boy years ago. Ever since the marriage, Agata had been very regular at Mass, and even the boy Francesco came and stood at the back from time to time. Well, he should encourage her, he supposed.

He was ushered into the study, a room he had visited many times in the past, and don Calogero stood to greet him, took his hand and kissed it. He must, reflected don Giorgio, want a positive outcome to the favour he wanted to ask. He was more intrigued than ever, and he realised that his own favour had a good chance of being granted, given that the boss seemed so keen to have this favour from him. Tiny glasses of vin santo were poured, which don Calogero knew was the priest's favourite drink. Calogero smiled impishly.

'We are both so grateful for all you have done for us,' he said. 'It was a lovely wedding, in a church that means so much to us both, and done by a priest I have known so long, and respect so much.'

Don Giorgio smiled to hear this. What a speech, and from an atheist too.

'And of course, there were all the added complications as well, all of which you helped to smooth out,' he said referring to his divorce and annulment. 'I mean, it was a bit embarrassing. The ceremony with Anna Maria was done by the Cardinal of Palermo himself and he had not done the proper paperwork, which goes to show that a Cardinal has not got a firm grasp of detail in the way a priest of great pastoral experience like you, don Giorgio, has. We are blessed to have you.'

He smiled and inclined his head. He was enjoying this, he reflected bitterly, because he knew just how much Calogero disliked him.

'How is your son?' he asked, thinking of the baby he had baptised. 'Quite an honour to have the mayor of Catania as his godfather.'

'Oh indeed. I thought it a cheek to ask, but he could have said no, I reflected, so I asked anyway. But he did not refuse, so we were delighted. He is an old friend of mine, really, I mean, we have known each other for years, and…'

'He was a friend of your brother, I seem to remember,' don Giorgio could not help observing.

'Yes, he was,' said Calogero smoothly, with the determination of a man who was not to be ruffled by the reference, the pointed reference, to the brother he had murdered, or whose murder he had commissioned. 'It has been some years since we lost my dearest brother, and the pain is real, though I have to say that much as I loved my brother, I feel the wound of his loss is being healed by the love I have for my wife, and she for me.'

He smiled radiantly at Agata, and she smiled back.

'I must leave you,' said his wife. 'Little Calogero is with signora di Rienzi, and I must go and pick him up after I have served the pasta, and I am having lunch with her.'

'They get on so well,' said Calogero appreciatively.

Don Giorgio raised an eyebrow.

They went through to the dining room, and the pasta was placed in front of them. Then Agata left, and they heard the door close behind her. Calogero poured the wine and began to serve the lasagne.

'Francesco is at university, the boys are at school, so it is just us,' he said. 'It is about the children that I wanted to speak to you,' he said. 'Not mine, though one day that may come. Other people's. Do you know this boy Nino Santacroce?'

'I know of him. The parents have been to see me. Both sets of parents.'

'I am glad of that,' said don Calogero. 'Both sets of parents came to see me as well. The boy is very young, younger than my Francesco, but from what I gather – I may have seen him, but I don't know him at all – somewhat in advance of his years. Not a bad boy, just an irresponsible one. And the girl, well, I know nothing about her. It is regrettable, it seems to me, that the boy's parents blame the girl, and her parents blame the boy. But no doubt you heard all this from them…'

'I did. And we have both heard it all before, when Traiano Antonescu met Ceccina; her parents were furious; his mother was philosophical, I seem to remember.'

'Yes, I remember that drama, and I remember how it ended. You married them, though you had to wait until they were sixteen. When children misbehave… I have done what the parents asked. I spoke to Nino. Not directly, you understand.' The lie came effortlessly from his lips. 'He wanted to see me, to make his case, no doubt, but I refused to see him. What was the point? There was very little for me to say to him. I conveyed my displeasure, and told him what he had to do, namely come and see you, tell you and indeed everyone else, that he was engaged to be married, and signify his intention to marry her in due course. That way, honour is satisfied. Of course, no marriage can take place for some time… But I hope this meets with your approval, don Giorgio, and when the boy comes to see you, you will understand, shall we say, where he is coming from?'

'I understand. He will be coming from you,' said don Giorgio.

'Precisely,' said Calogero.

'The girl's father is a policeman, and the boy's father was in Ucciardone. No wonder the two sets of parents do not get on. It will be some wedding. Though, in the meantime, the boy may lose interest.'

'Oh, he won't,' said Calogero with decision. 'He knows what I expect. There will be no problems there.'

'Then that is decided,' said don Giorgio.

He felt the temptation to derail everything by asking just what it was that Nino did for a living; but he was too keen to hear more from the boss about what he wanted. He sensed there was more. And there was.

'There is something else, that also concerns marriage,' continued Calogero. 'Another young couple. Not as young. Mimmo must be twenty-three and the girl is at least eighteen. They want to get married soon, as the girl is expecting a baby, and, well, there are complicating factors. You see, he is her father's half-brother.'

Whatever he had been expecting, it was not this.

'Her uncle?' asked don Giorgio, genuinely shocked.

'It is not as bad as it sounds,' said Calogero hastily. 'The two brothers in question share a father but have different mothers and they are twenty years apart in age at least. They have never met. The boy met the girl, and by the time he realised who she was, it was too late. He is a nice boy, but you know how it is, love or perhaps lust at first sight. Now he wants to make things right and marry her. It is not worse than first cousins getting married, is it? I mean the Kings of Spain all married their nieces, didn't they?'

'And produced monsters!' said the priest.

'Well, let us hope their baby is not a monster,' said Calogero.

'I am not sure about the answer to this,' said don Giorgio. 'I genuinely do not know. But one thing is certain: Not even you, don Calogero, can change the immutable laws of humanity about incest.'

'Nor would I want to change them,' he said quickly. 'All I would ask is for you to counsel this young couple and tell them what their available options are. And if you can see a way forward to their getting married, then I would be so pleased and grateful…'

'Who exactly are they?' asked the priest.

'Just a couple from Messina. He is the youngest son of the late don Carmelo, and she is the daughter of the eldest son. The late don Carmelo had a lot of children. It would be so nice for them to meet a sympathetic priest. May I tell them to get in touch with you?'

Don Giorgio assented.

'Now we can have the second course, and you can tell me what I can do for you?' said don Calogero, taking his empty plate and disappearing into the kitchen.

'Was it so obvious? That I had something to ask?' asked the priest when he returned with a platter of roast lamb.

'In my job, you recognise the symptoms,' said Calogero.

'And what is your job?'

Calogero looked at him.

'Property development. And easing people's hardships.'

'Ah, because that is exactly what I want to talk to you about. A certain person known to us both…'

'You mean Trajan Antonescu.'

'Actually, I meant his mother.'

'Ah, Anna Agostini.'

'Yes, Anna Agostini.'

'Father, she tried to see me when I was in hospital, when I really did not want to see her or indeed anyone else. She has asked to see me several times since, but I have said to her, and to her husband, who has also been in touch, that, well, I do not want to see her. You see, she reminds me of her son, and he reminds me of that dreadful incident, of which I am sure you have heard every detail. It is too painful to have such reminders. Besides, I know what she wants. She wants me to forgive him, and that is impossible. How can I? He nailed me to the floor. But even if I were to forgive that, how could I forgive the things that were done to others, which are not mine to forgive? The death of Luca Ginori's girlfriend, and her brother, and their baby, and Luca's father, his wife and their children? When Ginori tried to shoot Traiano, and succeeded in murdering Cristoforo alone, we tried to help Traiano, but we failed. If I had had him put down like a wild dog, eight people might be alive today. But I was too kind. I thought he could be helped. I was wrong. And what does Anna want me to do? Let him come back to Sicily? He travels as he pleases, I know, using false passports; but it is best that he stays where he is, in Africa, far away from all the people he has hurt.'

'I am not sure what Anna wants, apart from seeing you,' said the priest. 'I would imagine she is realistic about Traiano. She knows that he is lost. All she asked me was to arrange an interview with you for herself, and I told her that I would try my best.'

'Well, she asked the right person. I will see her. If that is all you want, consider it granted. It is such a great favour to ask? Is there nothing more you want, don Giorgio?'

'Nothing, nothing at all,' said the priest.

Chapter Two

As he looked at his wife, the mother of two of his children, don Costantino's heart sank. He could not help it. It was not that he found her unattractive, though she undoubtedly was. It was rather that he bitterly regretted the actions of his younger self. When he had arrived from Serbia to make his fortune in Sicily (and he had made it) he had been an outsider, a foreigner, seeking a way in, and she, this Rosa, had been a way in, young, beautiful and a relation of don Carmelo his father. So, he had taken that way in, and marriage and two children had followed. But the way in had been deceptive. He was still an outsider. She, no longer young, no longer beautiful, but still entitled and formidable, and she reminded him of this constantly, which was, he supposed, why he so very rarely saw her.

She stood at the door of the house, radiating discontent, a discontent that was focussed on himself, the man who had married her, given her the children, given her the house, given her everything. Her lack of gratitude was astonishing. He almost admired her for it. There was no hint of conciliation in her opening words, asking what he wanted. They had not lived together for many years, but they were still man and wife, and while she had that status, she seemed deny that she owed him anything.

'You know what I want,' he said, in answer to her question.

This was true. She did. Grudgingly, she opened the door, as if this were a concession too far, and allowed him to enter. He followed her into the kitchen and sat at the table. There was his son, Dimitri, untidy, unwashed, wearing a pair of shorts and a not too clean tee shirt, presumably, as it was 11am, just emerged from bed, with a cup of coffee in front of him. Dimitri looked up and scowled at him. He in return regarded Dimitri with cold eyes. Rosa, almost revelling in the way the son and father hated each other, turned to make some coffee for her husband. Dimitri continued to stare at his father without a word. He was now twenty, the idol of his mother. For the first eleven years of his life, he had been his father's idol as well. Then things had changed. From the age of twelve until the age of eighteen, he had been regularly and furiously beaten by his father, in an attempt to instil some sense into the boy. It had not worked. Dimitri was idle, spendthrift, given to the pleasures of drugs and the bottle and various women. He was an embarrassment and had on several occasions to be rescued from police stations where he had been held for drug possession, for dangerous driving, for drunk and disorderly conduct. Luckily, his father had influence with the police, though he was less and less inclined to use it, just as he was less and less inclined to shell out large amounts of cash for the boy. Indeed, don Costantino had made it clear to his son that the next time he was arrested he could expect to stay arrested, and he had also cancelled the boy's monthly allowance. This no doubt explained Dimitri's more than usually surly demeanour.

'How are you, Dimitri?' asked his father.

The boy looked at him with wordless contempt, and, seeing that his mother's back was turned, made a hand gesture that signified extreme disrespect. His father seemed unmoved. Dimitri got up from the table, leaving his coffee, and seeing his mother still could not see, did something even worse, pulling his shorts down for a moment and exposing his private parts. He then left the room silently, glad to see that his father's cheeks were momentarily flushed with anger.

A moment later his wife Rosa, as if unaware of the boy's departure, was placing some coffee before him, and sitting opposite him. She served the coffee not as a favour, but under protest, as if this were an imposition. He supposed it was. He had loved her, he had left her, he had loved another, and she could not forgive him, not because she loved him, but because his desertion was an insult. It made him think of his African wife, and his African children. How different they were. His lovely wife in Africa, who was always so glad to see him, his daughter, and his dear son Bosco, such a credit to him. And, of course, thanks to his most recent trip to Africa, another child on the way. Why he had to put up with Rosa's silent tantrums and Dimitri's rudeness, his did not know. He supposed he owed them a debt. Whichever way, they were his family, and they counted for something.

'Where is Maria?' he asked, conversationally.

'At university,' she said, in tones that closed off any idea of further pleasantries.

He sighed. He liked his daughter, and he hoped she, unlike her brother and her mother, still liked him.

'We need to talk,' he said.

'I know we do,' she replied.

'You saw this fellow?' he asked.

'I did what you asked,' she said. 'He was at the baptism of my cousin's child. I spoke to him. I invited him round. We are friends. He has been here several times. Dimitri likes him.'

'Dimitri knows who he is?'

'Yes, he has worked it out. Your brother. I mean, he is called Michele Lollobrigida, which is his mother's name, so that was not obvious, at least not at first, but he worked it out. They like each other. What are your plans?'

'You do not need to know,' he said.

'I have done what you asked,' she said. 'If you are planning on sending Mimmo to his death, I want to know.'

'Why? What do you care about him? Besides, what is this about sending people to their death? Since when did you care about that?'

'Your other half-brother, the one who drove his car off the cliff coming down from Taormina... After a time, you begin to sense a pattern emerging.'

'Don't you understand?' he asked wearily. 'When this Mimmo is out of the way, then the will can be unfrozen and then I get everything, which means you get everything, and the children get everything.'

She looked at him with a hatred she could barely disguise. It was a lie. The person who would benefit was his African whore along with her children. But she knew this was not a time to provoke him.

'When is Michele Lollobrigida next coming here?' he asked.

'I can find out and tell you, but... I don't want any blood on our tiles, and I do not want any shots being fired in our street, or bombs going off nearby.'

'There won't be any of that, I promise you. I will come round when he is here and take him away for a little chat, that is all.'

She nodded.

'He and Dimitri made some plans, I think,' she said.

She went to the kitchen door.

'Dimitri!' she called.

'Mama?' came the reply.

'When is your friend Mimmo coming round next?'

'We didn't make any plans,' he said.

'Well, call him up and ask him to come round on Saturday for lunch. That is when I am making lasagne. He will like that.'

'OK, mama.'

She returned to her husband.

'You heard,' she said.

'The reason that boy likes Mimmo is because he thinks it will offend me,' he observed.

He wanted to go to the boy's bedroom and beat him soundly, but he knew it was pointless, and besides, Rosa would object. He did not want to give her another reason to dislike him, so he drank his coffee, wished her good morning, and left. He would be back on Saturday.

Quarter of an hour later, washed, showered and dressed, Dimitri was leaving the house on his motorbike, heading towards the school in Messina where Mimmo taught mathematics. He arrived as the lunch break was beginning, and he told the lady on reception that he urgently needed to see signor Lollobrigida. After a short wait of about ten minutes, Mimmo appeared.

'The time is now,' said Dimitri. 'He is doing it on Saturday.'

Mimmo felt his guts grow suddenly cold, and his legs grow weak.

'OK,' he said.

They were soon on the motorway, heading south. They had to stop several times because Mimmo felt ill; he threw up the contents of his near empty stomach twice. Finally, after two hours, they reached Catania, and left the bike in the crowded via Etnea, just by the Post Office. They then walked to the Purgatory quarter and went to the gym. It was now about three o'clock, and the place was deserted. They spoke to the man on the door. When they said that they had come to see Francesco, the man betrayed no reaction. But he understood. He led the way down a corridor, and they came to a door, to which he applied an electronic fob. There was a staircase, which led to another door, which was also opened electronically. They were now in a subterranean changing room, equipped with benches and lockers, and piles of snowy white towels. From a room beyond came the sound of shower water. There were various boys and men milling around, some dressing, some undressing, some in their underwear. The man from the desk went into the further room. Shortly Francesco emerged, clad in a towel. He looked at Mimmo and recognised him and gave a brief nod; then he looked at Dimitri and realised who he must be; he nodded to the man from the desk, who left them. He told the visitors to take a seat and then returned to the shower.

The two sat there in silence. Mimmo felt that his world was ending, that it had ended. He felt sick and at the same time hungry. He felt that this underground chamber was the sort from which people might not emerge alive. He felt imprisoned, trapped, wondering if they had done the right thing. He could sense next to him that these feelings were not shared by Dimitri, who, if anything, radiated a subdued sense of excitement.

Francesco reappeared, after what seemed an age, wet and wrapped in a white towel, accompanied by another man in a similar state. Neither said a word. They shook hands. The other one introduced himself as Marco. Dimitri introduced himself. Francesco looked around the room, and the others who were there realised that he wanted to be alone with the visitors. Soon they had the place to themselves.

'Does Nino Santacroce know you are here?' asked Francesco, addressing himself to Dimitri, sensing that there was little point in trying to get any sense out of Mimmo just now. 'No? Good. The fewer people who know, the better. We were expecting you, but not right now, as you might have guessed. You catch us as we are, but prepared. We are always prepared.'

'My father came round to see my mother this morning,' explained Dimitri. 'He asked when Mimmo would be round our place next. We told him Saturday lunchtime, and he said he would come back for him then.'

'Then you did well to come here and find us. He makes plans, and so do we,' said Francesco lightly. 'But we stay one step ahead.'

'And if he catches up, I die,' said Mimmo.

'And so may I,' said Dimitri. 'He will know it was me who betrayed him.'

'Oh, he will go berserk when he discovers his prey has escaped him,' said Francesco. 'But don't worry, he won't catch up. We will stay one step ahead. We will protect you. Don Calogero will protect you.'

Marco did not say anything, but was clearly listening, as he dabbed his long wet hair with a towel.

'You do not need to worry about don Costantino Petrović,' said Francesco, now addressing himself to Mimmo in particular. 'Remember, we have an agreement. Remember what my dad said to you. He is always as good as his word. His guarantee is rock solid, and round here everyone does what he wants them to do. He does not even have to say it. In a moment, when I have dried my hair, and got dressed, I am going to take you somewhere safe. Somewhere no one will ever guess you have gone to.'

'Won't people wonder…?' asked Mimmo.

'People who know nothing may well wonder, but if they know nothing…. and the people who know, will say nothing. People, the sort of people we know, know the value of silence. There is someone I trust, someone whom no one will ever suspect. You will be safe. It may be some time, of course….'

'My job… My mother and my sisters….'

'Don't worry about any of that. Think of this as a little holiday. Listen, you did the right thing. The risk is minimal, and the reward is great. I won't say nothing can go wrong, but I will say there is no progress without risk. You just need to lie low for a few weeks, maybe only days, that is all. You are lucky. You don't have to do anything; you just have to let us do it for you. Trust us.'

Francesco was gathering his discarded clothes as he said this. They were put in a bag, presumably to be washed, apart from a black tracksuit, which he gave to Marco, who added it to a black tracksuit of his own, took them away, and returned empty handed. While he did this, Francesco applied the hair dryer to his long hair, and all conversation ceased. That done, once he was dressed, he announced they would leave at once, and that his motorbike was in the street above. He shook hands with Dimitri, as did Mimmo, and then left with Mimmo.

When they were gone, there was silence. Dimitri felt slightly disoriented. He was worried and frightened. What was he supposed to do now? Where were they taking Mimmo? What was going to happen to his father? Would they really….? And would he, his mother, his sister, ever forgive themselves for the part they were playing in it? But that was a minor thought. What if his father found out? Meanwhile, Marco sat on the bench opposite him and cleaned the gun, which, amidst all the clothes, neither he nor Mimmo had noticed before now. Dimitri was mesmerised by the gun. He watched him work with great interest.

'You like guns?' asked Marco.

'Yeah, why not?' said Dimitri.

'Used one?'

'Not yet,' admitted Dimitri.

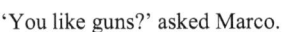
'Could you be trusted with one?' asked Marco.

'Of course.'

Marco nodded.

'Do you work for your father?' asked Marco.

'No. I am at university. Or I would be, if I went. But you know…'

'I don't,' said Marco. 'But he doesn't trust you, is that it?'

'He does not trust me, because he does not like me,' said Dimitri bitterly.

'Who cares who likes you or not?' said Marco, carelessly. 'It is trust, that is what matters. I mean, I know you will keep your mouth shut about this, because you don't want Mimmo to be killed and you don't want to get killed yourself, right?'

'My father wouldn't kill me,' said Dimitri.

'Yeah, right. He's killed all his other relations, hasn't he? But I am sure he would make an exception for you. And you, may I remind you, have decided to kill him, haven't you, or rather to get us to do your dirty work for you. Not that we mind. We will get our reward, and you will get yours.'

He smiled. He had finished with the gun and now moved over to the hairdryer. These was no more conversation. After what seemed an interminable wait, Marco spent more time tying his hair into a ponytail, while Dimitri sat disconsolately and silently on the bench.

In Piazza Armerina, Paoluzzu had been on edge all afternoon. It had been two weeks since the family of don Calogero had visited the restaurant, and all that time, he had been troubled by the request he had made to Francesco for a favour, namely the teaching of a lesson to Massimo, his former best friend who had stolen his girlfriend. He was not sure what he ought to do. Perhaps ring Francesco up and say he had not meant it, he had been joking, or he had changed his mind? But he did not have Francesco's telephone number, and besides which he had the fatalistic idea that he could not go back on his request now. He would look foolish, or cowardly, or indecisive, or unmanly, or all those things. He would lose the respect of Francesco. Besides, he told himself, Francesco would not do any serious harm to the man who had harmed him; and again, he reasoned, the man who had harmed him deserved to be punished for his behaviour, and she, the girl who betrayed him, ought to be made to feel that, in betraying him, she had done a very bad thing. She and Massimo had had no respect for him. That would change. And then, after thinking like this, he would start to have doubts once more.

Then that afternoon, two things had happened. He had been called to the phone in the restaurant, and had heard Francesco's voice telling him that he had done what he asked him to do, and saying that he would come to Piazza Armerina that evening, if Paoluzzu could make sure he was free. Well, he was not free, but he was the manager, and he supposed he could be free. The conversation was short. Later, when he had a few spare moments, he scanned the newspaper and read about the case of a young man of 22, snatched off the street in Catania, and taken somewhere and tortured, then dumped in a field on the slopes of Etna. The assailants were unknown, and the police had no lines of enquiry. He wondered what the torture had entailed. He was not sure if he were pleased or not. What if the outrage were traced back to him? He realised that he was a terrible coward.

They had to stop twice on the way to Piazza Armerina for Mimmo to get off the bike and throw up at the side of the road. It was a horrible thing to watch Mimmo make the terrible retching sounds, his helmet in his hand, while nothing came out. He said everything to reassure Mimmo that where they were going was safe, that he could not be found. For a start, he had switched off and handed over his phone, so there would be no electronic trace; besides which he had come from Messina to Catania on a bike wearing a helmet; and now, still wearing a helmet, from Catania to Piazza Armerina on a different bike. He could not be spotted. And he was going to people who were not connected with him.

They arrived a bit before six at the Trattoria Norma. Paoluzzu had been expecting him but was a little surprised to see Mimmo as well. The restaurant was shut, but the two visitors came in, and the manager sat them at a table, and brought some water and a bottle of wine. Mimmo, without a word, accepted the water with gratitude. He never wanted to ride pillion on a motorcycle again.

'So, what brings you here again so soon?' asked Paoluzzu.

'Girls, cousin, girls,' said Francesco with a smile.

Paoluzzu was glad to have the relationship recognised. He waited for Francesco to continue.

'Mimmo has got a girl into trouble and needs to hide from her father; and a girl has got me into trouble with my father. Mimmo's is the simpler case. He needs a place to stay for a week or so. I immediately thought of you.'

So, this was the favour being asked in return for the favour given. Mimmo looked harmless enough. Paoluzzu breathed a sigh of relief internally.

'Of course. He can stay with my parents, or upstairs here, there is a room not being used.'

'That might be best. The fewer who know the better,' said Francesco. He looked at Mimmo, who had said nothing. 'Go with Paoluzzu.'

The two of them disappeared. Francesco waited. After about ten minutes, Paoluzzu returned.

'He'll be Ok,' said Paoluzzu. 'He told me he just wanted to go to sleep.'

'Good,' said Francesco. 'Now, you need to spruce yourself up, and make some phone calls, as we are going out.'

'And you both wore helmets on the motorbike?' asked Marco.

'Yes, of course,' said Dimitri. 'As you told us to.'

'And you did what we suggested, you covered the numberplate of your bike with mud?'

'I did.'

Marco nodded. This was good. They were both in the bar in the square outside the Church of the Holy Souls in Purgatory. Each had a beer in front of him. Marco frowned.

'Do you like your father?' Marco asked.

'No,' said Dimitri. 'Not in the least. He never comes near us, except when he has to. He has humiliated my mother, and he wants to replace me as his heir with this kid in Africa. I mean, him having a second family is bad enough, but the thought of them coming to Sicily and becoming his first family, and us.... What he is doing is not right. And the way he has treated me... that is not right. And if he finds out that my sister has been seeing, and more than seeing, Mimmo, he will kill Mimmo, and that will not please her. So....'

'We will sort it out, we will sort it out,' said Marco. 'When do you see him, and more importantly, where do you see him?'

'I go to the flat he keeps in Messina, when I need to see him, and he sees me there, or they tell me where he is in Taormina, you know, one of the hotels. He has a few favourite suites. I go and see him at the suite. I don't like seeing him.'

'But you do, you see him, and he always sees you, when you ask?'

'He does. I don't like seeing him, but I have to see him from time to time. When I need money. He is mean and stingy, and he always gives me a lecture. I hate it!'

Marco considered. To ask for money, that would be humiliating. As it was, he himself was in the lucky position of being able to give his parents money. He never made them ask for it, either. He just left it on the kitchen table. No one ever mentioned it. He did so every week, on a Friday night. And at reasonably regular intervals, he went to Caltagirone, always bearing financial gifts, again, always unasked.

'You see,' explained Dimitri, feeling he could open up to Marco, 'He says I am no good, that I can't have a part in the business, that I cannot keep my mouth shut, that I am irresponsible, and that this kid in Africa, my half-brother, the one they call Bosco, is going to be better at things than me. That Bosco has guts, and I have not. It is humiliating and it is wrong.'

'Don Costantino has miscalculated,' said Marco. 'That is what I hear. I mean, he always goes everywhere with two Serbs in tow, doesn't he? It is as if he does not trust anyone. Perhaps he is right about that, but it offends people, his own people. And then this guy, your grandfather's son, the one who drove off the cliff, and the others who died during the picnic on Etna… people liked your grandfather a lot, and now, here he is killing his children… Don Costantino has made himself unloved and disliked, and no one will regret him when he is gone.'

'Still, he is my father,' said Dimitri uneasily. 'He loved me when I was little. He just could not stand me when I grew up.'

'That was his mistake,' said Marco. 'A son in Africa whom he hardly sees, and a son in Messina whom he does not get on with. How can anyone respect such a man? He can't look after his own children; how can he look after his own family? He's not….. responsible. He should have realised, when he got married, that he had duties, responsibilities. You and your mother are right to be annoyed with him.'

'Responsibilities,' said Dimitri. 'That is a big word. Are you married, or getting married?' he asked.

'No. You may be confusing me with Nino. He is having a child and marrying the mother, and he is hardly grown up. But he wants to do it for reasons of reputation, I think. Me, well, I have responsibilities. I have a son. He is eight. He lives with his mother. She is…. older than me. I go and see them every so often, and I make sure they lack for nothing. They are content. They don't live in this quarter, but away from here…'

'You keep them secret?'

'No, everyone knows I have a son. No one has met him, no one here, that is. It was her choice. And mine.'

'And Francesco?' he asked curiously.

'He sleeps with every girl he meets. But on top of that, he is in love with one girl in particular; he thinks we do not know, but we do. They used to live next door to each other. But it is a family the boss does not like, and the boss has other plans for him. He is important, so it matters who he goes around with. He is the boss's son.'

'He became the boss's son.'

'Same thing.'

'Has it made his head swell?'

'No. He is a nice boy. He is sensible. He has not let it change him. I knew him when he was still being carried around in his mother's arms. I am seven or eight years older. He was always a really nice person. His father had deserted them, and he and his mother had no money, none at all, though she worked when she could, and she also got a bit from don Traiano, being the second cousin of his wife. But I don't know how it is in Messina, and perhaps you would not know, but we all had no money in those days, but we all, well, we were friends. That is all I can say. I got my first job collecting debts for don Traiano; Nino, well, no need to go into that now, but he worked for don Traiano too. But none of us ever knew where the next ten euro was coming from. When you are born poor, you remember where you come from. Even Nino, who is perhaps richer than any of us.'

Dimitri took this as a rebuke and looked into his beer. After a few moments, he spoke:

'Have you got any cocaine?' he asked hopefully.

'Nino may turn up soon. He will have some, or if he doesn't, he will get it for you. Just be patient.'

'Can I ask something else? Can I meet don Calogero?'

Marco looked at Dimitri and considered.

'Generally speaking, he does not meet people, you know, as we do not want to establish lines of communication that others can trace. Plausible deniability. When what happens, happens, the chief suspects will all be people don Calogero has never met. He acts at one remove, always. But I know he will want to see you, get to know you, because you are the lynchpin of this matter, and afterwards, he will want to reward you.'

'Is that what he has said? In your hearing?' asked Dimitri, delighted.

'He thinks highly of you,' said Marco with ease.

'It is fixed,' said Francesco. 'That is all you need to know.'

Paoluzzu was sprucing himself up. This involved studying his face closely in the mirror for any signs of blemishes and applying a huge amount of gel to his hair. They had phoned the two girls, who had agreed to meet – not with much enthusiasm, it had to be said, but they had agreed, and on short notice too. Francesco knew what that meant. Ida was doing it to please her parents, and she needed an ally, this Claudia, the one Paoluzzu was after.

'Did you mention my name?' asked Paoluzzu.

'No need. We just let him know that he had offended a friend of ours. He won't do it again. We advised him to get himself the other side of the straits of Messina. You will not have to worry about him, trust me. Tell me, this Claudia and you....?'

'There is nothing to tell,' said Paoluzzu. 'She is very stand-offish. But now you are coming, and now she knows that we are friends, well, who knows...? What about you and Ida?'

'That is dad's idea, and perhaps her father's as well. I mean, I have got Petra, and that has been on and off ever since we met four years ago, and now it is really on again, but perhaps better not mention it tonight?'

'I know the value of silence,' said Paoluzzu.

Half an hour later, they were in a bar on the main square of Piazza Armerina, standing at the counter, each with a tiny cup of coffee. It was here that they had arranged to meet the girls. Above them was a television, barely audible, tuned in to a local channel. Very soon the news would be broadcast, and Francesco was studying the screen, but not looking at Paoluzzu. The news, as far as Paoluzzu could see, was the same as ever. It started with a murder in Catania. A tobacconist had been shot in Librino. He had been shutting up his shop at lunchtime, preparing to going home, when two men on a motorbike had gone past and shot him dead. The pictures were what they always were: two policemen guarding the spot; a long shot of the dismal road on which the tobacconist's stood; interviews with neighbours, none of whom had seen anything much; tributes from campaigners against extortion, who hailed the victim as a brave man for refusing to pay tribute to the local boss.

'What is the point of being brave if you end up dead?' asked Francesco.

The next item came up. Again, it was the usual thing: the inefficiency of the local hospitals and clinics. They both sighed, waiting for the sports news. But even that was uninteresting, relatively speaking, being a report on the Catania swimming team. They were fine fellows, but it was not football.

'You know Beppe Santucci? He goes to matches all the time, all over Italy,' said Francesco moodily. 'And he and his cousin, who is married to my dad's sister, go to all these marathons the cousin runs in, and they always appear on television with Alberto Whatshisname, commenting on the marathon, or the game that weekend.'

'Alberto? The one with grey hair? My mother loves him.'

'All mothers love him, mine included. She does not care about football, but when Alberto is on the screen, she watches with great interest. Well, he is the most attractive man in Italy. But why the hell they have Renzo Santucci and Beppe Santucci on, I do not know. Have you seen them?'

'Yes…. I mean neither of them are goodlooking, are they? I suppose they are rich, so people are interested. And he runs for charity, doesn't he?'

'Yes, the hypocrite, pretending to care about the unfortunate, when all the time the only person he cares about is himself. But they get invited on television and I do not. No matter how hard one tries, one is never invited to the party, is one? I suppose the answer is to stop trying, and to gatecrash. Just take it by force. But when you do get admitted, you are made to feel as if you are there on sufferance. For others, like the Santucci cousins, it's their birthright. But not me, not you, not even my dad. Mind you, I suppose people like me can do without being on television. Perhaps one day I will be - in handcuffs!'

Francesco laughed.

'So, you do not like the Palermo lot?' asked Paoluzzu.

'No. But don't tell anyone. They are arrogant. They are not like us…'

The girls of Piazza Armerina now entered, a few minutes later than agreed, for it was not a good idea to look or act too keen; that had been their game plan. They were both such beautiful girls, Claudia even more than Ida, because Ida was darker. Their appearance was very natural, and if they had spent time on their appearance, it did not show. If they had been aiming at effortless elegance, then they had surely achieved it. Ida was wearing a simple dress of midnight blue, with a leather belt, in order to show off her attractive waistline. On her wrist was a bracelet of large, dark blue ceramic beads. Claudia was in a pale linen dress, and her hair was drawn back, and she had a necklace of large ceramic beads around her neck, which were a glowing magenta in colour. Francesco recognised the beads. They came, he knew, from East Africa, from his father's hotel. He wondered if they had been a present from Paoluzzu, who might have brought them back with him, presumably for the girlfriend who had deserted him.

Francesco felt a little colour come to his cheeks at the realisation that these girls were intelligent and lovely, and not likely to be over-impressed by him. Colour came to the cheeks of Paoluzzu too, as he felt the wave of lust occasioned by the sight of Claudia hit him. His face burned, his guts turned to ice, and one part of him tingled at the sight of her. She, perhaps sensing his discomfort, regarded him with a wry smile. It was, Claudia reflected, nice to have power over a man. They greeted one another, and Claudia was introduced to Francesco.

Claudia had had plenty of opportunity before now to examine Paoluzzu, and she turned her gaze on the new friend, the one they called Francesco, whom she had already discussed at length with her best friend Ida. He was pleasant, though not handsome, but he had a nice face, and good hair, grown long. His eyes were clear and hazel; his nose rather big, and, like Paoluzzu, he was broad in the chest, and of average height for a Sicilian. An attractive boy, some might say, and the son, or rather stepson, of a very important man, perhaps spoilt rotten like so many other boys in similar circumstances. She noted the suit, and the expensive shoes, along with the modest but doubtlessly expensive wristwatch. He saw her look at his watch.

'I need a watch, because I don't have a phone,' he said, as if excusing himself.

'Then how do people get hold of you?' asked Ida.

'Oh, I am not hard to find,' he said. 'We have a landline at home. And I am never far from home.'

Drinks were ordered: four glasses of vermouth. Ida, the daughter of don Nunzio, was, on the whole, rather taken with these boys who gave the impression of being desperate to please. She had met don Calogero's family the other week, and met Francesco, and since then her parents had spoken of hardly anything else. Francesco was, according to both of them, who made the point separately, together and repeatedly, just the sort of friend for her. She was eighteen, nearly nineteen, and he was exactly the same age. He was the stepson of someone important; indeed, his stepfather was the most important man in Sicily. But he was only the stepson, which clearly mattered; if he had been the real son, it would have placed him out of reach. But he was slightly flawed, and that made him accessible. She was eighteen, nearly nineteen, and had never had a boyfriend; her parents were pushing her towards this Francesco, she saw, and she was content to be pushed, not because she wanted a boyfriend, but because she did not. And she could see that he was somewhat in awe of her, which was good. She was doing what her parents wanted, and that would keep them happy for now, indeed for some time.

'You are at the university?' she asked.

'Yes, information technology, but... it is not very interesting. I mean.... What about you?'

'We are both doing classics,' Ida said. 'It is very exciting. The Latin is nice, but the Greek is... immense.'

He nodded, not knowing what to say to this.

'I liked Virgil at school,' he said, feeling that this was an inadequate response.

He had, both girls noticed, a very strong Catania accent. In their different ways, they found it rather endearing. These boys, the restaurant manager, the boss's stepson, they were both rather unsophisticated.

Francesco saw how it was, almost immediately. Girls had, until now, fallen into his hands like ripe fruit, ever since shortly after his fourteenth birthday, when don Calogero had become his mother's lover. The principal girl had been, and still was, their neighbour in the Furnaces, Petra Costacurta; but there had been others, lots of others, here and there, all wanting a bit of the boss's son, something he had been happy to provide. All of which was well and good, as one did not know what the future would bring, but one did know that there would be no girls in jail. When one met a girl, one could tell whether she was interested, and they had all been interested, or nearly all – but now something had changed. Not these two, he sensed. They were not impressed by his shoes, his suit, his hair, his hazel eyes, his connection to the boss. They were immune to his charms and to Paoluzzu's as well, he could tell. They looked at them both as from a remote height; they were maidens at the top of a tower, looking at the world beyond their fortress with merry amusement. But they were beautiful, and all the more attractive for being out of reach. Ida was beautiful: her hair, her smile, her prefect lips, her dark eyes, her generous bosom. He felt his armpits beginning to prickle and sweat, and he felt a strong desire to put his hand in his pocket to make his testicles a little more comfortable. It was going to be that sort of evening, he felt, a rather different evening to what he was used to.

Claudia now asked Francesco how he had met Ida.

'My father is in business and knows her father,' he said. 'We were invited round last week to don Nunzio's house.'

'Is your father in paper?' asked Claudia.

He remembered just in time that don Nunzio, among other things, owned a papermill.

'Construction,' said Francesco.

'And you?'

'Well, I help him. I am studying information technology, and I have built the website of a charity that he is the head of. You may have heard of it. The Ancient and Noble Archconfraternity of the Holy Souls in Purgatory of the Noble City of Catania.'

'I haven't, I am afraid. Does the website get much traffic?'

'Thousands of hits a day. We are the biggest charity in Catania, and we are getting bigger. Our *donate* button never stops.'

'And what does this charity do?' asked Claudia, without much interest.

'It disburses money to those in need,' said Francesco, feeling he was being boring.

'That,' said Claudia, 'is nice. And what are you going to do next?' she asked practically.

'We are creating an app called Sicilia Historica; it is an interactive map with articles linked to every place of historical interest on the island. So, you know, you find yourself in Messina, and it tells you about the earthquake, or Scylla and Charybdis. My friend Nino is very clever, and he knows what to do; but really it was my father's idea. It is going to be huge, we hope.'

She looked, he hoped, a little bit more impressed by this.

It was a very strange evening, from Francesco's point of view. The two beautiful girls were polite and friendly, but he could see that their attention was more fixed on each other rather than on the two boys. The two boys were there as an interruption, perhaps a necessary one, for if girls wanted to walk around Piazza Armerina, they had to do so with boys at their side, or so tradition dictated, a tradition that was not quite dead yet.

Francesco had the sense he was being scrutinised by both Claudia and Ida. Ida was attentive, not to him, but to his clothes, his hair, his face, his demeanour. They walked, they talked, they went into another bar, they drank a little, they had something to eat, and then, at around ten in the evening, they parted. They did so, promising to meet again soon. The two boys walked back to Paoluzzu's house where the motorbike was waiting. Francesco felt no desire whatever to go back to Catania. In fact, he wanted to keep away from Catania for the next few days, largely because of the tobacconist from Librino, and also, perhaps, on account of the previous job, the man who had stolen Paoluzzu's last girlfriend.

'Are you staying or going?' asked Paoluzzu. 'There is a spare bed in my room.'

'I will stay, cousin, if you and your parents don't mind. I will need to check up on Mimmo tomorrow morning.' He paused. 'And maybe after that, I will go and see don Nunzio, you know, just to say hello.'

Paoluzzu took this in, and nodded, pleased. If Francesco was serious about Ida, that would only benefit him. It would mean Francesco would be spending more time in Piazza Armerina, more time with her, more time with him, and that Francesco's presence and visible friendship would only help to raise his status in the eyes of Claudia.

They went up to the flat. Paoluzzu's parents were still up, and Francesco had a polite conversation with both. He had known them both as a child in Catania years ago. The mother, he knew, was a relative, a first cousin, he thought, of his errant and absent biological father; he did not know any of his father's relatives, except by reputation and in a few cases by sight; none of them had ever done anything for him and his mother when they had needed help, but luckily none of them had presented themselves since then, when the situation had been reversed, of which he was glad. He treated the lady with calm politeness, calling her 'signora' as was right and proper. He could see her studying his face, as if looking for a resemblance to her absent, in every sense, cousin. The father, whom he addressed as 'sir', was a large, strong man, who was in his fifties and known to be 'unwell'; this fact was in the public domain; everyone knew that he did not work, and that he depended on his hardworking son, as did the mother. What form his unwellness took was not known, but meeting him now, Francesco assumed it was depression; luckily the man was not his relation, and it was not hereditary anyway.

The two young men, each in their own way, were quite glad to get away from the parents and go to bed. It was agreed that Francesco should go to the restaurant first thing in the morning to spend time with Mimmo; the cleaners would be there, and they would let him in; Paoluzzu would follow later, as he never went there much before ten. Thus, when Paoluzzu woke the next morning at about nine, it was to find his friend already gone. He heaved himself wearily out of bed and went to the kitchen in his pyjamas to have a glass of water. He was wearing a short dressing gown over his Calvins, and he was aware that his gelled hair was a terrible mess. He would have a shower soon, wash it, re-gel it, and all would be well.

But in stepping into the kitchen, he was immediately aware that all was not well. His mother was not there, as she usually was; only his father. His father's expression was thunderous.

'Massimo is dead,' said his father. 'It was on the television news this morning.'

Massimo was the best friend who had run off with his girlfriend.

'Massimo is no longer a friend of mine,' he said defensively. 'What do I care?'

'Aren't you going to ask how he died?' said his father.

Paoluzzu shrugged.

'They gave him a good kicking and ruptured something inside him; at first it looked not so serious, then, after a day or two, it was clear it was fatal.'

'Maybe he deserved a good kicking,' said Paoluzzu. 'He was not my friend, so what do I care?' he repeated.

'And that one is your friend?' asked his father.

He knew he meant Francesco.

'Yes, he is,' he answered defiantly.

'He will get you killed. He will get us all killed. He killed Massimo, didn't he? And you think they won't find out?'

Paoluzzu looked at his father with loathing and contempt.

'Do you think I want to be like you?' he asked with a bitterness he had not realised he felt. 'You are my father, and I will always love you, but I cannot respect you. I feel sorry for you. Everything we have is because I worked for it. I was in Africa for four years, working every day I could, saving money; and where did that job come from? From don Calogero, and I was lucky to get it. And then, when I was back, that bitch had been cheating on me with that bastard Massimo. Well, they gave him a kicking as a favour to me, and perhaps they kicked too hard, but I am not sorry, not sorry at all. No one will ever treat me badly again. No one. I am sick to death of being treated badly by everyone, and by you. That is over. If you do not like it, go back to Catania; me and my mother will stay here.'

'You are a fool,' said his father. 'It won't end well.'

His voice was subdued, his tone sad. He was not provoked. In his words were, they both felt, the inexpressible grief of being born Sicilian.

Paoluzzu say down at the table. There was silence between them that lasted some time.

'I did not mean for them to kill him,' said Paoluzzu at last. 'They must have got carried away, or it was an accident, or....'

'You have made your choice now,' said his father. 'I made mine many years ago. As you say, your mother and I depend on you and your hard work, and your connections. It is ungallant of me to complain about your choices, when I benefit from them. So, I will not be going back to Catania, but staying here, if that is alright with you.'

He nodded, not trusting himself to say anything. Then, after a moment, forgetting why he had come into the kitchen, he went to the bathroom to shower and do his hair. He felt nothing, he felt nothing at all, for his dead best friend, he told himself, though in the shower, and later standing in front of the mirror, he noticed that his eyes were welling up. Well, it was not his fault, not Francesco's fault, but entirely Massimo's fault for betraying him in that way in the first place. Far more worrying, surely, was the thought that the death of Massimo might be traced back to him. But it could not be. He had been here in Piazza Armerina, in a restaurant full of people. And if people knew that the person who had insulted and betrayed him was dead, well, so much the better. Others would think carefully about doing the same.

He went to the Trattoria Norma at about ten, his usual time of arrival. Francesco was there, with Mimmo, sitting at one of the tables, having coffee. There was a plate in front of Mimmo, who had clearly eaten something.

'I have been telling him that he will be fat by the time he leaves here, the food is so good,' Francesco said, as Paoluzzu approached. 'Not that he is staying long. We will have everything sorted out soon enough. Trust me. In the meantime, trust Paoluzzu. Trust the people here.'

He and Paoluzzu exchanged looks, but not words. He saw that Paoluzzu had heard about the unexpected death of Massimo. Well, there was nothing to be said. It had happened, that was all. But he could tell Paoluzzu was unnerved by the whole thing. Well, he wasn't, any more than he was unnerved by the death of the tobacconist of Librino. Nor was he unnerved by the prospect of the deaths to come.

'How were the girls you saw last night?' asked Mimmo who had recovered from being the vomiting wreck of yesterday.

'Gorgeous' said Francesco. 'But all Sicilian girls are lovely, don't you think? At least all the ones I meet. But the beautiful girls of Piazza Armerina are in a class of their own. For that reason, they are stand-offish. They are a challenge, which makes them unusual. And they are a cut above the usual sort of girl. They are very wise and learned. They are doing classics at the university. But the one called Claudia will not be able to resist Paoluzzu forever. As for Ida, well, the fact that I am here will please my father, and my mother. They both want me to meet nice girls. Now I have.'

'So, what do you make of Mimmo?' Calogero asked the next afternoon.

He was slumped on the sofa, the two younger boys sitting next to him, an arm around each. They were watching cartoons, which fascinated them. They were allowed to watch cartoons for an hour after school each day. On a wide armchair sat Francesco and Renato. Renato too was watching the cartoons with interest, though he was listening to his father and stepbrother as well and trying to understand what they were saying. He was enjoying his close proximity to Francesco, whom he loved almost as much as his father.

'When I left him, he was more or less calm. I think Mimmo is a huge coward. He is in no danger, is he, really? But he is terrified. No wonder he wants to get out, to sell up, and so cheaply. He did one brave thing…'

'What was that?' asked Calogero.

'Meeting this girl Maria, and, you know…. I mean that was daring, he knew who she was, I am sure, and he decided that there was something to be gained there. It was calculated.'

'Of course it was. It always is with these people.'

'Then, when it was too late to go back, to retreat in safety, he came running, in terror, to you.'

'He did. He is a coward, you are right. And we can and will exploit his weakness. And the other one, Dimitri?'

Francesco tapped his nose.

'I see,' said Calogero. 'Not the sort to be trusted.'

'Yes, a compete fool. Marco said that he told him that when he went to the school, there was no one on the lookout. Well, there was, wasn't there, and there had been for some time; our people, but he did not notice them. No observational skills at all. Not to be trusted. Besides, dad, he hates Costantino with a passion, as does the mother, as does the sister. As you will doubtless point out to me, it means he is not thinking straight. And Costantino has not been kind to him, has he, we know that… But I don't altogether blame Costantino for that. The boy must be infuriating, spending money, being idle, taking drugs. He doesn't realise it, but we know all about him; if he were cleverer, he would have guessed we had done our research. He is worthless. Susceptible to flattery as well. Vain and foolish.'

'Poor Costantino. Not lucky in his children. It must drive him to distraction, and we shall profit by that distraction. The people in his office, his men in the hotels…'

'They don't like him, dad. I am afraid it is a bit because they regard him as an outsider, a Serb. No one really likes the Serbs, not sure why.'

'Well, they are Serbs…' said Calogero. 'They are violent criminals, the lot of them. The thing is, will his Serb friends kick up a fuss? Or will they have too much to worry about when their protector is no longer there? You are right, they do not like him. They resent the insult to his wife. I have not met the signora Rosa, and I doubt I ever shall, but she is clearly a person to be reckoned with, like my mother and my sisters. They do not like this idea of the family from Africa coming over, not one little bit. Another greedy woman, another bunch of greedy children, and all the time there is only one cake, and they see more and more people wanting a slice. Besides, the people in Messina, they liked don Carmelo, and they never liked Costantino that much. Ah well, human nature. We would never have known all this, if it were not for all the complaints we have been receiving; it was nice and useful that so many came to us volunteering information. That too is human nature; some things, they can put up with, but not others.'

Francesco nodded. He understood.

'And how was your time in Piazza Armerina?' asked Calogero casually, as if this were the question he had not been itching to ask all day.

'Fine, dad, fine. She is a really nice girl. She brought her friend with her – she is that sort of girl. But that was OK and made things easier as Paoluzzu, the one from the trattoria, is in love with her. We had a nice time.'

'Ah, Paoluzzu,' said the boss. 'I read the papers; I saw the television.'

'It was an accident, dad. Marco and I got a bit too enthusiastic, I suppose, though we did not realise it at the time.'

The boss nodded.

'Is Paoluzzu a good boy?' he asked.

'Very, dad. A really good boy, works hard, does his job, well behaved, loves his parents. I saw don Nunzio as well. I went to call on him. He invited me to have coffee with him. Ida was out, but he was the one I wanted to see. I think he was glad I had come to see him.'

'Good,' said Calogero. 'When are you going there next?'

'Sunday.'

Calogero was pleased by this. His stepson was a good, obedient boy. That was what he had hoped for and expected, so he pretended not to be overly satisfied. He picked up the remote control and changed the channel of the television. The children protested at the interruption; their father wanted to see the local news. They hated the news. The news was boring. They groaned, but stopped protesting, knowing that their father would soon turn back to the cartoons.

The bulletin began, and the two adults watched in silence and without comment. The death of the tobacconist in Librino was still the first item on the news. Once more, they were told that two men on a motorcycle, both wearing helmets, had been seen riding away from the scene of the crime. There was more of the usual stuff, not photographs of the pavement outside the shop, the shrouded corpse, and the curious bystanders this time, but pictures of the victim's coffin entering his parish church. There were interviews with people. The tobacconist had been a good person, it was averred. A local politician was interviewed. (Calogero frowned.) The tobacconist had been leading a campaign against paying tribute to the local bosses. This was the price one paid for resistance. Then came an item about a local footballer who was injured, and who might, or might not, play that weekend, and on whose state of injury or not, much of the fortunes of the Elephants rested.

'Will the Elephants ever make us proud?' wondered Calogero sadly.

He turned back to the cartoons.

'Have you seen Nino Santacroce? How was he?' he asked, while the children looked at 'Road Runner'.

'Suitably penitent,' said Francesco. 'He has been taught a lesson by you, dad. I just wish that Marco and I could have added to the message.'

'You are jealous,' observed Calogero.

'A bit,' admitted Francesco.

'He is how old…? He thinks he can do what he likes. Well, he can't. None of us can.'

'Except you, dad,' said Francesco. 'You are different.'

'Exactly. He wants to be me. Well, he can't.'

'What has Nino done?' asked Renato innocently, not taking his eyes off the television.

The two adults exchanged looks.

'It is all over the quarter, so he will find out soon enough,' reasoned Francesco. 'If he has not found out already.'

'He has misbehaved, and he has been punished,' said Calogero.

'What did he do?' asked Renato.

'He…,' began Calogero, looking desperately at Francesco.

'He met a girl and slept with her, if you know what that means,' said Francesco.

'Of course, I know what that means,' said Renato.

'Well, that is not allowed, and unfortunately she is now having a baby, so your father has decided that he and she have to get married, when they are a bit older, of course.'

'I like Nino,' said Renato.

The adults exchanged glances again.

Renato fixed his attention on the cartoon. The two younger sons had been so engrossed by 'Road Runner' that they had been oblivious to this conversation. After a time, Renato whispered something to Francesco.

'You will have to ask your father,' said Francesco.

Renato nodded. Calogero ignored this exchange. The cartoons, at long last, came to an end. Calogero hauled himself off the sofa, kissed Sebastiano and Romano, and sent them off to do their homework. They trotted off happily. Renato hung back and approached his father.

'The answer is no,' said Calogero with more severity than he realised was wise. He felt riled. 'You remember what I said last time. You are almost twelve. You can't get into bed with me anymore, or your mother, or sleep in Francesco's room. If you really have to share a room, then go in with Romano or Sebastiano. But Francesco needs peace and quiet, and he is grown up, and he needs to be alone. As do you. You need to get used to being alone.'

The boy looked as if he might cry.

'You are almost twelve,' remonstrated his father. 'Grow up! Besides, Francesco may not be here this evening until much later. Isn't that right, Francesco?'

'Where is he going?' asked Renato miserably.

'That is none of your business. He is eighteen, he is grown up. He has not got time for you. He spends enough time with you as it is.'

The boy began to howl. Francesco went to comfort him.

'Renato, shut up,' said his father. 'If you do not, I will really give you something to howl about. Remember what is in that cupboard,' he said, gesturing to the other side of the room.

'You hate me,' said Renato, between his tears. 'Francesco loves me, but you are jealous.'

'Don't be ridiculous,' said Calogero, now in full despair. 'Look, come here, come here,' he said, embracing the child. 'Everyone loves you, me included. If you want to share a room with Francesco, then you can, tonight, but just for tonight. You are worse than your sisters when it comes to getting your own way.'

And worse than your mother Stefania, he could have added.

Renato smiled in triumph.

'Dad, please, don't give in to him,' said Francesco.

Calogero quelled him with a look, and Francesco accepted the inevitable. Renato hugged his father, and then hugged Francesco, then left.

'We have left Dimitri waiting long enough,' said Calogero.

Dimitri had been waiting for more than twenty-four hours, waiting for his promised meeting with the boss. He was, though he did not quite realise it, being left to stew, so that, when the meeting came, he would be suitably relieved and grateful. During this time, he had been entertained by Marco and Nino. He had been provided with lots of cocaine, he had been taken to eat in the pizzeria and the trattoria, and he had been given a hotel room to sleep in, and a girl to sleep with. He had passed the last couple of hours in the underground chamber, in the vigilant company of Marco the Dentist. He had been allowed some more cocaine, and his jaw was now delightfully numb, and he had even snatched a few moments of sleep stretched out on the bench. Marco's conversational possibilities were long exhausted. No overture to talking now made much progress. He had asked several times when the boss would see him. Marco said this would happen when the boss was ready, not before. The boss came when he could, and all of them, without exception, waited for him with patience. This was said without undue emphasis, but Dimitri took it as a gentle rebuke. He realised that his life was changing. These people revolved around don Calogero, and so, perhaps, would he. He was almost twenty-one years old and had lived his life in the shadow of his father, the father whom he loved, feared and hated in equal measure. That father was soon to pass from the scene, if all went well; and the huge gap he would leave would surely be taken by don Calogero. He had not thought of this before: he would be exchanging one father for another; one only discovered the consequences of one's actions after one had made the decision to act. He wondered how he would get along with don Calogero and felt unaccountably nervous; he wanted to ask Marco about don Calogero, but knew that Marco would not divulge anything of interest. Besides, what was the point, when he would soon be meeting don Calogero himself.

At last Francesco entered. He nodded to Marco, and he looked at Dimitri.

'Ready?' he asked.

Dimitri stood and felt a tremor of fear and anticipation. He followed Francesco out of the room. They went upstairs and into some sort of room that was plainly used as an office. There don Calogero was waiting. They stood and looked at each other. Dimitri took in all the details: the close-cut dark curly hair, the wide apart brown eyes, the smooth skin, the hint of a smile, the beautifully tailored suit, the crisp shirt, the wonderful shoes. He was tall, athletic and strong. Dimitri felt overwhelmed to be in the presence of such power.

'Have they been looking after you well?' asked don Calogero.

'Yes, sir, they have,' said Dimitri.

'Has Francesco? I hope you and he will be fast friends,' said don Calogero.

'I hope so too, sir,' said Dimitri. 'I would like that very much.'

'So would I, and as Francesco is such a good boy, it will happen, we can all be sure. Francesco, thanks for looking after our new friend. And tell Nino and Marco I am grateful. You can go now.'

Francesco approached the boss, kissed him, and left. The door shut behind him. Dimitri wondered if for one horrible moment he was about to be murdered, whether all this was a huge deception, worked by his father, Costantino. But the door was shut, he felt absurdly, and there was no escape. The boss indicated a chair he was to sit on and then sat down himself. The chairs were close together. Dimitri could feel the heat of his own body and felt the corresponding coolness of don Calogero.

'You need to get back to Messina, Dimitri, before anyone asks any questions. And you need to go to your father's flat, or wherever he is, as you normally would, as if nothing has changed, so as not to arouse suspicion, as I am sure they told you. We know what he is like. We know all about him.'

'All, sir?'

'Every detail,' said Calogero. 'Ever since your grandfather was blown up, along with all his legitimate sons and his chief collaborators; ever since then we have been hearing lots of complaints from Messina. It is over two years since your grandfather died, and in that time… well, don Costantino had a chance to show he was a good boss, but he has not done well. He has been cruel and arrogant to many of the people who did well under don Carmelo. He has treated your mother with a marked lack of respect, which many find unforgiveable. He has offended me as well, because he made no objection to the rebellion of that other Balkan person, Trajan Antonescu. Lots of people have come to Catania to complain about him, knowing that I alone am the one who can get rid of him. And now you have come, and Mimmo has come, and we will get rid of him, if you play your part correctly. I am sure you will. What he has done to others is wrong. What he has done to you and your mother is unforgiveable.'

Calogero put his hands of his shoulders and kissed his forehead.

'What your father has destroyed, I will restore,' he said. 'And all will be well.'

In a small flat, the next evening, near the Roman Theatre, off the Corso Vittorio Emmanuele, Nino Santacroce was in bed with his girlfriend. Through the wall came the sound of the RAI news, where her parents were watching the television in the kitchen. Penetrating the shut window came the sounds of the evening traffic from the Corso. The bed was not meant for two, indeed three, as the girl was pregnant, though nor showing very much so far. The discomfort was compounded by the bruises on his body, thanks to the beating he had received from the boss. He did not mind the punishment because of what followed it. He had been forgiven. He had a girlfriend, he had a child on the way, he had, he felt, prestige. He was a man. The boss had been pacified, he felt, as the beating was in fact a very pedestrian punishment. The boss, if he had been really annoyed, would have had him killed, but he had not. He rather thought that Francesco and Marco would have liked to have killed him, and resented the way he had got away with it. But there had been no real possibility of that, he was sure. He was the one that the boss could not do without. Marco pulled out other people's teeth and beat or shot them as necessary. Francesco was special because his mother was the boss's wife, but he, Nino, he was the one who knew Colonel Andreazza and the other policemen; he was the one who sold the pills and the other stuff. Anyone, he knew, could sell pills, but not anyone could command the attention of Andreazza. And Andreazza was key. Everyone knew that.

'Are you staying for supper?' she was asking.

'I have an appointment at about 7.30pm,' he said. 'I ought not to miss it. Besides, I think your parents, your father in particular, have seen enough of me for one evening, don't you think?'

'No, they like you,' she said.

'Oh, I am sure they will in due course, but for now they resent me, they think I have made a fool of them. But they will get over it.' He thought of the envelope he had left on the kitchen table. Its contents generally assured a degree of goodwill. 'I behave badly, and people forgive me, eventually. Your parents, my parents, even good don Giorgio will. Do you want to live in a flat on your own? I could get you one.'

'Without my parents?' she asked, for the idea was strange.

'I will get us a flat, you'll see. You won't have to live there just yet, but… when we are married….'

That was years away, they both knew. Still, it was worth looking forward to.

'Do you have to go?' she asked.

'In a moment, not just yet,' he said.

There was silence once more in the room. The traffic sounds and the sound of the television now seemed to become more intense.

'Thanks, Daniela,' he said at last, and extracted himself from her embrace and the bed.

She watched him as he got dressed, without bothering to wash. He was tall, slim, thin even, smooth, immature. It was obvious how young he was, how much younger in fact than he pretended to be.

'What?' he said, as he put on his shirt.

'Nothing,' she said.

'Aren't you going to get up?' he asked, looking for a hairbrush.

'I will stay here for a bit.'

His hair, she thought, which was long and thick and fair (for Sicily, at least), was more beautiful than any girl's. His dark blue eyes were perfect too.

He was in his suit, a nice herringbone pattern which she admired, and he had put on his shoes when he bent over to kiss her.

'When will I see you again?' she asked.

'Oh soon, soon,' he said. 'Say goodbye to your parents for me. I won't disturb them.'

And then he was gone.

The place he was going was the rather shabby square off the Corso Victor Emmanuele, towards the station and the port, piazza Cutelli, where, on a narrow side street, was an interesting bar, small, unassuming, the sort of place where no one noticed anything, and no one spoke about what they saw, even if they did see something. There, standing at the bar was a well-dressed and handsome man in his thirties, whose look was one of profound discontent.

'Hi, uncle,' said Nino, approaching this man.

'You are late,' said Colonel Andreazza, annoyed, but knowing he could not afford to show it. 'And don't call me that.'

'But you said I could. You used to like it,' said Nino unkindly. 'Sorry I am late. I was with my girlfriend.'

He smirked.

'Someone should shoot you,' Andreazza said, wishing that person could be himself.

'I am sure a lot of people would love to shoot me, including you, her father, and several others I can think of. But you can congratulate me instead, if you like.'

'I feel sorry for the girl's father. He is a good honest man, and now he is going to have you as a son-in-law.'

'I am glad you raised that matter. He is a good honest man who, like most good honest men, has sat at the bottom of the pile for far too long. He needs promotion. And as he is so good and honest, you cannot possibly find a reason not to, can you, uncle?'

'Very well,' said Andreazza. 'I will see what I can do. How is Calogero?'

'Last time I saw him, very well.'

'And when was that?'

'A couple of days ago. He likes me a great deal, a very great deal. I am the favourite. You had better remember that, uncle, the absolute favourite. It is not just that I do so much that is essential for him, which the various bosses in the various quarters do not do; but he likes me as a person. He admires my courage, my cleverness, my... well, the fact that I have no feelings.'

'Not even for this girl, my colleague's daughter?' asked Andreazza, his interest suddenly caught.

'She is a nice girl, and she is going to give me a child, and she is going to give me prestige and respectability – I can already feel both swelling to maturity around me – and she clearly adores me, which is very nice indeed, but I probably feel about her the same way men feel about their cars. She is a beautiful and admired possession.'

Andreazza reflected. He felt the same about his wife, he supposed.

'You are not the favourite,' he then said. 'That is the stepson. Or that murderous thug who pulls people's teeth out, whatever he is called.'

'Marco? Don't be ridiculous. As for Francesco, he is a nice guy, but... I am the one who really counts.'

'You should watch out,' said Andreazza. 'He likes cultivating rivalries; he likes picking people up and throwing them aside. You are in a very small pool full of piranha fish. Look what happened to Tonino Grassi. Look what happened to Trajan Antonescu. Francesco has an advantage over you. His mother is Calogero's wife; he's the brother of little Calogero. You... who are you to him? Nothing!'

Nino looked annoyed by this observation.

'Let us just wait and see, shall we?' was the best response he could think of.

A woman now entered the bar, just in time. She was middle aged and had dyed platinum blonde hair and a hard face. She approached.

'Auntie!' said Nino, pleased to see her.

Without a word, she opened her bag and took out a tablet. This was what they had both been waiting for, the book, the electronic book. She handed it to Nino and then withdrew to the other end of the bar, where she ordered a drink. Nino accessed the computer with practised fingers. He soon found the file he was looking for; he knew what the Colonel liked. He handed the book over, and the Colonel studied what was before him. The Colonel's eyes dwelled greedily on what it contained.

'Who was responsible for that killing in Librino the other day?' he asked, as if what was before him was of less than consuming interest.

'Are you investigating it? I would not bother,' said Nino. 'Well?' he asked. 'What do you think of this new boy?'

Andreazza nodded.

'Good. The details are there, the address. The boy and his mother are police informants, or so the story goes. Give this to the mother.'

He put something on the bar that looked like a coin but wasn't. It was a smallish metal disc, a token, made by the gunsmith of Librino. It has various marks on it as a precaution against forgery, including a number. Each token cost whatever Nino could get for it; he bought them back for much less, and the difference was the profit for him and the boss. Andreazza took the token, having memorised the address. He did not pay; that was for others. Nino beckoned the woman called Auntie and handed the tablet back to her. Auntie, who had advertised her presence by a Facebook check-in, would spend the next few hours in the bar, showing the book to various interested parties, who would then buy a token from Nino. The next day, at lunchtime, he would be in another bar, again advertised by Facebook, where people would bring the tokens back to him, and he would pay them. He dealt with the money, and only the money. Auntie dealt with the book, the catalogue of people of both sexes and varying ages who entertained strangers all over the city. They moved from bar to bar to avoid detection. The clients always knew where to find them, though; one simply had to watch out on social media, on which neither Auntie nor Nino appeared by their real names.

Andreazza prepared to leave, his business done. He had received the token, he had the address of the quarry he longed for, whose photograph was engraved on his memory. But before he could go, he had to consign the weekly report to Nino. This was verbal. Nino listened intently and asked a few questions.

'This guy the other day, the tobacconist, shot at lunchtime…?' asked Nino.

'Don't worry about him. No one cares about him. He brought it on himself. We will fill in a few forms, make the right noises, and then…'

'This other guy, the one who was badly beaten and died of internal bleeding, or whatever it was?' asked Nino. 'Massimo someone….'

'Forensics have drawn a blank,' said Andreazza. 'It was probably some jealousy between young men. Not an interesting case. They gave him a good kicking, and it got out of hand. Sad, but the case is going nowhere. What do you know about it?'

'Nothing,' said Nino. 'I mean, Massimo was from our quarter, but… I did not know him. I don't know anyone who did.'

'He's a no one then,' said Andreazza.

He made a dismissive noise and was then gone.

It was a large flat; the supper had been a delight, and the dining room was so large that they had had no difficulty all fitting in. The Black Widow Spider had been there, Calogero's mother, his wife, his three sons, his stepson, his former sister-in-law, the boys' aunt, Giuseppina, her husband Omar, her stepson Gennaro, her new child, a daughter called Amelia, with Calogero himself, eleven souls in all. Now, the soup consumed, the cold meats eaten, the cheese and the bread and the fruit all gone, the children had all gone to watch a film on television, the women had retired to the kitchen, and the three adult men had retired to the study. From a distance, the kitchen noises and the television noises were barely discernible. The windows were open, as it was a mild night. The sounds of the square rose from below. If the room was bugged, it was hoped that nothing could be heard. Nevertheless, they conversed in low voices.

'Boss, of course it can be done,' Omar was saying. 'But the question is, should it be done? Is it wise? What will be the consequences?'

'Everything has come together most unexpectedly,' said Calogero. 'My wife, I mean, my ex-wife, has her finger on the financial pulse and she will co-operate. This young man, who is a coward, Mimmo, is brave enough to come to us before Costantino kills him as he killed the other brother. Mimmo is in league with this soft boy Dimitri and his sister. They both need us, and the opportunity they present is enormous: we take over the entire business at a knockdown price. But I know what you are thinking, not the people in Messina, but the Serbs, the imports…'

'I am an import myself,' said Omar. 'But the Serbs….'

'Are not liked,' said Calogero shortly. 'Once their master is dead, they will need a new protector, and they will all come to me, begging my protection, kissing my hand. They have made lives here, and if it comes between choosing a good life working for me, or avenging their master, I know what they will choose. I mean, do they like Costantino? What have you heard?'

'He is not a man with the gift of making himself liked, boss,' said Omar reflectively. 'What I mean is, he dealt with don Carmelo, who was liked. He married don Carmelo's cousin or great-niece or whatever she is, and she is liked. I am not quite sure why, because donna Rosa is a little bit frightening, but people respect her, you know…. And the children, well, the girl is very sweet, and the boy… yes, he is a soft boy, and people feel sorry for him. He is a nice boy, Dimitri, but…'

'The two surviving male descendants of don Carmelo, Dimitri and Mimmo, Francesco is befriending them. We will be able to use them very effectively. The way we use Renzo Santucci.'

'What I have heard people say is this,' said Omar. 'That when Costantino's mother made such a fuss about don Carmelo making her pregnant, well, they paid her off, and she went back to Niš, and that should have been the end of her, and the child. But when Costantino came back, don Carmelo was too kind, he recognised him, he employed him, and in so doing he made a terrible mistake.'

'Oh, he did,' said Calogero. 'He nurtured a viper that bit him. He was kind, but he was never kind enough. His kindness was enough to fuel resentment, not to engender love. It was a bad mistake. He should have killed the child. Instead, Costantino killed him. Well, I suppose it was his fault really, and the original sin came back to haunt him: the rape of the mother. That has sealed the fate of his descendants, just as Antonio Santucci, killing his brother-in-law, damned his family.'

Francesco spoke.

'What about the Serbs in Africa?' he asked.

'They are mercenaries. We pay them a bit more, and they will accept it. They have got no loyalty,' said Calogero. 'Which is why they can stay in Africa. We do not want people like that here.'

'You are right, and they know this. That is why they will do their best to show their loyalty when the time comes. You watch,' said Omar. 'There is the African wife, though. I am not sure what influence she or her children might have.'

'Can we pay them off?' asked Calogero. 'The woman, the twins, the new child.... We can make her rich, by African standards. She will find that tempting, I am sure.'

'I know her. My guess is that she will find that irresistible.'

'Then she is no Agrippina,' said Calogero. 'So now we have to work out how.' He paused. 'As for the consequences, remember this. If his own wife and children and half-brother want him dead, will anyone miss him?'

'I will kill him with my bare hands,' said Omar.

'Me too,' said Francesco.

'And so say all of us,' said Calogero with satisfaction.

Night fell over the city of Catania. For Nino Santacroce, it meant work until the small hours of the next day; he was officially at school, though had not been regularly for at least two years; far more important to him was what one learned on the streets and what one earned in so doing: the girls, the boys, the pills, the things one sold, and what one gathered, the raw intelligence that he fed back to the boss, about what the police were doing, which of them were to be trusted and which not.

Night fell. For Marco, that meant sitting at home with his mother and sisters, surrounded by their chatter, saying nothing himself, eating the food provided, and drinking one judicious glass of wine. Afterwards, while the rest of them watched the news on RAI One, it meant making his more or less his daily phone call to the mother of his son, who lived outside the city, and speaking to his son, about his homework, about his school, about whether he was being good; he ended the call as he always did, speaking of the date he would next visit. After that, the evening meant going to the gym and doing his exercises until late, and then, if he were not needed, going home and going to bed, his thoughts centred on the boss, his needs, his family, protecting the boss, protecting those close to the boss, gaining the boss's favour through Francesco; and thoughts too of his own child and his mother.

Night fell and the traffic noises grew faint in the boss's flat as Francesco, in his pyjamas, brushed his teeth, with young Renato, grandson of the Chemist of Catania, his stepbrother, next to him. Very soon, they would be in the single beds alongside the opposite walls of Francesco's room, as Renato liked, and Renato's whim in this matter was law, Francesco knew. He could, perhaps, have phoned up Petra, and asked to go round to see her. He knew she liked to be phoned, liked to be pursued, liked to put him off and encourage him by turns, but liked him enough to sleep with him. Those occasions glowed in his memory. As he was the boss's beloved son, every girl liked him, and most of them wanted to sleep with him. The exceptions were the beautiful girls of Piazza Armerina, but he only liked one girl, and that was Petra, and he was content with the frustration of enjoying her favours fleetingly, sporadically and sparingly. He could not walk away from Petra; he was too obsessed by her. But he knew, as in the case of Renato, where his duty lay. He had to protect Renato, the boss's eldest son, who was just of an age to be entering into dangerous territory; and he had to protect him and Sebastiano and Romano, as well as his own brother, little Calogero, and to prepare them for their future roles. The two little boys were fine, the baby no worry at all, but Renato was wayward, one felt, and subject to irrational desires. Such a boy could be led astray, could become like Dimitri, a liability, and had to be protected. And from whom? Not his own father, who wanted to keep him safe from this world, but from those who would exploit him, which, to Francesco, meant one person above all, Nino Santacroce.

He distrusted Nino. Nino was younger, and, he feared, cleverer, more daring, more reckless, less hemmed in by the things that kept other people back from action. He himself was prepared to do anything for the boss and had had no compunction in shooting dead the man from Librino outside his tobacconist's shop the other day. The man had been warned; he had shown a suicidal lack of respect for the boss; an example had to be made, and it had been made. The man had his own stupidity to blame for his fate, and people should, rather than bewail him, bewail his pig-headed stubbornness. His worship of his stepfather was only increased by the fact that he was the one who dispensed life and death.

What he felt for Calogero, he recognised in Marco as well, but he did not see it in Nino. Marco was, in the boss's presence, respectful, silent, awe-struck. But Nino was playful, ironic, almost cheeky. He did not treat him as the godlike figure he was to the others, but as some kindly and slightly unpredictable employer, someone to be played, and even taken advantage of when not looking. Outwardly, he and Nino were the closest of friends, and so was Marco; but he did not trust Nino in the way he trusted Marco, and he doubted his sincerity. He feared that Nino's friendship was largely because he was the boss's son, and if it had not been for that, Nino would not bother with him at all. But the oddest thing of all was that Francesco realised with greater clarity than ever that he was jealous of Nino. He had everything, but he still envied Nino's way of living free from all ties. Well, not all ties. Nino had a girlfriend and a child, and would, at an early age, be married.

This matter of the girl Daniela and her pregnancy outraged him, puzzled him, left him unable to understand quite what it signified. He had not met the policeman's daughter, but had heard she was beautiful, a real asset to any man, any boy. That was one reason for jealousy. But it went much further than this. Nino had managed to acquire her so effortlessly, so young too. That was a sore point. Everyone knew that the boss had married at a very early age, as had Trajan Antonescu; it was a badge of honour. Marco seemed not to care about this, but Marco, of course, already had a child, not that any of them knew the child. As for himself, his interest in girls was overwhelming, and concentrated on one girl, Petra, albeit intermittently. They had slept together, and that had been wonderful, at least for him; but not, he felt, for her, for he sensed her occasional indifference to him. And he himself had other interests, other girls, and the beautiful girls of Piazza Armerina as well, not that they counted in the same way. Well, he was young, and he could have whatever adventures he pleased, he supposed. He would not be young forever, he would not be free forever, either, perhaps. But here was Nino, able to get a girl to fall in love with him, and to settle down. It was shaming, the difference between them. He himself would still be chasing Petra when he was in his twenties, and here was Nino already established.

And yet, and yet: he was the boss's son. Nino was not. There was nothing Nino could do about that. Of course, Nino was indispensable, but he was not the boss's son.

The boss understood this, Francesco was sure, for he was an excellent judge of human nature. The boss had punished Nino, which was his way of letting all three of them know that, despite Nino's latest achievement, it was Francesco and Marco who commanded. Of course, there were the local bosses as well, in each quarter, in each town, but these three were the inner family, the ones the boss saw regularly, the ones he trusted the most. The family, the family, that is what counted, thought Francesco.

After the tooth-brushing, it was time to go to bed and put the light out.

'Everyone is talking about Nino,' said Renato, with admiration and envy.

'He is a bad boy,' said Francesco.

'Why? He is nice to me,' said Renato.

'He... he is not a suitable friend for you. Your father would not like it. If he tries to make friends with you, tell me, and I will warn him off.'

'Is it because he has slept with a girl?'

'Yes, which is bad, but not just that. He is a bit wild.'

'He is going to be a policeman. Is that wild?'

'No. Not really. It is his character.'

'How is his character different from anyone else's?' asked Renato reasonably. 'Have you slept with a girl?'

'Don't ask questions like that. Your father would not like it, and neither would your mother. Your father in particular. Remember what he keeps in that cupboard in his study.'

'Papà is strange,' said Renato. 'That is what my grandmother says. That is what my mother says. That is what I think. But I love him. I am not sure if he loves me, though.'

'You must not say that. Of course he does.'

'How do you know?'

Francesco sighed.

'You are the eldest son, aren't you?'

'I thought that was you,' said Renato.

Francesco sighed.

'Yes, in a way. But you are the one that counts, and I have to look after you.'

'That is what my sisters told me,' said Renato. 'Well, I am glad I have someone to look after me.' He paused, and Francesco thought for a moment he might have gone to sleep. But no such luck. 'Has Marco slept with a girl?'

'Why do you ask? It is not a proper question. Your father would not like to hear you ask it. Marco is older than me. He has a son.'

'Has he?' asked Renato in surprise.

'I thought you knew. He does not live here. I don't know anything about him. Now shut up and go to sleep.'

Chapter Three

Mimmo started. The knock on the door had been very gentle, but he had not been expecting it. He had, in the relatively brief time he has been in the upper room above the Trattoria Norma, grown used to being alone. He had woken to the sound of church bells; Paoluzzu had looked in on him before the busy midday shift, but apart from that he had seemed cocooned from the world. Paoluzzu had, as promised, brought him something to read, some old school texts, the only books, Mimmo assumed, that Paoluzzu owned. He had been reading *The Betrothed* when the knock came, and for a moment, he held his breath. Then he reasoned that if someone had come to kill him, they would hardly knock first. The door opened, and Francesco put his head around it.

'Did you sleep well last night?' asked Francesco. 'Paoluzzu let me in,' he added by way of explanation.

'Not really,' admitted Mimmo. 'I thought you were someone coming to kill me,' he added miserably. 'I can't sleep, I just think of him, you know....'

'Don't worry about him,' said Francesco. 'Soon he will be history. Besides, he hasn't killed you, has he, which means that he cannot. He must know by now that you have disappeared. You have been away for several days. But he has no idea where to find you, where to look even.'

'What is going to happen to him?' asked Mimmo.

'Do you really care? Do you really want to know? You don't know him at all, do you? What is going to happen to him is what happened to lots of other people thanks to him, like all your half-brothers. You do not need to worry about don Costantino, trust me. He is not worth it. Very soon, you will not think of him at all.' He smiled. 'I think you are supposed to say, 'Thank you' at this point.'

Mimmo laughed.

'It all seems so... strange. I was just an ordinary schoolteacher. Yes, I know my father was don Carmelo, but we hardly ever saw him. Now I am in a different world - no job, no mother, no sisters, no friends, except you. I don't understand how I got here.'

'Then let me explain,' said Francesco. 'You got here because you made love to don Costantino's daughter, your own niece. I think that is what sparked it off. Of course, you can back out, if you wish. You can send Daniela and her mother a message saying you are going away, that you don't want her or the baby, and that you will never return.'

'I can't do that,' he said.

'It would not be gallant or brave,' agreed Francesco. 'Besides, wherever you went, don Costantino would find you, and then…. Now, get yourself ready, and come and join me downstairs, and then we shall have lunch.'

Within ten minutes, they were at table in the Trattoria Norma. Wine and mineral water were brought without their having to ask for it. They were strangers, but people knew better than to notice them, let alone stare at them. The place was full, which gave Mimmo the impression he was hiding in a crowd. He felt very hungry. They both decided to have the lasagne as it was Sunday.

'Can you take a message to Maria, just to let her know I am OK, and that I have had to go away, because…. I have been worried about her,' said Mimmo. 'I know that Dimitri will have told her that I am OK, but…'

'You do not want to tell her why you have gone away in great detail,' said Francesco. 'I mean, you do not want to explain in detail what is going to happen, but you can see her soon. Tomorrow in fact. This evening, late, I am taking you back to Catania, and putting you in a flat, one of the empty flats we have; then on Monday morning, you are meeting with the priest, don Giorgio, thanks to my father arranging it, and she will meet you there.'

Mimmo's face lit up with relief and happiness. Then he reflected.

'How much longer have I got to hide like this?' he asked.

'For as long as is needed,' said Francesco. 'We will move you around, but it won't be forever. You have been missing her?'

'Yes. All I want is to be with her. I know that I should feel sorry for what I did, but I can't. I would do it all again, even though, if I had been wise, I would never have had anything to do with her, and would have gone away, changed my name, forgotten who my father was, but… none of that was possible after I had seen her, even though I did not know who she was. And then when I did find out, I did not care. This don Giorgio, is he a nice man?'

'Very nice. I like him. Everyone does. He is very kind. You will like him. He owes my father lots of favours too, so he will want to help. If anyone can, he can.'

Mimmo looked reassured.

'I should have gone to Mass this morning. Maybe I will go this evening. Are you out with these girls and Paoluzzu later?'

'Yes, I am. They are my excuse for visiting Piazza Armerina. My father approves of Ida, and I can see why, and I have to make him happy. But she does not find me very attractive. You know how it is; you can tell if a girl is interested, and she just isn't. But I like her, and she interests me. Her father and my father, well, they are in similar lines of work. And I think her father wants her to be interested in me, you know… People can be a bit dynastic, if you know what I mean. You should know that: don Costantino only married signora Rosa because she was a relation of don Costantino…'

'Dynastic? Incestuous, you mean,' said Mimmo gloomily. 'I worry about the baby,' he added. 'But it is no worse than first cousins…'

'How were you to know?' asked Francesco, thinking at the same time, he himself would have known, instinctively.

Mimmo had thought about that first time he had met Maria. They had encountered each other without being introduced. He had not known she was Maria Petrović; she had not known he was Michele Lollobrigida, though, had she known that, she would not have deduced from it that he was the half-brother of her father. But even if they had known, the bolt of love was too much for any reasoning to moderate it. Within a few minutes, all was clear between them; within the hour they had made love; within the hour, the child had begun its existence. She had been a virgin; he had not, though he might as well have been, so little was his experience, so little was his cynicism about the flesh.

Francesco wondered as well. Could it be true that Mimmo cared so little about the world that he set it all at naught for the sake of Maria and the child? Was it a case of all for love? Well, he supposed he himself had strong feelings, too, for women, and for one in particular, for Petra. But that had not stopped him, in the past, taking other chances when no opportunity with Petra seemed feasible. One day he would get married, but all that was way in the future. He wasn't uxorious as Mimmo clearly was, Nino would be, and the boss, his father, certainly was. Even Paoluzzu was terribly monogamous, he reflected. He looked at Mimmo and wondered what his half-niece had seen in him. Maybe no girl had ever looked at him like that before now. But as for him, Francesco reflected with an internal smirk, girls looked at him with interest all the time.

'Are you going to settle down with someone?' Mimmo was asking.

'Oh eventually,' said Francesco. 'People expect it. But not for some time.'

'I have met your father, of course, and I realise just what it is about him,' said Mimmo. 'He thinks strategically. My father was lazy and careless, and it cost him his life. He also brought Costantino into the world, and not in a good way. He paid for that. He was too careless with his affections. When we are married, Maria and I will leave Sicily and go somewhere we are not known and live a nice quiet life.'

'Is there such a thing? And where will you find it?'

'Somewhere like Orvieto. Or maybe Florence. I mean, I will have the money, won't I? We will be well off and far away.'

Francesco wondered. Was he sincere in wanting this? Or was this all a calculated stance, was he playing a deeper game, was he not to be trusted?

'Orvieto, Florence... I have never been to the continent. One day we will go, but my parents have a very young baby and another on the way, and... well, the continent can wait. So can France and England and America. Of course, I could go on my own. Maybe one day I will go on a trip. The thing is,' continued Francesco, as they finished the lasagne, 'I think you will get bored there and start wanting to come home. I mean, a nice house, a job, a wife and children, but... well, this is home, and you are don Carmelo's son. Donna Rosa, your prospective mother-in-law, saw you coming. Have you thought of that?'

'I have thought of it a great deal, and I know it is not true,' said Mimmo with some spirit. 'You see, donna Rosa, who is my cousin, as she is the daughter of a cousin of don Carmelo – it is a huge family, with many branches, and we do not all know each other – donna Rosa knows more murderous thugs than you do, if that is possible. That includes her own brothers. If she wanted someone to be her champion, she would have chosen one of them, not me. I am not the ideal choice at all. I never wanted to have anything to do with this. When I met Maria, I did not know who she was, I did not realise she was his daughter, and the whole thing was spontaneous, not calculated. Hence the baby. Nothing was planned, not even that. If you think I am some masterly plotter, I have to disappoint you. This was something both Maria and I were thrown into.' He paused. 'Is it safe for me to go to Catania?' asked Mimmo, suddenly worried by the prospect.

'You are safe with us,' said Francesco. 'If Costantino has people asking questions, trust me, he will get no answers from anyone in Catania.'

Don Giorgio was waiting on Monday morning, as agreed, and permitted himself a raised eyebrow when two young men came to the small booklined room he used as a study behind the sacristy of the Church of the Holy Souls in Purgatory. He liked Francesco, who was so polite, so respectful, so eager to please. He liked him and felt sorry for him, given that the person he was usually so eager to please was Calogero, his mother's husband. Don Giorgio had baptised Francesco eighteen years previously. He had known both parents and had heard of the father's defection with sadness but not surprise. The man had abandoned Agata and abandoned the child as well. No wonder the child had taken to Calogero the way all fatherless boys seemed to do. He felt sorry for him, for he feared that it would end badly.

The second, somewhat older young man seemed nervous and diffident, lacking in confidence, giving the impression that he had made a mistake, moreover one of the worst type, the sort that could not be undone. Don Giorgio understood. After greeting Francesco, he told Mimmo to sit down.

'So, they tell me you have become a father,' he said with a smile. 'Congratulations. I gather the circumstances are difficult, but we will think of the child and try our best.'

Don Giorgio looked at Francesco.

'I will wait for you in the Church,' said Francesco, knowing what was expected of him. 'When she arrives, shall I send the young lady in?'

'Yes, do,' said don Giorgio.

He and Mimmo were left alone.

'I gather you are in a bit of trouble,' said don Giorgio sympathetically.

'I am one of a large family,' said Mimmo. 'I mean there is my mother and my sisters, but my father, we hardly ever saw. We were his illegitimate children, the youngest of several illegitimate families that he had. The eldest illegitimate child is don Costantino Petrović, of whom you have heard, perhaps, and I am the youngest, or so I was always led to believe. I was brought up to call don Carmelo my father, but only in private, I hasten to add. In public, I was the son of my mother's husband, a signor Lollobrigida, whose name I have, and whom I have never knowingly met. He lives somewhere in Lombardy, if he is still alive. Don Carmelo was my father as far as I was concerned, though he is not on my birth certificate. All his other sons are dead, apart from don Costantino, the most recent in an accident coming down from Taormina, an accident that was not an accident. I am in trouble because I am the last surviving brother, but I am also in trouble because Maria, my girlfriend, is pregnant and, well, she is my half-brother's - whom I have never met - daughter. I did not know we were related when I met her. If I had… but we were not brought up together, we never met, and as soon as we did, we fell in love, and the next thing was… I want to marry her. I have done some research. We share twelve and a half per cent of our DNA, the same as if we were first cousins. One can marry one's first cousin, can't one?'

'It is generally not advised,' said don Giorgio. 'The Church and the state do not allow it.'

'But in this case, it is too late,' said Mimmo. 'The child is there.'

'Indeed. But even if the Church were to give a dispensation to allow first cousins to marry, I am pretty certain the state does not allow a man to marry his own niece.'

'Dear don Giorgio,' said Mimmo. 'That is something I have thought of as well. Everyone knows that I am don Carmelo's son. Everyone. But only in the Sicilian way. It was supposed so by all. But there was, is, no proof. He was rich, he was generous. But we do not have his name or his surname, me or my sisters, on our birth certificates. He, he did not want that. We have my mother's legal name, I am called Michele Lollobrigida, so there is no legal proof that I am related to don Carmelo at all. According to my birth certificate and my baptism certificate, I am the son of someone else.'

'But he *was* your father.'

'I am mentioned in his will as his son, but that was a surprise, as I was not part of his world.'

'You are now. You have asked don Calogero for help.'

'My life was, is, in danger. What would you have done, Father?'

Don Giorgio sighed.

'The same, no doubt,' he said. 'I am sure you are right to be frightened of don Costantino, who has murdered so many people, given that you stand between him and complete possession of a fortune. And you are right too that probably the only person who can protect you is don Calogero. That is how it works. The police…. Well, I would not have wanted to go to them, for what use are they? How many murders have they ever prevented? I cannot say you have done right, but it is understandable. Your predicament was acute.' He sighed once more. 'If only doing the right thing was easy, but it never is, it never was. I know don Calogero wants me to help you. He told me as much. And no doubt you will pay him back handsomely.'

'If I inherit anything from don Carmelo, I have promised to sell it to him,' said Mimmo. 'At a very good price too. I don't want it, any of it. He can have it all.'

'He would take it all eventually, even if you did not offer it to him,' observed don Giorgio. 'He takes everything he likes the look of. Everything. He will never be satisfied. Until he has it all. But he is nearly there.'

'Don Giorgio,' said Mimmo. 'I just want a quiet life, that is all. A quiet peaceful life.'

'We all want that. Sadly, few of us get it. This other boy, Maria's brother, Dimitri, how will this affect him?'

Mimmo was suddenly defensive.

'Why should it? I mean, we are friends, and he loves his sister, and he loves his mother. He wants us all to be happy.'

'And he loves his father?' asked don Giorgio, aware that this was cruel. 'Have you asked don Calogero to kill don Costantino? Because if you have, you are an accessory to murder.'

'I have not. I have asked him to protect me from don Costantino, that is all. If Dimitri has asked him something…'

'Live men do not leave inheritances.'

'The inheritance is the one left by don Carmelo, my father. Currently, the will is frozen, and it has been so for the last two years. I do not mind; I have enough to live on. I do not care about the money, I care about the child and I care about Maria. Please, don Giorgio, I need your help, we need your help, me and the mother of my child. If don Costantino finds out, he will separate us, or worse. But if we are married…. Well, in that case, what can he do? What God has united, let no man divide.'

Don Giorgio thought he could see the desperation in his face, that of a young man who only wanted to be married, and who did not care if he was killed or not afterwards. He thought too of the advantage that would accrue if he helped the young man, what it had been that don Calogero had promised him. And the damage had been done, thanks to the strong passions of two young people who ought to have known they were uncle and niece but did not.

'This can be sorted out. You need to get a residential qualification here. Don Calogero will rent you a flat, I am sure. Then you need to go to the commune and tell them you wish to marry Maria. Who appears as your father on your birth certificate, you say?'

'My mother's husband, whom I have never met.'

'Well, he may be unknown to you, but he is useful. When you have done the papers at the commune, you come to me, and we do the papers here, and all is in order. The wedding, I would ask, ought to be very quiet, no more than a dozen people.'

'Whatever you say. I will go to the commune as soon as I can.'

'Don't worry, don't worry, everything will be fine,' said the priest. 'These people, well you know what they are like. Occasionally, they notice people like you and me, but they soon lose interest, don't they, and forget all about us, which is welcome.' He paused. 'Others are not so lucky.'

He smiled blandly, but he was disturbed. There was a knock on the door, and a young woman, who could only be Maria, entered. The young couple embraced. The priest explained what had been decided, speaking of birth certificates and baptism certificates. The girl, who was really very pretty indeed, burst into tears, and kissed the priest's hands gratefully. Mimmo did the same. The priest then dismissed Mimmo and sent him into the Church, so he could talk to the young lady alone.

Mimmo went into the Church, where Francesco was waiting, as he had said he would be. He was gazing up at the altarpiece, the Spanish Madonna, with rapt attention, and for a moment did not notice him. Then he turned and smiled.

'Well?' he said, 'I told you he was nice, didn't I? And that he would want to help.'

Mimmo nodded gratefully.

'Can I take Maria back to the flat after this?'

'Sure. As long as she was not followed. She's hardly likely to betray you. Besides, in a few days' time we will move you again. Have fun while you can.'

'It is not that, it is…'

'Oh, it is that,' said Francesco with a laugh.

A few moments later, don Giorgio appeared with the young lady and then dismissed them. Francesco made a move to go as well, but the priest detained him. Francesco looked a little uneasy for a moment, then smiled. He and the priest sat down in front of the Spanish Madonna.

'It went well, Father?' asked Francesco.

'Oh yes, I think I can help him, the situation is not ideal, but there are ways around it. But why are *you* helping him?'

'He is a nice guy, Father, and… well, don Costantino his half-brother is not a nice guy.'

'So, sticking up for the underdog again, eh? And yet,' the priest pointed out, 'you and don Calogero have been doing business with don Costantino, who is, or was, your friend. Now you have started to protect his enemy. Why? What has changed? Because you are not protecting his enemy out of the goodness of your hearts, are you?'

Francesco did not have an answer for this. He felt his cheeks burn.

'Father, you know what these people are like,' he said. 'Don Costantino is not a good person. He would do serious harm to Mimmo, and to his daughter, and has already done serious harm to his own son. People like that... well, you need to come between them and their victims. People like that are out of control. His cruelty to Dimitri, his own son...'

'And are you the ones to punish don Costantino for his crimes?'

Francesco was silent for a moment, then spoke.

'If someone were to do so, would anyone mind? Would anyone miss him? Would his son, his daughter, or his wife?' he said at last. 'Father, the world is full of bad men, and worse, bad men who cannot control themselves. Some can, others can't... if there were one less monster in the world, would that be a bad thing?'

'So, they are going to kill don Costantino. Does this Mimmo know?' he asked. 'Or maybe I should say that you are going to kill don Costantino. I did your baptism, Francesco, but I will refuse to do your funeral.'

Francesco was silent. What he was thinking was that they had miscalculated in introducing Mimmo to don Giorgio before the murder; they should have left it until afterwards.

'Tell your father,' said the priest, remembering the promise that he had extracted from don Calogero, 'that Anna Agostini will ring him later today. And tell him something else: I am doing this wedding because there is a loophole and because it is on balance the right thing to do. I am not doing it because I want to do your father a favour.'

Francesco nodded. The priest made a sign that Francesco could go. He left. Don Giorgio wondered what he could do, if anything at all. They were planning to murder don Costantino. He could not keep this information to himself. And yet, warning don Costantino seemed impractical. He looked at his watch. He had time for a cup of coffee before his next appointment, one which he was looking forward to. And he had time to phone Anna Agostini and tell her to phone the boss, as he had agreed to see her.

At noon he was in Church, and the other young couple came. The girl, Daniela, was modest and shy, and he liked her at once, even if this were their first meeting, as she did not come from the quarter. The boy, whom he had baptised, he knew well. He took the girl aside to the study on her own to hear her story. It was soon told: she loved Nino, he was so good and kind to her; she loved the baby already, it had changed her life; her parents were furious, but, as they were all Catholics, they thought, or had come to think, that the best thing was her marrying Nino, which was what she wanted too. She was a little surprised that don Giorgio made no effort to push back on this. Instead, he seemed happy with idea of marriage, when they were eighteen, though he also warned her that it would have its challenges. She nodded. Her father had said exactly the same thing.

Then, sending her out, he saw the boy. He did this in Church, which, they both knew, was less likely to be subjected to electronic surveillance. Daniela waited at a distance, while don Giorgio took a chair in one of the side chapels, and Nino knelt at the polychrome marble altar rails, like a penitent confessing his sins. Or so anyone entering the Church would think.

'How is your mother?' asked the priest.

'Upset, but happy, you know…'

'And the others?'

'They are all furious. Her parents, well, can you blame them? I am not ideal, am I, Father? Don Calogero is furious. He thinks it is a cheek that I have done what he did and what Antonescu did: father a child at a very young age. He thinks it represents a claim to power. As for the people I work with, they respect me for it, which sort of proves his point. But the ones who are most angry are Francesco and Marco. You see, they despise me because of what I did with all those policemen and others, because Antonescu told me to, when I was too young to know any better. They treat me as if I were a dirty thing, a, I can't bring myself to say it. Not that they dare to say it out loud. But if I was that, I was made to be that; I did not choose it for myself. As for Daniela and the child, I am happier than I have ever been. I like her, I like her a lot, I love her, which is something I have not told anyone else, but you, Father. And she knows the dangers; she knows that I am a bad boy in a risky business, but I have told her that one day I shall get out.'

'Yes, but remember what happened to Paolo Bednarowski, and what happened to Tonino Grassi,' cautioned the priest.

'I think of nothing else, Father,' said Nino. 'I want my child to have a father, unlike Tonino's daughter.'

'What happened to Tonino?' asked the priest, not for the first time.

'Something bad. They left no evidence. No one speaks about him, not even his parents. Of course, I am an only child, and leaving here would not be so bad. Daniela is also an only child, and her father a policeman.

They would be able to look after us, I am sure. That was the mistake Paolo made and Tonino made. They did not want to say goodbye. I do. There is a whole world beyond Sicily. My parents could come; her parents could come. What is there here for us?'

'They are planning something,' said don Giorgio. 'I think I know what.' He explained what he had gathered from Mimmo, while Nino listened attentively. 'But there is a weak link: Dimitri, the son of Costantino.'

'I know who you mean. Dimitri Petrović. I don't think he is a strong character, from what I have heard. He is a bit of an embarrassment. As for their plans for don Costantino, that does not surprise me one bit.'

'You have heard something?' asked the priest.

Nino nodded.

'They intend to act soon, I fear,' said don Giorgio. 'Very soon.'

He was displeased to receive the phone call from Anna Agostini, and even more displeased to agree to meet her. He could not be bothered to go to Syracuse, but he allowed her to come to him. He did not want to see her at home, or anywhere in the quarter, so he thought it best to nominate a new restaurant (one in which he had a controlling stake, as it turned out) along the via dei Crociferi. He invited her to meet him that very evening. She would, he knew, bring neither her children nor her husband, and that was a relief to Calogero. He knew people liked and respected the husband; the children, especially the eldest, who had been fathered by Turiddu, he had no desire to see. Turiddu was long dead. He did not want to be reminded of him. The child must be quite old by now, he thought, growing up, looking like Turiddu. What a horrible thought.

He had first had to do with Anna when he had barely been in his teens, and she in her twenties. They were both older now, but as she came into the restaurant, even though he had avoided seeing her for some time, he noticed, with a trace of annoyance, that she was still a beautiful woman, and that she was ageing well. She was somewhat younger than his ex-wife Anna Maria Tancredi. He had always had a thing for older women, he reflected, at least when he was younger. He was very content with Agata and his present marriage, though. To his annoyance, the head waiter himself brought Anna over to the table, no doubt thinking that he was doing him, don Calogero, a favour, and that Anna was somehow important to him. Well, she was, but only in a negative sense.

'It is kind of you to see me,' she said, as she sat down.

'Don't thank me, thank don Giorgio,' he replied, a trifle rudely.

'I already have. I called to see him on my way here from the station. It was very kind of him to intercede on my behalf.'

She smiled. The menus came. They both studied them.

'The spaghetti with truffles sound interesting,' he said. 'But if you have come here to intercede for your son, I am afraid you are wasting your time. What he did to me was beyond forgiveness, not that he has asked to be forgiven. He is too sensible to ask for the impossible. Besides which, all that nasty business... I was sorry when your grandson was killed, truly I was, as I have children of my own, and Cristoforo was a sweet boy. I was sorry when Ceccina left him, and I did my best to try and get her to return, but she defied me. He has suffered, I admit, but the revenge he took was too much. It was distasteful. It was counterproductive. It was, I suppose I should use the word, wrong. It was only thanks to the greatest good luck, to Francesco going against my orders, that I survived. Have you thought of a second course?'

She had. The waiter returned. The orders were taken. A bottle of white wine was brought, examined, accepted. He tasted it and made the right noise. She accepted a glass. It was still early. The place was empty.

'Everything you say is true. His life is ruined, that is all I would add. We went out there to see him, Alfonso and myself and the children, but really, he showed he did not want to see us. It was a mistake going there, really, and a mistake taking the children. They asked about their elder brother, and one had to try to explain, explain the impossible. Of course, they do not know, must not know. His actions were monstrous, but there again, he has become a monster. I speak to him on the telephone from time to time, even though he finds it difficult. I want him to come home. He is my son, after all. He says he cannot, because you will not allow it.'

'Well, that is true. I do not allow it. But even if I did, he would not come. Besides, that was what was agreed between us. He would stay there. Africa would be a cage for this beast, your son. And don Costantino agreed. I am not breaking that agreement. You are wasting your time.'

'He does not have a life there...'

'He has plenty of life there. He is a mercenary, a hired killer. That is the right place for him. That is what your beloved son is like.'

'That is what you made him,' she retorted.

'This conversation? Again? Did I make him kill that man Ginori and his whole family? And when your son became a monster, did anyone suffer from it more than me? I did everything for him, and look what he did for me.'

'I admit you have suffered,' she said. 'Just as you have made others suffer,' she could not resist adding.

The spaghetti came, and they stared across their plates at each other.

'If he came back here, it would only be to try and kill me, or my children,' said Calogero. 'Not that that would bother you.'

'When I say come back, I don't mean here necessarily,' she said easily, ignoring his remark. 'I mean Romania. Why can't he go there? He has relations there.'

'Whom he has never met.'

'He speaks the language,' she continued, ignoring his interjection. 'He could have a life there in the way that he can't in Africa.'

Calogero sighed.

'What sort of life is the man capable of living? He has killed children, for God's sake!' he said, lowering his voice to a furious whisper. 'You think that he can somehow be rehabilitated, that decent people would want to have anything to do with him? You are his mother, I know, but even you... Even you cannot believe in redemption on this scale. You should regard your son as dead to you, just as he regards himself as dead to the world, I am sure. You have other children. Be grateful for that. And remember that he does not like you, or me, or anyone he associates with the past, with the time when he was happy. Why do you think he tried to kill me in so vicious a way? Because he loves me, or loved me, and he could not bear to remember it a moment longer. Your son is in hell. Leave him there. Tell me, do you hear from Ceccina and the children?'

'We speak on the phone, but we never meet. I keep on hoping she will come back down to Sicily to see her parents, but though she talks of it, she never comes. Neither does Pasqualina or that husband of hers. It was all too much for them, the tragedy of little Cristoforo.'

He felt he ought to ask after her children, but he could not face doing so. The memory of Turiddu troubled him still, even after all these years, just as the memory of Traiano troubled him; this meeting was an unwelcome reminder of all the things he wished he could forget.

'At least Ceccina has plenty of money. I believe your son is generous to them, even if they have nothing to do with him.'

'They are well off, very. Occasionally I speak to Ceccina's mother, and she tells me that they have a nice house, a nice life; the children go to good schools. It is always possible she may find someone else, or so I thought, but perhaps not, as she has three children. What I did pick up is that she never mentions their father to them, and the children never ask. They never come to visit the grave of Cristoforo. It is as if they prefer to forget him too. That surprises me.'

'He is in the Church, isn't he? Like Stefania,' said Calogero with a touch of sadness. 'Why did he do it? Why did he kill that family whom he had never met, and Ginori's girlfriend and baby? And the people he used to do these things… why, why did they help him? You think I am a monster, don't you, but there are certain things that I disapprove of, and this is one of them, useless slaughter.'

'It was wrong,' she said.

She could say no more, for at that moment, the main course arrived: a Florentine steak for him, veal cutlets for her.

'It was wrong, as you say,' he said, when they were alone again, his tone lightly ironic.

'But is there nothing to be done?' she asked. She paused a moment. 'Do you know this woman, the wife of don Costantino Petrović?'

He regarded her with interest. So that was what this was about, something had happened that had occasioned this new approach.

'The one they call donna Rosa, the one from Messina?' he asked innocently.

'No, the one in Africa, who has twins. They are quite big now. She is having another baby as well.'

'I don't think I have ever met her. When I was out there, the very night your son tried to kill me, the boy was being circumcised. He was, what, ten years old? Older than Omar's son Gennaro, I think.'

'I met her when I was there,' said Anna, 'the African wife. She is… formidable.'

'Go on,' said Calogero, knowing that Anna was now unveiling her leverage. 'Don Costantino seems to make a habit of marrying formidable women. Perhaps he is attracted to them.'

'She is ambitious for her children. You see, we have spoken. The twins are now at least thirteen. The girl is beautiful, as you would expect a half-Serb half-African girl to be. She is already grown up. Her mother says she is a woman. The boy, Bosco, he says he is a man. I believe he has proved his manhood in that disgusting way teenage boys have. Some of the Serbs took him to the capital and arranged that for him. But the girl is a virgin, naturally, for now. But the mother has plans for both of them. She wanted me to persuade my son to marry her daughter. That is why we have been speaking on the phone.'

'You spoke to your son about it?'

'Of course. He was horrified, just as I was horrified. The girl is thirteen. He has no intention of touching the girl, this girl, any girl. The whole thing fills him with horror. Ever since Ceccina left him, he… well, you do not need to know. But he can't go down that path ever again. But the thing is this. He cannot refuse outright, and for two reasons: if he refuses, then the mother gets offended, and the boy gets offended, and he makes two enemies. And of course, behind the mother and the brother is the father. This is Costantino's idea, he thinks. The other thing is, if he refuses to marry the girl, the mother, and one assumes the father, will offer her either to his friend Slobodan or to his friend Darko. So, he is spinning it out, as he does not want to offend the girl's family, and he does not want either Darko or Slobodan to have her. That is what he told me.'

'How many cows is his daughter worth?' asked Calogero. 'I mean, Costantino is not giving away this gorgeous girl for nothing, is he? What does your son say?'

'He does not tell me anything,' she said. 'Except that he does not want to have anything to do with this offer. That he wants to get away from the girl makes me think he might want to leave Africa.'

Calogero was thoughtful. He had thought that he ought never to have allowed this meeting. He had always refused to see her for this very reason, that if he did, she would succeed in persuading him to do something he ought not to do – to concede. Yet what she was asking was very little; and what she had just told him was a great deal. He ought to be grateful. But it was the principle of the matter that rankled, the realisation that he was open to persuasion.

'Look,' he said, 'your son has numerous false passports and goes wherever he likes. He is a professional killer. Oh, don't look surprised. I am told these things. His main patron is not me anymore, it is don Costantino. But…. Look, tell him to leave Africa at once and go to Romania. But tell him to leave at once, without delay, without packing, without asking questions. He is very rich, he can do that, as money is portable, Anna Maria looks after him. Next week may be too late. You have persuaded me; now you have to persuade him. See if he will listen to you. I doubt he will, and if he doesn't, well at least you will have tried, and it will not be your fault.'

'It? What is it?' she asked.

'You should know better than to ask. I have given you what you wanted, so be grateful.' He paused. 'Why is he still alive? Because I have been tolerant. And because don Costantino finds him useful and profitable. But the moment don Costantino is no longer there, he will no longer have a patron, and all the people he has offended will take their revenge.'

She understood.

They finished dinner early, neither had a dessert, and after their coffee, they rose to leave, thanking the manager of the place effusively for a wonderful meal. He placed Anna in a taxi to take her back to the station and her train to Syracuse. Then he walked down the hill towards the via Etnea, and across that road into the Purgatory quarter. He walked into the square in front of the Church of the Holy Souls in Purgatory, which was floodlit, thanks to the generosity of the Confraternity of the Holy Souls, thanks, in fact, to himself. Taking advantage of the illumination, some thirty boys of varying ages were playing football, or watching the game, amongst them his own three sons and his stepson. It was like this most evenings, and there were even proper, though moveable, goalposts. There was the tiniest pause, a sort of jolt to the rhythm of the game, as he entered the square, barely perceptible, except to an expert. He pretended not to notice, and so did the rest of them. He came to stand on the steps in front of the church, where the spectators were sitting, and his eyes travelled around looking for the person he sought. He was easy to find. He was the only black boy in their midst. His gaze met that of Francesco, and he indicated that he wanted Gennaro. Gennaro, who was rapidly substituted, came over. He and the boss sat on the steps apart from the others.

Gennaro felt pleased and flattered to be called to the boss. This had not happened before. It was an honour. Of course, he was often with the boss, who was his honorary uncle, just as the boss's children were his honorary cousins, thanks to their aunt, Giuseppina, being his stepmother. But still, to be singled out in this manner was an unusual privilege.

'You like it here?' said Calogero.

'Yes, boss.'

'You miss Africa?'

'No, boss. It is nicer here. The food, the people, and the way everything is so well organised. I am very lucky.'

'I bet Bosco is jealous. You were great friends, weren't you? You were circumcised together, along with those two Serbs, Darko and Slobodan.'

'Bosco says he is coming here soon, boss, as soon as his father calls for him; but he has been saying that ever since I left Africa to come here. His father never does call him. It is because of don Costantino's wife, his wife in Messina. But Bosco says he is going to get rid of her, and her son. Bosco says he is a man, and he is going to kill Dimitri and have no rivals. He says Dimitri is not a man because he is not circumcised.'

Calogero laughed, which was a good thing, as Gennaro realised too late that the same criterion must apply to Calogero too.

'What else had Bosco told you?' he asked. 'Tell me everything, I am interested.'

'That his parents want his sister to marry Antonescu,' said Gennaro.

'His parents? Are you sure it is both of them, not just the mother?'

'It is both of them. Bosco too. But Antonescu keeps on putting it off. It has been going on for months. First, they said he would have to be circumcised, and he agreed, then he said he wouldn't, and they said he wouldn't have to, as it did not matter. Then they had to agree on what the celebrations were to be, small or big, and they could not agree on that. Then finally they said he should sleep with her, they sent her down to his bungalow, but he sent her back, saying he was not ready…'

'Usually, it is the girl who is reluctant, Gennaro, but sometimes men are. They find that beautiful girls bring too many reminders.'

Gennaro nodded sagely.

'But it won't happen now, boss.'

'Why not?'

'Bosco says that one of the men has already taken advantage.'

Far to the south, in the thick darkness of an African night, Trajan Antonescu pushed his plate aside and thanked his hostess. His thanks were polite but perfunctory. He didn't care what he ate, he had not cared ever since his son had been killed, and his wife had left him. She had been a wonderful cook, but that was all part of the lost world of which he was resolved not to think, the world which he was determined to forget.

He had been away, but he had come back. When he came back, he always came to see the woman he called Mama, the African wife of don Costantino; this was partly out of politeness, but also so he could talk to Costantino via her computer; but first there was always the ceremony of having to sit at her table, eat her tough meat and rice and beans, accompanied by a bottle of mango juice. Mama herself never ate in his presence, but she observed him, to check he left nothing. He remembered vaguely what Mihai had said to him, how he had to watch what he ate, because of his colostomy. Mihai would have been horrified by the cuisine that Mama prepared. But some months ago, he had had his colostomy reversed by a surgeon in the capital; he had been told it was possible, and though he did not care one way or another, he had had it done. After all, he might live for many more years, not that he wanted to live, not that he had anything to live for.

It was a hot night, as every night was hot in this part of Africa. He was wearing a pair of flip-flops, a ragged pair of shorts and an open Hawaiian shirt that had faded through many washes, which exposed all his scars, surgical and other, to view. His head was shaved, and now the sun had gone down, bare. His face was covered by a short dark beard, though his chest, arms and legs were smooth and very pale apart from the livid scars. If anyone from Catania or Palermo were to see him now, they would have some difficulty in identifying him as the Traiano Antonescu they had once known. He was physically different; he was mentally different. He could not stand the thought that once he had been a man with a full head of black curls, like his son. He had to forget, and the best way to forget was to bury his old self.

Mama had watched as he ate, and so did her son, Costantino's son, the boy Bosco. The boy's sister was somewhere in the house, doing whatever girls did – he did not know what – he had had a daughter once, but no more – but Bosco saw the visitor as an endless source of fascination. He said nothing and stared at him while he sat at table. Bosco was a confident child, and for a variety of reasons. He was tall, strong and big for his age. A few wiry hairs had appeared on his chin; not many, but just enough, to prove his precocious manhood. He was the son of an important, though largely absent man, in whose absence he was, in his own eyes at least, considered the man of the house. He was half African and half Serbo-Italian, the grandson of a great man, the late don Carmelo. He was young, very young, but had already proved his bravery on the night that Traiano had so savagely attacked don Calogero. He had not flinched under the knife that had cut into his flesh. He was, in his own eyes, the rightful heir to his father.

Trajan found the intensity of the boy's attention somewhat disturbing. He did not like the boy. He did not like being reminded of his own lost son, who would have been a bit younger than Bosco, but whose age was now rather vague to him. He did not like the way the boy had not learned what the men had learned, namely that he wanted to be alone, he did not want to be the object of any attention or any curiosity. Bosco intruded. He did not like that. So did his mother, but that was easier to deal with.

'You had a good trip?' Mama was asking.

'Yes,' he admitted, nodding idly. 'I will tell your husband about it soon.'

He had been back less than a day and he had already allowed the trip to slip from his mind. His work kept him sane. It was remunerative as well and required meticulous planning. His reputation was growing, he knew.

People from all over the continent applied to don Costantino in Sicily, and don Costantino passed on the details. No doubt some men met interesting people through their work; well, so did he, but he never met them for long enough to find them interesting. The latest had been an American family of five, in a luxury game lodge. It had made the newspapers as such things did, no doubt, not that he was interested. But what it did was straighten out accounts in New York, or Chicago, or Cincinnati, or somewhere else he did not care about. He had entered the lodge as a tourist, done what he had to do, then left quietly, leaving no trace beyond that provided by one of his many false passports. Dark glasses, wig, hats, clothes, these made him invisible. That is what he wanted to be, unseen; that is what he was, except to this very annoying child-man, Bosco.

'Was it just work?' Mama was asking.

'Just work,' he said, knowing what she meant.

'You are sad, don Traiano,' she said. 'You should have listened to me. My daughter was ready and willing. You would have liked her; she would have liked you.'

'That I doubt,' said Trajan, without emotion, yet aware of the past tense, and aware too of Bosco's eyes on him.

'But you did not want her,' said Mama accusingly. 'She would have given you lots of sons. She is a good girl. She can cook and clean and look after a man. But now she will do that for someone else.'

'I don't want lots of sons. I do not want even one son, Mama,' he replied. 'And I do not want anyone to look after me. You're a matchmaker, Mama, but I do not want a match. I like being alone.'

She shook her head sadly, not at the thought of him being alone, and the waste of a fine man, he guessed, but because all that money was going to waste. He was, indeed, making lots of money. He supposed that don Costantino told her so, and to her mind, it was a pity that their daughter did not get the chance to enjoy it.

'It is not good for the man to be alone, said the Lord God,' she pronounced sententiously.

Once more she sighed. He supposed she assumed that he spent his time like the other men, with sex workers or an unofficial wife in the capital city. Well, let her think that. He did not care. He had no feelings, sexual or otherwise.

'Why are you looking at me?' he asked, turning to the boy.

Bosco did not flinch.

'Because you have offended my father,' he said. 'You did not want to marry my sister. And now…'

His mother frowned.

'When your father is next here…' she warned the child.

'It is true! It is all his fault!' protested the boy. 'And if my father comes home again, I shall go and hide in the bush, and he won't find me and won't be able to beat me.'

'You will see him in Sicily,' said Trajan, evenly, avoiding the subject of the girl's fate. 'He will beat you there, perhaps. Are you looking forward to going to Sicily? Has a date been fixed?' he asked, turning to Mama.

'Oh, it has been discussed for months, and whenever a date is agreed, he then changes his mind. He is frightened of *her*. What a pity that you have not met her or her children and can't tell us what they are like. I know he does not like them, but he fears them, though why, I do not know. He should beat her. He is sick of her. She has not given him good children. This Dimitri…. I have heard he is a bad boy. A coward. Disobedient. Not like my Bosco.' She smiled, then frowned. 'But Bosco needs to go to school, be educated, learn the Sicilian ways, the Serb ways. He is old enough. Costantino will eventually send worthless Dimitri away, you watch, I am sure of it.'

This prospect did not interest Trajan at all. He was just waiting for eight o'clock, which was the usual hour that Mama and her husband spoke. This conversation was just a way of filling in the time that he had to wait. He suppressed a yawn.

'When I get to Sicily, I am going to kill Dimitri,' said Bosco.

'You should not talk like that,' said his mother.

The boy ignored her, and stared at Traiano, daring him to contradict him.

The impasse was broken by the sound of the computer ringing. It was don Costantino calling. Mama went to the computer to talk to her husband, and the girl appeared to talk to her father. Trajan went out to the veranda of the small house and sat on the step, looking out into the thick African darkness. He could hear the distant sound of the sea; the place was idyllic, and it was no wonder that the hotel was always full. It was a rare moment of peace, but far too brief. The boy Bosco came out and sat next to him.

'You are not talking to your father?' asked Trajan.

'No. It is always the same. Mama wants to go to Sicily, and he says yes, and sometimes he says when, and then he changes his mind and says not yet. Mama then cries. She wants the new baby to be born there, not here. She wants me to have my inheritance. She hopes the new baby will be another boy.'

'Do you want a brother?'

'It would be nice. I want my inheritance. I don't want it to go to Dimitri.'

'You have never met him. I am sure he is perfectly nice.'

'My father does not like him, or his mother, or so my mother says.'

Families, thought Trajan, who no longer had one.

'But he likes your mother, and he likes you.'

'When he comes here, he goes into her bedroom first thing, and they do not come out for ages. And then when he does come out, he gives me a good beating. Each and every time. She tells him things about me, and he says I am unruly and need to be taught a lesson.'

'Well, you do,' said Trajan. 'You need discipline. All men need discipline, and you say you are a man, don't you?'

'What are you going to talk to my father about?' asked Bosco with a degree of slyness, for he knew the answer to this question. 'Is it about Darko?'

Trajan stared into the darkness, saying nothing.

'What are you going to do about Darko?' asked the boy.

'You know about Darko?' asked Trajan.

'I was there; I saw it all happen,' said Bosco. 'We were playing football on the beach and then we went for a swim. Something happened, and Darko and Slobodan started to fight in the sea; then they got out and carried on fighting on the beach. Darko stabbed Slobodan, and then the others managed to separate them.'

'It could have been serious. He stabbed him in a nasty place.'

'It was serious. He wanted to kill him. He would have killed him if the others had not intervened,' said Bosco.

'Weren't you frightened?' asked Trajan.

'He wasn't trying to kill me,' said Bosco. 'I like Slobodan, but he is good fighter, and he was able to defend himself with his bare hands, and the others were able to help him. As for Darko, I feel sorry for him, but he should not have done what he tried to do. That is why he is in the cage. And he is there waiting for you to tell him what you are going to do; but first, you have to speak to my father.'

'And what do you think your father will say?' asked Trajan.

'It depends, I think, on what people have said to him, what Darko's friends, if he has any, will say to him. If his friends know, if he has been able to communicate with them.'

'After Darko stabbed Slobodan, he was taken straight to the cage and has been there ever since. He can't communicate with anyone, unless someone has undertaken to take a message for him; and how would they do that? We have no phones here. Unless someone went to the hotel on his behalf and phoned his relatives in Belgrade or wherever they are, or if someone came here and used Mama's computer. But Slobodan is now in the city, having his wound treated in hospital, and no doubt he has been speaking to your father, and his friends. Which of them has more powerful friends, do you think?'

'Why ask, when you already know the answer to that?' asked the boy. 'Slobodan is my second cousin, and he is the great-nephew of a hero of the war. Darko, Darko is no one at all. That is why you will take him out of the cage and hang him. In fact, I am surprised you have not done it already.'

'You don't understand a thing,' said Trajan. 'You are a silly little boy. None of this concerns you.'

'The only thing that can make a difference is what *she* says to my father,' said Bosco. He meant not his mother, but his sister. 'It is all your fault. If you had taken her, this would not have happened.'

The cage had once been used to contain a crocodile. It was just under six foot long and a couple of feet broad. It was like an open-air coffin. It was dark by the time Trajan Antonescu came to the cage, and the surrounding buildings were quiet, though he could tell - one could always sense these things - that his visit was expected, not just by Darko, but by the others, and that they were watching him, waiting for the inevitable outcome.

Darko did not speak. He merely looked up at the man who held his fate in his hands. Trajan did not speak either, but he proffered a bottle of water through the bars of the cage, and Darko greedily drank from it.

'Why did you do it?' asked Trajan, referring, they both knew, to the stabbing of Slobodan. He spoke musingly, not expecting an answer, knowing that there really could be no explanation to such irrational behaviour. Indeed, why had Darko stabbed his best friend and tried to kill him? For the same reason that he himself had nailed his patron, don Calogero di Rienzi, to a wooden floor and left him to die. There was no hatred that could compare to a love gone wrong.

'These quarrels between friends,' said Trajan. 'Well, he is going to survive, thankfully, not that that will make much difference. It was a nasty wound. You could see the bone. Horrible, and I have seen lots of wounds, as you can imagine. But they have patched him up in hospital, and no doubt, from his hospital bed, he has been on the phone to don Costantino; and maybe your relatives and friends have done the same. Do you think they have?'

Darko was silent.

'Has someone taken a message for you?' asked Trajan curiously.

The whole place was silent and deserted. Darko's cage smelled foul. He knew what that meant. The other men had turned against him; they had been out in the heat of the day to torment him, urinating against the side of the cage, standing on the cage and squatting. He wanted to hold his nose. He felt that Darko was resigned to his fate.

'I tried to speak to don Costantino this evening. I was at his wife's house. But... Mama and her daughter spoke to him, over the computer, and then when it was time for me to do so, the connection went down. Which means... well, you know what it means. In Africa, when that happens, it could come back in a matter of hours, or it could take days, weeks even. So, I was expecting don Costantino to tell me to take you out of the cage and hang you from that tree over there, which is what all the men want, I am sure. But as it is, they will just have to wait. Maybe a day or two, maybe more. You may in fact die in the cage. Of thirst, or of something else.'

'What?' said Darko, suddenly interested. 'If not the rope, or thirst, what?'

He spoke with supreme indifference.

'Despair,' said Trajan. 'Some people die of it. But others live with it, for years. Don't you want to live?' he asked.

Darko was silent. That was answer enough, Trajan reflected.

Then Darko spoke.

'Someone has taken a message. You guessed rightly,' he said at last.

'Bosco?' said Trajan.

'Bosco's sister,' said Darko. 'This was when you were away. She likes me. I like her, and the boss promised her to me.'

'What? She liked you? Maybe she liked Slobodan more? I mean …. Well, whatever she is, she is too young for this sort of thing, to have men quarrelling over her.'

'She is a good ten years younger than me, but I was prepared to wait. She is his daughter. Her mother wanted it too. Why else do you think when the doctor came, and when we had the circumcisions…? That was Mama's idea. It has been planned from that far back. You see, she picked me, as she wants to have a nice husband. She knows I would make a nice husband. Then Slobodan had to interfere.'

'Oh, more than just interfere. He has had her,' said Trajan. 'You were a good friend to Slobodan, weren't you, but he took advantage, just to torment you, and you ended up stabbing him.'

'I lost my temper. He hasn't had her. He was paying attention to her. Bosco told me. I had to warn him off. No more than that. I had to finish him off.'

'Oh, did you? Then why did you fail?'

Darko looked at him venomously. One could tell, despite the darkness.

'You spoiled it,' he said. 'It is all your fault. He was wearing swimming shorts, and I wanted to stab him just where all the veins and arteries are and watch him bleed out very rapidly. But the blow landed on a bottle top he had in his pocket. A metal bottle top. The blow glanced off that and hit him where death was not instantaneous.'

'He was lucky,' said Trajan, who knew where the most vulnerable parts of the body were from experience. 'A bottle top, eh? I wonder why he kept it. It must count as a miracle. But as for me spoiling it…'

He shrugged his shoulders, but he knew what Darko meant. The shorts had saved Slobodan's life, and it had been him, Trajan, who had ordered the men to swim in shorts, which they had not done before.

'And you were carrying the knife in the pocket of your shorts, were you?' he now asked. 'So, who do you thank for that? You are a murderer. You had the knife, you planned this, and you were jealous of Slobodan, whom I bet the girl preferred to you. And if Mama regards you as a friend, why didn't she tell me that just now? And if the girl prefers you, why hasn't she said so and pleaded on your behalf? All this jealousy is ridiculous. Both you and Slobodan have wives in the capital. And Costantino has promised you his daughter…? I do not believe it. I think this is something cooked up by that child Bosco. You should not have listened to him.'

'You will hear it from don Costantino himself,' said Darko.

He got up and left Darko, left the stink, and decided to walk home through the thick African darkness, towards the bright lights of the hotel. He did not like Darko, he did not like anyone, but that was not what troubled him. He did not like the idea of disunity in the ranks, and what Darko had done, trying to kill Slobodan, was unforgiveable. But the real blame lay with Mama, promising her daughter to one man, namely himself, and to Darko as well, perhaps; or perhaps the blame lay with the interfering boy Bosco, or even with the girl herself. He himself had no family, no attachments, and these tangled relationships annoyed him. He had no sexual feelings at all anymore, and the thought of this rivalry over a girl, if that is what it was, annoyed him. The whole world, or at least the male half, was chasing girls, and it was an intolerable distraction. Mama and her children were going to Italy soon, though just when remained opaque; but to have the interfering woman away from their camp, from their men's work, would be good. Mama liked Darko - did she really? She had played Darko off against Slobodan? Well, she and Darko had to be taught a lesson. He needed to speak to Costantino and tell him to keep his wife in order.

His own quarters were a simple wooden cabin right on the edge of the hotel buildings, a wooden cabin so bare that one would not normally know it was inhabited. He had a bed, a chair, a couple of books, a veranda that looked out onto the sea, that was all. Of course, he had a place in the capital as well, a small place, where he kept his weapons, his passports, his clothes, the things he needed for travelling. But this, this hut on the beach was the place where he could be alone and feel his solitude.

But his solitude was, for once, to be interrupted. Hanging back from the circle of light that radiated from the veranda were three Serbs. A delegation, he could see at once. He knew what they wanted. It was so obvious.

He saw from their faces that they knew that he knew what they wanted, that the purpose of their visit was transparent. They never came to his hut, they never intruded; he was the boss; he liked it that way, and they respected that. But now they were here, and the reason was serious, at least to them, serious enough to intrude in this unprecedented way. There was an air of ill-disguised desperation about them. He marvelled at how much they wanted Darko dead.

That was what they wanted, but the fiction had to be preserved that this was somehow incidental to their visit. He beckoned them forward, sensing their relief that he had come. He sat on the chair, and as there was no other seating, they sat on the wooden boards of the veranda. There was an awkward silence. In the distance was the sound of the sea, a comforting rhythmic sound.

The silence persisted. What indeed was there to talk about?

'Slobodan doing well?' Trajan asked at last.

'Yes, boss,' one of them replied.

They had heard. He was in hospital, patched up, recovering, his African wife and three children had been to see him and comfort him. Slobodan was the most prolific of all the Foreign Legion, having fathered three children, so far. They all had African wives, and many had half-African children. Some of them were polygamous as well and had two African wives. Well, they had money, how else were they to spend it, and it was generally agreed that wives in the capital (only don Costantino had one on the base) were a good thing, safer than the alternative, casual pick-ups or the sex one paid for. Of course, all sex had to be paid for, but that was a fact of life. The wives, the children, the sex, these were things that the men spoke of constantly among themselves, when they were here at the coast, guarding the hotel. The wives, the children, these were the reward, as well as the money, for the work they did. But they knew that the boss was celibate, the only celibate in their private army, and that one could not discuss these matters with him. They knew there were things that could not be mentioned.

'Did you see the football, boss?' one of them asked.

'No,' he replied, closing off another avenue of conversation.

This was one of the things that the men, Italian and Serbian, all shared, a mania for football. They followed their home teams and the teams they admired from other countries as well. They spent hours discussing Barcelona and Manchester United, as well as Red Star Belgrade, Inter Milan, and Roma. But for the Serbs, it was Red Star Belgrade that mattered above all others. Trajan understood why: the Yugoslav war had been sparked off by a riot at a match where Red Star had played against Dynamo Zagreb – no football had actually been played that day, he thought. But whatever football the men were asking about now, he had no idea, and no interest. He did not like games of any sort. The obsession of both Serbs and Italians with football, watching it, and playing it on the beach and in the central space where the cage was, mystified him. They would play for hours, with intense seriousness. He could not share this. He knew that this puzzled the men. He looked at them now: their ugly shaved heads, much like his own, the way they wore ragged shorts, just as he did, the way one of them, the one who had asked about the match he was not aware of, had a face covered with dark thick stubble. Well, he had one thing in common with them. He had seen them in action. He knew that, like him, they were completely ruthless.

'Did you have a good trip, boss?' one of them now asked.

'Yes,' he answered. 'You noticed I was away?' he asked.

'No, not at all, it was just that, well, yes, it was just that when you were away that Darko tried to kill Slobodan. If you have been here, perhaps he would not have dared.'

'True,' conceded Trajan. 'But I was not away for long, was I?'

He remembered his trip, to the capital, then on to southern Africa and to a fine hotel where an important American was on holiday with his wife and three children. He had allowed himself a slight beard for the trip, and travelled as a tourist, under one of his aliases, with a hat, dark glasses and a very cunning wig. He had spent one night in the hotel and been back at the airport and flying out of the country perhaps before the bodies had been discovered. It was the sort of clinical, surgical, operation in which he excelled. He had picked the lock of the hotel room, entered the suite on silent feet, and then used a hotel steak knife to achieve his end. The Serbs, and most of the Italians, lacked the skill he had perfected: a complete and utter indifference to what he was doing, and who he was doing it for.

'I wonder when our next trip will be?' said one of the men, thinking this worth saying, just to let the boss know they were eager, but not expecting any information to be forthcoming.

Trajan understood. He knew to what they were referring. Last year, he had been meeting his contact in a bar in a shopping centre on the capital, when he had seen, in the same shopping centre, one of the Serbs, his African wife and his child. Of course, they all wondered about this. Where did the orders come from? And who was his contact whom he met every two weeks for lunch at the Village Market, the shopping centre with the bars and restaurants quite near all the embassies in the capital? In fact, since being seen, he and his contact met in different places.

'It depends where we are asked to intervene,' he said noncommittally.

This is what the men did; part of the time was spent on the base, as they called the hotel at the coast; part of the time was holiday inland with the wives and children in the capital; and part of it was in the field. He had taken them all on field trips many times. He knew they were seasoned killers, all of them, even the youngest ones; they had all been killers before coming to Africa, indeed, that is why they had come, to escape the police in the Balkans, Sicily and elsewhere. They were ruthless, but not necessarily efficient, to Trajan's mind. Whenever they did land clearances, which were a feature of African life, the men would go slightly wild. They enjoyed themselves too much, he thought. They had no indifference to the work but took to it with enthusiasm.

'Boss,' said one of them, finally getting to the point of this visit, the point he had been patiently waiting for, 'Boss, we want to hang Darko.'

He nodded.

'Of course you do,' he said.

He explained his failure to talk to don Costantino. He sensed, as he did so, that this was not having the desired effect. The men were silent, unconvinced. Their faces seemed set, grim. After he had explained how he had failed to speak to don Costantino, he waited for them to speak, to accept the delay. But the silence continued.

'Boss,' said the youngest of them, an eighteen-year-old who went by the name of Zoran, looking at the others, seeing their slight nods, knowing he was the spokesman for the group, but clearly nervous about this prospect, for they all respected and feared don Traiano, and did not want to contradict him, 'Boss, we want to hang him now. Tonight. And not wait for don Costantino.'

The silence became profound. Trajan realised he was standing at the edge of an abyss, and below him was something he did not quite understand about the politics of Serbia.

Zoran tried to explain, in a faltering voice, sensing the encouragement of the other two. He was not sure he knew how to express what he felt, what they all felt.

'You know who Slobodan's great-uncle was?' said Zoran.

'Of course,' said Trajan, knowing whom he meant.

'He was a hero,' said Zoran. 'People say bad things about him, but to us he was a hero - he is a hero. And Slobodan is like him, very brave, a good fighter, a man other men will follow. We all like him, boss, and the way that Darko has behaved… well, he does not deserve to live a moment longer, and that is the opinion of us all. Let us take him out of the cage right now and string him up. The men are not going to sleep until they see that.'

'Slobodan is a great guy, we all agree on that,' said Trajan slowly.

He considered the case. He considered what they were telling him, and what they were not saying, which was equally important. They wanted Darko dead, that was clear, and they wanted him dead at once. Darko had no friends, not now, anyway. Once he had been the friend of Slobodan, but not anymore. They had quarrelled about this girl, Bosco's sister. That was trivial, perhaps, but Darko's attempt to murder Slobodan so openly was not trivial. That had been a naked power grab, an attempt to assert leadership. These men were saying that they did not want Darko as their leader, and they did not want Costantino to intervene. Goodness knows why they hated Darko. Perhaps they preferred Slobodan? He did not care either way, but he acknowledged Darko's ambition, which was clearly a threat. But in the end what mattered was that Darko had attempted to kill Slobodan, whose life had been saved by a bottle top. What possible doubt could there be? Darko was guilty of attempted murder.

There was one thing he was sure of, however, the more he thought of it. The men did not want Costantino informed of the decision, they wanted no appeal to Sicily or asking of permission, because they plainly feared that permission would not be given. And this meant something, he knew. It meant that the attempted murder of Slobodan by Darko was not just a simple quarrel, even if it looked that way. It was quite possible that it was a targeted assassination inspired from afar. He could see what the men thought: that Darko had acted under instruction, and that the person who instructed him had been Costantino, who would no doubt now give the order that he was to be spared. That was why the men did not want Costantino informed. That was why the men were so nervous, fearing that at any moment, the line to Messina would be restored, and the instruction would come to release Darko from the cage. That was why Darko was so defiant, he now thought: it was the confidence of a man who knew that the boss who ordered him to do what he had done would rescue him. But if that were the case, he would need to tread carefully, for he did not want to make an enemy of Costantino.

He sighed internally to himself. The years he had spent in Africa with these Serbs... the Sicilians were different. The Sicilians were disciplined and did not let their emotions get the better of them. But with the Serbs it was always personal. He saw that. He had known it for some time. The Serbs, cooped up here in their training camp, were difficult to handle. They needed discipline. They were all enthusiastic fighters, but that enthusiasm had to be channelled. When they were off the base, on leave, with their wives and girlfriends, that was different: there they could make babies to their hearts' content, live the simulacrum of normal lives. When on a mission, there they had to be focussed, driven; they had to be sharp in their actions, ruthless, sticking to the minute-by-minute schedule that such raids had, doing what they came to do, no more. Perhaps they were able to do this because the fear of death impelled them, or the excitement of such raids. But when on a mission they obeyed orders, minutely, and that was the reason they had hardly lost anyone on a raid. But here on the beach, it was different: they played football, they trained, they swam, they ran, they trained some more, but that was never enough. They were on a short leash, and the tensions rose. It had happened before now, that men had been sentenced to be beaten, or put in the cage for fighting with each other, or for other infractions, such as drunkenness. And there had been the man sentenced for theft, who had been dropped out of a plane into the bush. The men accepted this discipline, but there was a price to pay. He had nothing against Darko, he realised, and nothing for Slobodan; but he had to give the men what they wanted. He stood up and gave a nod. The men knew that he had agreed to give them what they wanted. He would explain everything to Costantino afterwards.

From the shadows, Bosco watched. He had not liked Darko, ever; he had not liked the way he looked at his sister, the way he had been so close to his mother. He liked Slobodan, and he knew that his sister did too; she had never wanted to marry Trajan, she had always hoped for Slobodan, even if he already had a wife and children. She would not be sorry that Darko was being dealt with in this way. Slobodan had already made love to her, and he had used this to taunt Darko, who had then tried to kill him.

He was glad now that the men were crowding round the cage, and extracting Darko, who made no protest, neither resisting nor co-operating. Bosco felt a strong interest in what was about to happen. They were tying a rope around Darko's ankles and dragging him across the ground to the tree with the low hanging but strong bough. Once there, across the sand, they hoisted him up, so that he was suspended by his feet, his head a few feet above the sandy ground. Darko made a noise like a cough, or perhaps a groan. To stop his hands moving they were pinioned with another rope to his back. The men settled down on the ground at a little distance to watch. Someone brought some beers. Trajan Antonescu, seeing all was done, and having no interest in the inevitable outcome, walked away, to go home, to go to bed. After a little while, Bosco approached. He looked into the eyes of the upside-down face, read their defiance, and smiled.

Chapter Four

'Dad,' said Francesco, standing at the window, looking out at the square, 'I think you should see this.'

'See what?' asked Calogero, who was at his desk.

He came to the window and looked down. He saw a huge black car, indeed two of them, and out of them pouring seven or eight men, and not just any men either, but men who seemed determined to have their way. All the men had beards, neatly trimmed haircuts and sharp suits, along with gleaming shoes. In their midst, black-bearded, was the Serb, don Costantino, the man from Niš. Calogero frowned. This was the man he was conspiring to kill. But no one could have spoken, he was sure of that. The fact that don Costantino was coming to see him, unannounced, this was a sign, surely, that he did not know, he did not suspect. For if he had, he would not be coming to see Calogero, he would have ordered his death. But this was not it; this was not death; this was a man coming to talk; indeed, this was a man coming to ask for help.

'Just keep calm and act normal. Ask your mother to make some coffee for the three of us. Were you going out?'

'I was...'

'Stay here and you will learn something,' commanded Calogero. 'Something important, perhaps. Think and act strategically,' he added.

Francesco went and told his mother about the coffee. While he did so, the doorbell rang. He tried to calm himself, and returned to the study, pretending that all this was normal. He opened the door.

'I am so glad to find you in,' don Costantino was saying. 'You must forgive me for turning up unannounced. But as you know, if we telephone ahead, we do not just tell our friends we are coming; we tell everyone else too. And... well, it is best they don't know, as they would only start to speculate, and we do not want them to know what we are thinking. Ah,' he said, looking at Francesco. They shook hands. 'It is about my son Bosco and his mother and sister that I want to speak. You know them, of course, as you have been to Africa.'

Francesco almost winced at the mention of their trip to Africa, for that was when Trajan Antonescu had tried to murder don Calogero. He looked at his father, who remained impassive, giving nothing away. Why had don Costantino mentioned it, if not to humiliate don Calogero, to remind him of his weakness, his brush with death, his, worse, his only miscalculation to date?

'Yes, sir,' said Francesco quickly. 'I was there for his initiation into manhood, as they call it.'

They sat down. Calogero said nothing but smiled at the Serbian boss from Messina. He was giving nothing away, nothing at all, but Francesco could read his mind and knew how much his father hated this man. He disliked beards, and the Serb's beard was black, bushy and gleaming: not the sort of well-trimmed beard one saw as one walked down the via Etnea, but a huge statement of a beard, a challenge to all who saw it. All the men in Messina had these beards; well, they would soon be shaving them off in a hurry, Francesco reflected, when their master was dead.

'Bosco has grown by leaps and bounds since then, which is why I want him over here now, so I can keep an eye on him. I have been hearing about him from his mother of course, and she has been tyring her best, but... there are certain things a mother cannot do. He needs to go to school as well. Bosco told me over the phone the other day that he is ready for his first killing; as for his first sexual intercourse, that has already happened. I am most displeased, as every father would be. The boy thinks he is grown up, but he isn't.'

Don Calogero nodded sympathetically.

'One of the men, Slobodan - if you remember meeting him - was entrusted with the task of taking Bosco to the dentist in the capital. He did so. But they also went to some sort of establishment and fixed him up with a girl. Now I want to send him to boarding school, in England perhaps, but if he has had those sorts of experiences, it is not nice, not nice at all. He needs a strong hand. He is growing selfish and spoilt and a little bit dangerous. You see, he returned the favour to Slobodan, and enabled Slobodan to sleep with his own sister, my daughter... That infuriates me. I had other plans for her. And my wife, my African wife, allowed this to happen. She can't control the boy. He is of an age, as was I, as were you, Calogero. One starts young, eh? Don't you agree, Francesco? But he has learned everything Africa has to teach him, and now I will bring him over here, and train him myself. And if he comes here, his mother has to come, and if she has to come, his sister has to come; and that means that my wife here gets very annoyed and upset, as do my two children. Ah, Calogero, how lucky you are with this young man!'

Don Costantino smiled expansively.

'Yes, Francesco is excellent,' said Calogero generously. 'I trust him entirely, and if I ask him to get anything done, he and his friends get it done for me. They are all wonderful young men. But I have daughters too, who are not easy, and three young boys; the eldest must be just a bit younger than Bosco, and he is showing signs of not being easy. The others are spoilt, but Francesco works for a living, that is the difference.'

Don Costantino nodded.

'I know that you have this boy over here now, the one called Gennaro...'

'A great little fellow, a bit younger than your Bosco too,' said Calogero. 'My children, my sons at least, all love him and look upon him as a cousin.'

'That is nice to know,' said Constantino. 'The fact that he is obviously not from here…. You may ask yourself why I am discussing these family matters. I want Bosco to come over here, and I want to make him my heir.'

Don Calogero nodded slowly.

'You already have an heir, as I am sure you have not forgotten.'

'I am in no danger of forgetting it. I have daily reminders from him and from his mother. She is a pain in the neck. We have not lived together for years, but the complaints, the demands for money, the sense of outraged dignity. She thinks she did me a favour by marrying me. It is true she was a cousin of my father's, but I do not owe my position to her. Not in the least.'

'You owe it to me and your own bravery and ingenuity,' said Calogero.

Costantino laughed, remembering the picnic on Etna.

'I want to divorce her and marry my African wife properly. I want to legitimise her children and delegitimise Rosa's. I will pay them off. Dimitri will not like it, not like it at all, but I will pay him off on the condition he goes away. America, somewhere like that. Somewhere far away, where he will not embarrass me.'

'If that is what you have decided, I will approve,' said Calogero. 'Dimitri has embarrassed you?'

'I have tried everything,' said Costantino. 'His rebelliousness detracts from my authority. If I cannot handle my own son, people will think….. He enrages me. But if I give him a couple of million euro on condition he never bothers me again, it will be money well spent. But he will be back for more, I am sure. But one day he will have Bosco to deal with. That may make him think. He may well understand he is better away from Sicily, safer that way. If he is sensible, he will, but that is the one thing he is not….'

There was silence between them.

'So, you do not love Dimitri anymore, and you want never to see him again. Is that it?' asked Calogero.

Costantino considered.

'That is not the entire story,' he conceded. 'You are a father too, you know how it is. The moment they placed the child in my arms after he was born, I fell in love with him. He was so beautiful, so sweet. You know the feeling. And he was that way until he was about eleven, then he became unruly and disobedient. I have reasoned with him, I have beaten him, I have tried everything, hoping he would abandon his sad attitude of opposition. But nothing works. It pains me to lose him, it pains me a great deal, but in the end, if he goes to America and has a life there, it will be better for him, and better for me. But I will miss him, even though he has given me so much pain. You never get over the love you have for your children, do you?' He looked at Francesco. 'Do you cause your father pain?'

'No, sir, not if I can help it,' said Francesco.

'Then you are lucky,' said Costantino to Calogero. 'I hope he always stays good and obedient.'

There was silence.

'Forgive me, Costantino, but you didn't just come here to ask me to approve your domestic arrangements, though I greatly appreciate that you have done so,' said Calogero. 'How we look after our families is important. If Dimitri is not an asset, it really is the kindest thing to send him away. But there is something else you would like to discuss, I feel.'

'Indeed, there is. I mentioned Bosco's twin sister. My African wife has had ambitions for her, as she is now, in African terms, marriageable. And certain men had ambitions in regard to her. You may remember both Darko and Slobodan?' he asked, looking at Francesco.

'The two who....?'

'Yes, and with that in mind. They had African wives already, both of them, but both thought they would be suitable sons-in-law to me. They are both about ten years older than my daughter. Her mother made a sort of promise to Darko, and I agreed, simply because Slobodan, well, he is the great-nephew of a great man, he has a sense of entitlement, and I did not want to give him a greater status than he already has. He might be a rival to Bosco in the future. So, I chose Darko, who agreed to wait. But Slobodan did not like this, and he decided to force the pace, shall we say, make the girl his, though Darko soon realised what he was up to. Now, to summarise, Slobodan is in hospital, thanks to Darko stabbing him in the groin, and Darko has been hanged.'

'When did this happen?' asked Calogero.

'The hanging? A couple of nights ago,' said Costantino slowly. 'My wife told me. She blames Bosco, thinking he told Darko what Slobodan was up to, and this provoked the quarrel. But she is mistaken. Bosco told me, I told Darko, and I ordered him to kill Slobodan. I am fond of my daughter. I had my reasons. Slobodan was too ambitious. He offended me. And I promised Darko to look after him. But Slobodan was lucky, and the men wanted Darko to hang, and Trajan Antonescu allowed it, without consulting me. The computer was not working that evening.'

Everyone was silent.

'Antonescu should have asked my permission,' said Costantino. 'I would not have given it. People here and people there know that Darko was my man. They know that Slobodan is a puffed-up idiot with little more than his family connections to recommend him. No one, not Slobodan and certainly not Antonescu, has the power to hang a man, without consulting me first, phone lines working or not. The damage has been done, but someone needs to be taught a lesson.'

'And that someone is Antonescu?' said Calogero.

'Yes.'

'You clearly want to undertake a lot of changes, Costantino. To divorce one wife and bring in another; to send away one son and bring in another; and now, to kill Antonescu, the man who allowed your man Darko to be killed. Of course, some people might question your domestic changes. They might feel that Rosa, a relation of the late don Carmelo, deserves better; and they might think you are being unfair to poor Dimitri. Antonescu has no friends in the world except me, ironically, and if I give him to you, no one, but no one, will question your dispositions. If you kill Antonescu, you will be all-powerful, given that Antonescu is a very important man, who has made a fortune for us all. He is an asset. But, I freely admit, his elimination is well overdue. Yet, his contacts, his work, both have been valuable.'

'Naturally, Calogero, if you give me permission to eliminate Antonescu, I will compensate you,' said Costantino. 'I come with an offer. I will give you one of the hotels in Taormina. You choose which one.'

'Ah, the same fee I had for allowing you to eliminate don Carmelo. That is a handsome offer, a fine offer. I accept it. But… you may find Antonescu hard to catch.'

'I know that you have told him he may never come back to Italy, so I was thinking that he needs your permission for one last visit. I intend to invite him for consultations about Africa, about our business there.'

'And he will come, do you think?' asked Calogero. 'Does he trust you?'

'He will come if you tell him to. He trusts you. You have left him alive so long… You forgave him, in a manner of speaking.'

'Oh, I forgive nothing,' said Calogero. 'I just wait till the opportune moment. I am patient. Tell me though, most people would be very frightened of even trying to assassinate Antonescu. One should not underestimate him. Promise me this.'

'What?'

'That you will do it yourself.'

'That is what I intend,' said Costantino.

Once more, there was silence in the room. It was interrupted by Francesco.

'Forgive me, sir,' he said, addressing the Serb, then turning to Calogero. 'Dad, let me do it.'

Calogero considered.

'You?' he asked, thinking of the boy's mother in the kitchen, thinking of the danger that Traiano presented. 'No. Don Costantino has said that he will take care of it, and take care of it, he will.'

'You have a son to be proud of,' said Costantino enviously.

Costantino stood, ready to leave. Calogero stood and held out a hand. Costantino took it and they shook. It was all arranged then. Without saying more the Serb left, with Francesco, at a sign from his father, seeing him to the door, and indeed his car.

They went down in the lift together.

'Sir,' said Francesco swiftly. 'I will disobey my father. When Antonescu comes, and I believe he is coming soon, I will kill him for you. I will bring you his severed ear in token of his death.'

'Can you do it?'

'I am a relation of his wife's. He would never suspect me. It will be David and Goliath all over again. Sir, trust me.'

'By all means, do your best,' said Costantino. 'If you can, kill him. Bring me his ear. I would like that.' He paused. 'Tell me, do you know my son Dimitri?'

'I have met him, sir. In a nightclub.'

'Yes, that is where people are likely to meet him.'

They were now in the square, and the cars and the bearded bodyguards were waiting. The other Serbs looked at Francesco, taking in all his details. He looked at them.

'You will hear from me, sir, I promise,' said Francesco.

'I'll expect you,' said the Serb, before entering the car and being driven off.

Above their heads, Calogero had been at the window, observing. The suited and bearded ones were standing by the cars in various relaxed attitudes. One of them was standing leaning against the wall of the church, smoking. Another was, hand in pocket, idly scratching his testicles. A third was looking at himself in the car wing mirror, arranging his hair. Two others were drinking coffee from small plastic cups. Some were idly watching the girls crossing the square, who walked past them knowing they were being watched. Others were observing two little boys kicking a ball against a wall. It was a calm and relaxed scene. Then suddenly, it changed. Coffee cups were thrown away, cigarettes dropped, all attention was focused on the man who approached them, don Costantino, and all stood to attention and became tense. Next to Costantino was Francesco. A few moments later, they were all in the cars, and the cars were leaving.

'I was watching,' said Calogero, when Francesco re-entered.

Francesco waited for him to go on.

'That man is nervous, which, from our point of view, is excellent. He goes around with this huge entourage, and why? What is he afraid of? I think they are all from Serbia, these bearded creatures. Like him. His nephews and cousins. Why? Because he does not trust us, and he does not trust Sicilians, and he does not trust anyone working for him whom he inherited from his late father. Don Carmelo was fat, he was lazy, he was given to worldly pleasure, but people liked him. This chap, not so much, and he knows it. So, what is he planning? He wants to reassert his authority by killing Antonescu, the man who has defied him, to show everyone he will take no nonsense. It is a good idea. To be frank with you, Francesco, killing Antonescu is a brilliant move; the very fact that he has remained unkilled until now is something of a reproach, I suppose. He thinks he will kill Antonescu with his own hands, and then no one will be able to defy him, no, not even me. But we are one step ahead.... I see it all now, what we have to do. Do you?'

'I think I do, dad. You want to use Antonescu to kill Costantino.'

'I am confident I can,' said Calogero. 'He always loved a challenge. And he will do it, for me. Oh, does that surprise you? It shouldn't. But you will see.' He looked at Francesco seriously. 'Traiano is dangerous. He has no ties to any human being, which makes him very dangerous. No, I am not quite right. There is one person he cares about in an entirely negative way – me. Hatred is a love gone wrong, and his love has gone seriously wrong. Despite what you think, he will never kill me; but he might kill you, to make me suffer, so you must be very wary of him, do you understand? Leave him to Costantino. He will relish the challenge. And vice versa. One of them will die: Costantino, I hope. But you, yes, I know, the tobacconist in Librino… I know, I know, but you are still too young. Your mother loves you too much. I love you too much. Ah poor Costantino, loving Dimitri so much, and Dimitri not loving him. But you and I are different, thank God. And his ridiculous ambitions for the boy in Africa, old enough to kill at whatever age he is. Well, you are old enough to kill, you have killed, but don't attempt too much too soon. And how is that girl, don Nunzio's daughter? When are you seeing her again?'

'She is well, dad, very well. I am planning on going there this weekend. And she will be down in Catania next week some time too.'

'Well, if something comes of it, I will be pleased. She is beautiful, and you are a young man, so if you make love to her as teenagers do, she would be ideal for you, and I doubt don Nunzio would object. She is a good girl, I am sure, the sort that does not ask questions.'

Calogero was silent, pondering something. Francesco dreaded the question, knowing what he was thinking. He was going to ask about Petra, but he did not, thinking the question counterproductive. Instead, he smiled. Francesco felt the huge relief at not having to lie.

In the Furnaces, the door opened, and Francesco was hit by a huge wave of discontent emanating from Petra.

'I was expecting you the other day,' she said.

'My father asked me to do something for him, and I could not get away.'

'You are eighteen. You can do what you like, surely. You can tell him to go to hell, for a start, can't you? My brother did.'

'He did not. No one tells my father to go to hell, least of all me. I don't want to tell him to go to hell. Anyway, I am here now.'

She grudgingly stood aside to let him enter the house. He could tell that her mother and her sisters were not there, and he had got her on her own. This was most unusual. Generally, his visits to the house were conducted under the critical eye of one or both sisters, or the mother, signora Costacurta. The empty house was an opportunity. He saw that the same thought had occurred to her as well.

'I have got about an hour,' he said, hopefully, and immediately realising that this was the wrong thing to say.

Her look was thunderous. She led the way to the kitchen.

'What have you to do next?' she asked.

'I have to take my stepbrothers to have their hair cut, then I am seeing the others, Nino and Marco, then on Saturday I have to go to Syracuse with the boys, which will take all day, more or less. They are being photographed by Alfonso Agostini.'

Petra was suitably impressed.

'Nice,' she said. 'You never take me to see anyone,' she added, with returning bitterness, as she busied herself with coffee.

'Whenever I suggest we go anywhere, you always say you are too busy,' he pointed out.

This was true. He had suggested trips on several occasions, to Taormina and further afield.

'Not those sorts of trips,' she said. 'But going to Syracuse and back in a day might be nice, with your stepbrothers.'

She gave him the coffee.

'Look,' he said, 'tell me if it is a crime to want to spend time with you, and to want to sleep with you.'

She looked at him with exasperation.

'How is Nino Santacroce?' she asked, changing the subject, adding. 'He is so beautiful.'

'Nino is very pleased with himself. He has got a girlfriend, and he has a child on the way. My father was very angry, but Nino has been forgiven, as he knew he would be. He is clever, he calculates well. Even the girl's parents seem to have forgiven him. Lucky Nino. He now has a reputation for himself, a good reputation. He has become respectable at long last. People did not respect him much before this. Now they will; they will admire him for having a child, getting married…'

'And the other one?' she asked, referring in this manner to Marco. 'Is he pleased with himself?'

'Marco is less demonstrative,' said Francesco. 'He… One can never be sure what he thinks.' He finished the coffee. 'I don't know why you are so interested in them. It is not as if you know them.'

'They are your friends,' she said. 'They interest me because they tell me about you.'

'They are not really my friends,' he said. 'I mean, I spend time with them, but, well… You could ask me about Paoluzzu.'

'Who is he?'

'He manages the Trattoria Norma in Piazza Armerina, near the Roman Villa. He is a cousin of mine. I met him, well I have always known him, but I met him more recently when he was working in Africa. He's nice. You would like him. He is an ordinary boy.'

'So, is that why you are always going to Piazza Armerina? To see this Paoluzzu?'

'Yes. He is nice. Look,' he said. 'Tell me if I am wasting my time. Tell me to go away, if that is what you want.'

She looked at him and felt sorry for him. He was so sweet. A few times, she had given in to him, and given into her own desires, for she found him attractive; but one thing troubled her.

'I like you,' she said. 'Of course I like you. It is just that…'

She approached him as he leaned against the kitchen counter and let him put his arms around her. She heard him sigh deeply and she felt the power of his desire, the heat of him, from under his clothes. They kissed.

'It is just that what?' he asked.

'Where is Tonino Grassi?' she asked.

'I have told you, I do not know. I hardly knew Tonino Grassi. Wherever he is, he is not here. Why are you so interested?'

'I was fond of him,' she said. 'Have you asked around, have you tried to find out?'

'You were not that fond of him, or he of you,' said Francesco. 'I have not asked.'

'Why not?' she asked.

He looked at her and said nothing; then he turned away.

'I asked my brother, and got the same response,' she said sadly.

'Can't you drop the subject?' he asked. 'Wouldn't it be better to let it go?'

'Why? How many other subjects are we supposed to drop? How many other things and people are we supposed never to mention?'

He affected indifference.

'It is the way it is. Where do you think the money to buy this nice house came from? Your brother, of course, and before you met Tonino, neither you nor he had two cents to rub together. Why not keep quiet and be grateful?'

'I have spoken to Emma Santucci. I went over to Palermo to meet her.'

'You have done what?' he asked, appalled.

'She thinks he was murdered by the police. She thinks he was murdered. She is at least half-right.'

'Please leave it alone,' he said. 'Can't you see…?'

'No, I can't see. See what?'

He shook his head in disbelief.

'I don't want to spend the rest of my life being told I cannot ask questions,' she said. 'I don't want to be like your mother.'

That reference offended him.

'You can ask questions, just not about this,' he replied coldly. 'Stop fishing. Stop trying to squeeze me for information I have not got, for stuff that is not your business, and for stuff I would not tell you about even if I knew it. When I say I do not know, it means I do not know; when I do not want to discuss something, it means I do not want to discuss it. Is that why you let me get into bed with you, so you could pump me in this way? Is that the price I have to pay for the favour? Can't we just go to bed, now?'

'I liked you,' she said.

'Then you should show it,' he replied.

'I don't want a boyfriend who keeps things secret from me.'

'I don't have secrets. There is nothing to know. You know me, the whole me,' he countered. 'You know me better than anyone. You mean a lot to me. I am not holding anything back.'

He seemed almost tearful. She knew what he was referring to, the way they had made love in her bedroom the last time. She stubbornly held to the ever more tenuous belief that he was a nice boy.

'Where were you when they shot that man outside his tobacconist's shop in Librino?' she asked.

'I was on my way to Piazza Armerina to meet Paoluzzu,' he answered levelly. 'What, you think I go round shooting people on a motorbike?'

'I didn't know you knew people in Piazza Armerina until you just told me.'

'That is not a crime, is it? I told you. He is a guy called Paoluzzu, a bit older than me, he works in a restaurant there, I met him when we all went up to visit the Roman villa. He is a nice boy, an ordinary boy, just like me. We have become friends.'

'But you are not an ordinary boy,' she said. 'I don't believe you shoot people from the back of a motorbike, no, but maybe you know people who do that sort of thing. I think you make yourself useful to the man you call your father, don Calogero di Rienzi.'

'But you say you like me, and yet you think I am a friend of murderers,' he said with bitterness, his passion now just a distant memory. 'For goodness' sake, be realistic. When I was a tiny boy, five or six, I would go into shops and go to the market and steal stuff and bring it home to my mother, because we did not have enough to eat. I bet if you had been a boy, you would have done the same for your mother. Does that make me a thief and a criminal? Well, if it does, I do not care. Lots of boys did much worse, much worse. Nino used to sit in men's laps and let them put their hands down his trousers, for God's sake, or so I have heard, all because he and his mother had no money. And your beloved Tonino, when he lived here in Catania, used to deal in stolen pills and other stolen medical goods from the American base, or so I have heard. He did it for the money which he gave to his mother, and to you and your sisters and your brother. And when he disappeared, where did that money go? To you, among others. So, please do not look down on me, or the criminal classes.'

'Are you? A criminal?'

'You think I am. You have slept with a criminal. Well done! You are not much of a judge of character, are you? First Tonino, who left you, and now me, and goodness knows who else in between.'

'I did not sleep with Tonino.'

'Well, that is nice to know.' He remembered something Marco had said to him, when he and Marco had discussed Petra. 'More fool Tonino. He should have done. Look,' he said, feeling his passion return. 'Enough nonsense. I want you, and I want to have you now. Let us go upstairs and go to bed. I don't care if your mother and sisters come back any moment now. I don't even care about the boys' haircuts. Just give me what I want and give it to me now.'

His face was red with passion, she could see.

The trip to Syracuse was on an altogether larger scale than had at first been envisaged. Because Francesco had only got home after his visit to Petra long after supper was over, and long past the time for the boys' appointment with the barber, and because the boys could not be disappointed, his mother had resolved to take them herself to the barber by the Opera. As she was doing so, she had met Nino Santacroce in the square outside the Church, and he had offered to make himself useful and accompany the boys. Delighted to hand over the responsibility, and seeing how Renato's face lit up at the thought of spending time with Nino, she accepted his kind offer. But as Nino walked with his three charges towards the Opera House, Marco spotted them and joined them, asking them where they were going. He was not going to pass up this opportunity to spend time with the most important children in the quarter, and he was determined that the three boys should not be monopolised by Nino.

The barber's was a hole in the wall near the Opera which, the boys knew, their father had frequented from boyhood, and their long-deceased grandfather before him. They had made an appointment, and the owner made a show of cutting their hair himself, leaving other, less important, clients to his assistants. No trouble, no attention was to be spared. The assistants, much younger men, looked on with awe at the way Romano and Sebastiano were treated, and, looking to their own advantage, offered to cut the hair of both Nino and Marco. Both politely declined. Nino was blessed with long, voluminous and fair locks of hair that reached down to his shoulders, when not tied back in a ponytail. Marco was less blessed, but his hair was long and full too, in the manner of an early nineteenth century poet. His hair, though, Nino had found out, thanks to Francesco telling him, was tinted, made a more interesting shade of brown by chemical means, just as Francesco's, which was naturally lank, had to be gently frizzed on a regular basis. Both attended the same hairdresser as Francesco's mother, Agata. Nino, who had no need of this intervention, found their homage to fashion, indeed to vanity, rather amusing. All the men who worked for don Calogero had long hair, just as all the men who worked for the Serb had long luxuriant beards and, it was said, tattoos, both of which were forbidden in Catania. In Palermo, it was different: Beppe Santucci and his friends had short back and sides, like American servicemen; and in Africa they had shaved heads, because of the dirt, the fleas and the lice.

While Romano and Sebastiano were seated in the barber's chair, and the barber flitted between one and the other, Renato sat on the bench, his eyes supposedly fixed on this operation, while Marco and Nino conversed over his head in low voices. All the time, however, Renato was listening.

'Where is Francesco?' asked Marco.

'Petra, I assume,' said Nino with meaning. 'He must have let the time escape him.'

Marco nodded.

'I told him, you know, don't take any nonsense, you are the boss's son.'

Nino nodded.

'Looks like he took your advice,' said Nino.

His hand was gently laid on one of Renato's shoulders, proprietorially and protectively. Without giving away that he had noticed this, Marco felt the most terrible jealousy. Perhaps he should not have come. To see the beautiful little prince like this, so intimate with Nino, pained him. That should have been his role, he felt, the protector of the boss's eldest son. The sensation of jealousy, something he was not used to, as he had been brought up as the centre of attention from his mother and sisters, and the person everyone feared among his male contemporaries, the sensation of jealousy was like a physical malaise creeping over him. He wanted to be the one whom Renato looked up to. Nino had taken his place. But it worked the other way, as well: he wanted Nino to pay attention to him. Nino paid attention to the child, but not to him; Nino paid attention to Francesco, but not to him; to everyone, it seemed, but not to him. Nino took him for granted. He wanted to be noticed. But he felt so tongue-tied and inarticulate, so limited, so stupid, that he did not know how to earn his attention. It was not often that he was alone with Nino, not often they conversed; usually Francesco was with them; so, this was an opportunity, but he did not know how to take it.

'Do you think she will be a thing from now on?' asked Marco, meaning Petra.

'Probably. He is very keen on her. Have you seen her? Well, you can see... she is gorgeous. He's liked her for a long time. But she has been stand-offish, unless that has now changed. We will have to get used to it. It's good, I mean, he needs to make the right choice, being who he is. You know…'

Marco nodded, not quite seeing the significance of what he said.

'Are you sure he is with Petra, and not in Piazza Armerina?' Marco asked. 'He has been there a bit recently. I mean, why go there…? Who has he got there?'

'No idea,' said Nino.

The boy spoke.

'He has got a friend called Paoluzzu, and he goes to see a girl called Ida who is the daughter of don Nunzio,' said Renato.

'You have met these people? He has spoken of them?' asked Marco with wonder.

'Yes,' said Renato.

'He's kept that quiet,' marvelled Nino. 'Though not quiet enough.'

They were silent. The only sound was the clipping of the two younger boys' hair.

'And your girl?' Marco asked. 'How is Daniela?'

'She is well, she is well,' said Nino with satisfaction. 'The baby will be here next year, around Easter.'

'Weren't you surprised, I mean, the baby….'

'No. I just think, you know…. I am not, you know…. What about you? How is the Widow?'

Marco considered for a moment.

'She is fine,' he said, wondering what Nino knew about the Widow. 'I mean, you know…'

'And her children?'

'They are all fine,' answered Marco shortly.

'What is your little boy called?' asked Renato suddenly.

Marco went scarlet. He had not realised they knew.

'He is called Bruno,' he managed to say.

'We ought to meet him,' said Renato. 'You keep him away from us,' he added, almost accusingly. 'How old were you when he was born?'

Marco could not answer.

'Not much older than me and my little one, I imagine,' said Nino easily. 'Now stop being curious,' he said to Renato. 'If Marco does not want to say, he does not want to say. You're twenty-five, aren't you? You should start looking for a wife,' he said, addressing Marco.

Marco felt uncomfortable.

'All in good time,' he said.

He was self-conscious about his family life. His mother and his sisters raised the subject periodically, when they felt bold. He explained it by saying to them, and to himself, that he was shy, diffident, and ill at ease, all of which was true, and that he was happy with Bruno and his mother, the Widow.

'What about you?' Marco said in return. 'How old are you?'

'Older than him,' said Nino, gesturing at Renato, who looked up at him. 'Younger than you, and younger than Francesco.'

Marco tried to work this out. He thought Nino was about sixteen or seventeen at the most.

'And you and Daniela… I mean, she is your one and only…?'

'Sure,' admitted Nino. 'We have been together for a long time. We met when we were both thirteen,' he added. 'It is wonderful.'

And what were you doing until you were thirteen, thought Marco, knowing the answer to that question. What Nino Santacroce had got away with! Working for Antonescu as a boy prostitute, now selling pills, and selling the services of prostitutes and all the while everyone thinking he was so nice, so sweet. He felt, at that moment, he hated him; it was, of course, envy and jealousy at work, and a sense of injustice. Nino paid attention to others but not to him. They were not friends.

'If you want to have a look at the book sometime….' Nino was now saying. 'It would all be free for you, because everyone knows who you are. I don't let any of our guys look at the book, as I don't want them bothering the girls, but if you… You are different, being a friend.'

'Thanks,' said Marco, his hurt feelings much assuaged. 'I might like it, once in a while….'

The boy Renato, who had been studying his younger brothers as they had their hair cut, now looked up at Marco with curiosity. Renato was enjoying himself. It was nice to be here between these two, to feel Nino so close. He liked the warmth and smell of the barber's shop, the fuss that was being made of his brothers, the closeness and warmth of Nino, the feel of his suit, the aroma of his well-washed long hair, and the feel, under his jacket, of what he knew was his gun. All the men around him carried guns – his brother did, Nino did, and so, he was sure, did Marco. Shifting his seat, he casually rearranged his body, drawing closer to Marco, resting his head against him, and once more feeling the hard heavy metal of a weapon under his jacket. Marco was ugly and, he thought, stupid, and he did not like him as much as he liked Nino; but he could tell Marco envied his affection for Nino, and he could not resist the prospect of making Nino jealous. He snuggled up to Marco. Marco, momentarily taken aback, was pleased, while Nino frowned.

'We are going to Syracuse tomorrow,' said Renato. 'You should come. You should both come. I am sure Francesco would like it.'

'Why are you going?' asked Nino.

'Uncle Fofò is taking our photographs. He does so every year. My father likes it. I like it too.'

'Will you see the signora?' asked Marco, looking at Nino.

'Yes, and Salvatore and William. We like them both.'

The two boys were done, their hair cut. It was Renato's turn to take the chair. He did not stir from his seat.

'I have changed my mind,' he said. 'I like it long. Like yours,' he added, smiling at both Nino and Marco.

Then the child's attention wandered.

'You can afford to get married?' asked Marco.

'Yes,' answered Nino, with satisfaction. 'I mean, I give a lot to my parents and other relations, but I have saved up too, and the signora looks after it for me. And I have bits in accounts here in Catania too.'

'How much have you got?' asked Marco.

'Two or three hundred,' said Nino, not having to specify that he meant thousands.

This was, of course, a lie. There was no need to make Marco jealous. He had at least twice that amount, all the fruit of hard work over the years, a lot of money, even after paying the bosses their cut.

Marco looked impressed and at the same time not so very impressed.

'What about you?' Nino asked.

'A bit more than that,' said Marco. 'Also with the signora. But I have been working longer than you, though I have my mother and sisters to look after. As well as Bruno and his mother.'

Both were silent, calculating which one of them was the better paid, and which trade was more profitable: the selling of drugs and human flesh, or the punishment beatings and shootings. But it was not just the money that exercised their thoughts, though money was important, as they both knew, contemplating the idea of being without it; it was the prestige that the money represented. Marco's prestige was enormous: he was older than Nino by several years, being in his mid-twenties; he was physically strong, intimidating just to look at; he was a ruthless killer, one who could dispose of someone without ever having a moment of regret or shame, let alone guilt. The sweeter things of life, he had to the full, namely the company of his mother and his sisters, and the Widow and her son, his son too. He did not need women in the way others did, he did not need their company or their conversation (his mother and sisters and the Widow were different.)

He knew he was awkward, not good at talking; he knew that he was a man of the most astonishing ugliness, which the Widow, inexplicably, had once found attractive. His entire emotional life was seemingly bound up in the boss, the boss's son Francesco, and the boss's younger sons as well. The boss, his approval, his approbation, that was all he cared about. He had that approbation. So why should he feel so irrationally jealous of Nino? Why did he feel this strong desire to kill him?

The boss had warned him about irrationality. He had told him, on the several occasions. late at night, when he had been summoned up to his study and sat opposite him on the sofa, that irrationality was the greatest enemy. One must be cold and deliberate in all things: think things through and only do what will bring you advantage. Only kill when it was beneficial; never kill out of rage, or hatred, or spite or revenge. Kill others to advance yourself, or to protect yourself and your family and friends. Don't fall in love with women, let them fall in love with you, and don't ever allow a woman to tell you what to do. Use the woman in your life to advance yourself, the boss explained, to add to your prestige; have children too, to add to your prestige. Found a dynasty; marry like royalty. Of course, that explained the boss's first two marriages, not his third; and as for not being told what to do by a woman, the boss seemed to have forgotten his mother and his sisters, and indeed the signora his second wife, and possibly his first wife as well. But the message was clear; do not be led by your passions, ever.

Marco regarded Nino through narrowed eyes. Was this a passionate attachment he had to the girl Daniela, or was it a calculated move? He thought the latter. Nino would have imbibed the same lesson from the boss. The girl, the marriage, the child, there were all ways of putting his past behind him, and the not so far off days when Nino spent his time sitting on the lap of Colonel Andreazza, whose hand went down his trousers. They all knew about that. It was shameful, but somehow to be forgotten and forgiven. And as for marrying like royalty, the father-in-law would be useful, perhaps.

'How is your future father-in-law?' he now asked.

Was the question pointed, Nino wondered? He knew that Marco was not as stupid as he looked. It would be a mistake to underestimate him.

'He is fine,' said Nino. 'I mean not at first, he was a bit difficult, but he seems to be OK now. And you know I am going into the police, so the fact that he is a policeman helps. It is not quite what he would have chosen, I am not at first sight the ideal son-in-law, but he now sees the advantages.'

Marco grunted. The haircuts were over, and it was time to go home. So, they walked back to Purgatory, with the two younger boys on their backs, and Renato walking between them.

Darkness had fallen over the quarter, and in Calogero's flat, everyone was asleep, even if it was not late. His wife Agata, pregnant, had gone to bed early. The two little boys, Sebastiano and Romano, were asleep, and so was Renato. He had been allowed to stay up late with his father to watch television and was now asleep in his pyjamas next to his father. The sound of the television was off, the subtitles were on, and the only sound in the room was the gentle breathing of Renato. Calogero felt the boy's warmth pressed against him and felt at that moment that he doubted his own judgement. He did not doubt his own commercial sense, not at all. He worked with trusted people, most importantly his own ex-wife Anna Maria; his investments were showing an excellent return; the Furnaces, the Catania Waterfront, the restaurants, the gyms, the pizzerias, the trattorias, the hotels, the bars. The outlay had been daring, the drug money was being laundered, and he was the richest man in Catania, and possibly in Sicily; the only ones richer were Renzo Santucci and Beppe Santucci, and they were, in his brother-in-law's case, effectively neutered, or in Beppe's case, too young to worry about. No, business was good. What was worrying was the nexus between the commercial and the personal. His daughters were a worry, or had been. He had now realised that they inherited their mother's rebellious streak, and he had ceased to worry about it. Besides, they were girls, and though women could be business-minded, as his ex-wife and his sisters undoubtedly were, his two daughters, he felt, would prefer to enjoy the advantages of having a rich family rather than throwing themselves into the maintenance of a great fortune. Besides which, the girls, Isabella and Natalia, seemed not to notice where the money came from; they had learned well from their adoptive mother, Anna Maria; they were effortlessly rich. It never occurred to them, as it did to their father, more or less daily, that once there had been little money at all, and that the Chemist of Catania, their grandfather, had started with very little indeed. Well, they were spoiled. But he was glad of it. They would live the lives of rich young women, and they were both being educated in England as well. Sicily would in the future always be home, in one sense, but in practical terms not more than a holiday destination. They would grow distant from what he sometimes felt was the family curse.

There was no family curse, of course; he was not superstitious. He was rational. He did not believe in the sort of things that most Sicilians believed in, the sense that one was either blessed or cursed by cosmic powers, and only the Madonna could protect you from one or assure you of the other. He did not believe that, even if he never passed the open door of the Church, and saw the Spanish Madonna in her glory, without feeling a certain something. But the truth remained that his father had died young, his brother had died young; Gino Fisichella had died young, Alfio Camilleri had died young; Sandro Santucci had died young, and so had Carlo Santucci, not that those deaths had had anything to do with him. His father's death had been an accident, albeit self-inflicted, blowing himself up with his own bomb, the sole costly mistake of an otherwise very careful man. His brother's death had been necessary, for his brother had been a liability, and he did not regret that, nor did anyone hold that against him. Of course, they all knew, and he knew that they knew as they never mentioned his brother's name in his presence, or, he assumed, out of it. It was as if his brother had never existed. If only he had in fact never existed! But no one reproached him, and he certainly did not reproach himself.

But Renato, so calmly asleep next to him, Renato worried him. He was the grandson of the Chemist, and the son of the late Stefania, the mother whom he had never known. Looking at him now, he was reminded of his first wife, her stubbornness, her mule-like independence of spirit. If she had loved him, which he doubted, she had determined never to show it, and this child was the same: he displayed a stubborn refusal to love and to obey. In that he was like his mother and his sisters. But, and this was what gave him pause now, he was like his father too; he recognised himself in the boy. His own father had been distant, and frequently absent, on the continent, working. He himself had tried to be the opposite of distant, but the boy Renato was, unlike Sebastiano and Romano, much easier children, resistant to intimacy. He was a rebel. Well, he supposed he too had been a rebel at that age, stealing car radios, stealing from churches, and doing other things that now caused him to wonder. Renato was almost twelve, tall, physically confident, in one sense; but childish, spoilt, whiney, tearful and complaining. The boy was approaching manhood, but was not acting like a man, and perhaps never would. There was something weak about him; he was susceptible to influences, the influences of others. Not his father's influence, the only influence his father wanted him to have.

He looked down at the sleeping boy and wondered. He looked like his mother, and the long hair, dark in his case, accentuated that. There was less than a year between him and Sebastiano, but the differences between them were quite pronounced. He wondered if the boy felt what he had felt at a similar age, namely the desperate urge for sexual expression. Would he soon start chasing girls? In a way that would be reassuring. But would he, in a year or two, be like that drug-raddled fornicator, Dimitri, the son of don Costantino? That would be one outcome, though not a good one. Would he imbibe the values of the quarter, the values of himself, of Francesco, Marco and Nino, the values of the bosses of each quarter, and the men who worked for him? But there was nothing tough about him, his father felt. He would not make a good leader. He was too emotional, too crucified by his own feelings. That was why he had decided to send him away to school in England. Sebastiano and Romano, Anna Maria's children, would go to school in England, live abroad, live with money. Little Calogero would stay, and with Francesco to help him, inherit his father's role. But he knew that Renato would use this decision against him, but that was something he would have to bear. Francesco would do his best, he was sure, to ameliorate things.

He heard the door of the flat open, and then heard the sound of footsteps, contrite and embarrassed ones, coming towards him in the silence, if footsteps could be thus characterised. Francesco stood before him, apologetic, penitent, having promised to be there to take the boys to the barber, having broken his appointment, and having come home a good five hours late.

'I am sorry I am so late, that I didn't keep the appointment,' he was saying in a low voice. 'I... I was distracted.'

'By Petra?' asked Calogero.

'Yes,' he replied hurriedly. 'Then signora Costacurta came home, and she invited me to stay for supper, and it seemed rude to rush away.'

There was silence between them. Of course, he had done wrong. He had disobeyed his father, which ought to be punished. Then there was the whole matter of Petra Costacurta, who just happened to be the sister of the new husband of Calogero's ex-wife. Of course, Calogero knew that Francesco had known her for some time, and he had not specifically forbidden the association, yet he had made it clear he did not like it. The boy's attitude revealed that he knew this; his apologetic stance, conveyed a sense of guilt for taking up with the girl so definitively against his father's wishes. For it was clear that the boy found it impossible to lie.

'It is such a little thing to ask for,' said Calogero. 'One asks one's children for so little, and one gives them so much. I know how Costantino feels. Dimitri is an unworthy son. My daughters defy me, this child defies me, and now you defy me as well. I am constantly amazed by how beautiful Renato is when he is asleep like this. He reminds me of Stefania, another person who did not love me. I gave her everything. Poor Stefania. He must have his hair cut. Is it too much to ask? He is meant to be a middle-class boy, not a gangster.' He sighed. 'Sit down,' he said to Francesco. 'We will discuss Petra Costacurta on some other occasion.'

Francesco sank onto the sofa.

'Your little brother had his instructions,' Calogero remarked, still looking at the sleeping child. 'As you were not there... Nino and Marco took him to the barber with his brothers. He's rebellious, and I am not allowed to cane him, as my mother won't allow it. Neither does Anna Maria, for that matter, or his aunts. He manipulates them all. And now he has manipulated Nino and Marco as well. I believe in telling people what to do straight up, not manipulating them. Oh well. He is like his sisters in that regard. Does he like Nino and Marco?'

'He does. Nino especially.'

'Marco is a good man. Nino, well, we need him and we value him. But I am not sure they are ideal friends for my son at his tender age. But I trust you. I trust you to look after him. Now listen, there has been a development. You know I saw Anna Agostini, as a favour to don Giorgio, and told her that her son could come back. I was in further communication with her, telling her that her son must come back immediately. That Costantino wanted to kill him, in short, because he had allowed the hanging of this man Darko. I put it to him, through her, that he needed to see Costantino to iron out the difficulty between them. The thing is - and I admit I am surprised - he is on his way back already. He is on a flight right now. He will be here tomorrow morning.'

'You are surprised?' said Francesco. 'I am shocked. I am horrified. Why is he coming? I thought he was sick of Sicily and just wanted to hide.'

Calogero looked at his stepson.

'Oh, that is what he said, and that was what he hoped we would all believe. I don't suppose he is homesick, and I don't believe he cares about his mother. He does not have those feelings for her, or for anyone. He is coming back for me.'

'He tried to kill you.'

'I had not forgotten. He tried and he failed. I know you came to the rescue in time, but if he had wanted to kill me, really wanted to do so, wouldn't he have killed me? And if I had wanted to kill him, wouldn't I have done it? What you do not understand, dear Francesco, is that Traiano and I hate each other with a passion.'

'Oh, I understand that,' he said.

'And that hatred is simply a great love gone wrong,' said Calogero. 'But you are too young to understand. He is coming back either to kill me, or to ask for my forgiveness.'

'You would forgive him?' asked Francesco, shocked.

'There would be conditions,' said Calogero. 'Nothing is unconditional.'

Nothing, nothing at all, was unconditional. Francesco understood. He carried the sleeping Renato to bed, and placed him under his duvet without waking him, and then undressed and got into bed himself, determined to sleep after such a day, but troubled by the many things that weighed upon him. There was Renato, there was Calogero, there was Nino and there was Marco, and now there was Trajan Antonescu, somewhere above their heads, flying from Dubai or wherever it was, on a false passport. He understood what he had to do. He understood his mission, and that was to kill Antonescu. He knew his father had forbidden him to think of it, to do it, even to try. It might be dangerous. But he would do it. It might even cost him his life, but he would try.

He remembered something his father had told him some time ago. Calogero had told him so much, had educated him, but this lesson he now remembered more clearly than all the others, because it now seemed to be the most applicable lesson of all. He had told him that some years ago, when Beppe Santucci had been about thirteen, he and Renzo Santucci and Trajan Antonescu had driven from Donnafugata to the house of Antonio Santucci in Castelvetrano, in order to tell Antonio about the engagement of Renzo to Calogero's sister, Elena. They had arrived and walked into a tense situation: Antonio had just fired a shot at his elder son Sandro. What they should have done, according to Trajan, was seize the moment, shoot Antonio with the gun, shoot Sandro, shoot Beppe, shoot the housekeeper, and then leave the gun in Antonio's dead hand, making it look like a family massacre followed by suicide. But they hadn't. They had missed the moment. If they had have taken it, so many problems would have been solved. Of course, Sandro Santucci was dead, but Beppe lived on, a potential rival. The moment had been missed. Tomorrow, a moment might come, and he was determined not to miss it.

But this thought was followed by the remembrance of the sweet things that had passed between him and Petra. At last, at last, she was his, or so he thought. There had been something about that afternoon that had been different to the previous occasions when they had slept together. He had got the impression that he was accepted, not simply there on tolerance. Perhaps she liked him, perhaps she even loved him. Maybe he loved her. Whatever he felt, he knew he could not do without her. And when they had emerged from her bedroom, he had not left the house furtively but had come down the stairs without trying to hide anything, and signora Costacurta had invited him to stay for supper. That too was important; she accepted the fact that he had slept with her daughter, was sleeping with her daughter, and would continue to do so.

But dad did not like Petra, ironically because of the brother, whom Petra never saw, and whom she heartily disliked. But nothing was unconditional. He had said no, but he might change his mind. He had promised to take an ear of Antonescu's to don Costantino. Antonescu had two ears, at present attached to his head in the aircraft in the skies above. But… the ear of Antonescu might just buy him the approval of his father with regard to Petra. And there was a greater prize as well – don Costantino himself. He had to make it happen; nothing was unconditional.

His last thought before falling asleep concerned Paoluzzu, whom he would see, perhaps, all being well, tomorrow, along with the beautiful girls of Piazza Armerina. He thought of Ida, and her friend Claudia, so very different from Petra, and presently was asleep.

Chapter Five

Compared to the claustrophobia of Catania, one felt one could breathe in Syracuse; there was a strong sea breeze, and on both sides they were surrounded by the blue sea. The buildings were not as high, or dark, or decayed; the sunlight sparkled on the bright white stone of the Cathedral Square. They had parked the car and left the motorcycle in the Archimedes car park, and walked along the sea road to where signor and signora Agostini lived in the Giudecca, in a large spacious flat with views of the sea, full of beautiful furniture and works of art, but dominated by the signora herself, whose monumental beauty filled whichever room she was in.

She was old, approaching or even past fifty, but her full dark hair, her lips, her eyes, her figure, all retained their power to charm and to draw the eye. She felt the eyes of the three young men upon her and noticed that her husband had seen it too; and she for her part looked at them with an appraising eye and judged them: there was Marco, huge, somewhat menacing perhaps in different circumstances, with a face as unattractive as a plate of half-cooked meat; there was Francesco, a nice boy, clearly, the son of a nice mother; and there was young Nino, beautiful to look at, and, she felt, clever as well. She knew them all, though not intimately; she knew their families and had known them from years back. She could, she felt, place them all in the web of relationships that dominated the Purgatory quarter, from which she had escaped. She knew whom she had escaped from too – Calogero; but these boys were all in thrall to him, she could see, without having to ask, for she understood it instinctively.

Her husband Alfonso examined the three visitors as one might examine exotic creatures displayed in a zoo. Their suits, their long hair, their shoes, all told the same story: these were Calogero's men. His eyes briefly rested on Nino, the beautiful one, the only one whose suit had a waistcoat (an adorable affectation, he felt) and the only one whose hair had not had to receive the obvious attentions of a hairdresser. He was clearly intelligent, one could see that from his eyes, and he was, of course, a former prostitute, as one could see from the way he sensed Alfonso looking at him.

'So, I have heard the news,' Anna was saying, knowing this was expected of her. 'Congratulations!'

The boy had become a man. Nino smiled at this. The other two looked momentarily displeased.

The elder son of the house came in. This was Salvatore, who had once been a small blond boy, years ago, like his father, the forgotten Turiddu. He now had thick dark hair, and, like Alfonso, thick and heavy glasses. He was older than Renato, and younger than Nino, wearing jeans, and a sweatshirt which advertised the cult of Saint Lucy, the local saint, in front of whose altar his mother and the man he regarded as his father had met. He was young, he was innocent (this was what both his parents loved about him the most) and he was studious. It being the weekend, he was not smartly dressed, and there was stubble on his chin, something that the others noticed with disapproval and a mild jealousy, for they were not allowed to go about unshaven. The two youngsters, Sebastiano and Romano, did not seem to notice the stubble, but Renato, more aware of these things, did. Then the younger son, William, more their age, entered, darker than even Salvatore his brother, but without the awkwardness of the teenage years upon him. William, less self-conscious, greeted his 'cousins' with enthusiasm, and Salvatore followed suit. It was never quite clear how the bond of cousinage had been established, for there was no real blood relationship between them, though Francesco was the third cousin of Anna's grandchildren, who were now living in far off Verona.

The children talked among themselves, and the three young adults made conversation with Anna and her husband, or at least Francesco and Nino did; Marco, as usual, was silent. Alfonso studied the three of them carefully under the cover of conversation. He was taken with Nino, whose beauty was arresting, and who had been, he knew from his wife, a boy prostitute of some sort, under the control of Traiano, his own stepson. He was talking now of his impending fatherhood and marriage, informing the signora, making sure, Alfonso felt, that they all now knew that he had put his old ways long behind him. The elder two, he could tell, were a little bit jealous of this. But Francesco seemed to make an effort and put this jealousy aside. He was older than Nino, and he was the boss's stepson, so did it matter if he were less goodlooking, and less far along the path to being the father of a family? He did not need to prove himself, he seemed to say. And then there was Marco, whom Alfonso had never seen before. Marco was, in his judgement, astonishing. His ugliness commanded as much attention as Nino's beauty. His face, in repose - and one wondered if he was even following the conversation - was terrifying: it was not that he was cruel, or could be cruel, because he probably wasn't. He exhibited rather a complete indifference to human feeling of any sort, even perhaps his own. It was fascinating that someone so monstrous could be still recognisably human, though only just; and that someone so monstrous could be there, in their midst, listening to their conversation, moving among them. Such creatures, one had always hoped, belonged in Hell, or in some place far away. But this was Sicily. He looked at his elder son, Salvatore, with his thick hair and his thick glasses and his stubbly chin, such a nice, innocent and studious boy, so eager to please, so well behaved, whose main concern was doing well in his physics homework, which he was due to tackle today. And he looked at William as well, and he felt a sudden fear for them both.

In sharp contrast to either of them, and in sharp contrast to the two younger sons of Calogero, was the boy Renato, Calogero's eldest. Not quite a teenager, like William, but not like William in other ways either. His interests were clearly focused on the elder three; on his stepbrother, on Nino and on Marco, and theirs on his. This was the eldest son of the boss, and they knew it, and Renato knew it himself: this was a very special little boy who was growing intolerant of the restraints of childhood. Alfonso's own children were biddable, even Salvatore, and would be for the foreseeable future, he was confident; but once more he was filled with fear.

It was decided that they would go to the studio to take the photographs. They said goodbye to the signora, and they said goodbye to William and Salvatore, who had their own Saturday activities: the physics homework, the football, the piano lessons. They went to the studio, a short walk from the Giudecca, just round the corner in fact, where Alfonso announced he would photograph the three brothers after he had photographed the three "brothers". The three suited men stood together against a plain background, arms over shoulders, united against the world, their faces telling their own terrible stories, or so Alfonso thought. One day he would publish a book about the gangsters he had known, and it would make him famous, he was sure. But when would that day come, he wondered? When they were all dead, he supposed. After this was done, he could see that Francesco was waiting for instructions, and he gave them, as quietly as he could: his stepson, who had arrived past midnight, was in the ground floor flat of the building by the fountain of Arethusa. He handed him a key. With a look to Marco, that he was to continue what he was doing, and a similar look at Nino, he slipped away. Alfonso got ready to shoot the little boys.

It was a very short walk to the fountain of Arethusa, just across the Cathedral Square, and then along to the beautiful waterfront of Syracuse. He had not been to the house before, but he found it without difficulty. In the short time the journey took, he felt the blood pound in his veins, he felt himself grow cold despite the fair day and his heavy suit; and he felt the gun beneath his jacket, and the flick knife in his pocket. The gun had never felt so heavy. He knew what his stepfather had told him to do, the message he had been commissioned to deliver, and he also knew what he wanted to do, a desire that seemed, for a few moments, impossibly strong. He should go into the flat, find Traiano, preferably in bed asleep, and shoot him dead.

He wanted to shoot him, he wanted to kill him, he had wanted that ever since Africa when he had saved Calogero's life. He hated the Romanian for that. But he hated him for another reason: he hated him as Calogero's past favourite, the position he now occupied, and he was filled with dread at the idea of a reconciliation, if that were possible. And Calogero had hinted it was. But if he were to kill him, then that would solve the problem. It would also raise his reputation in the way no other murder would; it would make the tobacconist of Librino look like the small fry he was. Traiano was a major figure, a feared man, hat spectral figure as well. To kill him would make himself, Francesco, important and indispensable. If he dared do it; if he dared disobey Calogero; if he dared tell Calogero that he had a conversation with Traiano, that they had quarrelled, and he had killed him, if he dared to present Calogero with this fait accompli. How angry would Calogero be? Would Calogero forgive him? It was a risk, but there was no progress without risk.

What would the signora think? What would her husband think? He did not care. Why should he care about them? Their feelings were hardly his concern. Indeed, the signora had no real relations with her own son, so why would she care? And as for his cousins in Verona, they would be glad and relieved. Everyone would be, including the boss, after the initial anger.

He went into the building, using the right key (there were two) and found himself in the hallway. The door he needed was at the end of the corridor. The blood pounded in his ears, but he was calm. Then the door opened, and there stood Traiano.

'They sent *you*,' he observed, with mild surprise.

'Yes,' said Francesco, not knowing what else to say.

'I heard you come in the first door,' said Traiano. 'I have good ears. It is something you learn. I know that Costantino wants to kill me. So, I am alert. It's a reflex, not a choice. You might as well come in.'

He followed him into the dismal, poorly lit ground floor flat. There was a sitting room, and a sofa, on which Traiano sat. He indicated a chair for Francesco.

'You have grown, cousin,' observed Traiano. 'Last time I saw you, you were just a teenager. Now you are wearing a suit, and you have long hair. What a change.'

'We last saw each other, two, or was it three years ago?' said Francesco.

Traiano shrugged with indifference. He did not care when he had last seen Francesco. He did not care about anything much anymore. And if he thought Francesco had changed, Francesco thought the same of him. He was clad in a pair of shorts and a tee shirt, the clothes he had slept in. He looked unwashed and uncared for. He was completely bald; though muscular and strong, he was pale, a man who rarely experienced the sun on his skin. His face was wizened, his eyes dead, his once handsome face ruined.

'I gather Costantino wants to kill me, but I am presuming Calogero does not. After all, if he did, he would have come himself, not sent you. So, what does Calogero want? I presume you are here to tell me.'

'He wants you to kill Costantino.'

Traiano raised an eyebrow.

'Can't he get one of your lot to do that? Have you killed anyone yet? Mind you, Costantino is something of a challenge, surrounded by bodyguards, and as suspicious as hell. He wants me dead because I allowed them to hang Darko, who was his man, whom he had authorised to kill Slobodan. Yes, I quite see that someone should kill Costantino. He is out of control. He is not reasonable. He is a megalomaniac killer. Bad combination. Yes, I will kill Costantino. Why not? That is what I do. I kill people. Calogero knows that. If anyone can kill Costantino, it is me. The only thing is…. What is in it for me?'

'A reconciliation,' said Francesco. 'He will forgive you for Africa, he will allow you to come back to Sicily or wherever you choose to live. He will take you back into his favour.'

There was a long silence, while Traiano considered this.

'Do you know the history of this place?' asked Traiano at last. 'There is no reason why you should. It all happened many years ago when you were a little boy. I myself was younger than you are now. This building belongs to Calogero, and he gave it to my mother to keep her quiet – how he loathes her, or more accurately, how he fears her. This flat is rented out to tourists, and it so happened that it was free right now, quite by chance, so I cannot suspect my stepfather sent me here deliberately, besides, I don't know if he knows….. But it is strange to be back here. It was here that Calogero and I killed Michele Lotto, the wild Romanian. He was… well, never mind who he was, he is forgotten now. Have you ever seen Calogero naked?'

'No, of course not.'

'It is a fine sight, I assure you. We hid our clothes in that cupboard there, and we lay in wait in the bathroom at the back, stark naked. We waited for hours. Then Lotto came in with my mother, and we heard them do what they did on the bed, and then Lotto came into the bathroom, and we killed him. There was blood everywhere. Calogero was coated with it, and so was I. So, we showered it off and waited for dark, and then wrapped him in a carpet and put him into the harbour, while my mother had her photo taken in the fountain by my stepfather, attracting quite a crowd, despite the late hour, as she was stark naked too. Perhaps you have heard the story, perhaps not. But you have felt its effects. You knew when you first met him that Calogero was a powerful man, and you knew that instinctively because he was the man, not that you knew it, who had had the courage to kill Michele Lotto, the wild Romanian. All his power, all his reputation, all the admiration he receives, comes from that. He was daring, he took the opportunity, and he seized the moment.'

'As did you,' Francesco pointed out.

'As did I. Quite correct. As did I. Calogero can never regret it, and I can never regret it either, because there was never another way for me, at least not one that I ever saw open to me. But how I wish things could have been different, that I had never ended up in that bathroom waiting for Lotto to appear, naked next to Calogero. But perhaps I am being overdramatic. Truly, I am not complaining. It is what it is. I am who I am. As for being reconciled to Calogero…. Have you seen my mother, my stepfather, my brothers?'

'Yes, I have, just now.'

'And how are they? Actually, do not answer that. I have not seen them yet, apart from my stepfather, and I think I will not see them. You see, I do not care for my mother who was the one who threw me in Calogero's path. I also think that she and my stepfather probably do not want me to meet Salvatore and William again, and think it better that their sons forget me. A lot of people want to forget me, I imagine. I bring grief and pain. I am a hired assassin, useful to many, but loved by none. As for being reconciled, as you put it, to Calogero, I have to say that I do not want to be reconciled to him, to any living human being, to life, to my fate, to anything. I am beyond reconciliation. I loved him, once, but there is no going back to that. I loved him so much. Do you love him?'

'Of course.'

'As passionately as I once did? As completely and unquestioningly?'

Francesco did not answer.

'Beware,' said Traiano. 'I am your future. You who are now as I once was, will be as I am now.'

'Can he rely on you to kill Costantino?'

'Given that Costantino wants to kill me, why not?' said Traiano. 'But it is not unconditional. I will require at least half a million euro.'

'And you would do it soon?'

'Yes.'

'How, may I ask?'

'I will ask for an interview, which he will grant, that is all. He wants to see me, and he thinks it will be his great moment to kill me. But I shall strike first.'

'Risky,' said Francesco.

'I have taken many risks,' he said.

'Will we see you in Catania at all?' asked Francesco.

'No, you will not see me again.'

Francesco nodded. He stood up diffidently.

'So, this is good-bye,' he said. 'No one knows I am seeing you, apart from your stepfather. If they knew I had seen you, they would ask how you were… people like my mother, other people you once knew.'

'Once knew, but know no longer,' said Traiano. 'I am a ghost from the past.'

'You say that Calogero loved you….'

'I didn't say that.'

'What I mean is, I used to love you and admire you. I am sorry that… well, that we are saying goodbye, and forever.'

'You have your consolations. Lots of money and a nice suit.'

'Yes, but...'

He approached Traiano. Traiano stood still. Francesco put his arms around him and brought his mouth close to his ear. They stood together like that for a moment.

'Good-bye,' said Francesco.

The gunshot was muffled by the clothing, by the proximity of bodies, by the closeness of the gun to the flesh. But the bullet found its true path, straight to Traiano's shattered heart.

A phone call had come from the flat to the studio, saying that Veronica, Anna Maria's faithful attendant was there, ready to drive the three boys to Donnafugata for the rest of the weekend, as arranged. The photographs were taken, and the joy of seeing Veronica and their mother quite distracted the three boys from the fact that Francesco had gone somewhere and not returned. Nino offered to take the three boys back to the flat and then return. When he did come back after fifteen minutes, he went into the studio to find Marco and Alfonso Agostini alone. Marco was sitting under the camera lights on a hard metal chair, while Alfonso studied him through the lens. Marco was regarding the camera steadily, and in his concentration, he ignored Nino's entry. Nino watched, fascinated. It was clear to him that the pose had been held for some time. Marco, still concentrating on the camera, was now aware of Nino watching him, a little annoyed by his presence, but determined not to show it. Nino was amused somewhat by the sight of him: his thick ugly face; the monumentality of his body enclosed in its suit; the long flowing hair.

At last, Alfonso declared he had all the shots he wanted, and Marco swiftly got up and stretched himself.

'I'll send you the prints,' said Alfonso. 'I mean, I will send them to you separately.'

'No need,' said Marco.

'So why did you do it?' asked Nino.

'I asked,' said Alfonso.

'Of course,' said Nino with a smile.

'Now you,' said Alfonso, indicating the chair to Nino.

As the minutes passed, neither of them mentioned the absence of Francesco or wondered out loud what had happened to him. Eventually, it was time to leave, the photographic session over, but still no one mentioned the missing third man. Marco and Nino walked to the Archimedes car park in silence. The motorcycle was there, to which they had the key, but the car was gone.

The children away, and that included Francesco, Calogero and Agata had gone out to lunch in one of the many restaurants he owned in the city, then gone home and gone to bed, where despite her pregnancy, they had spent the afternoon making love. Afterwards, Calogero had slept, then got up and had a shower and a cup of coffee and then wandered down to the bar in the square to smile at people, to shake hands and to pat young heads. He was talking to a group of men, basking in their admiration, conscious of the young children looking up at him with adoration, and feeling totally relaxed after his great lunch, and his more than pleasant afternoon, feeling so happy to be in his own quarter and among his own people, when he spotted Nino at the other end of the bar. He felt a faint flicker of surprise. Nino approached.

'You handed the boys over safely?' he asked. 'You saw the Agostinis, you met Veronica?'

As he spoke, he kept on looking round the room.

'Yes, boss, all went to plan, except that Francesco left us at some point, and he did not come back.'

'Did he tell you what he was doing or where he was going?'

'No, boss, and we did not ask.'

The boss nodded, smiled briefly, and let Nino go. He wondered what had happened to his stepson. Whatever it was, it had clearly involved a change of plan. The supposition he had had was that Francesco would return and report back, but he had not returned. As he was smiling at someone, talking of the retail outlets opening on the Catania Waterfront, alongside the largest pizzeria perhaps in Sicily, a sudden thought occurred to him. Had Traiano killed Francesco? Had he killed the one person he loved so much, out of rage, out of jealousy, out of revenge, in order to cause the maximum pain to him? The thought took him like a jolt, though he continued smiling and talking. If he had done something like that, how would he ever pacify Agata? How would he ever forgive himself for sending Francesco as a messenger in the first place? Had he miscalculated?

He spent about an hour in the bar and then went up to the flat, where his dear wife was setting up a very light, but nevertheless delicious supper.

'Is Francesco here?' she asked.

'No. I think he might well have gone to see that girl – again. He's young, he is in love, you know how it is.'

'Which girl do you mean?' she asked.

'The one in Piazza Armerina, of course. And he is very friendly all of a sudden, with that young man there, the one they call Paoluzzu.'

'If only he had a mobile phone, then we would be able to find out where he had got to,' she said.

'And so would everyone else,' he remarked, sitting down at the table in the dining room and looking at the Parma ham with interest.

After supper, while she was in the kitchen, he went to his study to phone Syracuse. His anxiety increased as he heard the phone ring in the large flat in the Giudecca. Eventually it was answered, by him, thankfully, not her.

'Hi, Fofò,' he said. 'Is Francesco with you?'

'No, I have not seen him since he left to meet up with his cousin.'

Alfonso knew not to mention names on the phone. You never knew who was listening, or rather, you did.

'You have seen the cousin?'

'I did, when he arrived, though we were expecting to see him this evening but have not. I went round to where he was staying, to check, you know… He had a key, but we have a spare, and when there was no reply, I went in, and he was not there, and his stuff was not there, not that he had come with much in the first place, and, well, he must have decided to leave without telling us. To tell you the truth, I was not looking forward to him meeting the boys, and having to explain where he had been, what he had been doing. And he was not eager to meet them, I suppose, or their mother. Understandable.'

'I see, I see. Was there anything unusual that you noticed? You know, anything out of the ordinary?'

'Well, yes. The place used to have a carpet, but it does not anymore. I mean, I think there was a carpet; it looked a little bare, and it struck me that the carpet was missing. I could not put my finger on it at first. But then I saw the floor was bare, but why should anyone take away, let alone steal, a not very nice made in China carpet?'

'Someone must have taken it away to clean it,' said Calogero. 'Forget about it. The cousin is a very fly-by-night person, isn't he? He comes and he goes. If anyone asks, best to say nothing…'

'Understood. Anna is disappointed that he has not come to see her, but….'

The conversation ended, on his part, with a cold feeling of dread.

As they were going to bed, his wife mentioned her son.

'I am sure he is off with that girl,' she said, sadly. 'Not the one in Piazza Armerina, but the other one. He was wearing his very best suit, wasn't he? He wanted to impress her. If he is out all night… well, boys will be boys, but he has never done that until very recently, and I feel a bit sad, him and her, when he should be here with us. I like signora Costacurta, but I am not sure this Petra is right for him. She is two or three years older for a start.'

He took her in his arms, to reassure her.

'Boys will be boys,' he agreed, 'But he needs to be reminded not to upset his mother in any way or worry her. He's eighteen, I know, and we know what eighteen-year-olds are like, but one always hopes one's own beloved boy will be different. I will speak to him, and tell him he has to behave in a way his mother and I would like… You know I can be firm, and young men need a firm hand.'

He smiled, and she was reassured.

It had been done without much planning, an inspired action, he hoped, rather than a purely impulsive one. But it was done now, he told himself, and there was no point wishing the impossible, that it be undone. His initial reaction had been expected: his breath had come in short swift pants, and he thought for a moment he might pass out. Then he had felt a little sick, and finally he had felt the overwhelming desire to relieve himself. But all these things passed, as he knew they would, and he had struggled only briefly to reassert his calm and his rationality. The body was still in his embrace, and gradually he released it and let it slide to the floor, where it rested on the carpet. The eyes were sightless, but open, the chest wound was small and neat and thank goodness there was not much blood, indeed hardly any. The face had changed, the skin tone too, and the bowels had opened, and there was a smell, a most unpleasant smell. But it was clear that Trajan Antonescu was already with the angels. His own clothes were unstained, thank the Lord.

After a few moments, he left the body and the flat, locking the door behind him. The first thing he did was to lean over the railing of the fountain of Arethusa and drop the gun into the pond, where it would be lost in the mud and the papyrus, and surely never recovered. He did this without anyone noticing, just letting the gun gently fall out of his hand and disappear without a splash. Then he walked back to the Archimedes carpark and fetched the car. He had to concentrate hard on how to get back to the flat, as the road system of the island of Ortygia was very difficult, and he drove round the one-way system twice until he eventually got to the road that overlooked the fountain and the sea. Here he parked the car illegally – nothing unusual about that in Sicily – and went back into the flat. A moment later he was out of the flat, carrying a suitcase stuffed full of Traiano's things, which he placed in the boot. Then he came out with the body wrapped in the carpet, which he placed on the back seat. It was as heavy as a sack of coal, and he understood what people meant when they spoke of a dead weight. There were people around, who must have noticed him, but no one 'saw' anything, he was sure, as his demeanour was perfectly normal. He was just another man moving house or vacating the flat. He made sure the flat was properly locked up, that he had left nothing behind, and then he drove off.

He told himself there was nothing to fear. The flat was cleaned regularly, he was sure, by someone employed by signora Agostini, and it would be cleaned and cleaned again before anyone suspected it was the scene of a crime. The sound of the bullet had been muffled, and the bullet that had passed through the murdered man's body had lodged in the upholstery of the sofa where no one would ever find it, he was sure: the entry mark looked like a cigarette burn, of which there were several. He reassured himself. All would be well. He was calm. He would not let himself fail. There was too much at stake. He thought of Petra.

The drive was a long and slow one, along lonely and unfrequented country roads, as he was in no hurry, and he wanted to avoid any possibility of the highway police stopping him, which would be fatal. He knew he should head for Etna, but that was what he was determined not to do, as he knew that everyone would expect that. Instead, he headed into the centre of the island, vaguely heading towards Caltagirone, and then up to Piazza Armerina. He was sure there was some place near there that he could find. In fact, he was drawn to Piazza Armerina. Quite near the town, near the famous Roman villa, he stopped at the Trattoria Norma. It was getting late, past two o'clock, but there was still time for lunch. He locked the car, obviously, but left it, as if it contained no special load, in the furthest reaches of the nearly empty car park under the trees at the back, and then went into the restaurant. The place was very quiet, and preparing to shut up for the afternoon, but there was Paoluzzu, as he had very much hoped.

'I wasn't expecting you,' he said with a smile.

'I am the sort of person who just turns up,' said Francesco. 'But my friends do not mind.'

'Of course, they don't,' said Paoluzzu. 'But you will have lunch, won't you?'

'Sure,' said Francesco.

He went to a table and Paoluzzu came to take his order. He indicated that he would only drink mineral water, and that he would have the lasagne, which had been so good on Sunday last, followed by the Milanese cutlet with some caponata on the side, as he was by now very hungry.

Paoluzzu came with the lasagne and stood by while Francesco tasted it. The restaurant was by now completely empty. The lasagne was good; one had to give them that.

'What is happening?' asked Paoluzzu. 'Why are you here?'

'Why should anything be happening?' he replied. 'I just felt like seeing you, that is all. Perhaps affairs of the heart drew me. How are the girls?'

'Have you come to see them too?'

'No. Not really, just you. But of course, it would be nice to see them too. Have you seen the girls, the two beautiful girls? Have you made any progress with Claudia?'

'Not exactly,' said Paoluzzu. 'She is like Mount Everest. A challenge. You think you are making progress, and then you slip down a glacier or something.' He paused gloomily. 'But if you make progress with Ida, it will follow that I will make progress with Claudia. Those two do everything together.'

'They even screw boys together?'

'No, they don't screw boys at all; but if one did, the other would not want to be left out. But I think I am more desperate for Claudia than you are for Ida.'

He considered this as he finished the lasagna. Then Paoluzzu brought the cutlets and sat opposite him.

'This caponata is perfect,' he commented. 'You know I have this other girl; she is called Petra. She is… quite difficult. She has her challenges. She has lots of stupid ideas. She asks too many questions. She is the sister of the man who married my father's previous wife, which is not a help. Getting to spend time with her is very difficult. It is like getting through Checkpoint Charlie, if you know what that is. But when you get through, oh God, it is worth the wait and the hassle and the frustration. She is heaven on earth. One girl is much like another in some ways, but she is really different, really special. But… my dad is right; she is potentially trouble. She told me the other day that she - well never mind. She met up with a girl called Emma Santucci.'

'The sister of the man who is always on the television talking about football? - Beppe Santucci?'

'Yes. It is a danger signal. Emma is his sister, but she was in love with a boy called Tonino Grassi, and…'

'I remember him,' said Paoluzzu.

'Then you know,' said Francesco. 'Petra knew Tonino and used to go out with him, though they never slept together, as Tonino wasn't really that keen on that sort of stuff, but still… I knew him too; he was a nice boy. But he is gone now and must be forgotten. And dad is right, there are girls and girls, but… Ida is special. She is beautiful, she is bright, she is intelligent and educated, you could take her anywhere; and she is don Nunzio's daughter. She knows what is what, I am sure. So, in a few years' time, when I have got over Petra, when I am ready to settle down, Ida would be perfect for me, and me for her, because, well, dad, I suppose… And if Ida chooses me, then Claudia will choose you, I am sure. You think I bring weight to the equation, but I think the opposite, that you are the big attraction. Those two are such friends, and we are such friends – what I mean is two girls like that will want to marry two boys who are friends. It appeals to their sense of neatness. And as for being like Mount Everest, well, that takes time to climb, and the view from the top will be as great in a few years' time as it is now. We have got time. And if we see a few other girls in the meantime, as I fully intend to do, then no one can blame us. Not that anyone would dare, not even my father. I mean, we would not blame ourselves.'

'Are you seeing others, apart from Petra?' asked Paoluzzu.

'Of course I do, but it is not important. We will go after Claudia and Ida together, and we will get them in the end. They like to be like Mount Everest, cold and inaccessible, but they will give in eventually. Trust me; Ida and me, it is written in the stars; and Claudia will not be able to resist my best friend. I mean, you are my best friend, aren't you?'

'Of course, I am.'

'I want a favour,' said Francesco. 'In the kitchen, do you have some of those small freezer bags? Can you get me one without anyone noticing?'

'Sure,' said Paoluzzu, surprised that that was all he wanted.

He removed the plate which had borne the cutlets and the caponata and returned a moment later with a small cup of coffee, and surreptitiously handed over the freezer bag, which Francesco put in his pocket.

'Paoluzzu,' said Francesco. 'There is something else. Can you find me a length of washing line? - Just a metre or two would do - or some string, or something like that?'

'Sure,' said Paoluzzu, who remembered seeing a ball of twine in the kitchen, which the chef sometimes used to tie up joints of meat.

'Hand it to me when I leave,' said Francesco. 'What are you doing this afternoon?'

'Nothing. Going home, resting, looking at the computer and my phone.'

He had finished his coffee.

'I'll come round. I will see you in an hour or two. Expect me.'

Then, the string secured, he left.

He drove half an hour to the north, and he arrived at the place he had been thinking of: the very mouth of hell itself, the lake of Pergusa, the place where the god of the underworld had snatched Persephone and plunged the whole land into winter. To his delight the fine day was clouding over, and by the time he was driving alongside the lake, a light rain was falling. He thanked the Madonna for his luck. It meant the lakeshore was deserted. Eventually he found what he was looking for, a track that branched off from the main road and led to the water's edge. By now the rain was torrential, which meant that visibility was minimal. Once more, he thanked the Madonna.

The smell inside the car was becoming intolerable and he opened all the windows to try and clear it. He unravelled the carpet on the back seat, took out his knife and made the freezer bag ready. It was not as easy as he had expected, cutting off a dead man's ear, and it took some time. At last, he had the trophy in the plastic bag, which he sealed. Then he rolled up the carpet and bound it up with the twine. Then he took off all his clothes, even his underpants, and dragged the rolled and bound carpet towards the lake shore a few feet away, right into the lake. He dragged it out as far as he could, feeling the soft slimy mud on his feet, around his ankles, feeling himself sink into it. As he had hoped the carpet became waterlogged and heavy, and the body lay on the bottom in the thick mud without any need to be weighed down. The lake was shallow, and he advanced about thirty metres from the shore. Then he waded back. He stood in the rain for a few moments, then got back into the car, soaking, and put on his clothes as best he could. Then he drove back to Piazza Armerina, confident that the rain would obscure all tyre marks. He had already marked the place that he needed, which was conveniently close to where Paoluzzu lived. Everything was working very well, and the day was not yet over.

It was about five o'clock when he rang Paoluzzu's doorbell, and was admitted, wet, dripping and mud stained.

'What happened?' asked Paoluzzu.

'Don't ask, I got caught in the rain. Then I fell over in some mud. Don't tell my mother, she will be furious! But I have ruined my suit, I think. Can I use the bathroom? Are your parents here?'

'Watching television. They won't disturb you,' said Paoluzzu. He went to tell them, and then came back, finding Francesco already in the bathroom. He was taking off his shoes.

'Have you got one of those rubbish bags?' he said. 'My shoes and clothes are all soaked and muddy. And I need to borrow something to wear.'

He came back with the plastic bag and a dressing gown, his own. The jacket and the trousers of the nice suit were indeed ruined by mud and damp, and he watched Francesco get ready to peel them off and put them into the bag. Before taking off the trousers, he emptied his pockets and that was when Paoluzzu saw it: not the fat wallet stuffed with damp notes, or the car keys, but freezer bag he had given him and its contents which, for a second, he did not recognise. He left him, allowing him to take off his trousers alone.

Half an hour later, Francesco was scrubbed, washed, perfumed and dressed in clothes belonging to Paoluzzu; luckily, they were the same size. Paoluzzu had already phoned Ida to say that they were coming round shortly. Francesco was now in the kitchen, drinking some coffee that Paoluzzu had made for him, and speaking to his mother on the landline.

'Ma, I am fine, don't worry. I decided to come to Piazza Armerina. I am with Paoluzzu, and he has invited me to spend the night here. We are going out with those girls. Yes, tell dad, I am sure he will be pleased. Yes, they are very nice indeed. You met them. Yes, he is very nice indeed. You met him. You do? You thought he was handsome? I will tell him.' He winked at Paoluzzu. 'I didn't see it myself, but I sort of see it now. OK, ma, I will be back tomorrow sometime. It is nice here. Paoluzzu is a really nice boy. Yes, I know... You will meet him again when he comes to Catania; and you will meet the girls again too, I am sure. There are lots of beautiful girls in Piazza Armerina. No doubt about it. Yes, yes, good girls too. Look, ma, I must go. I must not keep Paoluzzu waiting.'

He smiled at Paoluzzu, who was looking at him strangely. Then he dialled another number, one he knew off by heart. It was the bar in Purgatory.

'Hi, it's me. Is Marco there, or is Nino there? OK, thanks... Hi. Listen. Can you tell Dimitri that I want to meet him tomorrow in Messina at about 9am? Let's say in the Cathedral square? OK. Thanks.'

'Who is Dimitri?' asked Paoluzzu a touch aggressively.

'No one in particular. Some guy in Messina. I owe him a few favours, or he owes me a few favours. Something like that. Not a nice guy, really. Not like you. But listen. I need to get the car from the garage. I have stolen something.'

'What? The car?'

'No. Some stupid tourist left a case unguarded, and I saw it and put it in the car boot. But I haven't had a chance to look at the contents. Have you ever stolen something?'

'No.'

'I am a habitual thief. I have been stealing since I was four or five years old. It's become a habit. Sometimes I steal things that I do not need. This suitcase may be a case in point. We will go to the garage, and we can examine it, and then go and pick up the girls at don Nunzio's place. How about that? Oh, and can you do something for me? Can you take my suit to the dry cleaners, and can you put my other clothes in the wash? Then maybe next week you can bring them to me when you come to Catania?'

'Yes, sure,' he said.

There was only one thing that mattered, as far as Paoluzzu was concerned. The only thing that mattered was getting the girl. And not just any girl, the girl, Claudia. It had to be her. Once it had been just another girl, but now Claudia had become central and very quickly too.

From the age of about eleven and a half, he had noticed the girls around him, and they had noticed him. He had seen them with wonder and desire; they had looked upon him as somewhat dangerous, a temptation to be avoided. He had done his best to try and hide his burning desire for them, and gradually some of them had let their guard down and approached. Ah, the sheer delight of those early encounters. Then, at the age of thirteen, he had met the girl who had, not broken his heart, he was honest with himself, but smashed his self-esteem. For the first year, it had been a marvellous adventure, the kisses, the embraces, the way she put her hands on the bare flesh of his back, under his shirt, as he kissed her. A few months after his fourteenth birthday, things had gone much further, and by his fifteenth birthday he had long cast away his despised virginity. After that, after that arrival at fulfilment and bliss, he felt he could put up with anything, because she wanted him, she had given herself to him. He could put up with his father's moods, his mother's tears, getting the belt every now and then, the boredom of school, the boredom of life in Sicily – anything, because he had her, because, though no one else knew it, he was a man.

He had thought that he was doing so well, and he had gone to Africa a few months after he left school because the pay was so good, and he was grateful for the offer of a job, grateful for the generosity of don Calogero. Then he had been brutally reminded that he was not in fact doing well at all. He had come back from time to time for joyous reunions, but then, after four years away, she had dropped him without explanation, though the reason emerged pretty quickly. It was banal: she had found someone else, and that someone else was his best friend Massimo. He could not understand it, how it had meant so much to him, and so little to her. He had been expelled from Eden to a solitary life, one tormented by the memory of what he had lost. He had become depressed, angry, hopeless. His fury and his sense of hurt at Massimo's betrayal had been almost as strong. He had loved her, and he had loved Massimo too.

A few months after this black depression had descended, when things might have begun to get better, they had got worse. At least he was in Africa where no one witnessed his humiliation; but then his parents asked him to come back to Catania. This, he simply could not face and found hard to explain to them. But his parents, somewhat to his surprise, understood. They wanted him back; they were getting old; they had applied to the boss, and the boss said he would give him the necessary recommendation for managing the Trattoria Norma outside Piazza Armerina, where Paoluzzu could move with his mother and father. This was the favour that he had earned from the boss by being his eyes and ears in the African hotel for so long.

He loved his mother and pitied her hard life; he loved his father, he felt sorry for him too, but at the same time, he knew that his presence angered him, and vice versa. He often wanted to hit his father but could not; his father had hit him, frequently, in the past, but not now, now that he was the one who was bringing in the sole income. He was glad he was no longer in Catania, away from Massimo, away from her above all, and if Piazza Armerina was boring, and the work at the Trattoria Norma time consuming, well, one day perhaps, he would escape, but for the most part he worked, and tried to forget the past.

Then he had met Francesco again, and he had realised what form escape could take. There was something about Francesco, he had realised the first time they had properly met back in Africa. He was nice, he was friendly, he was eager to please, he was a relation, but above all he was lucky, as he had the favour of don Calogero. That, that was everything. That was transformative. That was what made the boy that no one had ever noticed, up till now, special. And when he had seen him again, in the Trattoria Norma, by then he had become an obvious rich boy from a rich family: you could tell by his clothes, his shoes, by the way the skin of his face shone; you could tell by the look of his mother and his stepfather, and the three younger children, for only the rich could afford so many children. But, and this was the interesting thing, Francesco had not always been rich; he and his mother had been desperately poor, and he had conquered poverty, escaped its grasp, thanks to his mother marrying don Calogero, but thanks as well to Francesco's determination not to be poor forever. It was, in the end, a matter of will.

That evening, as they went to the garage, and as they got into the car and examined the stolen suitcase, Francesco had explained that there were moments one had to seize: he had been leaning out of the window, trying to see or hear what was happening in the quarter, when, at just that moment, he had seen don Calogero di Rienzi leaning out of a neighbouring window. He had always known don Calogero, but that was the moment when their relationship, that between a boy of fourteen and a man wanted by the police, began. He had taken the moment. Don Calogero had liked him, and he had determined to make himself worthy of that liking. Moreover, he could see that don Calogero had liked his mother, and he had been pleased by that as well. From that moment he had known that his fate was entwined with that of the man who was to be his stepfather, and he was determined to make the relationship as close as possible.

'Why?' Paoluzzu asked.

They had stopped the car in a quiet place and were going through the contents of the stolen suitcase.

'It was not ambition; it was not a desire to better myself; it was simply the desire to please him. It was, you know…. It was as if that was the moment, and if I missed it, I would regret it forever. He is such a man, when you are in his presence, you just feel it. Didn't you notice, when you saw him in Africa, when you saw him again at the trattoria? He makes you feel good about yourself. That is why all of us, me especially, would do anything for him. Anything, anything at all. He is the most important person in the world. No one else counts. That is why I work for him.'

'Are you paid well?' asked Paoluzzu curiously.

'He gives me an allowance. A couple of thousand a month.'

Paoluzzu was shocked by this. All that money without having to do anything for it. Francesco sensed it.

'And on top of that, various presents. Talking of which, do you want these clothes? You can have them. I am not sure I want them. I will take the passport.'

He had looked at the passport. It was in the name of Gaetano Salimbeni. It might be useful one day, or he might destroy it.

The clothes, Paoluzzu noticed, were nice, most of them famous labels.

'Are they traceable?' he asked.

'Not really. You say, if anyone asks, that you bought them in the market in Catania. That is full of stolen goods. Put them through the wash. That will be enough. You can keep the case as well. It is a nice one. I don't need it. Do you want the electric razor? They are expensive. Again, if anyone asks, you bought it second hand. But who is going to ask?'

'Only my parents,' he conceded.

It was an odd thing, this receiving stolen goods, but what could happen, what could go wrong? The shirts were nice; the razor, a thing of beauty. He wanted them badly. The suitcase too was sleek, expensive, understated. Why shouldn't it be his? Of course it was illegal, and that in a way thrilled him. Francesco did not care about the law, and why should he? Maybe there were other illegal things that Francesco did too. In fact, there must be, and he did wonder about the wet muddy clothes that he was supposed to wash or send to the dry cleaners on his behalf. But what could he have done? There was the freezer bag with its contents too. It was best not to know.

These thoughts were banished by the meeting with the girls and their driving to a restaurant in the countryside in Francesco's car. After all, who cared about legality when you were in the back seat of the car with Claudia, conversing with the others and all the time feeling her presence, and for a fleeting moment, her hand on your knee? Who cared about anything else? He would get the girl, he would get the girl, sooner or later, and that was all that mattered, and oh God, she was beautiful, and, he could hardly believe it, she was don Nunzio's daughter's friend. He knew don Nunzio, of course, as he was the owner of the Trattoria Norma, and he found him a rather distant and fearful figure (unlike don Calogero) but don Nunzio would have to be warmer to him sooner or later, as Francesco's friend, as his daughter's best friend's accredited lover.

The evening passed delightfully. It was eleven by the time the girls were delivered to their respective homes. They planned to meet again the next week.

Francesco was in the Cathedral square in Messina in very good time. The place was sunny, warm, and people scurried across the wide, open space going to Mass, as it was Sunday. No one paid him any attention, he was sure. He was simply an eighteen-year-old boy hanging around in the square, early on a Sunday morning, perhaps waiting for someone, as so many did. And sure enough, the someone arrived in due course, looking tired, looking a little nervous.

He embraced Dimitri.

'You need to leave everything to me. All you need is to act well, OK?''

Dimitri felt something inside him go cold, but he nodded.

Chapter Six

In the end, he decided a forthright approach was the best way forward.

'But what are you going to do?' asked Dimitri, several times.

'If you ask me that one more time, I am going to break your jaw, that is what I am going to do,' said Francesco without emotion. 'Is this the house? Good. Go in and act, the way I told you to. Take this and use it the way I told you to. Then, when things are as they should be, come down and get me.'

Dimitri nodded dumbly.

The place where don Costantino lived was a flat in the city centre, a nice block. It was large, and it suited him. There was a kitchen with a balcony, and beyond the kitchen, a room and a bathroom for a maid, and it was here that the two bodyguards slept, sat, waited, watched television, played on their phones, and otherwise killed time, until the boss wanted them, which was not often. The bedroom had two beds and was very small; the bathroom, even smaller; one could barely get into it and close the door without bruising oneself. At least in an army barracks, one had room, if no privacy; here one had neither privacy nor space. The kitchen, where they usually sat, and which was rarely used for more than making coffee, overlooked a narrow dark street, and the constant noise when one opened the door to the balcony was unsettling. Both boys (they were in their twenties) found the place claustrophobic and very dull. But the job was well paid, and they guarded the boss in shifts, which meant that they did not have to be there for endless days, but had the consolation that a relief would eventually take their place, sleep in their beds, wash in their bathroom and sit in their kitchen. A maid - a real maid - came in and cleaned the place between shifts, thank goodness.

Sundays and weekends were particularly dull. About once a month, sometimes more often, on Saturday nights, the boss would come in with a girl he had picked up in one of his hotels or clubs and go to bed with her for an hour or two, then kick her out and expect one of the bodyguards to put her in a taxi. It was a different girl each time, though there was a pattern: tall statuesque blondes from Moldova alternated with dark luscious girls from Brazil. Sometimes, you could even hear the boss's grunts, and the bedsprings squeaking, which occasioned a little resentment; last night had been just such a night; the sex worker had left at about two in the morning, and the men had had to stay awake until she was off the premises; then one could sleep while the other kept vigil. Neither of the men had been in Africa, but they had heard about life there. Endless games of football and swimming on the base; endless fun off it with compliant and enthusiastic black girls. Both had cousins there, cousins who spoke well of what they were able to do off the base; cousins who hinted that the various jobs they did, which involved real fighting, were enjoyable, exhilarating and wildly profitable. Both were very much hoping to go to Africa one day. It would make more sense than passing one's life here in Messina.

For indeed, their life was passing them by. They did not like Sicily. The Sicilians, they knew, did not like them. They were suspicious of Serbs. They were suspicious of the boss, of course, even if he were half-Italian. They took the side of his wife and children against him. This had seemed so unreasonable to them. Of course, they all liked Dimitri, but one could see that he was not worthy of his Serb ancestry; indeed, he was only a quarter Serb. Serbs were warriors; the sons of warriors; men of action. You could see that Dimitri was none of those things. The boss must be bitterly disappointed in his eldest son; no wonder he was calling the African family over. But they had heard the disquieting news from Africa about the attempted murder of Slobodan and the hanging of Darko.

Neither of the two bodyguards on duty this Sunday morning had known either party, but both were well-known to them by reputation. This fame was one of the reasons why the news had spread so rapidly to Serbia and to Sicily. Slobodan was the great-nephew of a war hero who had been assassinated in a Belgrade hotel in the 1990s, one of the men who had fought to defend Serbian homes from the infidel and the Croat. Building on this ancestry, Slobodan had gone from success to success, fathering several African children, distinguishing himself in battle, making huge amounts of money. All this, of course, aroused jealousy; and while there was a natural supposition that Darko had deserved to be hanged for trying to murder a comrade, there was a more troubling explanation, namely that their boss had incited Darko to murder Slobodan and then washed his hands of him. A further complication came in the consideration of the role of the daughter, the African daughter and her mother. Had Costantino promised his daughter to one man, or the other, or both? Had he engineered the quarrel by promising the daughter to Darko, knowing that Slobodan wanted her, and would have her whatever Darko said? Had Darko attacked Slobodan because he had found Slobodan with the girl? Had the boss wanted to get rid of Slobodan as a threat, a potential rival? Had he tried to use Darko for this, and then abandoned him? This is what they could not understand: that a quarrel, perhaps about a girl, had involved the boss, because the girl was his daughter, was clear enough; but whom had the boss betrayed? - Darko? Or Slobodan? This morning, it was the subject of conversation. The one with the blond beard thought Slobodan had been hard done by; the one with the back beard thought that the unlucky fellow was Darko, left to hang by his feet from a tree, until he died some twenty-four hours afterwards. But whatever had happened, one was gravely injured and the other dead, and somehow, obscurely, they knew the boss was to blame. Of course, the boss was not there in Africa, and the business of Africa was left to don Traiano Antonescu, a Romanian, whom they all instinctively distrusted. But the boss was ultimately responsible for what happened, as it was his choices that shaped everything. He had taken on the African woman, had children by her, not promoted Slobodan, or not promoted Darko, allowed one to be hurt and the other to hang. It was clearly not a well-run operation. And of course, it was the same in Sicily.

Clearly, the boss was nervous, nervous that somehow they would one day get him, whoever they were, though that was not hard to guess, for he had only one real rival. The constant presence of the bodyguards told you something; it told the bodyguards themselves something unsettling: they too were at risk. And yet it was Sunday morning, you could hear the sound of the bells of Messina Cathedral. All was at peace; but beneath that peace was the threat of war, of violence, of destruction.

The doorbell rang, and the two men - the dark one and the blond one - tensed for a moment, looked to their weapons and went to the intercom. But it was only the boy, Dimitri, come to see his father, after an absence, they sensed, of some time. Dimitri was spoilt, lazy, a wastrel, but they all liked him. He was let into into the building, and a moment later there was a feeble ring at the door of the flat. He was admitted; he greeted the two men as he always did, by name, kissing the cheek of each. They had known him for a couple of years, and they had always got on.

'Is he up yet?' Dimitri asked of his father, a trifle nervously.

They knew he always found seeing his father difficult. The last time he had been here, there had been a tremendous row.

'Not yet,' said the blond one.

'Was he alone last night?' he asked.

'Not entirely,' said the dark one.

'That is why he is still in bed,' said the blond one. 'He is tired.'

'OK,' said Dimitri with seeming resignation.

They knew what he meant. He would wait. When don Costantino had been with a girl the night before, he tended to be more amenable in the morning. Whenever Dimitri came to see his father, he usually ended up provoking him and getting a beating. That was why he didn't come very often, the men knew. He only came when he had to, which meant when he wanted something, which meant when he wanted money. They felt sorry for him. They too had been beaten by their fathers, but they were different. Dimitri was a rich, spoiled kid, not as tough as them.

The two men were clearly not expecting the boss to stir for some time, for both were still in their boxer shorts and tee shirts, not their usual black suits, white shirts and dark ties. (Don Costantino had the affectation of going round like a politician.) They began to make coffee for the visitor. They had not frisked Dimitri for weapons; they never did, as he was the boss's son.

'There is someone downstairs who wants to come up,' said Dimitri, as casually as he could. 'Francesco, the boss's son from Catania.'

The two bodyguards nodded. They remembered him from their visit to Catania, and his words with the boss as the boss had got into the car. They buzzed him up. And a moment later, he was at the door, and then in the kitchen. The blond one frisked Francesco, running his hands along his clothing, checking for a weapon. They did this to all visitors. Francesco smirked as the man touched him, catching his eye. The man looked away, embarrassed. There was, of course, no weapon.

'Look, I will go and see him,' said Dimitri with decision, when this was over. 'Then I may come back for the coffee. Can I leave Francesco here with you? He has something for my father.'

Turning towards the door, as if to make his mind up to see his father at once, Dimitri hesitated. Then he began to tremble, and he sat down on one of the kitchen chairs and began to sob uncontrollably, holding his head in his hands. The bodyguards and Francesco exchanged hopeless glances with each other. Francesco put a comforting hand on the distraught boy's shoulder.

'It is going to be fine,' he said soothingly. 'Trust me. We all get beaten by our fathers. It is natural. It hurts at the time, you bet it does, but then it is over. Look, you need to see him, you need to be brave.'

'I love him,' Dimitri managed to say. 'But I am a bad son, a very bad son, so he hates me.'

'Yes, but we are going to sort it all out, aren't we? Look, you go in there, think of your mother and your sister, and stop crying, be a man. You have got to be a man, Dimitri, you have got to be a man!'

He stroked his cheek. Dimitri dried his tears and stopped crying. He did not speak, he just nodded. He looked at the two bodyguards, and then at Francesco. Then he stood up and left the room.

'Poor boy, eh?' said Francesco.

'He is nice,' said the blond, 'But, you know, he is spoilt.'

The other nodded vigorously in agreement.

'Could you put on the coffee?' asked Francesco.

The dark one found the coffee pot, filled it with water, put in the ground coffee, tightened the screw, and then placed it on the gas and lit it. All this was done in silence. They were waiting, perhaps, for the sound of raised voices and the sound of a leather belt falling on human flesh. The silence continued. They sat round the table. Francesco leaned back in his chair, his legs spread wide, wearing Paoluzzu's clothes, projecting an air of calm and confidence. No one said a word.

'Here is something,' said Francesco, taking his wallet out of his pocket, opening it, and revealing the freezer bag which he placed on the table.

The two men looked. One looked revolted by what he saw, the other, the blond one, concerned.

'Whose?' he asked.

'Antonescu, removed yesterday.'

'Is he …?' asked the dark one.

'Well, he is not walking around minus an ear, that is for sure. He arrived the night before last, and I saw him yesterday morning, and the result you can see. He had nice little ears, didn't he? He was supposed to be the best killer in the business, but he did not see me coming. He came here on a false passport, so the police will not have any idea that he has been killed as they did not know he was here in the first place. Look, here is the passport.'

He took the passport out of his other pocket, and placed it in front of them, next to the severed ear. They looked at it with horror. Somehow the passport seemed more terrible than the severed ear. Behind them, the coffee machine began to make its familiar noise. One of the men took it off the gas, switched off the gas, and then sat down again.

Judging that they had had enough time to think, Francesco spoke.

'I have a message from my father,' he said. 'It requires an immediate response. Some of his men are coming here, and they are going to arrive very shortly.' He looked at his watch. 'When they arrive, they will kill you. You can, of course, resist, but it will be futile. They will kill you. However, he grants you your lives, and will look upon you favourably, if you do the following: get up, dress, and leave this building. Get the hell out of here, and do not look back. Then sometime next week, come to Catania, and I will arrange for you to be compensated.'

No one spoke. Francesco maintained his relaxed pose. The two men looked at each other, perhaps calculating where their weapons were. Then, suddenly, they stood, went to the bedroom for their outer clothes and their shoes and silently and swiftly left the flat.

Francesco allowed himself a long sigh of relief.

As don Costantino woke up, there was a gradual realisation of previous sexual satiety, the reminder of the previous night's sexual intercourse. He swam into consciousness, aware of his state of arousal, vaguely reminded of the woman he had perhaps loved once, but loved no more, his wife in Messina, the formidable Rosa; the woman he did love, the mother of his children in Africa; and the sort of women he habitually slept with when he was away from her, the Moldovan girls, tall, blonde, statuesque, who worked in his clubs and his hotels, or the Brazilians, like last night's girl, who brought an enthusiasm to entertaining the boss that was quite gratifying. Oh God, the Brazilian girls, they were such fun!

This pleasant idyll was interrupted by a soft knock on the door and the entry a moment later, without permission, of his son Dimitri. With an annoyance that approached fury, he rapidly removed his hands from beneath the bedcovers and ruffled the sheet to hide his state of arousal, pretty confident that the boy, stupid as he was, would not realise what he had been doing.

Dimitri was not stupid, and he was clever enough to pretend not to notice what the sudden withdrawal of his father's hands from beneath the sheets, and his heightened colour, meant. Of course he did, as it was something he himself did most mornings. How funny and strange that he should catch his father in such a shameful activity. He remembered the time when he had been twelve or thirteen, having a private moment in his bedroom at home, when his father had caught him and given him a good beating on his bare buttocks with his belt. That had not been pleasant.

'What do you want?' asked his father with distaste. 'I haven't seen you for days, and now you turn up all of a sudden... Look, go and wait in the kitchen. I need to get up and have a shower. Then we can talk, and you can ask me for money, and I will say no. I am sick of your demands!'

'I have not come to ask you for money,' said Dimitri, though the truth was, he did need money, he always needed money. But the thought occurred to him that he might have plenty, and very soon. He thought of all the girls and coke and respect he would enjoy and smiled. 'I have come to tell you something important.'

'What?' asked Costantino.

'Antonescu is dead.'

'Is he?' said Costantino, feigning complete lack of interest. 'Who killed him?'

'Don Calogero, of course, though not in person.'

'And who told you?'

'Francesco. The stepson of don Calogero.'

'I know who he is. Has he brought some sort of proof?' asked Costantino, his interest now aroused.

'He has brought his passport and his ear. He is waiting in the kitchen, waiting to show you.'

There was silence between them for a moment.

'He's here?'

'Yes.'

'So quick,' said Costantino, marvelling. 'Send him in to me. You go and wait in the kitchen. I need to speak to him. This is men's work, not for boys. Go. What are you waiting for?'

He added an imprecation to send Dimitri on his way. After a further moment's hesitation, he left.

'He wants you,' he said as he entered the kitchen.

Dimitri noticed the two bodyguards were gone. He took out the flick knife from his pocket and handed it to Francesco, who took it without a word, along with the freezer bag and the passport, and made his way to the bedroom. Don Costantino was standing there wearing a silk dressing gown. The bed was rumpled and crumpled, there were clothes strewn everywhere, and the curtains were drawn, blocking out most of the light of day. They looked at each other. In his pocket, Francesco was aware of his flick-knife without having to touch it. He was aware too of the sheer size of the Serb, his massive physique, and he knew that surprise was everything, indeed his only advantage. He casually threw the passport onto the bed. Costantino picked it up and examined it. He looked a carefully at all the entry and exit stamps. He recognised it as one belonging to Antonescu, a record of his travels, something Antonescu would not have parted with willingly. Then Francesco took the freezer bag from his pocket and threw that on the bed. Costantino picked it up and examined it with great interest. He felt the absolute joy of every violent man at the elimination of a rival. Darko was avenged, his own authority reinforced. As he looked at the bloody and severed ear, barely recognisable as something that had adorned the head of Antonescu or indeed any human being, so strange did it look, he was unaware of Francesco's hand going to his pocket again, drawing out the knife, flicking it open, and plunging it into his back; with the pain came the thought that he had been taken by surprise and that it was now too late; he turned to defend himself and received another wound in the chest; rage and terror were his lot, to be rapidly succeeded by the cold onset of unconsciousness and death.

In Piazza Armerina, Mass was over. The two beautiful girls, Ida and Claudia, stood on the Cathedral steps, wondering what to do next. Usually, at this time, they took a little walk, before parting and going their separate ways home. With younger siblings trailing behind them, they would discuss the things that interested them: a pair of shoes that one of them had seen; their clothes, make-up and hair; and of course, boys.

'Well, do tell me, what do you think of him?' asked Ida when she was sure her younger siblings were out of earshot.

'Of Francesco di Rienzi?'

'No. Of *him*.'

'The manager from the Trattoria Norma? Paoluzzu? I am surprised you seem to imagine I think anything of him at all.'

'Of course you do, I know you do. You told me you did. Don't tease me.'

'Well, he is very sweet, very nice, quite good-looking…'

'Only quite good-looking?' said Ida, pretending to be shocked.

'Well, some might find him attractive,' conceded Claudia.

'Do you prefer the other one's looks?' asked Ida.

'The other one has nice hair and a merry, round face, but yes, Paoluzzu is the better looking.'

'He's gorgeous,' said Ida. 'The sort of shepherd that the Greek poets of Sicily wrote about. You know, Theocritus….'

'You are being very bucolic,' said Claudia, 'But who cares about Theocritus, or even Bion, or even Moschus, when one is so devoted to Sappho?'

'No one, least of all you, should doubt my intense devotion to Sappho,' said Ida. 'But as you know, my father and mother only let me out of their sight because of you being there and because of Francesco di Rienzi being there. You protect me from him, and he protects me from goodness knows what, though I can protect myself; and as for Paoluzzu he is there to make up the numbers. Francesco is a catch, at least my father thinks so. It is all because of his father, this don Calogero, one of the richest men in Sicily. Though, I have to say, that coming from such a rich family, despite the nice clothes, Francesco is quite humble really. And he is best friends with Paoluzzu, who is even more modest.'

'They have not known each other well for very long,' pointed out Claudia. 'And he is a stepson not a son. His stepfather is very strict with him, I get the impression. If his stepfather tells him he must pay attention to you, that is what he does, even though his heart is not completely in it. But it is Paoluzzu whom you want to talk about, is it not?'

'Yes. Do you think he has, you know, done it?'

'Yes.'

'How do you know?'

'There was some girl I knew or heard about who went out with him for some time. From what I heard... then she dumped him. That's why he came here, to get away from her and from Catania. But I think he is the patient type. He hints at things, and he sends me modest photographs on his phone.'

'He looks so sweet in his underwear,' admitted Ida. 'Though I think he hoped to somehow impress. It is, of course, futile, but we did giggle, didn't we?'

'Boys are just after one thing,' said Claudia. 'He says he is not, but you can tell he is. His eyes tell another story.'

'And what do we girls want?' said Ida.

'Each other,' said Claudia.

'But somehow, we have to make our peace with men and our peace with the world.'

She sighed. Next to her, Claudia sighed too.

When Dimitri got to Catania, at about lunchtime, he did what he had been told to do. He parked the car in the square outside the Church of the Holy Souls in Purgatory, in the space that was reserved for the boss, and left the key, as instructed, in the footwell. He then got out of the car feeling self-conscious, nervous and afraid, and went into the bar to have a drink. Dimitri drank a lot, for man of his age, but he rarely drank at this time of the day, but he stood at the bar and ordered some bourbon, which was what he usually drank, sweet stuff, sophisticated stuff, the sort of thing that impressed the girls, or so he thought. He knocked one back and then asked for another. There were few people in the bar, and those few men drinking coffee, waiting for their womenfolk and children to come out of Church. The same scene was being enacted in squares outside churches all over Sicily on this Sunday morning; but this felt so different. He felt alien. He was numb. He was, on reflection, surprised at the way he had managed to drive the car all this way without having an accident. Within himself, he felt fear, resentment, rage and guilt. There was, of course, no going back. This was it. This was how he would feel for the rest of his life. He needed to find the big guy, Marco, who would take him to the place where Mimmo was hiding. Then he needed to tell Mimmo that he need hide no more, that the danger was passed. Then he needed to tell his mother and his sister. He looked at the television, which was showing a Papal Mass from the Vatican. Soon the whole world would know. And what would happen then?

He needed to find the big guy, and there was no sign of him in the bar, so the best place to look was the gym. He needed to see him, and he was also feeling desperate for some cocaine. He left the bar, paid for his drinks, and came to the gym. The man on the door looked up at him with something like surprise, but when he asked for Marco, he led him into the gym. There was Marco, huge and sweaty, working out at one of the machines.

Dimitri approached and whispered in Marco's ear.

'Message from Francesco. They are dead, both of them,' he said.

Marco continued his exercises, with an imperceptible nod. Dimitri retired at a little distance. Then, after about an interminable ten minutes, Marco left the machine, with no sign of hurry, and left the gym, Dimitri following.

'You are sure?' he asked in a low voice.

He stank of sweat.

'Of course I am. I saw Antonescu's ear, his severed ear. And his passport, or what was supposed to be his passport.'

Marco looked impressed.

'And the other one?'

'With my own eyes,' said Dimitri. 'I need to tell Mimmo, and then I need to go back to Messina and tell my mother and sister. Mimmo's safe now.'

'We all are,' said Marco.

He mentioned Mimmo's address. As Dimitri prepared to leave, he asked a question.

'Where is Francesco?'

Dimitri shrugged.

'I left him at Riposto. I am not sure where he is going or why he wanted to stop there.'

Marco said nothing and let him go.

He was drinking his coffee in the bar some minutes later, his long hair still damp, and his eyes on the door of the Church of the Holy Souls in Purgatory, when he saw what he wanted to see, the figure of Nino Santacroce emerging from the church, looking about him as he stood on the steps, and then realising he was being looked at, and by Marco too, and coming towards the bar. Nino was always aware of his surroundings, always alert to who might be looking for him, and Marco was unmistakeable; he made no sign, he gave no outward indication, that he wanted to speak to him, but you could just tell that he did; he didn't need to show it, one read his thoughts.

Nino slowly came over, letting Marco know he had seen him, and at the same time letting him wait.

'Who are you waiting for?' he asked.

'My mother and sisters are in church,' said Marco. 'They will be out soon. You left early.'

'I did,' said Nino. 'I like church, but not more than about forty minutes of it. Daniela and her parents are there.'

'Is the boss?'

'I think they have gone to the Furnaces, to Our Lady of Loreto, to worship the picture they like so much. They go there when the children are in Donnafugata.'

He paused, knowing that this was not the reason he had been summoned.

'Your greatest enemy is dead,' said Marco.

'And who is, or was, he?' asked Nino without interest.

'Trajan Antonescu, of course,' said Marco. 'Who else?'

'Ah, of course,' said Nino, echoing him. 'Who else? And you know this because…'

'Dimitri told me. He did not do it himself.'

'Of course not,' said Nino. 'Now we know where Francesco has been.'

'There's more.'

'More?'

'Don Costantino.'

'My goodness. How?'

'We don't need to know,' said Marco. 'Best we don't either, when people come asking questions.'

'Will this Dimitri keep quiet?'

'Yes. He is more frightened of us than them, isn't he? And so is Mimmo, who was nowhere near the scene of the crime, who has never met don Costantino. He has gone, with Dimitri, back to Messina. So far, there is nothing, nothing at all about it on the television. There may not be for some time. This may be the peace before the storm.'

'There will be a storm?'

'Bound to be. The police, the television, but the boss as well. He won't be pleased.'

Nino understood. More immediately, Marco was not pleased. By this one stupendous act, Francesco had shown himself to be more capable than Marco. He had eclipsed them both. Oh, he was clever, there was no doubt about that, he had done something daring, killed Antonescu, and killed Costantino, both terrifying men. He must have had a lot of luck. He and Marco would have to live under his shadow from now on. That might be hard, especially for Marco.

'Look,' said Nino, aware that the congregation was coming out of the church. 'Let us meet later, OK? Do you know where he is?'

'Dimitri last saw him in Riposto. He will keep cover for a few days. I am sure of it. And you know what that means? We will have to tell the boss.'

Marco looked even more glum that usual.

The boss was, at that moment, at Mass in the new church of Our Lady of Loreto, in the Furnaces, the new housing project that had made his fortune. It was officially called the Catania Garden City, but that name had never caught on, and the Furnaces it remained, the name it had borne when, as a hellish and ruined landscape, it has been used for the manufacture of bricks. The church of Our Lady of Loreto, patroness of aviation, was a pleasant modern building, which had cost an absolute fortune, thanks to the marshy landscape and the expensive underpinning, none of which had any existence except on paper, and which had allowed millions of euros to be washed. Calogero liked the church, and it reflected his taste and his aesthetic sense, which was, he thought, good. The church was a double cube with an apse, and in the apse, above the main altar, was its chief glory, the supposed eighteenth century copy of Caravaggio's *Holy Family with Saint Laurence and Saint Francis*. This was the painting stolen in the 1960's by the members of the Santucci family and entrusted to their banker, his ex-wife's father, and kept so secret that in the end, only she had known of its existence. Now it was here. It had been carefully 'faked' thanks to the expertise of the art historian Ruggero Bonelli, who had arranged to have a few extra details added that were not supposed to be in the original. A lot of very sniffy art critics had condemned it as a bad copy, which was very helpful, did they but realise it; in a few decades people would realise that it was a good copy, and a few decades on from that, that it was not a copy at all. And when that happened, Romano and Sebastiano who would inherit it, would be rich. What a glorious future!

Mass was boring, as it always was, very boring, always the same, but at the same time he enjoyed being there, in front of his own painting, knowing what he knew, his wife Agata and baby Calogero next to him. And it was nice to be in a church that he himself had built, and at such advantage to himself. And it was nice to know that everyone present knew it: he was their benefactor, and a benefactor of the Church, and a benefactor of Catania. He was in a good position. And after Mass, they would drive home for lunch – his mother was cooking, to give Agata a break, and lunch would be excellent. After that, his mother would take the baby, and with the other children away in Donnafugata, he and his wife would have a lovely time together. He was looking forward to that. Every now and again, she turned and smiled at him, and he smiled back. She knew he was looking forward to the afternoon. How he adored her, how he loved being with her, and the children, and how he loved being with her alone! And she adored him too.

The Mass ended, and the congregation spilled out into the October sunshine. The Church was built on a little hill, on the highest point in the Furnaces, and commanded a pleasant view of the park, the cleaned-up watercourse, and the various gardens. The trees had been transplanted from elsewhere, and the bougainvillea was still in bloom. It was a green and colourful spot, the work of his excellent garden planner, Gabriella Bonelli, sister of the man who had been so helpful over the painting. And there indeed she was, Gabriella, with her baby and with an older woman, whom he recognised as signora Costacurta, the baby Gabriella carried being the daughter (he could never remember her name) of the odious Costacurta who had married his ex-wife, Anna Maria.

He took signora Costacurta's hand and wished her good morning, while Agata kissed her (they had been neighbours), and he kissed Gabriella's cheek.

'The little one will be seeing her father today?' he asked, knowing the answer.

Costacurta was banned from Donnafugata when his and Anna Maria's children were there, as he was not allowed to meet them. So presumably, if he was not in Donnafugata, he was here in Catania, in the Furnaces, seeing his mother, and his former girlfriend Gabriella and their child, but luckily not at Mass.

'Yes,' said Gabriella, who, he could tell from her tone, liked the father of her child as little as he did. 'He comes over now and again. Is Francesco not with you?' she added a little pointedly.

'He is eighteen, you know how it is,' said Calogero easily. 'He is a law unto himself. Goodness knows where he is right now. He is off chasing some girl in Piazza Armerina, I believe. But he is a good boy.'

This perfect lie was pleasingly enunciated. Indeed, the opposite was true: Francesco's entire existence was regimented by his stepfather, who was both angered and puzzled, if not already worried, by the boy's absence.

'Isn't Petra here, or Cosima or Luisa?' asked Calogero, hoping he had got all the girls' names right, turning to their mother, signora Costacurta.

'You know what girls are like,' said the signora. 'They really are a law to themselves.'

She smiled at don Calogero, glad as she was to have his attention. Like her daughters, Petra especially, she was not pleased with her son, who hardly ever came to see them. Today's visit merely served to underline the infrequency of his attentions. The fact that he had given his mother and sisters the house they lived in was overlooked, something that he resented; but the signora and her daughters thought that the very least he could have given them was a house. After all, who was he supposed to look after, if not them? But the signora was glad to see don Calogero, who did not like her son, pretty obviously, as it gave her a chance to let this important and powerful man know that she and her daughters' allegiance lay with don Calogero, not with her son. They knew where the real power lay.

He smiled back at her, graciously. He had, he knew, a very beautiful smile, the sort that melted women's hearts. He didn't care about the signora one way or another, though he supposed if he had any sympathy, she might qualify for some. She had had a hard life; four children; a husband who had deserted her; she had always been nice to Agata, when Agata had lived near her in the Furnaces, though one assumed that she had been guided in that, less by altruism and more by knowing who Agata was to him; but still, Agata liked her. Her husband had deserted her, and now her son was far too busy for her or her daughters. Mind you, he had bought her a house with the money that he had stolen off Tonino Grassi, poor boy. Roberto Costacurta was a lowlife piece of scum, and he would settle with him one day. He felt a fierce pleasure in the thought that his ex-wife had chosen to console herself with so very worthless a character. Well, Roberto did not care for his mother, so Calogero was content to smile on the signora now, if only because she reminded him of how much he hated her son.

'We have been seeing quite a bit of Francesco,' the signora was now saying conversationally.

The smile did not leave his face for a moment.

'That is nice,' he said encouragingly.

'He and Petra,' she said, not needing to say more, her tone conveying everything. 'Of course, she is a bit older than him, but he is such a nice boy and so grown up. You must be so proud of him, don Calogero.'

'I am, signora, I am,' he answered.

The boy in question was in the railway station in Riposto, waiting for the train, the Circumetnea. He was not sure where he was going or what he was doing. After the burst of activity in the last twenty-four hours, he felt slightly lost, at a loose end. His main task was to find a place where one could have something to eat. The station buffet had sandwiches, all very expensive, which, he supposed, did not matter. He had enough money to buy an expensive sandwich. The days of his youth, when he could not buy expensive things, were long gone. He had a thousand or so euro in his pocket. He usually did. So, he bought a sandwich and a bottle of mineral water and waited for the train. The only difficulty was the presentation of a fifty euro note, which the man on the cash register looked at with distaste. The counting out of the change took ages. He experienced this as something novel. In Catania, he never paid for anything, because the places he went to were owned by his father, or were places where they knew who his father was. The man eventually handed him his change, and he accepted it with thanks. He was, of course, invisible, which was what he wanted, wearing Paoluzzu's clothes, an ordinary Sicilian boy. No one was looking at him. He was, dressed like this, no one special. He had put on Paoluzzu's clothes, and at the same time Paoluzzu's status. How very curious it was not to be looked at, not to be the centre, in fact, of any attention at all. He had forgotten what it felt like.

Sitting there anonymously with his sandwich – ham and mozzarella and tomato – he could start to look at the world as it really was. The railway station, the view of the mountain, the ancient train carriage that waited on the tracks; no one would expect him to be here, and indeed no one was here, except a few tourists. He had bought a ticket, along with his sandwich, and one set of tourists had clearly found the way tickets were sold difficult; they were, he was sure, German or French, they had that air of discontent about them. He didn't like them. They were not smart. There was, by contrast, an English couple nearby, who were smart, as the English always were. He liked the English, and he could speak their language. His little brothers would go to school in England, just like his stepsisters, and live amongst such beautiful, civilised people. This was something he shared with his father, a profound Anglophilia. According to Calogero, the very best time in Sicilian history had been the short period in the Napoleonic wars when Sicily had been under the unofficial rule of the English. Maria Carolina and Ferdinand had lived in Palermo and spent much of their time in the little Chinese Palace they had built for themselves, leaving the tiresome matter of administration to Admiral Nelson and his men. Then, after 1815, Sicily had reverted to rule from Naples. What a pity, poor Sicily. He was fascinated by the way Calogero knew so much about Sicilian history, how much he felt for all the characters in the island's story, how much all this mattered to him. Nelson, for example, the Duke of Bronte, one- armed and one-eyed, the lover of the beautiful Emma, the most beautiful woman of her time, the friend of Queen Maria Carolina; yet a woman who had been a prostitute at the tender age of eleven or twelve. What a story! And to think that dottoressa Tancredi had a portrait on her wall of Emma Hamilton, not that he would ever see it, being banned from her presence; not that he wanted to meet the dottoressa, but he would have liked to have seen her pictures in Palermo.

When he had been a teenager, he had not really wanted to go to school, but he was glad, now, that he had done so. Calogero had come into his life and forced him to do so. It wasn't good to be ignorant. He was glad he could speak English, and even a little French, and that he knew about information technology and Italian history and geography and literature. He was glad that Calogero had been firm; the belt and the cane had done him a lot of good. He marvelled at the fact that Calogero had not been to school much, and yet was so cultured and knowledgeable about everything that mattered. Of course, he could not speak English, he abominated computers, but he had an appreciation for art and history that was awe-inspiring. Not being ignorant himself, he wanted his son to be educated as well. When he had been at school, every evening he had had a brief time with his father in his study, during which he would be quizzed about what he had learned that day. Now that he was at university, it was different, as he was studying information technology, and that was a subject they could not discuss; but Calogero still asked him about the books he read, the music he listened to, and any pictures, monuments or churches he had seen. If one was going to lead, one had to have a cultured and cultivated mind, that was Calogero's implication. You had to impress in your conversation. Hence their trip to the Roman villa at Piazza Armerina. One had to be the sort of person who knew these things, not some ignoramus. God only knew, they had been kept ignorant and oppressed for generations in Sicily. It was time to rise above all that. And Calogero had certainly risen.

It was time to get onto the antiquated train. Again, this was something he had always wanted to do, to take the Circumetnea to visit these small town at the foot of Etna, to admire the views of the mountain, to see the plume of smoke coming from its peak. To be a proper Sicilian, you had to understand the mountain, you had to love it. It was part of your education. Of course, his education was different to that of Calogero's other children, that was clear. He was meant to understand Sicily, to experience it directly, to be a true Sicilian. The girls, well, they were in England and might never come back. They were like the dottoressa, the sort of people who worked at one remove from the coalface, the sort that never got their hands dirty, the sort that had to be protected. He, Francesco, was the barrier between them and the real family business, he was the cordon sanitaire (he liked that phrase) between their income and its source. They would enjoy the money and the power, as would their three younger brothers, while never knowing first-hand where it came from.

Well, he knew. From the age of about sixteen, he had known too that one day he would do what his father had done, that is, kill other men. He did not have a very clear idea of how many men Calogero had killed but he knew it was several. These things were not spoken about. The man in the shop in Corso Vittorio Emmanuele had been the first, or so it was assumed, when Calogero had been sixteen. Alfio Camilleri and Gino Fisichella – who had killed them, who had wanted their deaths? And Rosario di Rienzi, how had he died? And there were others too, he knew. A man called Ino, and

Michele Lotto the wild Romanian, that Trajan Antonescu had spoken about. They had stabbed him and covered themselves with blood; his father preferred the knife to the gun. It was more intimate, he supposed. He himself preferred the impersonal nature of the gun.

The train gave a jolt and very slowly began to move. There was a little stir of excitement among the tourists in the carriage.

The killing of the tobacconist of Librino had been perfectly executed, he reflected. His father had trained him on what to expect, on how to get used to the idea, and he had practiced with the gun, and Marco had been with him. But he had pulled the trigger, he had been the one who had seen the man, just for an instant, and then fired, and watched him crumple, before the motorbike sped away. His acquaintance with the man had lasted seconds, and the sheer ease of it had been a shock. But Marco had been pleased by the way he had conducted himself, and so had his father, and he himself had felt a real sense of achievement. He had become a man, in the same way Marco was a man, in the same way his father was a man. That was what a man was, someone who defended the territory, someone who defended his family and interests, someone who would defend little Calogero, as he certainly would one day.

He remembered when he had first gone to bed with Petra, after endless preliminaries. When it was over, when it was done, she told him he was now a man. He had smiled, and sort of agreed, without quite assenting to the idea. Boys were sleeping with girls all over Sicily, but they were not men. Dimitri slept with hundreds of girls, no doubt, and even cowardly, fearful Mimmo had slept with his girlfriend, but they were not men. One became a man when one fearlessly killed one's enemy, and when people knew you were prepared to do that, that you were fearless, you were determined. Nino Santacroce might well have fathered a child, but he was no man, he was sure of that. He had a gun, which he carried as a mere ornament, which he had never used, and probably never would. He did not need to worry about Nino; he had proved himself in a way Nino never would. He had even outdone Marco. And he had outdone and outshone the person he was most envious of, Giuseppe Santucci.

This was something that no one knew, not even his father, because his father, he was sure, would not approve. According to don Calogero, you should not hate anyone, not even your worst enemies. This seemingly admirable Christian attitude was in fact based on calculation and self-advancement. To hate your enemies was to let your emotions be involved and was to warp your judgement. Francesco knew this, but he could not help himself. He loathed don Giuseppe Santucci and he loathed don Renzo Santucci as well. He knew this meant he did not think logically in their regard. He wanted to kill them both so badly. He had not hated Antonescu with the same fervour but rather saw him as a wild dog that needed to be put down; he had had no feelings towards don Costantino at all. That had been a business decision, a strategic decision: it would win them control of the Messina operation.

As for Antonescu, that was revenge for what he had done to Calogero; it was also a desire to get rid of the man who had married his mother's second cousin and let their child be killed; it was also to do with the fact that Antonescu had been such a friend to Costantino and to both Santuccis, originally, certainly to Beppe. Those two had been very close, but it had not ended well, had it? Beppe Santucci would be displeased when he realised Trajan Antonescu was no more. He wondered how he would take it and to whom he would attribute the disappearance. To whom, if not to don Calogero?

The train was heaving and straining its way around the base of Mount Etna, rising slowly, and stopping about every five or ten minutes. The views of the mountain and the lava fields were very pleasant, the names of the villages such as Piedimonte and Linguaglossa seemed poetic, though the places themselves seemed deserted, forgotten. But that was good. He wanted to be somewhere far away, somewhere no one would think of looking for him. This place, right at the foot of Etna, this was just such a place.

Were they looking for him? He had to assume as much. They would be looking, wondering, trying to piece together what had happened. In the first place, Antonescu's stepfather who had given him the key to the flat where Antonescu had been, he would realise something had happened. He would go to the flat, see that Antonescu was gone, and his things gone, and the carpet had gone, and work out what had happened. Perhaps. But would he tell anyone? Would he tell his wife? Would he tell the boss? Or would he be glad his stepson was no more? And Francesco realised that he had an advantage. Antonescu had never been there in the first place; the man he had killed and buried in the lake had entered the country under the name of Gaetano Salimbeni. Antonescu moved around the world without leaving a trace; men like that could disappear easily.

The train arrived at Randazzo, after a good hour of straining uphill, and here he decided to get out, having nothing better to do. Quite a few of the tourists did the same thing, and it was now getting late, and he very much wanted a cup of coffee. The town was picturesque, built of lava, with narrow streets that overlooked a valley, at the bottom of which was a river running through a rocky and almost barren landscape. He did find a bar, but though Randazzo was pretty, it was lifeless. Perhaps all these tourists were hikers. He could not understand that: the desire to wander through the countryside, to tire oneself out in this way. There had been a big battle here in the Second World War; he had heard his father speak about it. He stood at a viewpoint and wondered about the battle, and how difficult it must have been to fight over this terrain. And how useless. The Germans had lost by then, that was clear, so why fight on? The Fascists were doomed, so why fight on? Why fight for a losing cause? Why fight for any cause but the only cause that mattered, your own?

The British and Canadians had fought at Randazzo, just one of their battles up the eastern side of Sicily, but in the west, there had been hardly any fighting at all, because the Italian troops had run away and the Germans had as well, told to do so by the men of honour, saving the Americans much pain and much blood. The Americans had been practical about it, letting Lucky Luciano out of jail for just that purpose, and he had arranged it all. What a great man. The British had been less than practical. And as he stood there, the English couple from the train were there next to him, at a little distance, talking in their own language. He strained to overhear what they were saying. Their accents were impenetrable. He looked at them once more, admiring their good looks. The girl was ravishingly beautiful; his eyes took in all her details, her nice well-rounded bottom, the smooth delicious curve of her breasts, the way her blonde hair hung down to her shoulders, her lovely, almost sculpted and make-up free face. Then he saw that the man had seen him looking at his girlfriend, and was smirking, and had recognised him from the train.

'Hi,' he said in a friendly manner.

By Sunday afternoon, Alfonso Agostini was beginning to panic. He knew he had to do something, and that he could not put it off forever. The only good thing was that his wife was too busy with all the usual weekend things - with the two sons Salvatore and William, with going to church, with getting the lunch ready - to care much about the fact that Traiano had arrived, taken up residence near the fountain of Arethusa, and then failed to appear. Or rather, she chose not to show it (he read her mind) because this was the sort of behaviour she expected from her eldest son. He had ignored her for years. They had gone to Africa to see him, and he had ignored her there; now he had come to Sicily, and he had ignored her once more. It hurt her, Alfonso knew, it hurt her very much; and it hurt her that her own son, ignoring his mother, had always had time for his stepfather. It had been Alfonso who had picked him up at the airport, and Alfonso who had taken him to the flat, and the same Alfonso who, on Sunday, admitted to her that Traiano had gone.

'Gone?' she had asked. 'Gone where? And what do you mean, gone?'

She was in the kitchen, stirring the pasta sauce as she said this.

'His stuff is gone, all of it,' he explained. 'The place is empty.' He looked towards the door, towards the next room where the two boys were waiting for lunch, reading their books. They both hoped they could not overhear. 'I mean, is this something he would do, just disappear like this?'

'It is typical,' said Anna. 'He did not want to see me. I suppose I should accept it. Besides….' She motioned with her head towards the boys. 'It may be better that they do not meet him; he clearly does not want to meet them, so we should be grateful for that. I mean…'

He knew what she meant. They were both terrified of their sons coming into contact with criminals. And one criminal in particular.

'He is probably here to do something that he does not want traced,' said Anna. 'We had better just forget he was ever here.'

He nodded. He tasted the pasta sauce. It was good. It always was.

In Catania, that very afternoon, at about four, Agata asked:

'Where is Francesco, do you think?'

She had not asked about her son all afternoon; her mind had been on different things, but now, those desires satisfied, the nagging question of her son's absence had come back into her mind.

'I sometimes wish he had a mobile phone,' she said. 'Then we would know where he had got to.'

'And so would everyone else,' said Calogero, making his usual observation. 'Besides, even when youngsters have mobile phones, they can neglect to answer them. If he had one now, he would not be answering, I am sure.'

'He was not home last night.'

'He is eighteen,' said Calogero.

'Still….'

'Look, he is probably in Piazza Armerina, pursuing don Nunzio's daughter. Didn't he phone you from there yesterday afternoon?'

'He did. But he would not have stayed the night, not with her, anyway.'

'No, but he may be with his friend Paoluzzu.'

'Does he, does he sleep with girls?' asked Agata.

Calogero sighed.

'He tells you everything,' she said. 'You two are so close. But he never tells me anything. You two are always plotting something.'

'He is a normal eighteen-year-old. He likes girls. And yes, we have discussed it. There are lots of things he does not want his mother to know. There are lots of things I don't want my mother to know, for goodness's sake. Like this.'

The sails were swelling with what he poetically called his second wind. The thought of her son was banished from her mind.

'I hope you told him…' she said, after about an hour, returning to the same subject, her son.

'Told him what?'

'That whoever he meets, his mother and you will always be more important.'

'He knows that. We have talked about it, you know, what really matters in life. He loves you passionately. His mother counts for everything. No girl will ever take your place.'

'He is not going to have a baby with the first girl he meets, is he?' she asked anxiously.

'No. We talked about that. He is not having a baby with anyone. He has got enough small brothers to look after.'

'He might be jealous of Nino Santacroce.'

'Well, he might, but he and I have spoken, and he knows what I expect.'

'I am glad you take a firm line. So many young men have no one to guide them. I don't think he is in Piazza Armerina. I think from what signora Costacurta said, that he has gone somewhere with Petra.'

'He likes Ida. Petra, not so much, at least not anymore. At least that is what I think, but it may be wishful thinking. Look, stop worrying; when he returns, I will make him explain himself, and I will tell him that he must not worry his mother.'

'Good,' she said. 'Be firm.'

It was early evening when, freshly showered and dressed, feeling content, but still worried by Francesco's absence, that he went to the window of his study and looked down at the square in front of the Church of the Holy Souls in Purgatory. There on the steps, waiting for his attention, were Marco and Nino Santacroce. He could tell they were uneasy, and that they had probably been waiting some time, and that they were filled with dread. With a slight motion of the hand, he indicated they might come up. A few minutes later they were in the study, looking embarrassed and, he was glad to see, pale with fear. Something had clearly gone seriously wrong, and they knew, he could tell, that they had to tell him about it, and that to put it off would just make things worse.

Nino was the more articulate, and he was the one who spoke.

'Boss,' he said, 'Dimitri Petrović was here. His father is dead; Mimmo and he have gone back to Messina.'

'He is sure he is dead?'

'He saw it with his own eyes. Don Costantino is dead.'

'Who....?'

'Boss, it was Francesco. He went to don Costantino's flat with the son, he persuaded the bodyguards to leave, both of them, and then when Costantino was in his dressing gown, defenceless, he stabbed him.'

Calogero permitted himself a raised eyebrow.

'And the body is still in the flat?'

'With the water running in the kitchen and the bathroom,' said Marco, knowing this was important. 'I did not ask, but I am sure the drain was blocked.'

'Very clever,' said Calogero, looking at him. 'Where is Francesco now?'

'Dimitri left him in Riposto.'

The boss nodded.

'Boss, it gets worse,' said Nino apologetically. 'He left us in Syracuse and according to Dimitri, he killed Antonescu.'

There. It was said.

Calogero said nothing, betrayed nothing, but the silence was tense.

'So,' he said at last, 'You go to Syracuse with my sons, and you let Francesco slip away, and he kills Antonescu, and God knows what trail of evidence he leaves behind him… You,' he said, with cold venom, addressing Marco. 'I trusted you with him, to educate him, to look after him, to prevent him making mistakes, and you let him do this? And you,' he said, turning to Nino, 'You are supposed to be clever, and you let this happen? Don't you realise my son's career, my son, please note, his career might be over before it has even begun?'

Neither of them could speak. Francesco was his own master, and it was not their fault, but the boss was clearly in no mood to hear that.

The rhythms of Sunday night settled over Catania. Because most of the places where he sold pills and drugs and other things were shut on a Sunday, Nino Santacroce was at home with his mother and father; he had seen Daniela his girlfriend and her parents at lunchtime; the evening of Sunday was when he was supposed to devote himself to his own parents. They had eaten, and he had gone to have a shower, and examined the stripes that the boss's cane had left on him, in the bathroom mirror; then he had emerged in his pyjamas and his dressing-gown to watch television. The pain he felt was extraordinary, and the humiliation intense, but infinitely worse than both was the fear that he might have lost the boss's favour. He needed the boss's favour more than anything. The boss's favour was the most important thing, the only thing that mattered.

As he sat on the sofa, looking at the television screen, trying to pretend that he was interested in this programme about football, he could feel his father paying him no attention at all, and his mother looking at him with anxious concern. She knew he was unhappy, he could tell, but he could not bear her sympathy. He was indifferent to his father, who had been in jail for most of his early childhood, but towards his mother, he felt furious resentment. She should have paid him more attention when he had been younger. She should not have trusted Traiano Antonescu and allowed him to exploit her only child. When Andreazza and others had put their hands down his trousers, where had she been? And surely she had known? She ought to have known; either she had known, which was unforgiveable, or she had chosen not to know, which was equally bad. Now, she pretended to care. Well, it was too late. Here they sat, the three of them, pretending to be a family, but it was a farce. He knew that. He knew he was intelligent, and he knew he was good-looking, and he knew he loved Daniela and she, him; but there was something else about himself that he recognised, that no one else around him had: he could see things for what they were.

His eyes had been opened early. Too early. The very first time he had been left alone with Andreazza, he had known then that he was there to be exploited and used by others for their purposes. What exactly was going on about him, he had not quite surmised, but they needed him, they needed to use him, as the boy Paolo Bednarowski was too old for their purposes; and Antonescu had needed him to induce Andreazza to do whatever Andreazza was needed for. And of course, when they no longer needed Bednarowski, they had got rid of him.

He had not particularly liked Paolo, whom he had thought was aggressive and surly; a good footballer, a handsome boy with blonde hair and blue eyes, he seemed to remember, whose mother went with men for money; well, maybe Paolo had had something to be surly and angry about; he himself had always avoided that mistake of showing anger. There was no point to it. No one was interested in your anger; and your anger only marked you out as difficult. He had not liked Paolo, but when they had killed Paolo and his mother – a national scandal, as they were supposedly under police protection – he had felt sorry for them.

It had been the gravedigger of Bronte, the one called Pio Forcella, who had taken charge of their bodies and overseen their cremation in Rome, far away. No one had wanted them. That had struck him as tragic, not to be wanted when alive, not to be wanted when dead. The sheer lack of love was desolating. One should not expect love, there was so little of it about, and none available for Paolo and his mother. And they would do the same to him.

'Did you go to Mass?' asked his mother, turning her attention away from the television, without moving her eyes.

'Yes, with Daniela and her parents,' he answered.

'Where?'

'In the quarter. The Holy Souls in Purgatory.'

'How was it?' she asked.

'Maybe you should go and find out, ma.'

'You know I do not go,' she said defensively.

'You went in Pordenone,' he pointed out.

'Everyone goes in Pordenone. They want to look respectable.'

She had in fact gone to Mass in Pordenone when they had been staying with her sister. It was sort of expected up there, in the north of Italy, a foreign country.

'Did you go to Holy Communion?' she now asked.

'That is none of your business,' he said, trying not to rise to the provocation.

He knew this was her revenge, her needling him with the charge of hypocrisy. A drug pusher and pill pusher who went to Mass was always going to be vulnerable to the charge of hypocrisy. And he was banned, he knew, from approaching the sacrament, as he was involved in immoral activity, as well as sleeping with a girl who was not his wife. Though, God knew, He surely did, that those who did go to Holy Communion were probably up to much the same thing. But his mother wanted to remind him of his moral depravity, he knew, to caution him against taking the moral high ground with her. Both she and his father had separately told him, when the news of the child had emerged, what he had to do: persuade her to abort. They had both been very angry, in their own ways, when he had refused, steadfastly refused. They still resented this, he could tell. They had both taken the same line: he was too young, he was ruining his life, the girl was manipulating him.

Well, he knew the truth. The child had been his idea, the result of his craving, his longing. She had, of course, assented, but the idea had been his. Of course he was young, but he was old enough to know what he wanted, and he was rich enough to look after Daniela and the child. Both his mother and his father had spoken separately about the merits of aborting the child; his mother had spoken of how easy it was for a woman to do this, and his father had stressed how convenient it was for a man; which had made him wonder, with resentment, how many of his brothers and sisters had ended that way.

'I don't know why you want to get married at all, let alone in Church,' said his mother, renewing the attack. 'I blame that priest,' she added.

She had, he realised, turned into an anti-clerical, which was somehow his fault.

'I am a Catholic; you had me baptised,' he replied evenly. 'Where else am I to get married? If you were happily married, you would understand why I wanted to get married.'

His mother was silent.

'Someone should give you a slap, a hard one,' said his father.

'Yeah, right, someone should, but not you, you would not dare.'

His father looked resentful. He remembered the last time he had tried to hit his son, when his son had resisted. That had been some years ago.

'They are going to cut off all that lovely hair when you become a police cadet,' said his father.

Nino looked at him with contempt. The usual gibe that his son was a long-haired sissy. It rather missed the target, he thought. He had spent his early years watching policemen do disgusting things, so having long hair did not embarrass him. In truth, he was looking forward to getting rid of it, looking more normal, growing a beard, forbidden by the boss, shaving under his arms, ditto. Oh, he could not wait to be a policeman. Neither could Daniela. Her father, one of the policemen whom he had seen do disgusting things was, he felt, less enthusiastic. His future father-in-law regarded him with embarrassment and dread, but this ensured his deference and co-operation. He had a permanent hold over him, and he was not sorry. His future mother-in-law had no idea about her husband, which had at first surprised him, but now no longer did.

He looked at the television. They were talking about that day's football matches, mentioning all the usual teams; it was very rare the Elephants ever got a look-in. They were the only team he cared about. Why on earth should anyone in Catania give a damn about la Fiorentina, Lazio, or Roma? Though some of them were good players, no doubt about that, the best in the world; many of them had long hair, like himself. Some of them looked beautiful, as all men should, but few actually did. Antonescu had never cared about football. Antonescu, the man who had ruined his childhood, but who had also made him rich, by introducing him to this world, Antonescu was dead.

It was very curious that someone like Antonescu could be dead. Antonescu had been one of those people who was so completely strong willed; he had not hated or feared him, merely accepted him and his orders without question. Antonescu had been like God. And now he was no more. He was not quite sure what he felt. Was it relief? Was it a sense of justice done, for, after all, if anyone deserved to be killed, it was Antonescu? Or was it a sense of almost sadness, that Antonescu had ended like this? Of course, Antonescu had always been bad, when he had known him, very bad, but at the same time, he had had some qualities to recommend him, surely? He had been very fond of his wife and children, enamoured of them, especially the little boy who had been murdered, his eldest, Cristoforo. But he had not cared about other children, had he? He had not cared about him, when he had pushed him towards Andreazza. He wondered if Antonescu was at peace now; his life must have been torment after the loss of his son, his wife, his other children. If Francesco had killed him, it had been because Antonescu had allowed it, losing the will to live.

While Antonescu had not been part of their lives for some time, but Francesco was a present reality. He had killed Antonescu; he had killed don Costantino. He had, he was sure, killed the tobacconist of Librino. But he was equally sure that while don Calogero had primed him to do the latter, with the help of Marco, he had not authorised the murder of either Antonescu or the boss of Messina. Those two killings were his own idea, his own bid to show how clever and daring he was; and something else as well: his bid to outflank Marco, the brutal killer; and his desire to get rid of Antonescu, the former favourite of the boss, his desire to have no rivals.

He had known Francesco for a long time, from before he had become the boss's stepson. In those days, he had been a nice boy, just another boy in the quarter. Well, he still was. He admired him for that. Many boys would have been changed by wealth and position. From being a nobody, just Agata's son, to being the most important young man in the Purgatory quarter, the one whom everyone wanted to be friends with, well, he had handled that well. He gave the impression that he was still ordinary, that he was one among the young men of the quarter, no one special. Hence the tobacconist of Librino: he had wanted to show that he did not mind getting his hands dirty, that he would muck in with the rest of the people who worked for his stepfather, people like Marco. But this, killing Antonescu, killing the boss of Messina, went too far. His stepfather, he was sure, would be furious with him.

Well, don Calogero was already unhappy, that was for sure. He had expressed his discontent when he had told Nino and Marco to put their hands on the back of the sofa in the study and given them both the taste of his cane. Nino resented this in a way that Marco did not; Marco was too slavishly devoted to the boss to resent anything, as indeed was Francesco. It was unexpected, this double murder and disappearance on Francesco's part. No doubt the boss would be terrified that Francesco would end up in a police cell somewhere. How would he explain that to his wife? How would he himself feel, given how much he loved the boy?

The football programme ground on, and there was no interrupted news flash as he half expected there to be. Indeed, the programme ended, and it was time for the news headlines, but once again, he was disappointed. No body had been discovered in either Syracuse or Messina. There were no flashing blue lights, no police standing around or pieces to camera, as there surely must be when a person as big as don Costantino died. Perhaps the body has not been discovered? Or perhaps the police were keeping this quiet for reasons of their own? Whatever it was, it seemed destined to be a dreary Sunday evening. He wondered about phoning Daniela to wish her good night and perhaps getting dressed again and going over there for the night. He went to the phone, which was in the hallway, and just as he was about to pick up the receiver, it rang.

He picked up. It was the barman from the bar, asking if he could come down. He knew this sort of request would not be made lightly, so he said he would be there in ten minutes. He went to his bedroom, and got dressed, then left the flat without a word. He felt that the dreary evening might be about to get interesting.

On entering the bar, he saw why he had been called. The place was nearly empty, and the barman did not have to explain. There were two of them, pretending to look at home, pretending to look normal, but so great was the effort they made, they stood out to even a casual observer, as not quite right, not fitting in. They were foreigners, the Balkans written on their faces; and the same faces had a peeled look: these were two heavily bearded men who had shaved in a hurry to try and disguise their appearance, and only succeeded in making themselves look more odd. These were two of the men he had seen guarding don Costantino when he had come to the quarter. These, he guessed, were the two men who had failed to protect him from Francesco.

'Well?' he asked.

'We want to see don Calogero,' said the blond one. 'Are you a friend of Dimitri?'

'We are all friends of Dimitri,' said Nino casually. 'He was here earlier, and he told us… told us the news. I expect you already know the news.' He glanced towards the ever-present television. 'It is not out yet, is it? But when it is, your fellow Serbs are going to come looking for you, aren't they? So, you have come running to don Calogero, to save yourselves…'

'We were promised…' said the dark one.

'Promised the world, I do not doubt. But…. I am not sure what authority Francesco had for making promises.' He looked at the barman. 'Is Marco around?' he asked.

'No. We were waiting an hour, trying to find him. That was why we eventually called you. Marco is off somewhere.'

Nino nodded. After their beating, the boss had held Marco back, to give instructions. Marco had rushed off to follow those instructions, and Nino knew what they would be. Marco was looking for the Serbs, and these two in particular; he need not have bothered going to Messina, as they had come to him. And he had missed them. What a piece of luck.

It was too dangerous to speak there. Someone would see them. The Church door was still open. He gestured with his head, and walked towards it, confident they would follow. They did. He sat near the back and saw them enter, making the sign of the cross in that strange way Serbs had. Luckily the church was deserted and dim. The two Serbs approached. He spoke to them in a whisper.

'So, they have not discovered the body?'

They shook their heads.

'He likes to spend Sunday quietly. They won't know he is gone before Monday morning. Usually, he spends Sunday at home watching television, making phone calls….' said the dark one.

'You are sure he is dead?' asked Nino. 'That this is not a trick?'

They both nodded dumbly. They had not witnessed the death, but they had no doubt it had taken place.

'Whatever Francesco promised you is worthless,' said Nino. 'Don Calogero, unless I am very much mistaken, has already sent someone to Messina to kill you. You see, he needs you silenced because you know it was Francesco who did it, and you have the power to have him found guilty of murder. Where do you come from in Serbia?'

'Novi Sad,' said one.

'Sarajevo East,' said the other.

'Well, that is where you need to go, and now. Before it is too late. You will be as safe there as anywhere else. There you will have friends to protect you. Here you are exposed…. You are all exposed. Your only friend is dead, and you betrayed him. His African wife, his African children, all left defenceless. Get away while you can.'

'But we helped Francesco. He owes us…' said the blond one.

'There is no gratitude. You fell for a trick. Trust me. I know how that feels. Get out while you have the chance. Get down to Syracuse or Pozzallo, take the first ferry south, then take refuge in Serbia. Save yourselves!'

The blond one sat on the bench, held his head in his hands and began to mutter imprecations.

'Don Calogero will clean up after his son. I am sure of it. You will be swept away,' said Nino.

The Serb with dark hair, who had been feeling fragile for some time now, broke down in tears.

'We should not have listened to him,' he sobbed.

'Indeed. But it is too late for that.'

A figure approached in the darkness. It was don Giorgio.

'I was just shutting up,' he explained. 'What have we here?'

'Lost souls from the Balkans, Father,' said Nino.

Chapter Seven

The English couple, contrary to what he had heard about English people in general, were very friendly. They had fallen into conversation, and they had complemented Francesco on his English. They had spoken at length, then gone for drinks, then gone for dinner together. He supposed, as he woke up the next morning, contemplating the light playing on his bedroom ceiling, that they found Randazzo as dull as he did, and that their chance meeting had enlivened the experience of being there.

After they had parted – he had told them he was staying the night in Randazzo, without saying exactly where – he had walked around the darkened town and checked out all the empty properties, closed up for autumn, until he had found one he liked and whose lock seemed vulnerable. He had easily let himself in, gone up the stairs, without switching on any lights, and found the main bedroom and gone to sleep. The bed had not been made up, but it was reasonably warm and comfortable. Now as he lay in his borrowed bed, he stroked his chin, realising that he could not shave, and wondered about his breath, having no toothbrush or toothpaste. No comb either. Well, he could always buy one. Perhaps the bathroom here was well provided for, however, as he was on the run, he did not want to leave his DNA everywhere. But how would anyone know he had been here? He had disappeared off the face of the earth.

There was a bathroom, and there was a toothbrush, and an immersion heater, so he was able to have a warmish shower. He then went down to the street, shutting the door behind him, and heading to the main bar of the place for his coffee, and to watch the television. The place was reasonably full, and no one would notice him, and as it turned out, everyone was looking at the television. A lady was sharing her horror with the nation, describing how water had begun to trickle through the ceiling of her flat. She had gone upstairs, but no one had been at home. Water had been seeping out from under the front door. She had called the manager of the flats, the police, the fire brigade. But it had been a Sunday, and it had been ages before anyone had come. But at last, they had come, forced open the door and entered the flooded flat. The signora said her ceiling was ruined, her furniture ruined; there were sympathetic noises round the bar. Unlucky signora!

Bathrooms, by Italian law, had drains in the floor, as the fireman was explaining to camera, but in this case, someone had deliberately blocked the drain with a towel. The shower had been on, as well as the kitchen taps, and so the whole flat was flooded, and the body of the owner had been found slumped in the shower.

'Was it foul play?' was the question put to a uniformed man.

The policeman regarded his questioner with something approaching disdain. At present, they were keeping an open mind, he said. But his eyes spoke of the vision of horror he had witnessed: the flooded flat; the blood and water flowing; the naked body; the stab wounds. He had seen a lot in his time, but this had shaken him. He knew the man in the shower, known him better than he cared to admit. This death would be, he feared, the first of many.

A reporter was speaking to the camera now. The resident in the flat, who was presumed deceased, was Costantino Petrović, an Italian citizen, and a leading businessman in the province of Messina, with an interest in several hotels and other businesses in Taormina. It was not yet known what had happened to signor Petrović. Then, there he was, Dimitri, looking very pale, recounting that his mother and sister were distraught, and the entire family in shock. He did that rather well, Francesco thought; he was not acting; he really was shocked, and looked it. The man had no guts. In this case, that was rather useful for once. He had probably spent the last twenty-four hours vomiting. He nibbled his cornetto and wondered if he ought to have a second cup of coffee.

This question was settled by the entrance of the Englishman. Well, it was hardly a coincidence, as it was the best bar in the place, perhaps the only bar in the place. His wife was still in the place they had stayed the night, just opposite, putting on her makeup. Steve - that was the man's name - looked up at the television and asked what was happening. 'Nothing', said Francesco: some man found dead in his shower. It would all be forgotten by lunchtime. It turned out they were both taking the train towards Bronte, half an hour away, later on. Steve and his wife were going to see Lord Nelson's place. Francesco said he was going to see a family friend there, an undertaker, a friend of his father's. He had always been promising to visit. Steve asked what his father did. He was in property, said Francesco. He helped with the business when not at university. Right now, things were a bit difficult. He and his father had not fallen out, one never did that, but his father did not like his girlfriend who was a couple of years older than him, and who was the sister of the man who had married his father's ex-wife and whom his father could not stand. It was complicated. His father was his stepfather, he ought to clarify. But he owed him a lot, and when he told him that he did not like the girlfriend, and that he should pay attention to another girl, whose father was a business colleague of his father, he knew he had to listen.

Steve heard all this with sympathetic concern.

'But what do you want?' he asked.

'To please my father, of course. The thing is, my girlfriend does not like him, so I can't see it progressing very far. I mean, I like her, but I am not sure how much she really likes me, and I wonder if she would get over it. It is very complicated. So that is why I am taking a few days off, visiting friends. Then I will go home and, as you say, face the music. Tell me, what do you do?'

'I am a police officer. We both are.'

At that moment, his beautiful wife entered.

'In London?' asked Francesco.

'No, Liverpool.'

He had heard of the football team but otherwise knew nothing of the place. He smiled at the beautiful wife, and she smiled back at him. Then they spoke of Bronte and Lord Nelson.

The children had come back from Donnafugata late on Sunday night, full of their chatter about what a lovely time they had had with their mother, Anna Maria. The two little boys, Sebastiano and Romano, could not stop talking and giggling amongst themselves. They were glad to see baby Calogero, and to see Agata their stepmother, who they adored, because she was so kind and such a good cook. Renato seemed happy as well, but Renato, Calogero knew, was 'sensitive', in the way his two younger brothers were not. Renato understood more. The two younger ones had had supper and gone to bed, as they did on a normal Sunday evening, while Renato had noticed something different about the atmosphere in the house. But it was only the next afternoon that the difference in atmosphere became clear to him. His father seemed pensive, reflective, almost sad, quite unlike his usual self.

'Papà,' said the boy, 'Where is Francesco? Is he alright?'

'Why shouldn't he be?' asked his father.

'I just wondered,' said Renato.

The boy was sitting next to him on the sofa in the study, reading from his English book, an exercise he usually carried out with Francesco, who spoke the language with some facility. Calogero, by contrast, did not, and hearing his son read aloud was to be subjected to all sorts of horrid sounds that made no sense. What a barbarous language, but Renato had to learn it, as Renato was going to go to school there, like his sisters.

'I can't pronounce this word,' said the boy.

The word was 'thoroughfare'. It was, to Calogero's eyes, impossible. But Renato turned to his tablet, put the word in carefully, as the spelling was difficult, and then pressed a button, and out came the sound in a wonderfully strange accent. The accompanying text even explained what the strange word meant.

'You see,' said his father, 'You don't need Francesco or me. A computer can do it all.'

The boy looked at his father.

'Papà?'

'What?' he asked, sensing something was coming.

'Where is Francesco? He has been acting strangely recently.'

Calogero considered. What did the child mean? Had he noticed that Francesco had killed the tobacconist of Librino? Had the child understood? He hoped not.

'Look, you are going to be twelve very soon, aren't you?' said his father. 'When boys get to a certain age, they get interested in girls.'

Renato seemed unimpressed by this.

'Francesco is eighteen. He is probably more interested in girls now than he has ever been or will ever be. So… He has gone off somewhere chasing a girl. You remember the family we met in Piazza Armerina, the day we saw the Roman villa? They have a daughter called Ida, and I think he has gone there. So, if he has been acting strange that is the reason why. He is in love.'

'You mean like when a dog or a cat goes a bit strange, when they are on heat?'

'Well, I would not put it like that exactly,' said his father. 'But yes.'

'But Papà, he has already got a girlfriend, her name is Petra, and he and she sleep together already.'

Calogero was silent.

'What makes you think that?' he asked, as calmly as he could.

'I just know,' said the boy. 'I can tell. It is not that he told me, but from the way he talks, and the others talk. And he has got a secret compartment in the bottom of his wardrobe, which he thinks I do not know about. That is where he keeps his gun as well.'

'Do you know what sleeping with a girl means?' asked his father.

'Yes. What Nino and his girlfriend do. Which is why she is having a baby.'

'There are certain things that you are not supposed to know about,' said Calogero.

'Papà, do you honestly think I live in the dark?' said Renato. 'Didn't you know these things at my age?'

'Renato, that was different. We were very poor, and I had to learn to look after myself.'

'You were not that poor,' said Renato. 'Grandmother told me that you were quite well off, compared to most. You were wild, she said, and my grandfather tried to discipline you, but it did not work, as he was so often away. By my age, you had done a lot of bad things. Just like Francesco does bad things now, as does Nino, and Marco.'

'Look, when I was only seventeen, I was married to your mother, and Isabella was born soon afterwards. So, if Francesco has a girlfriend, that is not bad. He is eighteen... As for the gun...'

'Which is no longer at the bottom of the wardrobe. Wherever he is, he took it with him.'

'Are you telling me that Francesco is a bad influence on you?' said Calogero.

'Not really, Papà. The bad influence is you, surely.'

He sent the boy away to his bedroom to do his homework on his own. Shortly afterwards, the first of his visitors came to see him. He had asked him to come. It was Alfonso Agostini, the husband of Anna the former Romanian prostitute. He was shown into the sitting room by the signora and was joined a few moments later by don Calogero. They looked at the photographs of the children first, the official excuse for his visit, then Agata withdrew. Fofò sat in his chair expectantly, while Calogero took out a bottle of vin santo from the drinks cabinet and carefully poured two tiny glasses, one of which he handed to his visitor.

'Thank you for coming and thanks for the pictures, they are really good, as ever,' said Calogero.

'I was expecting you to call me,' said Fofò.

'You were? Why?'

'This thing in Messina. It represents a big upheaval,' said Fofò.

'Oh that. Yes, it does. Or maybe it represents the beginning of a calmer and better period. Don Costantino Petrović was a bad man, as you may have heard. He was a disruptor. Now he is gone, perhaps order will be restored. But for him, being killed like that, it was personally a big upheaval. What have you heard?'

'Just what I have seen on the television. But…'

'Of course it concerns you more personally, doesn't it? You are worried about your stepson, aren't you?'

'I was worried about your stepson, Francesco,' said Fofò carefully.

'Ah, so was I, but as it turns out, I ought to have been more worried about Antonescu. Francesco is fine; someone saw him on Sunday morning. My stepson is well, yours less so.'

'I do not know what to say,' said Fofò.

'Does one need to say anything?' asked Calogero.

Fofò felt a wave of desolation wash over him. He had loved Traiano so much. He had been so young, so beautiful, so affectionate, at least to him. It was impossible to think of him as dead and gone. But he was; he had been gone for years, ever since the little boy Cristoforo had been killed, ever since the marriage had died with him, ever since the last vestiges of humanity had been destroyed by his father's craze for revenge.

'If the little boy had not died,' began Fofò.

'Don't,' commanded Calogero. 'It is too painful to contemplate.'

For he had loved him too, once.

There was silence.

'What exactly happened?' Calogero asked. 'Just tell me the facts.'

The facts were simple. Traiano had been staying in the flat, having arrived the previous night. He had picked him up at the airport. Calogero knew, without having to be told, that the visitor would have arrived on a false passport, so no one would have known he was there. The next day, Francesco had left them to go and see Traiano. That evening, Alfonso had gone to the flat, and had found it empty, the carpet gone. He had told his wife that her son had left, and she had accepted this, partly because she knew he did not want to see her, and partly because she was relieved he would not see Salvatore and William. She had not really been expecting to see her son, and had known he had come back to Sicily, not for her, but for Calogero. Secure in this deception, Fofò had cleaned the flat himself as best he could and bought a new and identical carpet. He had also called in the lady who cleaned the flat between tenants and got her to clean it as well. It was now, he hoped, as if no one had been there; new tenants would arrive soon. He had, he knew, become an accessory to murder. But he was hopeful no one would ever know. He was telling the boss this as an insurance policy. Should he get into trouble, his lawyers and his influence would help.

'Where is the body?' asked Calogero. 'In the sea?' he asked, remembering Michele Lotto the wild Romanian.

'I don't know,' said Fofò. 'But he left with your car.'

'This news from Messina...'

'Anna had jumped to the conclusion that it was Traiano who did that, which is why she is convinced he has already gone away, and will never return.'

'Then Anna will be satisfied,' said Calogero. 'To tell you the truth, it is only a minor matter, but I would not like her to think that I lured him back so Francesco could kill him. The person who wanted him to come back was her, and Traiano himself. Luckily, if she thinks he is alive, she will not blame herself for his death. She should never have asked me to allow him to come back. But... neither of us were to know. Above all, I want you to know this: I was not to know that Francesco would take it upon himself to kill Traiano, against my express orders. I am very angry with him for disobeying me. Many have offered to go and kill Traiano, but I refused all offers. I was happy for him to stay alive. As it is, I am surprised that Francesco could kill him. Your stepson was a mass murderer, a very skilled and shrewd operator, and Francesco is an innocent by comparison.'

'Not so innocent,' said Fofò.

'Well observed,' said Calogero. 'One misjudges one's children all the time. They constantly surprise us.' He poured two more glasses on vin santo. 'How are your sons?'

'Both excellent. Both good, stay-at-home, sort of boys. Salvatore even looks like me, even if we are not blood relatives, not that he knows that, not that he ever needs to find out. William is a delight. They are both studious, and they get on with each other. It is very nice.'

'Are they good-looking?'

'Not really. Well, you can't have everything. They have not inherited their mother's beauty. That all went to Traiano.'

'They could have inherited yours,' said Calogero.

'They may in time,' said Fofò. 'Your eldest is a fine little fellow. Not so little. Anna says he has inherited Stefania's good looks.'

'And her wilfulness,' said Calogero. 'Anna Maria's sons are younger and much more biddable. Renato has grown up too fast.'

'As perhaps has Francesco,' said Fofò.

They were interrupted by the mother of the same Francesco opening the door, announcing that Nino Santacroce was there to see Calogero. Calogero admitted that he was expecting him. Nino entered, greeted the boss, and then greeted the photographer. Fofò prepared to leave, knowing that this was perhaps some business that he did not want to get involved in. He left the flat, took the lift downstairs, then, knowing he would have time before the next train to Syracuse, went into the Church of the Holy Souls to admire the Spanish Madonna. He was about to leave, when he met Nino coming in.

'You were not long,' he said to Nino.

'I just had to deliver a message. Well, two messages,' said Nino.

'I will send you the photographs I took soon,' said Fofò.

'I'd forgotten about them, sir, so much has happened in the meantime.'

'It has,' agreed Fofò, not mentioning his stepson. 'I was just here to pray for Cristoforo; he is buried in the crypt.'

'Ah, poor little boy. That was a tragedy, one among many,' said Nino.

'Yes.'

'Are you sad he is dead?' asked Nino, meaning Traiano. 'I presume you realise he is dead.'

'I do realise, and I am sad. He was, well, he was a charming boy when I first knew him. He liked me a great deal, which won my heart. And he... well, he loved his wife and children, didn't he? When he lost them, he lost everything.'

'He didn't like all children, though, did he?' said Nino bitterly. 'There was Paolo Bednarowski and there was me, and there were others. He used us. Yes, I know, he was a powerful man, how could we say no? - I was ten years old, my father was in prison, my mother needed the money, we were poor, and, well, he was charming, he was persuasive. And maybe I did not mind. Maybe worse things have happened to children.'

'I am sorry for you,' said Fofò, feeling this was inadequate. 'I am sorry he is dead, in the sense that I am sorry it ended like this, his life. But in many ways, I am glad he is dead, because his life was beyond redemption. It would not have got better. I am glad because his two half-brothers, my sons, now will never know him, which is good. I just worry about my wife, though I think she knows in her heart what has happened. Something like this was inevitable.'

'He blames me,' said Nino, pointing upward, meaning not God, but the boss. 'He said that I should have stopped Francesco. Or that Marco should. But now that Trajan is dead, they will blame the murder of don Costantino on him as well. And they will be able to do that quite easily, unless something goes seriously wrong.'

'You mean…?'

'Yes. They might catch Francesco. You never know. They might be looking for him right now. Goodness knows what evidence they have found already. They may have made arrests. They want to be seen to be doing something, I am sure.'

'If they arrest Francesco….'

Fofò contemplated the consequences of that for a moment. How would Calogero feel? How would his wife, the boy's mother feel? Who would she blame? And how would the signora Tancredi, the mother of the younger boys, react?

Calogero had left the house and was sauntering towards the Cathedral Square, along the via Etnea. His appointment was in the bar opposite the Cathedral, which was always full, and where clandestine meetings were easy to arrange. He did not like the fact that the police colonel, Andreazza, had said he would meet him there in twenty minutes, as if Andreazza were doing him a favour; he did not like this, though it was true. He was on the back foot, not a comfortable place to be, not a position he was used to. He despised the boy-loving Andreazza and hated to make use of him, but there was really no choice in the matter this time. Besides, Andreazza's weakness meant he was pliable and useful. And Nino, who he rather liked, had the run of the police headquarters in piazza Santa Nicolella; the future son-in-law of a policeman, a future policeman himself, and the man who supplied all the police with their cocaine, their girls, their boys, which amounted to most of them.

He entered the bar and saw Andreazza at the counter with a cup of what seemed to be tea. He ordered an American whiskey from Tennessee and stood next to him. He was aware that Andreazza was aware of him.

'What is the latest on the Messina case?' he asked.

'You know more than I do, surely?' said Andreazza.

'Maybe. I want to know what you know.'

'The flat where Petrović died is a real mess, thanks to the flooding. They think that there will be little valuable forensic evidence. But we have made arrests. The son, Dimitri Petrović. He was seen entering the place on the Sunday morning. He went to see his father regularly; people knew who he was. We have picked him up, and our witnesses say he was not alone when he called in on his father, and when he left some time later. That second person is the one we are looking for. He holds the key to the whole thing. The trouble is, no one recognised him, no one got a really good look at him. But perhaps you know who he was? But we may well find out, because we have made two further arrests. Petrović's bodyguards, attempting to leave the island, two Serbs, arrested at Catania Airport. Now, what do you think of that?'

'Well, that was a stroke of luck,' said Calogero sourly.

'It was. As soon as we knew that someone had killed the leading Serb gangster in Sicily, we decided to keep a watch on all ports for young Serbian men. These two are now in custody, and we are working on the assumption that they were Petrović's bodyguards, who betrayed him, and who were fleeing for their lives.'

'They fled rather slowly, if you do not mind me saying. If Petrović was killed on Sunday morning, and his body not discovered for some considerable hours afterwards, these people had ample time to get away. And if I were going to Serbia in a hurry, I would not be going via Catania Airport. I would be getting a boat to Malta and flying from there. But perhaps Serbs are a bit thick, eh? Now let me tell you something, which you can pass on to your police colleagues. The person behind this was Trajan Antonescu, whom you know, or whom you knew quite well. He landed in Sicily on Saturday very early, on a flight from Rome. He had come from Dubai, I imagine, and before that East Africa. He was travelling on a false passport, possibly under the name of Gaetano Salimbeni, but it could have been some other pseudonym. On Sunday morning, he killed Costantino Petrović. Now he is God knows where. He's an invisible man, and you will never catch him.'

Andreazza sighed.

'And why would Antonescu kill Petrović?'

He explained the Africa situation.

'So, this is the story I am supposed to sell?' asked Andreazza wearily. 'I mean, I can sell it, if that is what you want, but will anyone buy it?'

'It is plausible,' insisted Calogero. 'Get an arrest warrant out for Antonescu. Start a hue and cry. Give all these lazy policemen something to do.'

'As you say,' said Andreazza. 'If you think it is a good idea. You are the one who commands.'

Andreazza left. He ordered another American whiskey. God, the stuff was vile, but it suited his mood. He did not have long to wait. The Mayor of Catania entered, shaking hands, and coming to rest next to him at the bar.

'This is a mess,' said Volta. 'I saw Andreazza crossing the square. So, you must realise it is a mess. Is it one of your creation?'

'No, it is not,' he replied irritably.

'Then whose?'

'For goodness' sake, this is Sicily. It could be many people. I was his business partner, but he had a lot of enemies. He was a Serb. They kill each other for very little reason. He had lots of Serbs around him. I gather two are in custody. And if you need someone else, there is always Trajan Antonescu, who had a grudge against him.'

'He had a grudge against the whole world, but I am surprised you want to throw him under the bus, or at least in the direction of the forces of law and order. I imagine he is dead, and that this is a false scent to distract the police. You have done that sort of thing before, I remember, blaming Gino Fisichella for all sorts of things once he was safely dead. How long have we known each other? When will you ever tell me the truth?'

'My lies have made you rich,' said Calogero. 'But please, let us not quarrel. We need each other. The fact that Petrović is out of the way is very good news for me, and that means for you as well. Trust me. You will reap the benefit. You really will. And if I do not tell you the truth, it is merely to protect you from knowing things that would embarrass you. But I will tell you the truth now. It is a mess, as you rightly observe, and none of it is of my doing. I am a careful man, and I try not to make messes, because, well, because they need cleaning up. Best to not make a mess in the first place. Someone has killed Petrović, but not with my approval.'

'But you know who,' said Volta.

He ignored this.

'The mess has been made. The only question is how we clean it up.'

'We?' asked Volta.

'What affects me, affects you. First of all, this is a Messina business, not a Catania business. Such things do not happen here. That is the first point for you to emphasise. Secondly, Petrović was a Serb. That is very important. Not one of us. A savage from the Balkans, a man who murdered his own father, and now, well, may have been murdered by someone close to him. Look at the family, the wife, the son, the mistress in Africa, the children there. Jealousy is corrosive. A man with two wives, two families, it was never destined to end well.'

Volta, who was drinking a small glass of vermouth, nodded.

'You have had two wives,' he pointed out. 'No, three. That will be your destruction too.'

'Don't worry about me. I will survive.'

'This may finish you,' said Volta.

'Don't count on it,' said Calogero.

When he walked back to the quarter, there was Marco standing in front of the Church.

'Well?' he asked. 'The police have got the two Serbs, the bodyguards.'

'I looked everywhere, asked everyone, tried everything, boss. They had fled. They knew we were after them, the other Serbs were after them…'

'You failed,' said Calogero.

'Sorry, boss.'

'Let's hope the lawyers do better,' he said, passing on.

Bronte was boring. He spent the day with the English couple, visiting the house of Lord Nelson, which contained a not very interesting museum, made even less interesting by the fact that Nelson, despite being the duke of the place, had never been there. But the English couple were very nice, and they had a good lunch, and in the evening, he went to find Piuccio Forcella, which was not hard, and to invite himself to stay the night there. He knew Piuccio very slightly, and Piuccio knew who he was, and asked no questions. Then the next day, saying goodbye to the English couple, he decided to go back to Piazza Armerina, asking Piuccio to drive him there. He arrived at the Trattoria Norma at lunchtime and then went home with Paoluzzu. He was tired; he gave Paoluzzu his clothes back, asking him to put them in the wash; then he had a shower and a rest, and then dressed once more in new clothes, also belonging to Paoluzzu. He told Paoluzzu that he had quarrelled with his father, and would like to stay for a few days, without anyone knowing he was there; Paoluzzu's parents were to be trusted, they could know he was there. But the beautiful girls of Piazza Armerina, it was best he tell them nothing.

'Paoluzzu has messaged,' said Claudia, looking at her phone.

'He likes you so much,' said Ida.

'I know he does,' said Claudia.

'But I like you more,' said Ida.

'I know you do,' said Claudia.

The two girls giggled. They were in Ida's bedroom, 'studying', or at least that is what they had told don Nunzio and his wife, and the parents, who were very committed to their daughter's university studies, knew they were not to be disturbed, as did the younger children. Besides, the door was firmly locked. They were free to pursue their studies in peace. They had been doing this for the last three months.

'Does little Paoluzzu tell you how much he loves you?' asked Ida.

'All the time,' said Claudia.

'And you believe him?'

'He may think he does. But what he really means is that he wants to go to bed with me. But I believe you when you say it, and I feel it when you say it. When he does, well, I have to say I grin and bear it. He is a reasonably good kisser, but not as good as you, sweetest.'

'That is nice to hear,' said Ida.

She demonstrated her superior proficiency in kissing. For a moment, they both forgot about boys, forgot about everything, except the beauty of that moment. After a short while, it was necessary to return to real life and the boring subject of boys.

'The other one is very respectful,' said Ida, meaning Francesco. 'But that is because he has a girlfriend already, whom his father does not like.'

'He told you?'

'He did. We have to talk about something when gallant Paoluzzu is pursuing you. He even told me who she was, and why his father does not like her. She is Petra Costacurta, and her brother is married to don Calogero's ex-wife. I know, how complicated. And this Petra is a friend of someone from Palermo called Emma Santucci. And that family are the rivals and partners of don Calogero. They are all very friendly on the surface, but deep down they do not like each other, I reckon.'

Ida lay back on the pillow, her magnificent dark hair framing her lovely face.

'Business,' she said.

'What has that to do with us?' asked Claudia.

'A great deal. Everything. We have to live with these men. What does Paoluzzu say?'

'He says that he does not know when Francesco will be back, and can we meet up without him. And I am going to say, no, we can't, because if my father finds out, he will be annoyed. Very annoyed. I think he will accept that. He is quite timid, you know.'

'Except when....'

'Yes, except when.... Are all boys like that?'

'Yes. Or so I imagine,' said Ida.

'Oh, I saw a beautiful policewoman in the Via Etnea last time I was in Catania. I think they must choose them for their looks. Maybe we should become policewomen, what do you think?'

'The uniform…..' said Ida. 'But then men would tell us what to do all day, and that would not be so good. So, where has Francesco gone? People don't just disappear, do they?'

She looked at Claudia seriously.

'Some people do, I believe,' said Claudia. 'Some people just disappear and are never seen again. You know that.'

They were both serious now.

'You don't think that someone has killed Francesco, do you?' asked Ida.

'Would you care if they had?' asked Claudia.

'I think I would,' said Ida in all seriousness. 'I like him. I mean, not in that way, but he is a nice boy. And… there is the business angle. My father, my mother, he understands, because he has lived in the same world. Do you think it would be so very awful doing it with him?'

'It would be awful doing it with any boy,' said Claudia. 'I imagine thy grunt a lot and grind their teeth, and sweat, and horrible things like that. But if you had to do it with someone, then Francesco di Rienzi would be less unpleasant than most. He's eager to please; he is, what is the word I am looking for, amenable. I mean, if you were with him, you would tell him what to do, and he would do it. Not just in bed, but generally. Like your mother gives orders to your father, and he does what she says.'

'In the house,' Ida pointed out. 'Only at home. Not outside it.'

'But who cares what goes on outside the house?' said Claudia. 'I mean, that is their world, isn't it?'

They were both thoughtful.

'I would like to find out more about Emma Santucci,' said Ida. 'I mean, you cannot choose your father, but you can choose your husband, and the fact that your father is who he is doesn't mean you have to marry someone like him, does it?'

'You don't have to marry anyone at all,' said Claudia.

'We don't,' agreed Ida. 'But we don't have to tell them that, do we? I like keeping them guessing… I intend to bat them all away until they lose interest, or I get to thirty; then I might settle for Francesco, and he for me. He is very biddable, and the chances are the children will be pretty. And I would not have to do it very often, would I? I mean, after the children were born, he would develop other interests….' She paused. 'That murder the other day,' she said.

'In Messina? Or the one in Catania? The tobacconist of Librino?' asked Claudia.

'I mean, Francesco…. Surely not?' said Ida. 'Though Paoluzzu did say he had a gun.'

Claudia was thoughtful.

'I think we had better get dressed,' she said, picking up some items of clothing. 'Oh, I do like this bra of yours. You must tell me where you got it again.'

Claudia was asked to stay for supper.

'You have been working so hard,' said Ida's mother, as she served the vegetable soup.

'Sappho is a very hard author, signora,' said Claudia.

'But immensely rewarding,' said Ida.

Her mother beamed. It was such a joy to have a studious and beautiful daughter, who unlike every other girl in Piazza Armerina, did not seem to be boy mad.

'Are you seeing Francesco di Rienzi soon?' asked Don Nunzio after his first slurp of soup.

'Well, Papà,' said Ida, 'We just got a message from Paoluzzu, his friend; you know they are best friends, and Francesco does not have a phone. Paoluzzu said he was not going to be around for a few days at least. So, no. I won't be seeing him soon. I am not sure when the next time will be. Paoluzzu was vague.'

'Well, he is a nice boy, a good boy, and sometimes he may well have to do stuff that necessitates an absence.'

'Sir,' said Claudia, 'Has he been arrested, do you think, is he in jail?'

'My dear Claudia,' said don Nunzio easily. 'What on earth makes you think that?'

'Boys go off, they do stuff,' said Ida's mother. 'He is a good boy, I am sure.'

'Paoluzzu says he carries a gun, signora,' said Claudia.

Both parents looked at the younger children, who had not noticed this, so busy were they with their soup. The subject was changed.

After supper, while the signora cleared away, and the younger children went to watch television, the subject was resumed.

'Paoluzzu told you he had seen him with a gun?' asked don Nunzio.

There was no avoiding an answer, Claudia saw.

'Sir, that was the impression I got; that he saw his gun, or thought he had a gun, or something like that.'

'Boys are silly,' said don Nunzio, something his daughter and Claudia themselves believed. 'They like to boast. Perhaps Francesco boasted to Paoluzzu, and Paoluzzu passed the boast on, thinking it made him look important by association. Well, Paoluzzu should keep his mouth shut. Next time I see him, I may remind him of that. As for Francesco, well, he is a nice boy, and, I hope, not in any sort of trouble. Has he ever said anything to you that gave you the impression he might get into trouble?'

'No, Papà.'

'No, sir.'

'And he is respectful?'

'Very, Papà.'

'Good. Of course, he is not don Calogero's son, but he might as well be, so much does don Calogero love him and his mother. And I need hardly tell you, girls, that life in Sicily and life in Piazza Armerina in particular is… precarious. I mean, we are doing well here, I mean, I am doing well here, and so is your family, Claudia, but there are pressures on us all the time. We need the friendship of don Calogero. I need not say more than that. And if you and his stepson become friends, Ida, well, so much the better. Not that I… well, you understand. If you find out where Francesco is, please let me know at once. The reason I ask is that he seems to have disappeared. The reason I know that is because his stepfather, don Calogero himself, cannot find him. He told me so, because he sent a message asking whether he was here or not. If we find him and send him home, don Calogero will be grateful. And I do not need to explain to you what a difference the goodwill of don Calogero makes to us all. We may not notice it most of the time, but we must not take it for granted. Look, you had better tell Paoluzzu to come and see me, sooner rather than later.'

The girls both nodded.

Chapter Eight

Something truly disturbing had happened. The television was full of football and gameshows, and news about the latest eruption of Mount Etna, but there was nothing about the murder in Messina; nothing about the disappearance of Antonescu; nothing about the tobacconist of Librino either. It was all very worrying. There was clearly a news blackout. This did not mean they were not investigating; rather it meant the opposite – they were, and they were making progress, and they did not want anyone to know until they made their surprise arrests. For the first time in his life, Calogero felt a sense of dread. He had always been one step ahead of the police, indeed more than just one, but now it seemed they were one step ahead of him. He was being outmanoeuvred, and he was no longer in control, and all because of the ambitions of his stepson. It was quite possible what Andreazza had hinted; that Francesco might bring down the whole edifice though his amateurishness and his stupidity. He had told him; he had told him so many times that he was not to touch Antonescu. As for the hit on Costantino Petrović, that he had reserved for Marco, who was trustworthy, and for Omar, who was a man who could be relied on. But not for an eighteen-year-old boy; he had been assigned the easy task of silencing the tobacconist of Librino. That was his level.

To make matters worse, the women in his life were doing their best, without intending to, to drive him mad. Obviously Agata was worried about her son, and she was not stupid; she understood what had happened, without knowing the details. The boy was in hiding - that was clear enough - and might be arrested. She said nothing, but it was clear what she wanted, what he could not give her: an assurance that all would be well, that the boy would come home, that there would be no charges, that the police would charge someone else, the police would be made to see sense, or some clever lawyers would, at a high price, make the charges go away. But this was wishful thinking, he knew, even though the wife whom he adored, and who adored him, believed him to be all-powerful. He had once believed himself to be all-powerful, but now, his luck, his good fortune, was coming to an end, he feared.

If Agata was a problem, if her silence was a reproach, his mother, oh my goodness, his mother was much worse. She did not keep silent. She told him what she thought. She was very fond of Francesco, and she knew that he had done something, but she did not care what in her rush to blame not him, but his stepfather. Calogero had failed. He should have been stricter; sometimes this changed – he had been too strict. Whichever way, it was his fault, and Francesco's absence upset the other children.

Those other children, Renato, Sebastiano and Romano, had a mother in the shape of Anna Maria Tancredi, and the dottoressa had not held back on the phone. What, she had demanded, was going on? She meant primarily the demise of their business partner don Costantino. Of course, he could not discuss it over the phone, so he agreed to go to Palermo and meet her there for lunch. They had met at a small restaurant where they were both confident that nothing would be overheard, or if overheard, nothing passed on. He knew she was intelligent, and he told her the whole story, knowing that he might as well, for she would only find out for herself sooner or later. After he finished the narration, she was thoughtful.

'Well,' she said at last. 'Congratulations on hoovering up all these interests in Messina. As for don Costantino, we shall not miss him. Have the Serbs given any trouble?'

'The Serbs have been the easiest of people to deal with. The one in hospital in Africa, Slobodan, is a popular fellow. He is the one whom Costantino tried to have done away with. They are rallying around him. That is the situation there. The wife there is realistic enough to know that her main card has been taken away from her. Slobodan will leave hospital, and she will be dependent on his mercy. He may well be magnanimous. There's a daughter; there is a son - twins in their early teens. Slobodan has already adopted the girl. The Serbs over here know that the one person who holds their fate in his hands is me. They have come to see me to make their claims, to keep their jobs, all except the two bodyguards on duty. My fear is that those two have gone over to the police and fingered Francesco.'

'You must cut him loose,' said Anna Maria.

'That is easy for you to say.'

She sighed: 'I am not being personal. You can send him to America. This is business, after all. Or send him to Africa. Whichever way, don't let him drag everything down with him. Is it certain Antonescu is dead?'

'Yes. Just what happened is not clear, and there's no body, but yes, he is dead.'

'I will tell the wife, if you like. Her husband is dead, and her cousin killed him. Well, I do not need to tell her that, and she may not ask, as she will not want to know. How has his mother taken it?'

'I am not sure. I think we are letting her think he is not dead, just gone somewhere....'

'That is cruel,' said Anna Maria. 'But you were always cruel, weren't you?'

'I am the father of your children,' he said. 'I make lots of money for you and for them. Where do you think money comes from?'

She nodded.

'You were always good at making money,' she said. 'But listen, we cannot have Francesco near the three boys. You do understand that, don't you? You have to send him away or let the police lock him up. You cannot be sentimental about his.'

'I understand,' he said.

Then they spoke about the three boys and their education, and their going to school in England.

After lunch, he walked up the via Ruggero Settimo towards the Santucci offices to go and talk to his sister, her husband, and her husband's cousin. It was quite possible he might meet Roberto Costacurta, but if he did, he was pretty sure that Costacurta would find the meeting more painful than he would. As it was, on entering the building, he was told that his sister was there, and so was don Giuseppe, as they now called him. He went up, and there was Beppe, the person he wanted to see, sitting at a desk and a computer in a little glass office, making phone calls. He gestured for him to approach.

He was talking to a supplier about lemons. Unlike everyone else in the office, he was wearing, not a suit, or smart clothes, but jeans, a jumper, and a frayed shirt. His shirt hung out, and he wore trainers. His hair was neatly cut, and he had a small well-trimmed beard. His voice, as he spoke on the phone, was warm, and his lips were smiling. Only his eyes seemed dead. He was leaning back in his chair, and his feet were resting on the desk. With his free hand, he was scratching his testicles. Eventually, he put the phone down.

'The new factory. Preserved lemons. The struggle to get enough lemons to preserve! One has to keep the suppliers sweet. They are nice people; they are our people. They are only too willing to help. Most of them speak about my grandfather with awe in their voices. Anyway…' He got up, put his arms around Calogero and kissed him on the lips. 'You don't like the beard, I can see, but everyone has one, at least everyone round here. We have not seen you for months!'

They both sat down.

'New wife, new baby, well, second baby as well. It keeps me busy, and it keeps me at home.'

'That is what we hear. How many children have you got now? I have lost count.'

'Isabella, Natalia, Renato, Sebastiano, Romano, Giovanni and Tino, if you count them, and then little Calogero, plus the next arrival.'

'Nine,' observed Beppe. 'I admire your productivity. Your wife is well?'

'Very. How is your girlfriend?'

'Rosalia? She is in Naples. She will be back for Christmas. She works hard, much more than I do. I confess I neglect the university, preferring to do this. But not her. She is an intellectual.'

'She does not come back? You do not go there at weekends?'

'Too far. Why should I? We can speak on the phone. Unlike you, I am not sex mad. I mean, we have done it, to mark the territory, so to speak, but I don't make a big thing of it. I am not that interested. When we are married, we will have children, but before then, I don't see much point in these practice runs. I am happy without it. She knows that and accepts it. Her brother, my best friend, is crazy about this girl in Rome. They are still together, or rather not together, as she is there and he is here. He goes up to Rome whenever he can, and they spend the weekend in a hotel, in bed. Then he comes back here and is miserable. Poor Riccardo. I feel sorry for him. There are better things in life.'

'Like what?'

'Like walking into a room, and everyone paying attention. Like a whole room going quiet when you talk. Like you coming all the way from Catania to speak to me to ask a favour.'

Calogero laughed.

'How are the family?' he asked, ignoring this.

'The family? My mother is well, Emma is well, her children and her husband are fine, he is such a nice guy, better than she deserves; my cousin is as crazy as ever, but keeps himself amused. Your sister is fine, I am sure. Renzo spends an awful lot of time with Costacurta, as I am sure you know. They are inseparable. My father, the same as ever, never comes to Palermo. Muniddu is well. Yes, we are all well, and very close knit. My late brother Sandro is never mentioned; and neither is that little fellow who came among us, Tonino Grassi. His daughter, my niece, is sweet. I think Emma takes her to Catania regularly to see her grandparents, which is only right. And you? You did not mention your stepson. We heard…'

'I am sure you did,' said Calogero quickly. 'And that is what I came about. I may need your help.'

Beppe looked at him blandly, but Calogero could tell he was savouring the triumph. Here was the most powerful man in Sicily asking for his help. He felt the humiliation bitterly. But he did not show it. He smiled. But he vowed he would not forget this. The Santucci family were only there because they were manageable. But they seemed to be getting unmanageable, he reflected.

'Obviously we will help,' said Beppe. 'Just as you would help us.'

He was made to wait, and wait he did, his fears rising the longer he waited. Paoluzzu was not a very brave boy. He realised this now. The friendship of Francesco had made him feel as if he were brave, but all he felt now, having to present himself to don Nunzio, was a terrible fear. He was sitting in the hallway of the house, quite oblivious that this was the place where the best friend of the girl he loved lived, conscious only of the fact that this was the home of the ogre don Nunzio, who just happened to be her father. He tried to calm himself by thinking rationally, hard as that was. If don Nunzio wanted him dead, he would certainly kill him, but he had not done so yet, that was surely – he was not sure how the logic worked – an indication that he would not kill him ever. Besides, he was too unimportant to kill. Surely they would not bother. And what was he supposed to have done? He tried to think, but nothing came.

Don Nunzio's wife passed him several times, assuring him that her husband would be home soon, which was not very comforting, and asking him if he would like a cup of coffee as he waited. He politely declined: his bowels had alternatively turned to ice and at the same time rumbled threateningly: he felt the stab of terror. The signora's friendliness just made him more and more uncomfortable. Ida, he knew, was in Catania today, thank the Lord; he would not want her or Claudia to see him like this.

Don Nunzio arrived.

'There is someone waiting to see you,' his wife called from the kitchen.

'So I see,' he observed without emotion.

He opened the office door, and indicated that Paoluzzu should go in. He closed the door behind him. He took his seat at the desk, while Paoluzzu stood.

'You seem a nice boy,' said don Nunzio at last. 'My daughter and her friend Claudia seem to like you. I gave you your job at the request of don Calogero, of course, and I know about your parents. Nice people, good people. And then your head was turned, wasn't it, by that boy Francesco. Well, I understand. When I was your age, or a bit younger, my head was turned by boys of my age who seemed to have a certain confidence about them, who carried knives and guns, who used knives and guns, who had money and respect. So, I decided I would be like them; and I became like them; and I became even tougher than them. But you, my sweet handsome boy, you are not tough, are you?'

'I am just the manager of the Trattoria Norma, don Nunzio, sir,' said Paoluzzu, feeling he was expected to say something.

He had overcome the terrible wobbly feeling in his bowels, but nothing could stop the tears.

'Yes, that is your level,' said don Nunzio. 'You should not try to rise above it. You should not associate with people like Francesco. In fact, it goes further. Someone like Francesco should have stuck to his own level; but he did not; he rose, through accident, but he seized his chance; he rose. I suppose one should admire that. He is brave. He took the risk, and now…. And you told my daughter and her friend that Francesco had a gun, didn't you?'

He nodded mutely. He could not remember doing so, but he must have done.

'That annoys me. Not that Francesco has a gun - that is normal - but it is the sort of thing I do not want my daughter to think of as normal. I had thought he would be a nice friend for her, but…. You, Paoluzzu are a little fool. But he, Francesco is a much bigger fool. He rose, and now he will fall. Like that man who made the wings out of wax, what's his name? My daughter studies the classics, she would know.'

'Icarus, sir.'

'Indeed, Icarus. He is so famous that we are still talking about him, if indeed he ever existed. This Francesco too… do you know what he has done?'

'No, sir.'

'But you can guess?'

Paoluzzu was silent.

'Tell me what you know,' commanded don Nunzio.

Paoluzzu considered. Confession was the safest option, he realised.

'He had a gun, don Nunzio. I saw it. But he does not have it anymore. When he came here that day…'

'What day?'

'The day before the Messina murder, his suit and his shoes were covered with mud; and he gave me the suit to dry clean, and the rest of his clothes to wash, and he had a long shower, and in his pocket he had a freezer bag which I had given him, and in it was something that I recognised as a man's ear.'

'So, when they arrest him for murder, they will arrest you for being a co-conspirator or else an accessory after the fact. How would you like to spend time in Piazza Lanza, Paoluzzu?'

'Not at all, sir. Are they going to arrest him?'

'We must never underestimate the stupidity of the police, but it is always possible. One person is worried, and that is don Calogero. I was out today, but the message reached me from Catania that don Calogero wants his stepson at all costs. He wants to get to him before the police can. No doubt he will hide him away, better than anyone else can. Don Calogero has a fatherly concern for all his children. Where is the miscreant?'

'With me, sir.'

'Keep him there. Don't let him go away without telling me. I will tell his stepfather, and he will collect him. It may be in a day or two. I am glad you told me. I had guessed as much.'

There was silence.

'I am glad you are so co-operative, so weak,' said don Nunzio. 'I am glad that you have not thought to usurp my authority. I am glad you are so pliable. So many young men are not. Tell me, has Francesco touched my daughter?'

'No, sir, he is very respectful.'

'And have you touched Claudia?'

'No, sir, I am very respectful too.'

'Have you had a girlfriend?' asked don Nunzio.

'Yes, sir, I have.'

'I like Claudia; as Francesco will no longer be here, if you want to entertain her - nothing disrespectful of course - I approve. She needs a young man to go around with, a respectful one, one who respects her and respects me. You can come and have lunch with us one day soon, when Claudia joins us. My wife likes you, Paoluzzu, and I am sure Ida will too, if she does not already. I like you. You're not like all the other young men I know. Come here, kneel in front of me, and kiss my hand.'

Francesco was growing bored of the flat in which Paoluzzu lived with his parents. He had spent a lot of time asleep, a lot of time looking at Paoluzzu's laptop surfing the internet, he had even browsed the small collection of books in the room. He had looked at Paoluzzu's clothes, gone through his drawers, checked out all the secret things that Paoluzzu imagined would remain secret; when his parents were out, he had watched the television, wondering why there was nothing on the news about the Messina murder. Then, after less than two days of this enforced idleness, his father came to him, quietly, and surprisingly. The bedroom door opened, and don Calogero stood there.

'I guessed you would be here,' said his stepfather, as the boy stumbled to his feet. 'I mean, it is the most obvious place, if, that is, you are hiding from me. If you were hiding from the police, Catania would be better. The Purgatory quarter is full of little hiding places. But, anyway, here I am, and here you are.'

Calogero was not smiling. There was silence between them.

'I am sorry,' said Francesco at last.

'Words that always come too late, that come after the damage has been done,' observed Calogero.

'I did it....'

'I know why you did it,' said Calogero. 'I understand that. And yes, you took the opportunity when it was offered, while it was offered, before the offer was snatched away. You took advantage of a very small window before it closed. Well done. You are brave, even foolhardy. As for Antonescu and Petrović, well, good riddance to them. No one is sorry that they are dead, not even Petrović's fellow Serbs, two of whom have been arrested, and, I discovered today, charged with conspiracy to murder.

They were caught trying to leave the country. The police were on the lookout for any Serbs leaving the country after the murder of don Costantino. They are not entirely stupid. The two Serbs are in the frame for the murder. As is a third person, Dimitri. The three of them were placed in the flat at the correct time. He too is in custody. He is not strong. I believe the police think they will crack him. At least, that is the information I have, and it took me some time to get it, for the police investigation is watertight so far; no leaks, no speculation, no spinning, just silence. Very worrying. Even Andreazza did not have a clue what was going on. I had to go to Bonelli's old friend Pasquale Greco, the one who is in the fine art department, not immediately connected with a case like this, but who knew people who knew people… They are waiting to arrest the fourth person of interest, the one who left the flat in company with Dimitri, and that person is you.'

'But no one saw me leave, dad. They can't have done. I was just a normal boy walking down the street. And there can't be any forensic evidence linking me to the scene. The flood, the others who were there…'

'True,' agreed Calogero. 'They only have one way of linking you to the flat, and it's not forensic, or camera evidence: it is the simple fact that one of the three in custody may have spoken. Let us assume that. But which one may have spoken, we cannot at present know. The other two may not know either; maybe the police have told each one of them separately that the others have spoken, to prompt a confession.'

'I don't believe it,' said Francesco. 'The Serbs would never speak. They would go down for being accessories to murder first. Dimitri would never speak. It is not that he is so brave, but because he fears us more than he fears jail. Besides, who would ever believe that Dimitri would be man enough to kill his father, or the Serbs would kill their boss? Or that you, or donna Rosa would arrange to have him murdered by Dimitri of all people?'

'I don't entirely believe it myself,' said Calogero. 'But I am not inclined to take the risk. Tell me about the passport and the ear.'

'How do you know about them?'

'Dimitri told me when he came to Catania. Where are the passport and the ear now?'

'Gone, completely gone. I fed the ear to a hungry dog in the street in Bronte, when I stayed with Piuccio Forcella. As for the passport, I ripped it up, page by page, and disposed of each page separately, some in bins, some down the lavatory. Neither object exists anymore.'

'Thank the Lord for that. Did the dog really eat the ear?'

'It was a hungry dog, dad. A stray.'

Calogero winced.

'You see, they will arrest you for the murder of Petrović, citing Dimitri and the two Serbs as accessories or co-conspirators, in the hope that one of them at least will make a deal with the prosecution. At least, that is what I think they will do. But that is just part of it. There is also the tobacconist of Librino. The information I have is that you are in the frame for that.'

'They are bluffing,' said Francesco. 'They are pretending to have evidence they cannot possibly have. Marco and I were very careful. We were wearing nondescript clothes, and the bike was stolen. They could not see our faces, as we wore helmets with visors. We wore gloves. We dumped the bike near the Villa Bellini, we dumped the helmets and the gloves separately in public bins and then we stripped off completely in the gym and had long showers, making sure we cleaned ourselves very thoroughly, and we threw all our outer clothes down the shaft.'

'What did you do with the gun? Who saw you throw your clothes down the shaft and spend a long, long time cleaning yourselves?'

'Just our usual trustworthy friends. That was the day they brought Dimitri to see us…'

'And he was there?'

Francesco nodded dumbly.

'The gun. Did he see the gun?''

'We had to clean the gun,' said Francesco miserably. 'He was there. He must have seen it.'

'What did you do with the gun afterwards? Think carefully.'

'I took it upstairs and I hid it in the secret compartment of the wardrobe, under the bottom of the wardrobe in my bedroom, where no one could find it. After all, we know the police would never dare raid your flat, dad, don't we? It was completely safe there. And afterwards, I took it with me to Syracuse and used it on Antonescu and then threw it into the fountain, which is full of mud and weeds.'

'This secret compartment in the wardrobe, what else do you keep there?'

'Just stuff I do not want my mother to see when she is cleaning or tidying up. You know… you told me. When I meet girls. Male stuff. Embarrassing stuff.'

Calogero was silent.

'Well, the gun is beyond recovery, but they can compare the bullet used on the tobacconist with the bullet that killed Antonescu. Where did the bullet that killed Antonescu go?'

'I think it went into the sofa,' he said miserably. 'But I am not sure.'

'And where is the corpse?'

He went over to the laptop and opened the maps. He pointed to the place.

'About thirty metres from the shore.'

'We will find it before they do, and move it somewhere safer,' said Calogero, memorising the place. He sighed. 'We have got to assume that Dimitri is the traitor. The gun, the tobacconist, the ear, the passport… But time will tell. If the two Serbs and Dimitri are sent down for conspiracy to murder, it will mean they have not spoken. But the case may take years to come to court. I find it hard to think it could be Dimitri, if only because he would be terrified of his mother, and he would be worried for his sister and prospective brother-in-law. If he has betrayed us, then they all suffer, don't they? But the real conspirators were you and me, or so they will want to prove; the others were mere accessories. But if they get hold of you… no one will believe it was you on your own. They will believe it was me. As it is, if it is the Serbs and Dimitri, well, it is a little intra-Serb war, nothing to do with us honest Sicilians. I have to think of your mother.'

'My mother?'

'Yes. For you to be arrested, put on trial and then do hard labour for twenty years, it would not just punish you, it would punish her severely. And me. We have to spare her that. She has had enough suffering. Then there are the younger children to think of, and the baby she is going to have. And if they come for me as well… A person you have never met, Anna Maria Tancredi, is adamant that you will pull us all down.'

'She has never had cause to like me.'

'Indeed. But she is a good businesswoman. She does not particularly like me, either. But… I have spoken to Beppe Santucci.'

'About me?'

'About you, correct. It was that, or speak to the Arabs, or speak to the Serbs in Africa, or worse, in Serbia. The Santucci family have connexions with New York. So do I, but they are connections I share with them. Beppe will help. You will go to America, and soon. False passport; new identity. And then, when all this is over, when they release the two Serbs and Dimitri on bail, and then drop the charges for lack of evidence, then you can come back.'

'But they will charge me for the tobacconist of Librino,' said Francesco.

'Who else knew about that?' asked Calogero. 'Who did you tell?'

'Marco knew,' said Francesco. 'Obviously. He was there. You knew. But no one else knew. We never mentioned it, we never discussed it, apart from amongst us three. We kept perfect silence. The other boys would have been able to put two and two together, as would Dimitri, but no one knew.'

'The police think you were responsible for the tobacconist, but if there's no evidence that you did, nothing at all to link you to the scene, no forensic evidence, then it is all speculation, all wishful thinking on their part. They know you did it, but they cannot prove it. As for Antonescu and don Costantino Petrović, we will arrange it for them to blame someone else. Some Serb who had a grudge over the killing of this man in Africa. It can be done; it will be done. I can do it. We have lawyers; we have contacts; we have favours to call in. We will fish Antonescu out of the lake; we will get rid of that carpet; we will dump his body somewhere where it creates a sensation, or make him disappear. But we will handle all of this. It is what we do. It is a challenge, but one that we will rise to.'

The boy was thoughtful, subdued.

'I don't want to leave Sicily,' he said at last. 'I have never been abroad. America…. I don't want to leave my mother, I don't want to leave my brothers, I don't want to leave Paoluzzu and my other friends, I don't want to leave you…'

Tears flowed in abundance.

'Listen to me carefully,' said Calogero after a few moments. 'If you want to have the top position, you have to make sacrifices. Sometimes you sacrifice other people, and you put your feelings for them to death inside yourself. Obviously, there are certain feelings that cannot be sacrificed entirely: your mother, your brothers, your friends, and me. But it will only be for a time. You will come back stronger, and when you do, no one will question you. They will look upon you as my heir, my successor. But the one lesson you have to learn is discipline, to control yourself. You have been lucky this time. It wasn't disciplined, what you have done; it was not planned; it was the work of an inspired moment. But you have been lucky. When you come back, your reputation will be secure. They will know who you are. The Santucci family will know who you are and not dare to question you. Volta, the men of business, the police, the politicians. They will all know. A small sacrifice, going away, to be followed by a huge gain. Remember, I have chosen you, because you are your mother's son, you are my son, and I do not make bad choices. With Antonescu, it was malign fate, but before his son died, he was a good man. I should never have allowed him to marry and have children; I should have kept him close to me. But… It is too late for regrets now. You, you are different. You have learned discipline through this, and you will learn more.'

The boy nodded.

'What is in America?' he asked.

'A world of experience.'

'Friends of the Santucci family?'

'Yes.'

'And they would arrange everything?'

'Yes. A new identity.'

'Dad, I don't like Beppe Santucci, and neither do you. He's clever, he is sly, and he will use this for his advantage. Besides, he was a friend of Antonescu.'

'He was a friend of Antonescu, true, but he didn't have any feelings for him. He has no feelings for anyone.'

'Such men are dangerous,' said Francesco. 'I doubt he cared about Antonescu, but he is just the sort of man to avenge his death, not because he cares about him, but because he cares about his reputation. People would respect him for that. And he is the man to help me, you think?'

Calogero sighed. Francesco was clever; he knew that; but he showed new signs of cleverness now.

'Look, dad, have you noticed what I am wearing? No? Ever seen these clothes before now? No, you have not. They belong to Paoluzzu. We are the same size. We are cousins, after all. We even look alike. I think he is my closest male relative, isn't he? He is my second cousin, isn't he?'

'Something like that,' admitted Calogero.

Francesco went over to the chest of drawers and opened the top drawer. Inside was Paoluzzu's passport, and his identity card. He took them to his father. Calogero examined both. While he did so, Francesco took Paoluzzu's wallet, which had been on top of the chest of drawers, and examined its contents. It contained nothing of interest, apart from a bank card.

'I will need his phone too,' he said. 'But I am sure he will give it to me.'

Calogero handed back the documents.

'There's an age difference,' he remarked.

'I look older than eighteen,' said Francesco. 'I will cut my hair; I will grow a beard. No one will ever know. Besides, who checks these things? And you noticed the name in the documents. Paolo Rossi. One of the commonest in Italy. What better way is there to disappear?'

'Will he co-operate?' asked Calogero.

'Of course he will. We are friends. He loves me,' said Francesco. 'He owes me lots of favours.'

The boss sighed.

'Call him,' he said.

Twenty minutes had passed. The boss sat at the kitchen table with Paoluzzu and his parents. He had already made Francesco's excuses for not saying goodbye. The person who had brought the boss to Piazza Armerina on the back of a scooter was now taking Francesco away by the same means, heading north towards Messina. Francesco had nothing with him, apart from Paoluzzu's passport, identity and phone. The phone had the bank details. These things were the only things he needed for a new life away from Sicily.

'You must be very proud of your son,' the boss was saying to Paoluzzu's parents. 'I mean, it is not just that he is a nice-looking boy and a hard working one, but he has been a good friend to me and to my son. When he worked for us in Africa, he was someone we could trust. It goes further than that. He is someone we like. One of us. And he is doing well at the Trattoria Norma. I have been there. I like it a lot. Good food; but a trattoria is only as good as its manager, in my humble opinion. As it is, I would offer Paoluzzu a job at a bigger and better place in Catania, but I happen to know that he likes it here, well, for the usual reasons. As you know, he's met a girl. This Claudia…'

'Boss, I like her, but I am not sure she likes me that much,' said Paoluzzu modestly.

'Well, what will be, will be,' said Calogero, 'and I like to make plans. If Claudia has any sense, she will grab you with both hands, a lovely boy like you, don't you think, signora?' he asked, appealing to the mother.

'Of course, don Calogero, that is exactly what I think too. She would be crazy not to.'

'I am glad we think alike,' said Calogero. 'She comes from a good family, there is some money there, and I have heard she is beautiful, as well as being highly intelligent. I am sure she will warm to Paoluzzu and come to see what we all see, that he is a catch. But perhaps I should keep quiet on this matter, as I have not got a good track record. My first marriage – well, I do not regret it, three lovely children – but Stefania and I were very young, and you were living in Catania at the time, weren't you, and you will know that we married because she was expecting my eldest daughter. We were both seventeen… but I am very happy now. And Paoluzzu here is a second cousin of Francesco, which is another reason for me to value him. And the two of them are more like brothers than cousins. It is so nice to see. And because he likes Claudia, and he is best friends with my son, it follows that Francesco will like this girl Ida, who is Claudia's best friend. I can see two alliances, not one, on the horizon, and the double nature makes it more likely. Having said that, I wanted my eldest daughter to marry Beppe Santucci, but he has had other ideas. I was disappointed once, but hope not to be again. But one can never be sure of these things.'

His voice trailed away.

'You can be sure of one thing, boss, and that it won't be from want of trying on my part.'

'That is the spirit,' said Calogero.

He looked at his watch. It was time to go. He rose. Paoluzzu accompanied him out into the hallway, and then onto the landing outside the door to the flat.

The boss looked at him seriously.

'I have trusted you a long time, Paoluzzu, and I have rewarded you for that trust. Your father, I can tell from the way he looks at me, does not like me. Ah well, what does he know? Your mother is different. I have entrusted to you the most important thing I have.'

'Francesco, boss?'

'Yes and no. I mean my happiness, which depends on Francesco's mother, and also on Francesco. I am a man of the very deepest emotions, which are rarely engaged. My wife, my children, my sons especially, Francesco; they all mean so much to me. People may come sniffing round, wondering where he is… the police, obviously, but also people we think are our friends but perhaps do not wish us well. The Serbs, but perhaps people who are closer to home as well.'

'I will know nothing, boss, so I will have nothing to tell them.'

'They might approach your mother, or your father, or Claudia…'

'There will be nothing to say. Nothing at all.'

'This girl Ida…'

'I will talk about him to her, of course, but not say where he is, because I do not know.'

'Good. Remember what we agreed. Don't report the identity card lost or stolen, or the passport. Let him use them, and when you need one, well, how often will you need one? He may be back in about six months. Open a new bank account, at a new bank, for your own use.'

He leaned forward and felt a slight tremor as the boss put a wodge of tightly rolled banknotes into the pocket of his jeans. He felt his cheeks colour. Calogero smiled. He could trust Paoluzzu: he belonged to him, body and soul.

Don Nunzio was another who belonged to him, body and soul. He had come by motorcycle, helmeted, anonymously, and now he was here at the doorstep of don Nunzio, unannounced. He needed to make the most of his secret presence in Piazza Armerina. Don Nunzio himself had come to the door, which was surrounded by late-flowering oleanders; a child's bicycle lay on the path; from behind don Nunzio came noises of domesticity and young children. The expression on his face was one of immediate dismay – there was no time to prepare for the important visitor – they were *en famille* – followed by an expression of unalloyed delight. The boss of bosses dropping in like this was a sign of the greatest friendship.

He bent over and kissed the hand. Then he shouted to his wife that they had a visitor. He led the boss into the dining-room, where they were gathered. The wife of don Nunzio was ladling soup and looked up, alarmed, then comforted: there had never been a shortage of food in her house. The three boys looked up, startled, adoring, for they had seen don Calogero before now, and they knew who he was. The eldest, the girl Ida, looked up, amazed, despite herself, by the shock of admiration she felt for his good looks, his confidence, his clothes, his shoes, the way he transformed a room, simply by entering it. Don Calogero took the signora's hand and kissed it, as soon as she put the ladle aside. He did the same for Ida, remarking on how lovely it was to see her again; then he kissed all three boys, who received the attention with a sense of receiving a holy sacrament, while don Calogero remarked on how nice it was to see a proper Sicilian family at home, round the table. He accepted some soup. A place was made for him. He spoke to the boys about football, about the national team, and he asked the eldest whether he was going to go to university after school, or work for his father, or even, come and work in Catania for himself. He asked him if he were disciplined enough to work for his living just yet. The boy coloured and confessed his great desire to work for his father as soon as he arrived at the age of sixteen.

'Sixteen, that is the age of freedom, for boys at least,' said don Nunzio generously.

Ida raised an eyebrow, which don Calogero noticed.

'Well, I have son of eighteen, whom you all know, and he has been a bit wild in the past, but he has also been amenable to discipline when discipline is called for. He is settling down, I hope, into a serious young man. He's a brilliant coder. He and another boy, who is even younger than he is, have done the new website and app for the Most Noble and Ancient Confraternity of the Holy Souls in Purgatory. It means you can pray with the Confraternity, get daily updates to your phone, donate, subscribe, whatever. Since it started, it has become one of the most popular apps in Sicily, and not far behind on the continent. I do not understand it, I don't even have a phone, but they explained it to me. Then they have been working on Sicilia Historica, which means that whenever your phone senses you are near to some historic site it pings, and you get a little notification about the history of the place. That is a huge project. And then they want to do one called Sicilia Sanguinea, where you phone goes off whenever you approach a site of some ancient or not so ancient bloody deed. They stand to make a lot of money, or so they hope.'

'I like the Latin names,' said Ida. 'Though my main interests are Greek.'

'My name is Greek,' he said.

'I know,' she said.

God, he was beautiful, she could not help thinking to herself: the way he sat there, the way his body moved, the way, even, he spooned the soup into his mouth between those lips, the way he spoke, his gorgeous teeth, his dark and shining skin. And how old was he? Not more than thirty-five. If she were ever to stoop to sleeping with a man, this was the sort of man she would like to sleep with. He was charm itself.

'I like the Greek things in Sicily,' he said. 'The Arethusa fountain, I am very fond of. Years ago, I used to meet a colleague over lunch in Enna, and I would often think of poor Persephone being snatched away by Dis. That is a wonderful legend. I would like to go to that other mouth of Hell, the one in the *Aeneid*, the one in Cuma – Lake Avernus, or as you would doubtless prefer *Aornos*, the lake without birds. Are there birds over Lake Pergusa?'

The general opinion round the table was that there were. Her younger brother, the middle one, spoke of seeing a bird once when they had picnicked by the lake. In the midst of this conversation, she was impressed by his culture. He rather put her father in the shade.

'My son said,' Calogero now said, addressing Ida, 'that the very first thing he noticed about you was that you were so well-informed and intelligent, and that he wished he knew more about the classics.'

Ida heard this, thinking it a lie. No boy would ever appreciate intelligence before the way a girl looked.

'And he is really so good a coder?' she asked.

'Oh yes, and if you look at what he has created, he has aesthetic sense too. He's not just neat and tidy, but he knows when something does not look right. He knows things should look right. But he is from Purgatory, you see. We are the roughest of the rough and the lowest of the low, but we appreciate beauty, because we have grown up with the Church that contains the painting by Velasquez, the only one in Sicily. It is so beautiful, you cannot help being moved by it. And we have a new Church in Catania, dedicated to Our Lady of Loreto, with a copy of the famous Caravaggio in it. Like the Church of the Holy Souls, which was designed to frame a painting, this Church was designed for the painting, by me, in conjunction with architects of course; but it is a very simple design, a double cube, as laid down by....'

'Vitruvius,' she supplied. 'Or Palladio. One or the other.'

'And the gardens, you should see the gardens. They were designed and planted by a wonderful person called Gabriella Bonelli.'

'I know who she is,' said Ida. 'I read about her. It was in some magazine…'

She did not add that she had read about Gabriella and studied the photographs with such interest because she liked horticulture. Goodness, Gabriella Bonelli was beautiful!

'Would you like to meet her? I can introduce you,' said Calogero. 'And take you to see her work and the new Church. The next time you are in Catania…'

'I am there with my friend Claudia, every week, for university,' she said.

'Then we will arrange it,' he said. He saw her parents smile, and the three boys look jealous. 'We will also arrange for you all to come down. I have three boys, not quite your age, but still. And I know my wife is dying to see you again. It will be good for my boys to meet your boys again, don Nunzio. We need to stick together, and they need sensible friends, and the sort of boys they can look up to,' he added indicating don Nunzio's eldest son. 'But you mention Claudia. Paoluzzu, you know who I mean, is mad about her. She must know. You must know.'

'Oh, we do,' said Ida.

'He is a good Sicilian boy. He has worked for me in Africa; now he works here and works hard. He is good to his parents, and he wants to settle down, I am glad to say. And he is a beautiful young man, I am sure you will agree.'

The signora agreed enthusiastically.

The second course was delicious, and Calogero praised the tomatoes and the local cheese; the bread too was good, better, he said, than the bread of Catania.

'We must,' he said, looking at don Nunzio, 'talk about the paper mill. Perhaps go there later on. I feel I ought to get to see it, considering I own part of it.'

Don Nunzio nodded enthusiastically.

Supper over, don Calogero kissed all the children again, and then retired with don Nunzio to his study, where they could talk and drink whiskey. It was as don Nunzio supposed, he was being asked a favour, a big favour, and he was delighted; it would put the boss of bosses forever in his debt. After the business discussions were over, don Calogero mentioned something else. He wanted Ida to be his daughter-in-law. Francesco was away, but he would come back. And when he did… Don Nunzio was very pleased; he tried to hide his excitement; he wondered what his wife would say; she would be so thrilled. As for the girl herself, well, she knew what was expected of her, surely, and what the wellbeing of the family entailed. And Francesco was a lovely boy, though not as lovely, perhaps, as Paoluzzu, but lovely, nevertheless.

Night had fallen over Sicily, and over Piazza Armerina, and over the mouth of Hell and death's hunting ground, the territory around Lake Pergusa. Don Nunzio had assembled his six very best men, as he had promised the boss, men who could be trusted never to speak, men who would be grateful for any service they could render to him, don Nunzio, but especially to the boss of bosses, don Calogero. They were all young, all sturdy, all from Piazza Armerina. The eldest was about twenty-five and the youngest was don Nunzio's son, the fifteen-year-old, Ida's brother, who, his father thought, ought to discover just what the family fortune rested on. They came to the lake in a car, and in a van. It was dark, but they had taken the precaution of disguising the number plates of both with tape.

It was not hard to find the track that led to the waterside, or the bare piece of shore, between reed beds, where Francesco had said he had entered the water. The difficulty was finding the body, which might have moved of its own accord, although the lake waters seemed particularly still. The lake was shallow but muddy as well, and perhaps the mud had swallowed the corpse. If it proved impossible to find, so be it; if they could not find it, no one else would, so Calogero reasoned.

The van went to the water's edge, which was deserted and ill lit; the car stopped along the track, out of sight, blocking access, in case anyone should disturb them. Nunzio's son and one other man stayed with the car, to tell any nocturnal visitors that the track was closed and that their friends were night-fishing and did not want to be disturbed. If anyone did come down, they would understand, and they would say nothing. It was clear by the state of the ground, the tyre marks and other detritus, that people came down here often, which was good. The more mess, the less chance of any recoverable forensic evidence. The four men took off their clothes, left them in the van, and put on bathing suits and sturdy plastic shoes, and then waded into the cold dark water, while don Nunzio and don Calogero watched from the shore. As they waited, watching the men in the water, they discussed his son, fifteen-year-old Gabriele.

'He is a good boy?' asked Calogero.

'Excellent, they all are, all three of my sons. They know they have to work. Most of the time they do, on their schoolbooks, and in Gabriele's case, helping me; he was very keen. Fifteen is young, I know, but he is grown up. The other kids of his age respect him; they know he is my son; they know I am the biggest employer for miles around; they know, most importantly of all, that I am your friend, don Calogero. So, Gabriele has a lot to live up to. But he is quiet and respectful and behaves himself. He has recently started seeing a girl, but I have told him that he is not allowed to sleep with her, and if he does, I will be most annoyed, and he knows what that means. I don't have to beat any of them very often; it is enough for them to know that the stick is there.'

'Discipline, discipline,' agreed don Calogero. 'I had it at the hands of my father, and Francesco had it from me. Of course, he did not obey me on this, and that is displeasing, but at the same time, he disposed of Antonescu and more importantly of don Costantino Petrović, for which we should all be grateful.'

'And the Serbs? The Serbs all accept this?' asked don Nunzio, for this had been worrying him.

'The Serbs are an interesting lot,' said Calogero, 'But we have been lucky, and we have judged them well. When this man Darko tried to kill Slobodan, at the behest of Costantino, well, that was an act of jealousy. Slobodan is the great-nephew of a Serbian hero, that man who had the pet tiger, if you remember him; that was why Costantino disliked him; Darko disliked him because he had slept with Costantino's daughter, whom Costantino had promised to Darko as a reward for killing him. This man,' he said, gesturing towards the lake, meaning Traiano, 'he inadvertently saved Slobodan's life. If he had not been wearing shorts, with a bottle top in the pocket, Darko's stab would have killed him. Then poor Traiano made a mistake letting them hang Darko. That was fatal for Costantino. He had conspired to murder one of his own and then failed to protect one of his own. The other Serbs lost confidence in him. But it goes further: all the Serbs like the Costantino's children. The ones in Messina are liked as they are related twice over to don Carmelo, who is not forgotten. The girl is nice, and I have been helping her, I have let that be known, as has her mother, so the Serbs are grateful for that, as are don Carmelo's friends. The boy, Dimitri, he is terrible. He drinks too much; he does no useful work; he spends all the money he is given; he snorts cocaine all the time; he is a fornicator and a wastrel, but, but, the Italians love him, and the Serbs love him, I don't know why. And right now, he is in jail, and I am the only person who can get him out. So that counts for a great deal. So that is good. It means we have to put up with the boy Dimitri, but that is a small price to pay. And we have to put up with the son and daughter in Africa, thanks to Slobodan sleeping with the daughter. But they are all onside, and glad that we are absorbing the Messina operation. The two sons, the one in Africa and the one here, may grow resentful in time, but that is a problem for another day.'

'That is good news, boss,' said don Nunzio. 'As you say, this Dimitri is not disciplined enough to be a threat. And the one in Africa....'

'He may be a credit to us in time, you never know. The African operation is making a fortune for us. Our friends in the Middle East are very grateful for their services, and our version of the foreign legion rely on us for the contacts. And then there is the new project, the Catania Waterfront, which is huge in scope. Your papermill - you have the contracts for all my business, don't you, and the Santucci companies, and who does that leave…?'

'Not many, boss, not many.'

They both mused on their good fortune, staring intently out into the lake, watching the four men who were up to their shoulders in the water, feeling the lake bottom with their feet. The four men had been moving around, but now they came to a stop, and had clearly found something with their feet, something, one guessed, that was six or seven feet long and cylindrical in shape. There was a whispered conference between the men, and then an attempt to bring the thing, whatever it was, to the surface. Eventually they lifted up a rolled-up and tied-up carpet, which was very heavy, and brought it to the shore. It was clear, even before they reached the shore, that this was what they had been looking for. The smell told them that. They had thought to bring a sheet of plastic with them and placed that in the bed of the van with the rolled carpet on top of it. The four men then tried their best to dry themselves and rub off the mud and then dressed. The van turned round, while don Calogero and don Nunzio walked to the car where the other two were waiting. Then the cortege drove slowly to the main road and headed back in the direction of Piazza Armerina.

They turned off before reaching the town, heading up an unlit and narrow road, and then onto a road that was even more neglected and less frequented. Here they came to a pig farm, belonging to friends of don Nunzio. They were expected. A man opened the gate to them and waved them through. The van and the car stopped by a single light. They emerged from the vehicles. Hands were shaken with the host, but nothing was said. Behind a low wall one could smell pigs and hear them too.

'You have been up all night?' asked don Nunzio.

'More or less,' said the farmer. 'I don't mind. I like the isolation of this place, you know… By the way, I have something for you.'

He produced a small clear plastic bag from his pocket. It contained something small and white; only after a moment did Calogero register what it contained: teeth.

'A full set from last time,' explained the farmer. 'All thirty-two. But he was young, wasn't he? Anyway, *you* have them.'

He gave them to don Nunzio, who put them in his pocket, knowing that this was the only forensic evidence that the owner of the teeth had ever existed.

'The pigs can't digest them,' said the farmer, by way of explanation. 'Same with hair.'

The men had opened the van and taken out the plastic sheet on which lay the rolled-up carpet. One took a knife to the twine that bound the carpet, and the smell suddenly got worse. The body was revealed, the face grey and mottled with purple patches, and the skin on the fingers coming away.

The men surveyed it, and all instinctively made the sign of the cross. They had done this before. They used their knives to remove the shoes, cutting them away, then the rest of the clothes, until the body was naked. Then, they picked it up and threw it over the wall. There was movement in the pigsty.

'Gone by morning,' said the farmer.

Don Nunzio took out a roll of notes and handed them to the farmer.

'You'll burn all this?' has asked, indicating the muddy carpet and the sodden and ruined clothes.

The man nodded.

'When they are dry. And I will let you have the teeth' he said.

One of the men was sluicing out the back of the van. Hands were once more shaken. Don Nunzio and don Calogero got into the car and left, heading to Catania; he would be back home by dawn, where his wife would be waiting for him, and when he would reassure her that Francesco was safe.

Francesco was safe. He had arrived in Naples, after a five-hour train journey from Reggio. He had found a cheap hotel near the station and fallen into bed, exhausted, some hours before.

Chapter Nine

'Did you kill your father?'

'I told the other lot; no, I did not.'

'We know you did. Or rather, you conspired to kill your father. You did not wield the knife yourself, but you helped plan the whole thing. We have the transcripts; we can piece the whole thing together.'

The first speaker was Chiara de Donato; the second Dimitri Petrović; the third Silvio Pierangeli.

'Then why are you questioning me? You have the transcripts. You can work it all out. I have told you everything. Why aren't my lawyers here?' asked Dimitri.

He tried to sound reasonable, not arrogant, but it was an effort. He knew who these two were. They were magistrates with special powers, from the north of Italy, to judge by their accents. He had been warned about them. He had been expecting them. They had taken their time. He had been locked up in Piazza Lanza for three months already. He wondered why it had taken them so long. Was it because they were not really interested in the case?

Piazza Lanza was really not that bad, and the last three months had been more or less alright. He had not realised it before now, but if there was one place in which don Calogero di Rienzi was all-powerful, it was within the walls of Piazza Lanza. He had been wary of prison life, even frightened (he had seen films, though he had little imagination). But once inside, he had been treated with the greatest of respect by both the prison guards and the other prisoners. He had a cellmate, a youngster like himself, who acted as his servant, bringing him meals, looking after his clothes and polishing his shoes. The cellmate acted as a butler. He had food sent in every day, which was nice, and alcohol, proper wine, though disguised in soft drink bottles. He had a phone, and a tablet, on which he could watch films. His cell was never searched. Above all, he had all the cocaine he wanted; he had been very worried about that, but his worries were ungrounded. All in all, prison was not so very bad, thought he looked forward to the day of his release. Of course, there were no girls in prison, they could not get round that; but it was not altogether true to say that there was no sex. Still, it would be good to get out. He wondered if this interview was a sign of them giving up, their last throw of the dice, before they finally realised they were helpless and would have to let him go.

They were in a room in a police station in the suburbs of Catania, he did not quite know where, as he was unfamiliar with the environs of the city. But the room had a view, and one could see the mountain, now covered with snow. It was, after all, January. Luckily, the room was well heated, as was his cell, and relatively comfortable. He had even been offered coffee and cake. He understood their little game. They wanted him to make some sort of a mistake. He had been warned about this. He was not stupid.

'We have all the transcripts, and they are very long and very detailed,' said the man who identified himself as Silvio, in a weary voice. 'The thing is this: the man with a Serbian accent, he comes into the story rather late, doesn't he? Can you explain that?'

'No comment,' said Dimitri.

'I mean, the story… you were going to see your father on a Sunday morning, and you met this man with the Serbian accent outside the flat, and he said that he wanted to see your father and he had something for him, and you took him up. Then, when you got there, he went into the bedroom and killed your father and then left; oh, and the bodyguards did nothing.'

'Sir, you don't understand. I am sure it is in the transcripts, but perhaps I did not make it clear at the time. This man, I did not know him, but he knew me. He greeted me by name, and he seemed to imply he knew me and knew all about me. He spoke to me in Serbian, a language I do not understand well. He said he needed to see my father, and I had to take him in. The implication was that if I did not, he would force me. He was a frightening-looking man. Then he showed me that thing….'

'The ear?'

'Yes. I felt sick. I was very frightened. He said that Antonescu was dead, and he was dead because he had killed Darko, characters I had heard of but never met. That is not my world. I have been to Serbia, it is a nice place, but I have never been to East Africa, I have never met a gangster in my life. Until then, of course. This guy was terrifying.'

He felt he should not overdo it, so he felt silent.

'The thing is,' said Chiara, 'this man, whoever he was, killed your father. As for the ear, where is that now? Oh yes, the man must have taken it away with him, because we did not find it, and so we only have your word for its existence. As for this Serbian man, the only question is, did you co-operate with him unwittingly, or were you co-operating willingly? And the same goes for the two bodyguards. Did you usually go to see your father on a Sunday morning? Wasn't it a coincidence that this mysterious man met you when and where he did?'

'I went to see my father whenever I wanted to,' said Dimitri. 'He was my father. I could go whenever I liked.'

'You do not strike me as being an early morning sort of person,' observed Silvio.

'I went to see my father then because I needed money,' said Dimitri. 'Sunday morning, one was bound to catch him at home, and in a good mood.'

'Your description of this Serb is vague,' said Chiara. 'The same goes for the two bodyguards. Medium build, brown hair... How well do you know your father's two bodyguards?'

'Not well at all. They worked on a rota. It was always different men every time I saw them. These two, I had seen them before, I remembered seeing them, but I did not know them or their names. And yes, I have seen them in Piazza Lanza, but only in passing. We have not spoken. We have nothing to speak about. I am not interested in Serbia or Serb things or Serb history. I know my grandmother, and she is lovely, and I like Belgrade a lot, but I am not a Serb. I am a Sicilian, the son of a Sicilian mother, and my paternal grandfather was Sicilian too; three grandparents out of four were Sicilian. These Serbs and their quarrels mean nothing to me.'

'Your father's other family in Africa....' said Chiara.

'Oh signora, please,' said Dimitri. 'I have heard about them every day of my life, from my mother. My mother is a good woman, but she is stubborn, and she never lets anything go. So, my father took up with this woman, he was not faithful, it was an insult, a threat to us all, according to my mother. Well, I understand her point of view, but do not share it. My father liked women a lot. He was not faithful. It would have been a miracle if he had been. He had the African woman and lots of other women on a more temporary basis. He slept with dozens of women. So what? I would be the world's biggest hypocrite if I condemned him for it. Good for him. It is what we all want to do. When I get out of Piazza Lanza, it is what I am going to do or start doing again. OK?'

'Are you sad your father is dead?' asked Chiara.

'He was my father,' he said.

That was what he had said repeatedly until now, and he was sticking to it.

'And who do you think was behind this?' asked Silvio.

'People who wanted revenge for Darko,' said Dimitri. 'I suppose. As I told you, I know nothing about the Serbs, I was brought up by my mother, I know nothing about their quarrels, but everyone knows they love revenge above all other things.'

There was silence. Dimitri knew what it meant. He had known this some time. There were no CCTV images of himself and Francesco arriving at the flat. Thank God for that.

'Tell us about these three young men,' said Chiara, pushing three photographs over to him. 'Tell us how you know them.'

He looked at the photographs, and studied the faces of Marco, Francesco and Nino. He shook his head.

'We know about your very considerable drug habit,' continued Chiara. 'Did one of these men supply you with drugs?'

'I have never knowingly met any of them,' he said. 'Are they from Messina?'

'No, they are from Catania,' she said.

'Well then, how would I know them? I never go to Catania.'

In silence, Silvio pushed a laptop computer towards him. He pressed a button, and a video played. It showed himself and Nino Santacroce standing outside a nightclub in conversation. The video was dated to October the previous year.

'Whatever we were discussing, or doing, it was not illegal,' said Dimitri defensively.

'So, you do go to Catania?' said Silvio.

'They have the best nightclubs. And this boy, I met him in a nightclub, but I have no idea who he is. I have no memory meeting him.'

'But you did meet him,' insisted Silvio. 'And you do know who he is, and we know who he is. He is a person close to don Calogero di Rienzi.'

There was silence.

'Tell us about your sister,' said Chiara.

'What has she got to do with this?' asked Dimitri.

'Oh, everything,' said Chiara. 'You are fond of her?'

'Of course, she is nice, and she is my sister.'

'So how do you feel about the fact that her own uncle made her pregnant?' she asked.

A look of rage came into Dimitri's face.

'He is not her uncle!' he said, grinding his teeth. 'Mimmo Lollobrigida is not a relation of ours at all!'

'But he is. The police have been busy. Mimmo is the son of don Carmelo, your grandfather. We have DNA samples to prove it. We interviewed him, and he voluntarily gave us a DNA sample, so did your sister. We told them that they were going to be prosecuted. We have been busy while you have been on remand in Piazza Lanza. We have also cautioned the priest who was planning to marry them, don Giorgio, and we have also established that Lollobrigida, as he is known, is renting a flat here in Catania from no less a person that don Calogero. So, you see, we have put the pieces together: we know that you conspired with Calogero di Rienzi to murder your own father. Because of Mimmo, Maria and the child. Because of your mother. Because of the family in Africa. Because you hated your father as he tried to discipline you.'

'No comment,' said Dimitri between gritted teeth. 'And Antonescu? Was I involved in that as well?' he asked sarcastically. 'Did I urge people to cut off his ear?'

It was their turn to be silent. For the truth was, they had no clue about Antonescu at all. He could see that and felt triumphant.

'When did you first meet Lollobrigida?' asked Silvio.

'Mimmo? It was at a baptism, I think,' said Dimitri.

'He met you first and then your sister? You introduced them?'

'I can't remember. It was a big party.'

'You're lying,' said Silvio.

'Why should I lie about something like that?' asked Dimitri, confused.

Silvio was silent.

'Because you deliberately put your sister in his way, in the hope that she and he would get together, for your advantage. And when they did, you were delighted, weren't you? It meant you could get rid of your father, and Lollobrigida would inherit; because your father had decided to disinherit you and your sister in favour of the African family,' said Chiara.

'You think I....' began Dimitri. 'You disgust me.'

'You encouraged them,' she said. 'To commit incest. To break the law.' She paused. 'We have the transcripts, right here, of the texts you exchanged after that party. Let me see: *'Great to meet you, can't believe we have not met before... Does your sister have a boyfriend, I would really like to get to see more of her, but I am a bit shy... No, she is single, never had anyone, perhaps you will be her first, my mother and I were discussing how much we both liked you.... When are you coming round.... I will make sure Maria is here... She is shy, but if you are shy too, I am sure you can both overcome your shyness... The fact that you are a relation is really good....'*'

'You are twisting my words,' said Dimitri in fury.

'Then you admit they are your words?'

'Yes, but when I say he was a relation, I mean a relation of my mother, not my father,' protested Dimitri.

'That will be for a court to decide,' said Chiara primly. 'But in the meantime, you are already charged with conspiracy to murder, and with a new charge, which is conspiring against public morals and aiding and abetting incest, essentially prostituting your own sister. Sexual abuse in short. And not just you, but also Calogero di Rienzi as well.'

'You cannot do this!' he shouted.

'We can,' was her calm reply. Then she added: 'Why not tell us what you know, what we know you know, what we want to have confirmed, and what we know you want to tell us?'

'I want to go back to Piazza Lanza,' he howled. 'All this is rubbish...'

'Tell us about Francesco di Rienzi,' said Chiara.

There was complete silence in the room.

Dimitri breathed deeply and said: 'I want a lawyer.'

He smiled at them, sensing their disappointment. He was not going to talk. He was not going to be frightened into blurting out the truth. The strategy had not worked, on him, at least.

At the very same moment, police teams were interviewing everyone else involved in the case, both in Messina and in Catania. Incest was not illegal in Italy, and one could sleep with one's half-niece (though not many people knew this) or even your cousin or your sister, though it was not advisable, but there was a law about public scandal, and there were laws about pimping and prostitution and sexual coercion. The strategy was very simple: to accuse Dimitri and his mother, donna Rosa, of pushing Maria towards Mimmo. To accuse them of pushing Mimmo towards Maria as well, indeed of selling Maria to Mimmo, and to accuse don Calogero di Rienzi and the priest don Giorgio of enabling all this to happen. And the motive was to get hold of the inheritance of don Carmelo, which, once don Costantino was out of the way, would belong entirely to Mimmo, the last surviving son of don Carmelo. That was the strategy, but they had got precisely nowhere with Dimitri or his mother; indeed donna Rosa had been outraged by the very suggestion; but this did not put them off, as they were confident that in court Dimitri and his mother would look like exactly the sort of people who might run a sex ring of some sort.

Both don Calogero and don Giorgio had denied everything; don Calogero with a calm that was impossible to dent, with his lawyer next to him. He had not known that Mimmo was related to anyone in particular, let alone don Carmelo or the girl. Mimmo was just a poor boy asking for help, terrified of the rage of his prospective father-in-law, who had a brutal reputation. People like Mimmo came to him for help all the time.

As for the priest, he was more guarded, but he too spoke with a lawyer provided by don Calogero. He had asked to see Mimmo's birth certificate and that of the girl Maria; he knew that they were vaguely related through the girl's mother, but no more than that. The boy's birth certificate made it clear he was Lollobrigida's son. Any other questions he declined to answer, as they touched on matters in the internal forum. It was not true that he saw the couple as a favour to don Calogero; he saw any prospective married couple who asked. This was true, but he felt bad about making the assertion. The police had confronted him with the DNA evidence. He had taken refuge in silence.

Even more embarrassing for don Giorgio were the phone calls from the archdiocese. This had culminated in a summons to the archbishop's office and a threat of suspension. Faced with that, he had done the only thing possible. He had turned to the only help available. He had spoken to don Calogero. The boss was charm itself, though one could see that he was enjoying this little triumph. He promised to sort it out. Don Giorgio was accordingly summoned to see the archbishop himself, but the interview was gentle. It had been made plain to the archbishop that to discipline a much loved and popular priest, who, if he had erred had only done so out of compassion, would be unwise. Besides, who knew what don Calogero might do if offended? But if the threat of suspension had been lifted, don Giorgio felt it had been replaced by a greater weight, namely a reputation in the Church of being a priest in the pocket of don Calogero di Rienzi. For that was what he now was, as the archbishop had made clear. Before leaving, the archbishop had told him that he should go ahead and marry the couple, and that he would face no consequences. He realised, as he was told this, that a similar pledge must have been made to don Calogero. He was trapped.

The interview with the girl was the least satisfactory, from the police point of view. Maria wept and said she loved Mimmo, that she had had no idea; she had lost her father recently, and not in a nice way; all she wanted was to be with Mimmo, and for them to do what was best for the child. The police psychologist who was there did her very best to persuade her that she was the victim of a cruel trick, worked by the people around her; that Mimmo did not love her, nor she him; and that it would be best for all concerned if the child were aborted, given the high probability of it being unhealthy.

Maria dried her tears as she heard this and even began to nod in agreement. There was silence for some time while what was said was digested.

'It would be the kindest thing, for the child too,' said the psychologist.

The police then spoke. Had Mimmo spoken about don Calogero di Rienzi, or about her father, don Costantino? Had he mentioned someone called Francesco? How close was he to Dimitri?

She considered all these questions, and then, after a period of silence, rose and terminated the interview. She was not under arrest, and they had told her she could end the interview whenever she chose.

With the boy, it should have gone better than it did. They thought that intimidation was the best strategy.

Had he known his half-brother, don Costantino? He replied he had never met him, on any occasion, and he stuck to this assertion, every time the question was asked.

Had he met don Calogero? Very briefly, once, and don Calogero had been very kind and sent him to see the priest. Why had he gone to see don Calogero for advice on this matter? Dimitri had suggested it. So, he had conspired with Dimitri? Dimitri was a friend. And he was frighted of don Costantino, as were his children; but everyone knew don Costantino respected don Calogero. They were business partners. It was natural he should go to don Calogero.

He and don Costantino were in opposing camps in a court case. Did he want don Costantino dead? No, he did not. That was ridiculous. Did he know Francesco? No. Had he heard of Antonescu? No. Wasn't it a bit strange that he had got Maria pregnant at the very first opportunity?

He looked at them wonderingly.

They had fallen in love, he said.

'How many other girls have you slept with?' asked one of the policemen.

He considered.

'None,' he said, which was broadly true, though not strictly accurate.

'You expect us to believe that?' said one of the policemen, with a contemptuous laugh.

'Believe what you like, but it is true.'

'You people,' said the policeman, who, by his accent, was certainly not Sicilian. 'You start with your sisters, aged twelve, you move onto your nieces and your cousins, and you end up marrying your mothers. People like you, the scum of Messina and Catania, you have incest and crime in your blood. It is true, we all know it. You aren't Italian, you are a filthy Arab. You can't even speak proper

Italian, and you have not done an honest day's work in your life. You are a degenerate. I bet your parents were first cousins.'

One of the other policemen told him to shut up.

The lawyer, without emotion said: 'My client has the right to reply to that personal accusation.'

Mimmo spoke: 'I had my first complete sexual intercourse last year, when I was twenty-three years old. I have a high school certificate and a degree in Mathematics. I work as a teacher, and until very recently, I had not missed a day of work. I have never indulged in the kind of disreputable behaviour that you attribute to me. I don't tell lies. I am not an Arab; I am an Italian citizen like you; I am a Catholic. My parents were not related by blood. I have no criminal record, and neither do any of my immediate relatives.'

His tone was calm, and it infuriated the policeman even more.

'Are we going to sit here and listen to this little Arab boy insult us?' he asked.

The interview was terminated.

'We have been having a little difficulty,' said don Calogero di Rienzi, 'but everything will shortly be arranged once again as we would like.' He smiled broadly at the two guests. 'I am sure don Nunzio mentioned it to you?'

The two beautiful girls smiled back. It was so lovely here in Catania, in this huge beautiful and airy flat, where they had had lunch with don Calogero and his family, his ravishing and pregnant wife, his three sons, the baby and don Calogero's mother, a lady full of smiles and welcome, who had cooked, and magnificently so. With them too was Paoluzzu who was more or less overwhelmed to be there with the boss, at his table, in the bosom of his family.

'That poor girl,' said Agata with feeling. 'What they said to her....'

'That poor boy, and what they said to him,' said Paoluzzu.

'They have both sued, and they will both accept an out of court settlement,' said don Calogero. 'There was some silly argument about whether calling someone an Arab was in fact an insult, but it was clearly meant as such. They will be married soon, anyway, and the child is healthy, they have done all the scans, and there are no abnormalities. Don Giorgio has been told by the Church he can go ahead, and public opinion is on the side of the couple, and the state dares not interfere, and there is the fiction that Mimmo's real father was this Lollobrigida.'

'But it is not quite accurate calling them Romeo and Juliet, when Romeo and Juliet came from rival families, not the same family,' said Ida.

'Is it your favourite Shakespeare play?' asked don Calogero. 'Mine is *Richard II*, a story of rebellion. Such poetry, even if I have only read it in translation.'

'I like *The Merchant of Venice* best,' said Ida. 'Though I have soft spot for *Much Ado about Nothing*, which is set in Messina.'

Sebastiano and Romano were too busy eating to pay much attention to this, but Renato was following and thought it all very pretentious.

'I will be going to England a lot soon,' said Calogero, 'as the boys are going to school there in September. 'Their mother and I have agreed it. A place near Windsor. Very convenient for the airport. But you know, the lords of misrule made an attack, and we counter-attacked and we won. They chose targets that were too soft. Mimmo and Maria are too sweet, too innocent. As for Dimitri, well, his father had just died, so he was pitiable. The charge of conspiracy was ridiculous because there was no conspiracy. Don Costantino was killed by a discontented Serb. They have released Dimitri and the two bodyguards. Dimitri is a nice boy, but a bit spoilt.' He tapped his nose. 'You know what I mean.'

'You must miss Francesco,' said Ida sympathetically.

Renato was all attention. Agata looked momentarily tearful. Before lunch she had been reading the letter that Paoluzzu had brought, the third that her son had written. The boss too had received a letter.

Ida had had a letter as well and so had Paoluzzu. Paoluzzu's letter had been the most honest, describing life in Florence and detailing the two dozen or so girls he had slept with since his arrival there in late October. It was now April. Needless to say, despite the fact that Francesco had told him not to tell his father, Paoluzzu had. It had annoyed the boss, his son's sexual incontinence. His idea was that the boy should be spending his exile in solitary sadness. He should not be enjoying himself with, it seemed, American art students.

'He will be back soon,' said Calogero, looking at his wife, who smiled bravely. 'None of this is his fault. It is them, the lords of misrule, trying to punish me. But Francesco has done nothing, and though they have tried to fit him up, there's no evidence against him at all. He will be back soon, as soon as we are sure no one will arrest him. We don't want him treated like poor Dimitri.'

Everyone nodded.

Lunch over, he was driving the two beautiful girls of Piazza Armerina over to the Furnaces to look at the gardens there, where they were to meet Gabriella Bonelli, the creator of the same gardens, and also visit the church and see the Caravaggio (copy of) painting. The original plan was to drive the two girls over, but it seemed that Paoluzzu wanted to come too, despite never having expressed an interest in gardening before now. In addition, Renato said he wanted to come as well, as he liked gardens (again, this seemed a first), and besides, he wanted to see the Caravaggio. Calogero sighed and knew he could not refuse this request. The boy was being immensely difficult; there had been numerous quarrels of late, all to do with his unhappiness about going to school in England, his continual refusal to cut his hair, and his general rudeness to his father. Calogero could not stand this defiance, and he had caned the boy several times, about which he felt guilty, as he knew the dottoressa, the boy's mother, would not like it, and she was bound to find out. Oddly, Agata approved of this discipline, which had of course been employed on Francesco. He sighed again, this time at the thought of Francesco fornicating in Florence. It was so irresponsible. His daughters were a burden to him, and now his sons, as well, were going that way too.

So, they all went to the Furnaces: the two beautiful girls, Ida and Caludia, don Calogero, Renato and Paoluzzu.

Paoluzzu was so happy to be included in the group. To be in the boss's presence, to have had lunch with him, his sons, his wife, his mother, this had been an undreamed-of honour; it was to be admitted to the inner circle. One would have to be careful about talking about it later, in case others became jealous. But he had access to the boss, because Francesco was writing to him from his Florentine exile, and enclosing letters for his father, his mother and for Ida. These letters Paoluzzu brought to Catania, and, of course, divulged the things that Francesco said to him but did not include in the letters to his father. One knew, in the end, that the father was more important than the son. When you were in his presence, you almost trembled with excitement, with the sense of his importance, his power. It wasn't just the money, the clothes, the appearance of command, it was the sense of power, of being so close to the one whom everyone wanted to be close to.

They came to the church, which was open, and they went up together to examine the altarpiece, the supposed copy of Caravaggio's *Holy Family with Saint Laurence and Saint Francis*. They gazed at it in wonder, or at least the two girls did, while Calogero spoke of the painting's history, how it had come to him from Bonelli, who had inherited it, and how it was in fact the property of his ex-wife, Renato's mother. He said this easily and smoothly, with his hand on the boy's shoulder, feeling the boy's interest and resentment. Renato was now twelve, had grown, and from being difficult, his father thought, had become impossible. He had inherited his mother Stefania's looks, and her wilfulness, and it was more apparent by the day that he was only the half-brother of Romano and Sebastiano, for he looked less and less like his half-siblings, and he had outpaced Sebastiano in growth considerably. There was less than a year between them, but Renato seemed to be two or three years older. The boy, Calogero sensed with foreboding, was hurtling towards sexual maturity, young, too young, just like his sisters. He recalled the trouble Isabella had given him and sighed. He loved all his children, but this wilful child, perhaps more than others. But Renato, like Isabella before him, was determined to resist him.

Things had recently been complicated by the knowledge on Renato's part that he could play his mother off against his father. His mother, meaning the woman who had brought him up, Anna Maria, had made it clear that Calogero was not to hit the child, which Calogero resented, and which rule the child himself had goaded him to break. But things were complicated further by the boy's realisation that Anna Maria was not his biological mother and that the painting they were now looking at, which was worth so much, might one day belong to Romano and Sebastiano and not to him and his sisters. This had created furious discontent on Renato's part. In vain, it had been explained to him that he stood to inherit a great deal from both parents; it was the painting that was the sticking point. That was the prestige item, the great object of his desire. He had to have the painting, or at least a third of it. For he did not care too much about his sisters.

Leaving the Church, they went out into the sunshine of the fine spring day, and there was Gabriella, waiting for them. Ida and Claudia were introduced. Hands were shaken. They immediately headed towards the lemon grove next to the church, and Gabriella spoke of the importance of lemons, and the beauty of having a grove where people could help themselves whenever they wanted; and the symbolism of having it next to the church: the one, the source of spiritual grace, the other, the source of health and beauty, lemon juice being the original cosmetic.

The men hung back, and Renato stayed by his father.

'So….' said Calogero. 'You and her?'

'Boss,' agreed Paoluzzu. 'It is a thing.'

At that moment, Claudia turned her head and looked at him, almost crossly, certainly proprietorially.

'It took time and persuasion,' said Paoluzzu, 'but eventually, we got there.'

He knew the boss had read what Francesco had written to him.

'And the girl before?' asked Calogero.

'Forgotten, boss. We were together for almost ten years, all the time I was in Africa, I thought…. We started the night of my thirteenth birthday. But I hardly remember her now. I never thought I could forget her, but I have.'

'I like my men to be monogamous,' said Calogero. 'I was angry with Nino, because he was so young, but I have forgiven him, as he seems very keen on the girl, and they now have the baby, so… But I am annoyed with Francesco. I want him to settle down. I rely on you to be a calming influence on him.'

Renato was following this conversation closely.

'When will he be coming back, boss?' Paoluzzu felt bold enough to ask.

'Maybe in the autumn, maybe for Christmas. When they send the various cases to the archives, which my contacts will tell me about when it happens. Someone took a pop at a pathetic shopkeeper in Librino… but eventually they get bored and move on. The Antonescu case… that I am sure was some discontented Serb, the same one who did for Costantino, and who left the country the very day of the crime. Do you miss Francesco?'

'Of course. I want him back. So does she,' he added with meaning.

'She asks you about him?'

'All the time,' said Paoluzzu.

The conversation about lemons had given way to a discussion of oleanders, plumbago and pines. It seemed that don Nunzio had a plot of land, quite big really, outside Piazza Armerina, and Ida was thinking that before they began to build anything, they should plan the garden, given that plants took time to grow. Gabriella asked about the type of soil, but Ida was not sure what type of soil it was (indeed, she had been hazy until that moment about soil classification even being a thing.) Did one need planning permission for a garden, she wondered. Gabriella spoke of the various types of soil, a rather prosaic subject, but it was lovely listening to a beautiful woman speaking about such things: the soil, plants, trees, the idea of a Sicilian garden, a pastoral paradise. Ida had in mind a place for herself, a retreat from the world, a sort of Eden from which all unpleasant things would be excluded, by which she meant, principally, she supposed, men. Oh, if only Eve had had the place to herself. But God, or biological necessity, had decided otherwise.

Biological necessity. It seemed the beautiful Gabriella, who was single and happy to be so, had a child, and the father was a useless and worthless man called Roberto Costacurta, whose mother and sisters were very nice. Roberto was now married to Calogero's ex-wife, the dottoressa Tancredi, explained Gabriella, seeing the men were out of earshot. The dottoressa was supposed to be the cleverest woman in Sicily, and she was a great friend of her brother Ruggero, who was an art dealer, and whose client she was, but the dottoressa had shown limited judgement in marrying someone as worthless as Roberto. He had married her for the money, Gabriella was sure, and she had married him for his considerable looks, the only good thing about him. Their daughter, said Gabriella, was beautiful, and if one were going to have a child by a worthless man (though you only discovered generally too late how very worthless he was) one might as well have a daughter by a worthless and beautiful man. That was what men were: a biological necessity.

Ida smirked. Well, if they were necessary, she would acquire one, just as Claudia had acquired one. She and Claudia were as close as ever, and they had discussed Paoluzzu, and she had given her permission to her friend to, well, acquire him. She remembered how the two of them had gone to Reggio Calabria to see the bronzes of Riace and to visit the museum there. Paoluzzu was as beautiful as the bronzes that had been reclaimed from the sea, almost. The children would be very pretty, that was for sure. And Paoluzzu was submissive. He had told Claudia, perhaps to flatter her, but perhaps because it was true as well, that he knew she was better educated and far cleverer than he was, and that he would always defer to her judgement. Moreover, he was submissive in daily life, always asking her what she wanted to do. It was clear that he accepted the hierarchy of Sicilian life: that Claudia was to be deferred to as the friend of Ida, the daughter of don Nunzio, his employer. He was also full of deference to don Calogero, who had made it clear he looked on both girls with immense favour.

Paoluzzu was an acquisition, thanks to his looks, his deference, his connection to don Calogero, his friendship with Francesco. Claudia had reported that he was submissive to the point of not retaliating when slapped, and slapped hard, and that his horrible male genitalia were not as repulsive as they might have been. Nor was he over-hairy, which was a thing with men, particularly men from Sicily. Claudia had amused herself by pulling out some of the sparse hairs on his chest, which had made him scream and her laugh. But he had not stopped her.

And if Claudia could have Paoluzzu, then Ida could have Francesco. Don Nunzio and his wife, her parents, wanted it, as well they might. But if they could be ambitious, so could she. If one wanted to marry not for romantic reasons, but to have children, to have position, then marrying Francesco was a good idea, and Claudia's alliance with Paoluzzu made it more certain. But the person whose influence was decisive was the boss himself, and his wife. She had made a good impression on both, she felt. Why not marry Francesco? He was the heir, after all, the heir to all of this. He would control it all, and she would dominate him. They said the don Giuseppe Santucci was dominated by his young lady, just as don Renzo Santucci was by his wife, Calogero's sister, so why should it not be the same with Francesco? And if she needed him, he needed her, because he was a silly boy. He needed someone sensible. All men needed a sensible woman, really. Even clever don Calogero.

Francesco was the heir, thanks, no doubt, to his mother's cleverness, and to his father's affection for the two youngest children, little Calogero and the new baby, who was a boy called Piero; he would rule on their behalf. And the other children were clearly not suitable, particularly not this boy, the twelve-year-old Renato, despite the fact that he looked older, and had good hair, long hair, like his elder stepbrother. But there was something about Renato, she could not quite place it, though she compared him to her own fifteen-year-old brother, Gabriele, who was almost grown up, who was dependable, silent, trustworthy, as this boy was most definitely not. There was a reserve about her brother that meant her father trusted him, people respected him, young as he was. This boy Renato was not reserved; he was emotionally incontinent, the sort whose discontent showed in his facial expressions; he was, in an obscure way, dangerous, as his own father clearly recognised. Don Calogero, by contrast, clearly liked Paoluzzu, and she understood why. Paoluzzu was the confidential messenger. He was trustworthy. He had been so in Africa (he had told Claudia) and he was still receiving the messages from Francesco.

She did not know where Francesco was, but she could communicate with him via letter, via Paoluzzu. He was not on the run but had made a strategic and cautious withdrawal. He would be back. She did not care when; she did not mind his absence, the longer the better. But when he came back, then she would pounce, not that she needed to do. His father had chosen her, and Francesco would do what his father wanted. Her father had chosen him, Francesco. She knew, she had always known, that for her, and her brothers as they grew to maturity, these considerations were crucial, as they were to Francesco – pleasing the boss, when the boss was your father. The only real challenge was making the most of the situation. Francesco, she realised, was an opportunity, and one not to be missed. And he, she was sure, saw her in a similar light. He was not a full-blooded prince, after all; he had his charms, and he was very bright, but his position depended on his connection to his mother and his half-brothers, little Calogero and Piero. These were firm connections: everyone knew how the boss loved his wife and adored his little sons. But there might be challenges ahead, she thought, looking at Renato, who, she noticed, regarded her with an interest tinged with suspicion.

They were now discussing trees, and the challenges of growing Aleppo pines, which boiled down to this, the fact that no other tree or plant could grow under or near them. If one had some land, one could plant a small pine forest, but there would be no other vegetation, and no bird song; nothing could co-exist with the pine. It was a beautiful tree, but Gabriella preferred the oak and led them off to see a particularly fine example which had been transplanted when mature. Calogero, said Gabriella, with a smile, had been impatient; the tree had been a good twelve feet high when transplanted, and had been bought at great expense; it was now sixteen feet, and flourishing, which was a sign that the soil here was rich, and had been successfully decontaminated. They admired the tree, and Ida thought of all the mentions of oaks in Virgil, Theocritus and Bion. To have money meant you did not have to wait years for your oak tree to grow, which was a comforting thought.

She was aware as they stood around the oak, and as Gabriella spoke, someone had joined them, a woman a few years older than herself, holding a little girl by the hand. Gabriella, still talking, gave a little wave to this person, and Calogero, making no sign that he noticed her, concentrated his attention on the tree. But it was impossible to ignore the new arrival. The little girl ran to her mother when Gabriella had finished, and Gabriella scooped her up into her arms, explaining that this was her daughter (and of course, the daughter of the worthless Roberto Costacurta); she was a beautiful little girl, and excited universal admiration from the rest of them, even Calogero, who knew what was expected of him. The one who had brought her was her aunt, Costacurta's sister, the one called Petra.

Ida knew, of course, who Petra was. Claudia had been discussing Francesco with Paoluzzu, and while Paoluzzu had not been indiscreet about some things, he had let out that Francesco had a sort of girlfriend called Petra, of whom his father did not approve; this had all been passed onto Ida. Well, it was clear that don Calogero did not approve of Petra: his face, his carefully prepared smile, told that story. But Petra seemed not to mind. She was now explaining how the little girl, entrusted to her for a few hours, wanted to see her mother, and she hadn't the heart to say no, and she hoped she was not disturbing them; the truth was she was very keen to disturb them, she liked being a disturbance, that was clear. Ida and Claudia shook hands with her. Claudia mentioned they had seen her at the university, though not to talk to. It was interesting to put a name to a face, added Ida. Petra, for her part, registered the references to Piazza Armerina. They knew who she was, and she knew who they were.

Petra turned towards Calogero and said:

'I was just in Palermo.'

This was thrown down like a challenge.

'Seeing your brother?' he asked casually.

'No. I only see him when he comes here, and that is not very often. He does not have much time for us. No, I was seeing your cousin-in-law.'

He frowned, not quite sure whom she meant.

'Oh, you mean Emma Santucci,' he said at last. 'I hardly know her,' he added defensively. 'I didn't know you knew her.'

'Well, I do. She had a child with my friend Tonino Grassi, didn't she?'

She might as well have added 'the one you killed', but there was no need. Her tone said it all. She was holding him accountable, it seemed to him. He felt cold fury, but suppressed it and smiled, saying nothing.

'Where is Francesco?' she asked.

'He has gone away, but will be back,' said Calogero.

'In the same way as Tonino went away?' she asked pointedly.

Calogero looked at Paoluzzu, who spoke.

'He has been in touch, he has written. He is having a good time. He wanted to discover the world beyond Sicily. But he will be back. He wants us to keep it discreet where he has gone. But I have had letters, and he is fine. He and I are very close,' he added.

She was stung by this. He was writing to the friend in Piazza Armerina, if this is who this was, not to her.

'Closer than me?' she asked, stung by this assertion.

Paoluzzu looked at her and felt a stab of sympathy. So, Francesco had slept with her, but he had not mentioned her at all since he had gone away, had not said he was missing her. She was just a girl, a lover. Paoluzzu was a friend, and that counted for far more.

'We are friends,' said Paoluzzu shortly, meaning there was no more to be said. Everyone understood what this meant, except women, perhaps, who did not experience it.

Everyone knew, after all, what Sicilian friendship meant.

This was the only thing to say, but it was also the wrong thing to say, he realised as soon as he had said it. The two other girls looked somewhat cross and gave him looks that made him feel uncomfortable. But what else could he say? He decided he did not like Petra and the way she put him on the spot. Who did she think she was? As for the others, they knew the truth. One longed for women, one lusted after them, but in the end, it was your friends who were the most valuable. He loved Claudia, he was enslaved by her, but Francesco and his father, these were the two who were central to him, not her. And if she did not like being reminded of that, well, that was the way life was. At least here. In Sicily. They knew that, surely.

They did know that, and it was a bond between them, all of a sudden. The four women moved off to look at some bougainvillea. Ida might have disliked Petra, given her history, but the common cause all Sicilian women shared, namely the unreasonableness of Sicilian men, somehow united them. That was more important.

Left with the boss and his son, Paoluzzu felt awkward, as if he should apologise.

'What could I say, boss?' he asked. 'Besides, it is none of her business where Francesco is. It is none of any of their business what Francesco does. They should not ask questions.'

'You said the right thing,' said Calogero. 'But you will have to bear the consequences. I mean, for the next few months you will get furious looks and no sexual favours.'

Paoluzzu laughed ruefully.

'I don't know what you think about the air up in Piazza Armerina, boss, but sexual favours were not coming thick and fast as it was. But seriously, boss, I tell her little, and she doesn't ask much, except about Francesco, how he is, things Ida puts her up to. But they have never asked about, you know, sensitive matters. Ida has been well brought up by her father, and so has Claudia, she's from a similar family, and so am I, I know what is what, and that one should not gossip.'

'I know you know not to gossip,' said Calogero. 'You see,' he said, addressing Renato. 'Gossip is a sin. Don't do it. And when you have a wife or a girlfriend, make sure you do not tell her the things that do not concern her.'

'I know that, Papà,' the boy said a trifle sulkily. 'Everything is secret, and everything is to be kept from women and children.'

'Correct,' said his father. 'Women and children don't make good decisions. They are too emotional. But in the meantime, women and children plague us. I am so lucky in Agata, Paoluzzu, you cannot imagine. She is so nice, and she does not interfere. But my other two wives… The dottoressa was very commanding, which was fine, as a rich woman in her own right; one could hardly object, and it had its advantages and its consolations. But my first wife Stefania, we were together very young, and she was hard work, and she had her own ideas about everything, and was content with nothing I gave her. She was stubborn, and very sparing with her favours, and then after two girls and a long wait, finally Renato came along. That was when it was all worth it. Let me assure you, Paoluzzu, your wife will torment you and drive you mad, but the moment they put the son she gives you into your arms, everything will be worth it. For a few moments, at least. Then that son will grow up and begin to torment you. This one torments me. I love him so much, but he is like his mother, stubborn, and he refuses to love me.'

He looked at Renato as he said this. Renato looked back, defiant.

'You see, Paoluzzu?' said the boss. 'Now, you had better behave, as Paoluzzu is looking at you and judging you. Remember you are my son, and different standards apply to you.'

Calogero smiled. He had provoked his son to anger, he could see, but the boy had no response to make.

Meanwhile, among the girls, something had gelled. The bougainvillea was not very interesting, as it was not yet in flower, but Gabriella had explained why she had chosen it for the verges of the roads between the houses. It stopped people walking on the edges of the road and creating hard patches of dull brown earth. And bougainvillea needed very little water, like oleander. The colours, the colours were magnificent in the summer, and they should come back and see the place then. It was clear to Ida and to Claudia that Gabriella and Petra were good friends, and the bond between them was their affection for the little girl and their disdain for the little girl's father, who paid her as little attention as possible, and was similarly neglectful of his mother and sisters. Well, he provided money, of which he had plenty, but not his presence, not his affection. He dedicated all his time to the dottoressa and even when not with her, when free to do what he liked, he seemed to prefer to stay in Palermo rather than come to Catania. It was a shame, but they could do without him.

If Petra had a fault, it was that once she had decided about something, it was hard for her to dislodge that thought from her mind. Her brother had been complicit, after the fact, of the disappearance and murder of Tonino, and had robbed him; she was sure of that. They had got rid of Tonino; she knew it, and so did Emma Santucci, and the policewoman Antonella Sanzio, who knew a great deal about police inefficiency and corruption. And now, what had happened to Francesco? Was he really away, hiding somewhere, or had what had happened to Tonino happened to him as well?

It was clear Tonino was dead simply because he would never have so completely abandoned his own daughter whom he had loved. As for Francesco, sending letters from the continent via this man Paoluzzu, well, he had not written to her, had he, because Paoluzzu and the others did not know what had passed between her and Francesco. She flattered herself, perhaps, but Francesco had been obsessed with her ever since he had been fourteen. Would he have left her without a word, and written to these other, less important people? Or were these letters faked by the people who did not know the truth about his affections? (The idea that Francesco had forgotten her seemed too fantastic to consider.)

It was time for them all to go, as discussion of flowers was over. But Gabriella was invited to Piazza Armerina, and Petra as well; and Claudia and Ida said they would see Petra at the university too, no doubt. Don Calogero shook hands with them all most warmly, not realising, perhaps, that a coalition had formed against his interests. All the girls kissed and hugged Renato, which pleased him. So did Paoluzzu. And so, they parted.

Chapter Ten

Summer came, and with it the heat and the holidays. The five elder children of don Calogero spent the hot weeks in Donnafugata, at their mother's house. The two girls, Isabella and Natalia, had returned from their schools in England, content to enjoy the hot weather, to laze by the pool and to play tennis, as well as enjoy the superb food served by the devoted Veronica. The three boys, who were all going to go to school in England when September came, were content to use the pool, play tennis and football on their own, play games and read books; the two youngest were very keen on climbing trees in the orchard, where they did a great deal of damage, but Renato had grown out of this, and spent time with his sisters, who adored him, by the pool, contemplating the way he had grown – their heights were all marked on a wall behind a door in the house – his hair too, now well over his shoulders, which pleased him immensely, and his legs now getting hairy as well, which both pleased and alarmed him. He had been young when it had happened, but he remembered clearly the way that the first sexual experiences of his sister Isabella had caused such trouble in the house, and he was aware now of how his own nascent sexuality was creating a sense of worry in both his mother and his father, and a sense of admiration in his sister Isabella.

Isabella, who would be starting university in London that autumn, had long been viewed as a sex maniac and man mad by her father, an embarrassment to the family. Her mother had thought this unfair, and that Isabella was just a normal sort of girl. It all depended on what one considered to be normal, in Calogero's opinion, but he had lost that argument, and he was grateful that Isabella wanted to stay in England for her studies for which he did not mind paying. It pained him that his daughter was not more like the beautiful girls of Piazza Armerina. Natalia, less pretty, was better behaved, indeed if she had misbehaved, no one had noticed, so taken up were they by the bad behaviour of Isabella, something Isabella herself considered profoundly unfair. She loathed her father's injustice towards her, and was pleased that her little brother, not so little anymore, was going to be, in her estimation, an almighty headache.

The dottoressa took the view that the boy was a normal twelve-year-old, a bit in advance of his years; and then she took the somewhat contradictory position that the boy had a bad side inherited from his father. This stung Calogero. He himself was hard working and immensely successful, and Renato showed no sign of ever being either; he had inherited his bad side, if he had one, not from him, but from his mother Stefania; and it had been made worse by being spoiled by his grandmother, the Black Widow Spider, and his aunts Assunta, Elena and Giuseppina, not to mention the dottoressa herself. But the dottoressa took the position that both of them were rich, immensely so, and therefore the children had to be brought up as rich children were brought up. He assented to this if it meant sending them to school in England, while resolving that little Calogero and his other children with Agata would be brought up very differently.

He dreaded the future with Renato, the boy who bore the same name as his grandfather, the Chemist of Catania. He wished now he had called him something else. He remembered what he had been doing at the age of thirteen and pictured the boy on the edge of all those things. It was not the thieving or the violence that particularly worried him, but rather the thought of the child being no longer a child. He remembered what he had done aged thirteen with Anna the Romanian prostitute, and he shivered at the memory.

The child tormented him, and he realised it was because, strangely, the child was not good, not as a child should be. Francesco was violent, as well as a thief and a fornicator, but that did not matter, because he needed to be at least two of those things, and he was always kind and loving to his mother, and obedient to his stepfather. But Renato had no intention of submitting to his father. He had lost that battle, just as he had lost it with Isabella; the greater battle was with Anna Maria, and he had lost that as well. In fact, Anna Maria told him time and again, without anger, that he was a bad father. In that his children did not love and obey him, he supposed he was. He and Anna Maria disagreed about the children, but they no longer argued. They did not love each other so the arguments were purely cerebral, not passionate. He resolved, having lost the battle, to stop fighting the war.

Periodically, Anna Maria went back to Palermo, on her own, ostensibly for work, but really to see her husband, the loathsome Costacurta; sometimes she went and took the girls with her, and did not, according to the terms of their agreement, see Costacurta. Occasionally, he went back to Catania, for work, but really to see Agata, and spend blissful moments with her. Sometimes the boys came with him, and sometimes the girls, and sometimes all of them, to see their grandmother and aunts, to see little Calogero and baby Piero, and to see their various friends in the quarter. The girls liked to visit the quarter, to be 'home', particularly as it was no longer home; it was the place they came from, the place they had escaped. But Renato liked going to the quarter, because that really was his home, and there he saw his grandmother and aunts, and his cousin who was not his cousin, Gennaro, Omar's son, and Marco and Nino. The former had spent some of the summertime at the beach, but Marco hardly ever went anywhere, and Nino was there all summer, as his girlfriend Daniela had just given birth. When in Catania, Renato slept in the room that had been Francesco's, and which still contained all Francesco's stuff. In it, he had found the electronic key that opened the gym, and at various times he would take it and go down to the underground room where Marco, Nino and the others would meet.

It was here he met Dimitri Petrović.

All the boys were older than him, though some not that much older. All the boys knew who he was, and were respectful and wary of the boss's son, with two exceptions, the one being Nino and the other Marco. They, after all, were the most important boys in the quarter, and they had the boss's implicit permission to talk to his son, to befriend him. Marco was the boss's most trusted man when he wanted something done, and Nino, well, Nino was important to the boss too and licensed even to be cheeky to him on occasion, and to get away with what others would never dream of doing, at the price, of course, of the occasional beating. These two knew Renato and how to handle him; the others not so much; the others sensed Renato might be dangerous to them and were perhaps not brave enough to risk making overtures to the child. But Dimitri Petrović was different. He was vaguely aware that he had met him before, of course, but here he met him without his father, and here it was clear that Dimitri was very keen to be his friend. There was an intensity about him, a desire for his friendship, which was a little unsettling.

The first thing he noticed about Dimitri was what he was wearing: around his neck he had a large gold crucifix hanging from a weighty gold chain. In addition, there was a medallion of Our Lady of Lourdes, hanging from another chain, and a brown scapular. These signs of religious devotion were partially lost in a tangle of back curling chest hair. Once he had been rather unkempt in appearance, but he now had a neat haircut, and he had got rid of his beard. This quarter Serb three quarters Sicilian had intense dark eyes which were, once you noticed them - and Renato did - quite disturbing. The way he talked, too, was not relaxing in the slightest; his tone conveyed that the things of which he spoke were of the greatest importance. He had just been in the gym with Marco, lifting weights, something that Renato considered a waste of time, but which, Dimitri's tone conveyed, was a life-giving activity.

Renato regarded him attentively and curiously, thinking Dimitri reminded him of his uncle, don Renzo Santucci, whom his father often dismissed as mad. And it was very odd that at that very moment, Dimitri mentioned how he had met Renzo and his aunt Angela on a retreat for former drug-users, and how kind they had been, and how instructive it had been meeting them. Shortly after this, he had gone on a pilgrimage to Lourdes with a group from Sicily and met Angela Santucci again. Lourdes, he said, had been wonderful. It had changed his life.

Marco nodded and had said that he had heard Lourdes was remarkable and he wanted to go one day.

Later, he met Nino. They sat together on the Church steps, in sight of the windows of his father's flat. His father could no doubt see him but could not hear them. He recounted to Nino his meeting with Dimitri.

'He's become a religious maniac,' said Nino dismissively. 'He has even started going to Mass. He never went before. He wants to show everyone he is a changed man. They locked him up, but then they let him out, though he still has charges hanging over him: conspiracy to murder. He wants to show the world he is not that sort of person, he is just an innocent caught up in things he did not create. But it goes further. He has made friends with don Renzo and his aunt, has he? He is frightened. And he was friendly to you? Well, it makes sense. He is frightened the person who killed his grandfather and killed his father will want to kill him. He wants protection, that is all.'

'Will he get it?' asked Renato.

'We will see. Your father may decide he wants to protect him, give him protected status, as a compliment to donna Rosa, perhaps. As a way of showing he is the lord of not just death, but life as well.'

He looked at Renato.

'Don't be so serious,' he said, with a smile. 'Dimitri is fine, it is just that he is nervous, and perhaps guilty, and perhaps traumatised by seeing his father murdered, or knowing his father was murdered in the next room by the man he let into the house. What I mean is, Dimitri and the two Serb bodyguards are the witnesses who say it was a Serb who did it, and not someone else, not your brother. So, your father needs them. If it comes to a trial….'

'Will it?'

'It never seems to. This is Sicily. There is a statute of limitations, or there is not enough evidence, or people change their stories. But these people will not. Your brother has nothing to fear about the Petrović case or the Antonescu case. It was all this mysterious Serb, who was acting to revenge the one they hanged in Africa.'

'He's not my brother, he is my stepbrother,' said Renato.

'I thought you liked him,' said Nino casually.

'You did; you liked him. You are the one who liked him, and you betrayed him.'

'I thought you betrayed him,' said Nino.

'That does not count. I never liked him. He is an interloper, an impostor. I am the eldest son, not him. You know that.'

'I do,' said Nino. He paused. 'You told me about the gun, and I passed that on. The stupid police have told me that they have not found the gun, but they have found a bullet in the wall behind the sofa in the flat by the fountain of Arethusa, though no other forensic evidence, as the place had been cleaned so many times since then. But that is where he killed Antonescu. He would have been careful to get rid of the gun. You told me about the gun, and I passed it on to Daniela's father, and he will be very discrete about that. You told me about the tobacconist of Librino, which I already knew. But have you found out any more?'

The boy nodded.

'He is in Florence. That was what he told Paoluzzu. My father and Agata were discussing it. Agata is worried, but he has Paoluzzu's identity card and his passport, and he is using his bank account. He won't be in Florence forever, but he will travel around, and if he uses the passport, if they are told to look out for it…'

'They can arrest him,' said Nino. 'You have Paoluzzu's details, his name, date of birth, place of birth?'

Renato nodded again.

'It may not be soon,' said Nino. 'They don't check passports between France and Italy anymore.'

'I can wait,' said Renato. 'What is it my father calls it? A long game.'

It was a long game, and he waited, he watched, all that summer at Donnafugata. His father was there, some of the time, shuttling back and forth between there and Catania, where Agata, little Calogero and the baby were. His mother and his sisters were more frequently there, as Anna Maria had less work to do in the summer as it was, and could work from home too. Veronica was there, whom he loved and who loved him. His sisters spent their time lying by the pool, listening to music on their headphones, playing tennis, going to the beach, going out to dinner in nearby restaurants sometimes, watching the world from behind their dark glasses. His sisters, both in their different ways, adored him, as did their mother. He spent time with them by the pool, reading a book, wearing a pair of dark glasses himself; he played tennis with them, quite well too; he spent time in the kitchen with Veronica; and he spent time with his mother, in the glorious drawing-room, with the school of Murillo picture of the Madonna, sitting next to her on the sofa while she read, or dozed in the hottest part of the day, or watched DVD's of her favourite programmes which were designed to improve his English. Sometimes he played football and tennis with his younger brothers, who were almost like twins so much did they share. But he felt distanced from them, because though not much younger, they were his half-brothers, and they did not realise that adult life even existed. He did. Renato was like a man standing on a mountaintop, surveying the valley below, knowing that that was his destiny.

He was aware of the female adoration that surrounded him; and he was aware of the female dislike that was evident when his father came; Calogero was at Donnafugata on tolerance. Veronica did not like the signore, that was clear, and her lips had that compressed look whenever she saw him, or whenever he was mentioned. His sisters had long adopted, each in her own way, an air of not being impressed by their father, and of holding his treatment of Anna Maria against him. Anna Maria herself regarded her ex-husband as a fool who had failed to control his passionate impulses, quite ignoring the fact that such a verdict applied more to her than to him; but she tolerated him as a business partner.

The adult male part of the household was not much in evidence, being his father, only intermittently present. Renato adored his father and wanted to regain the position of beloved eldest son, which had been usurped by Francesco. His father came to spend time at Donnafugata with his children but gave the impression that he would rather be elsewhere, with Agata, with little Calogero, with the new baby, who had been born in mid-June, two months after Nino's son was born. He looked at his eldest son absent-mindedly, as if he had other, more important things to consider, which, in a way, he did. Agata was unhappy without Francesco. He too was unhappy without Francesco. He wanted Francesco back, but he had been told that he would, if he appeared, be arrested, for the murder of the tobacconist in Librino. Nothing, nothing at all, connected Francesco to the murder of Antonescu or Petrović; it was this unexpected thing, the murder of the tobacconist, which was proving so difficult. Or so he thought. Then Andreazza had come with disturbing news. The police, the useless police, had scored a success, raiding a flat, also in Librino, where a gunsmith turned starting pistols into something more deadly. The bullets he sold matched the bullets used to kill the tobacconist, and a similar bullet had been found in the wall of the place where Antonescu purportedly died. Moreover, someone had betrayed the fact that Francesco had had just such a gun. If they found the gun, now buried in the mud and reeds of the Arethusa fountain…. But who had known Francesco had had such a gun? Several people, all trustworthy. Several people including the not so trustworthy Dimitri. This gnawed at him. Had Dimitri betrayed Francesco, even inadvertently? Was Dimitri the one who was responsible for making his wife and indeed himself so unhappy?

Andreazza, though, had been soothing. They would abandon this line of enquiry soon enough, he was confident, because they had not found the weapon, which was surely in Syracuse harbour, irrecoverable. Calogero wished he could share his confidence. Andreazza said he thought the case would be abandoned in the autumn; then Francesco could come back, perhaps be interviewed, but nothing more, while the hunt for the mysterious non-existent Serb went on.

The tenth day of August, coincidentally the birthday of Giuseppe Santucci, was the date when all the associates throughout Sicily gathered for their meeting. The meeting this year would be heavily dominated by business concerns, and it was important to work out a strategy first; to that end he had invited, with the dottoressa's permission, of course, his sister and brother-in-law from Palermo, and Giuseppe Santucci as well. It was the latter who counted. Everyone knew that, even Renato.

A certain tension gripped the house at the thought of the visit. For a start, there were delicate negotiations to be done about the Catania Waterfront project and about the Furnaces; the settling of various loans; the dividing up of various profits. Every bit of business to be decided between Calogero and the Santucci family would take time, would be picked over very carefully. And the dottoressa would be in the middle of it, the mother of Calogero's children, not exactly neutral, which he knew the Palermo people resented. And not just the Palermo people, all the people, all the associates, would require something to be thrown their way, and that offer had to be worked out before the meeting. These sorts of financial negotiations were always nerve-wracking for Calogero. He preferred negotiations of the old-fashioned type, where the people who stood in your way surrendered to your will in abject humility. He liked dealing with dependants and clients, but he was not so at ease with dealing with equals. He could deal with the powerful people in Rome and elsewhere and enjoyed manipulating them. But equals needed careful handling, and luckily there were only two of them, his former wife and the mother of his children, Anna Maria, and this tiresome boy Giuseppe, as they now called him, Santucci. Then there was another class of people who were openly defiant, namely his mother, who made it clear she would do what she wanted, when she wanted, as she wanted, and his own daughters, especially the elder one Isabella. And now, most disappointingly of all, that camp of the defiant included his eldest, Renato, the boy who bore the name of his own father, the Chemist of Catania.

The negotiations were now over; everything was settled; at least the material things were settled. Anna Maria was satisfied that her investment was being rewarded; the other interested parties would have their own rewards, which included Giuseppe Santucci, and all the other associates. But now there was something else that had to be done, which was much harder. He had to sit with Beppe Santucci, whom he disliked so much, and he had to do his best to build up their friendship, even though this went against the grain, because on this friendship, so much hung. This was the axis on which everything depended, on which the whole of Sicily rested, the jobs and welfare of so many. War between them would ensure disaster. So, it had to be peace, for their own good and the good of all, and also for the good of the next generation.

The next generation's representative, his son Renato, was sitting next to him on the sofa, leaning against him, and he had his arm protectively round the boy, while Beppe sat in an armchair opposite him in the large drawing room of the house, where the Madonna, school of Murillo, a painting he had long considered inferior, dominated the room. Anna Maria was working in her study, the girls off playing tennis, and goodness knows where Renzo and his wife had got to. But the boy Renato had come in to join the two men, his father and his father's only rival, and he had not sent him away.

He reflected that when he had first met Beppe, Beppe had been the age Renato was now, a sweet little boy, who had now disconcertingly grown up into this rather challenging young man. In those days he had had a little boy's long hair and had been an engaging child. He remembered the time he had met him first, at Castelvetrano when they had driven over to announce to his relatives that Renzo was going to marry Elena. Now Beppe was tall and thin, angular, like his cousin Renzo, having all the family traits that made Renzo so unattractive; he had closely cut dark hair, and a very trim beard. Calogero loathed beards and forbade anyone who worked for him to have one, and he sometimes wondered if Beppe knew this (surely, he must) and had chosen to grow a beard just to annoy him. Or was he being obsessive?

Beppe's clothes too left a great deal to be desired. He never wore a suit but always wore jeans and trainers, and in the summer a series of undistinguished tee shirts. At Donnafugata he had been wearing some ill-fitting shorts and flipflops and an unfashionable bathing suit in the pool. All of this was unforgiveable, considering he was the richest man in Sicily. To make things worse, he had begun to speak (or so it seemed, for Calogero could not remember him speaking like this in the past) with a pronounced Palermo accent. If you saw him walking down the via Maqueda in Palermo, or if you heard him order a cup of coffee in one of the bars on the via Principe del Belmonte, you would think him just an ordinary person. And that, Calogero knew, was the entire point. It was clever, but it annoyed him.

'So, you have bought a salt pan?' Calogero was saying.

'Yeah,' agreed Beppe. 'It is quite a place; you should see it. And it even comes with a few buildings that can be converted into a boutique hotel. You know, it is fashionable. Like the Dead Sea. People go there and cover themselves in salt and they think it is good for them.'

'They do?'

Beppe nodded.

'And they were happy to sell?'

'Very. When they knew it was me. They know I am fair. And the other thing was the place had been making no money for years. But it will now. We are going to sell Sicilian salt, the large white flaky stuff, all over Europe and North America. And use it for the preserved lemons. The next thing I am looking for is a glass factory to make the bottles for the preserved lemons; really nice bottles, you know, the sort people will recognise as works of art. You should see the place where we are making the preserved lemons. Two hundred women working there. I decided that we would employ women, and in peak times, students on a temporary basis. It is good to see.'

'The first time I saw you, you showed me your father's lemons in Castelvetrano. What do you think of the lemons here?'

'Superb, Anna Maria is selling us her crop. Poor Papà, that was the day he tried to shoot my brother, and you stepped into the drama with Renzo and with Antonescu.'

He smiled, and Calogero knew why. That was the day that Renzo had failed to assert his authority, failed to take over the family. He could have shot the lot of them. But he had missed the opportunity. Calogero said nothing about this, but they both agreed on Renzo. He was a failure. They both despised him but tolerated him. Then Beppe frowned, remembering all the pain, grief and sorrow Renzo had caused. But even that had been put to good use.

'Do you miss Antonescu?' he asked.

Without having to look at him, Renato sensed that this question displeased his father, and that his father did not want to show he was displeased.

'I first knew Traiano when he was six years old, I think. I saw him grow up. I was fond of him. He was a bright fellow, a real spark of genius. But he became unhinged, didn't he, perhaps through no fault of his own. I feel sorry for his mother. But as for Traiano himself, he was not able to see things dispassionately. Few can take a step back from their own circumstances, but we all have to from time to time. As a result of that failure, he suffered a great deal, though other people's reputations came out of it enhanced.'

'You mean me?' asked Beppe.

'Of course I mean you,' said Calogero. 'And Muniddu. But not Renzo. One needs to be cold-blooded. To be too passionate is dangerous, and in this case it proved fatal.'

'What you say is true. And how is Francesco?' Beppe asked casually.

Calogero was annoyed by this and immediately felt himself become defensive. He was annoyed with Beppe asking, but he was more annoyed with himself. One had to be cold-blooded, and he knew he was failing in this regard. His chief failing was perhaps his passionate attachment to his wife Agata. How he loved her, how even thinking of her now made him long to be with her, made his blood run hot at the thought of her. How different it had been with Stefania, and even with Anna Maria. How desperately he had wanted a son with Stefania, and how disappointing it had been to have two daughters (one only realised how disappointing Isabella would be when she came to maturity) and what a struggle it had been to conceive Renato. And it had all been Stefania's fault, that was how he saw it now. The years before Renato's birth had been dry, sexless years. But now, life was so different. The only cloud was the absence of Francesco, whom his wife loved so much, and who he too loved so much.

'Francesco is travelling,' he said lightly. 'But he will be back.'

'I thought he was going to America. I was all ready to help when you asked me.'

'He changed his mind. He is a bit wilful, you know, being young, well, only a year or so younger than you. But generally, he is very obedient to me. I have trained him well, I hope. Tell me,' he continued, changing the subject. 'How are your family?'

If he meant his drunken father, or his sister, Beppe ignored this.

'Rosalia is well. She is in Naples and enjoying her course. I don't see much of her. I would love to go to Naples more often, but, what with the salt project and the preserved lemons and the office and being at university myself, I have little time. Little Emilio is a sweet child, and Riccardo, well, Riccardo has been a bit unhappy, and his father has been a little unhappy with him. I have been there to make peace between them. The thing is that it is over between him and this girl in Rome. She was not the right sort of girl for him, as his father pointed out; I agreed, though I did not say so, thinking things could be let to flow naturally, run their course. Well, I am as glad as his father is that it is over, though Riccardo is not, and I hope he meets someone better soon. That would be the best cure. I told him he should be submissive to his father, see the world with his eyes…'

'All boys should. I am sure he will. He is a good boy,' said Calogero. 'You see,' he added, addressing his own son. 'Be submissive and see the world with your father's eyes.'

'Were you submissive when you were a boy?' asked Renato.

'Your grandfather was often away from home, working, so there was no one to be submissive to,' said Calogero.

'I think you did what you liked,' said Renato. 'You got into fights, you stole things, and you slept with ladies, all when you were my age.'

'Who tells you this nonsense?' asked his father.

'Isabella,' he said. 'My grandmother, my aunts, Marco, Nino, people like that. They don't know the whole story, but they know bits, and I have put it all together.'

'No, you have not,' said Calogero calmly. 'You think you know, but you do not know. The person who knows is me. You were not there, none of them were there; my sisters were there, but they knew very little; and my mother even less. I was just a normal boy. My father, your grandfather, was hardly ever there, so perhaps I was a bit wild; maybe I needed the discipline he would have administered. We did not have much money. There were lots of fights in Purgatory in those days, so one had to look after oneself and one did. If I got into fights, I made sure I won them. Just be grateful you will never have to fight anyone. And if we stole things, it was only because we were poor.'

'You were not poor. Grandpa was a science teacher, wasn't he, at least to start with, and then he must have made a lot of money blowing people up for the Santucci family, for don Lorenzo and don Domenico. Your grandfather and great-uncle,' he added, looking at Beppe. 'Everyone knows about the Chemist of Catania.'

'Yes, everyone does,' said Calogero with great calmness. 'Everyone has heard the story without knowing the facts, and the people who never knew him have woven a tale that is a true as the story of

…. Robin Hood. People love gossip and fantasy. But you, my son, should not. You should ignore what people say.'

'Actually, you shouldn't,' said the boy reasonably. 'Because when people talk in this way, it gives you, Papà, the reputation that makes people co-operate with you. It makes you important. It makes me important. It makes all these people want to be your friend. Just like Beppe. Isn't that right?' he asked, turning to Beppe.

'Isn't that right, *sir*,' said his father correcting him. 'And you call him 'don Giuseppe'. Have some respect.'

'Oh, I do,' said the boy. 'When you were my age, you went to bed with Antonescu's mother. I heard my aunts talk about it, in whispered voices. And you never got over it. And I know what happened to Uncle Rosario….'

The boy was silent, because he realised that he had said enough, indeed too much.

His father did not reply but looked at Beppe.

'How many children are you going to have, Giuseppe?' he asked.

'Some, but it is a long way off, as we are not even engaged yet, but we will be soon; though we won't be marrying for some years. But some, definitely some,' answered Beppe calmly.

'Children are a trial,' said Calogero. 'A joy and a trial. This clever little fellow,' he continued, meaning his son, 'goes out of his way to provoke me at every step. I am not sure why. Maybe it is what he inherited from the mother he never knew. Maybe it is because I have not been a good father, or so he thinks. But he does not realise, at least not yet, that everything I have done is for him and his sisters and brothers. That they will live lives of comfort because of my hard decisions and my hard work. This boy is the child of the second richest man in Sicily, for I assume you are the richest, yet he feels aggrieved and ungrateful, and above all he is disobedient, and he fails to understand.' He drew his arm tightly around Renato. 'He fails to see that the decisions I make are for his good. You, Giuseppe, you know what our world is like, a world of competition, a world of rivalry, yes, I had a brother, you had a brother too, and an uncle, I seem to remember. We all have had friends and relations whom we loved in our own way, but who are no longer with us. It was hard for us, but maybe harder for them. But we chose this world; you chose this; you could have been like your sister Marina, in America. But no, you stayed, you took part, you gambled, you won. But this is not the life I want for Renato. Renato is not cut out for it. That is why he is going to school in England. This is not his world, Sicily is not for him, except as a holiday destination. He is soft boy.'

'I am not,' said Renato, between grinding teeth.

'Yes, you are,' said his father.

The boy burst into tears and ran from the room. There was silence for some time.

'Did you kill your brother?' asked Beppe.

'So it is rumoured. But it is not on my conscience, any more than Sandro is on yours. Or Tonino Grassi, or any others, the Ginori family, for example.'

'Some things are necessary,' said Beppe. 'As you know. I learned from you.'

'I am flattered.'

'Francesco....'

'I am confident that he will be back, and all will be resolved,' said Calogero firmly.

Towards the end of August, Calogero returned for a few days to Catania, to be with Agata, little Calogero and Piero; he felt he had been neglecting them. Renato came with him, but not the girls and the younger boys.

Catania, always so crowded, now seemed deserted, so searing was the heat, from which the only shelter was some air-conditioned interior or the beach, or the mountain. Marco was absent; most of the boys who filled the underground room in the gym were absent as well; one evening, late, Renato found the place seemingly empty, entering with the key that had been Francesco's. But he saw clothes that he recognised as Nino's on the bench, and that someone was having a shower. He sat down to wait, without making a noise. A moment later, the water ceased, and Nino entered.

'I thought I was alone,' he said, registering the presence, not exactly welcome, of the younger boy. 'Someone might come in,' he added.

'Someone did, I did,' said Renato, with affectionate contempt. 'Aren't you pleased to see me? You used to be. I mean when you used to kiss me and put your hand down my trousers. Yes, I know, that was the search for information, not the search for love.'

'Look,' said Nino, hurriedly dressing. 'That was a mistake. You are the boss's son. He would kill me, and more importantly, from your point of view, he would kill you. Well, not kill you, but send you away.'

'He is sending me away, haven't you heard?'

'How lucky you are,' said Nino. 'You get to leave. For the rest of us, it is not so easy.'

'Oh, you could leave,' said Renato, 'But I will always be his son. There is no escaping from that. Don't be sad or cross. How is your son?'

'Very well. The reason I am here is that the bathroom there is full of baby stuff, and I needed a bit of peace.'

He sat next to Renato on the bench and sighed.

'I don't hold it against you,' said Renato. 'I enjoyed myself. And the information I gave, I gave willingly. I would have given it without the favours you bestowed. You see, I hate him so much, I would do anything to make him suffer. I love him, and he does not love me at all.'

'Your father does love you,' said Nino.

'Not my father, you fool! Francesco. I loved him, but he never paid me enough attention. He cared about Petra, he cared about Paoluzzu, but he didn't care about me. That was unforgiveable. At least you did not ignore me.'

'You will grow out of it,' said Nino. 'You will get interested in girls…'

'That is what my father thinks, I am sure,' said Nino with a smile. 'That is why he is sending me off to a boarding school with 300 other boys.'

He laughed. After a time, so did Nino.

'Why did *you* hate Francesco so much?' asked Renato.

'Oh, the oldest reasons of all: jealousy and the desire for revenge,' said Nino.

'I know how old you are,' said Renato suddenly. 'You are a child like me. You are fourteen.'

'I was. I was fifteen two weeks ago,' said Nino proudly.

The heart of Sicily was burned brown by the heat of late summer, and on the other side of Mount Etna, far from the sea, as the very same evening brought some cooler breezes, a group of boys were playing football in the flood-lit courtyard next to one of the parish churches of the town of Caltagirone. As the game drew to a close, they were aware of the parents and elder siblings who had come to collect them as the session of play ended, and they were aware of one of the adults, a young man, an elder brother perhaps or even a father, who was a relative stranger, who was seen but infrequently at these events; perhaps one of the many Sicilians who worked on the continent, in Italy or Germany or Belgium or France. He was a big, silent man, and his attention was fixed on one child in particular. The way he looked at him made it clear to any observer that this was a special relationship. The boy himself had spotted the stranger, and knew he had to concentrate on the game, and could not break away to greet him, much as he wanted to. But at last, the final whistle blew, and he was free to run to the stranger. He threw his arms around him, and kissed him, and was so moved by joy that he was unable to speak.

'Does Mama know you are here, Papà?' he asked at last.

'Yes, I saw her, and she told me you were here, and I came to fetch you myself, while she did some extra shopping,' said Marco.

'She must be happy to see you, but not as happy as me,' said the boy. 'Are you staying long?' he asked.

'A couple of days. Then I have to work.'

'I wish you would take me with you,' said the boy, who was eight. 'I could help you.'

'No need. You need to stay here, go to school, and work hard at that. It is nice here.'

It was indeed. They walked down a quiet narrow street and came to the house, which he had entered earlier that afternoon, when he had surprised the Widow. He liked to surprise her, liked to keep her on her toes, liked the idea that she could not rely on the timing of his visits. The last had been three months ago. He had rung the bell, and she had answered. He had placed his bag on the sofa, and they had moved to the bedroom at once, where he had loosened his belt and experienced a few moments of blessed sexual relief. The Widow was now fifty, and he had first had this experience with her when he had been sixteen or so, which had led to the birth of the boy, who was called Bruno. She had been, in those days, but recently widowed, and left with two small sons. Marco, who made few demands of her, suited her. He had sent her to Caltagirone when the child was two years old; he had paid for everything and was extremely generous. His visits were irregular and infrequent. She knew he came for the child, not for her; he was a good father, and that was important; and he had been good to her other two sons. If he was a good father, she was a good mother, and her three sons her main concern. She had been very glad to leave Catania, a dangerous place, not for her own sake, for who would harm her, but for that of her three sons. The little boy was a delight, the elder two diligent and obedient; it was nice to be able to bring them up away from the temptations of Catania. Caltagirone was a quiet place, full of good people, the sort of place where little happened. Her boys were all of them doing well.

and could not break away to greet him, much as he wanted to. But at last, the final whistle blew, and he was free to run to the stranger. He threw his arms around him, and kissed him, and was so moved by joy that he was unable to speak.

'Does Mama know you are here, Papà?' he asked at last.

'Yes, I saw her, and she told me you were here, and I came to fetch you myself, while she did some extra shopping,' said Marco.

'She must be happy to see you, but not as happy as me,' said the boy. 'Are you staying long?' he asked.

'A couple of days. Then I have to work.'

'I wish you would take me with you,' said the boy, who was eight. 'I could help you.'

'No need. You need to stay here, go to school, and work hard at that. It is nice here.'

It was indeed. They walked down a quiet narrow street and came to the house, which he had entered earlier that afternoon, when he had surprised the Widow. He liked to surprise her, liked to keep her on her toes, liked the idea that she could not rely on the timing of his visits. The last had been three months ago. He had rung the bell, and she had answered. He had placed his bag on the sofa, and they had moved to the bedroom at once, where he had loosened his belt and experienced a few moments of blessed sexual relief. The Widow was now fifty, and he had first had this experience with her when he had been sixteen or so, which had led to the birth of the boy, who was called Bruno. She had been, in those days, but recently widowed, and left with two small sons. Marco, who made few demands of her, suited her. He had sent her to Caltagirone when the child was two years old; he had paid for everything and was extremely generous. His visits were irregular and infrequent. She knew he came for the child, not for her; he was a good father, and that was important; and he had been good to her other two sons. If he was a good father, she was a good mother, and her three sons her main concern. She had been very glad to leave Catania, a dangerous place, not for her own sake, for who would harm her, but for that of her three sons. The little boy was a delight, the elder two diligent and obedient; it was nice to be able to bring them up away from the temptations of Catania. Caltagirone was a quiet place, full of good people, the sort of place where little happened. Her boys were all of them doing well.

'Your father does love you,' said Nino.

'Not my father, you fool! Francesco. I loved him, but he never paid me enough attention. He cared about Petra, he cared about Paoluzzu, but he didn't care about me. That was unforgiveable. At least you did not ignore me.'

'You will grow out of it,' said Nino. 'You will get interested in girls…'

'That is what my father thinks, I am sure,' said Nino with a smile. 'That is why he is sending me off to a boarding school with 300 other boys.'

He laughed. After a time, so did Nino.

'Why did *you* hate Francesco so much?' asked Renato.

'Oh, the oldest reasons of all: jealousy and the desire for revenge,' said Nino.

'I know how old you are,' said Renato suddenly. 'You are a child like me. You are fourteen.'

'I was. I was fifteen two weeks ago,' said Nino proudly.

The heart of Sicily was burned brown by the heat of late summer, and on the other side of Mount Etna, far from the sea, as the very same evening brought some cooler breezes, a group of boys were playing football in the flood-lit courtyard next to one of the parish churches of the town of Caltagirone. As the game drew to a close, they were aware of the parents and elder siblings who had come to collect them as the session of play ended, and they were aware of one of the adults, a young man, an elder brother perhaps or even a father, who was a relative stranger, who was seen but infrequently at these events; perhaps one of the many Sicilians who worked on the continent, in Italy or Germany or Belgium or France. He was a big, silent man, and his attention was fixed on one child in particular. The way he looked at him made it clear to any observer that this was a special relationship. The boy himself had spotted the stranger, and knew he had to concentrate on the game,

She had had a husband, and he had died. She did not think of him often. The manner of his death had been painful for her. Then Marco had come along, and, though no more than a big child himself, had made love to her in the impersonal and hurried way that some men had. When she had realised the consequences of their encounter, she had informed him that she would get rid of it. He had forbidden this and made it clear that he would look after her and the child. That suited her. She was not interested in sex, or what magazines called a relationship; but she wanted security. He had offered security. Over the years he had always made love to her in the usual way on his visits, just to show that, well, they belonged together, as she was the mother of his child. But there was never any talk of marriage. That would have been ridiculous, she knew, instinctively. She also knew that he never looked at other women. He had not said so; she just knew.

She was, of course, completely right. Marco felt no desire for any woman at all, even the Widow herself. He made love to her on his visits as a matter of form, almost a matter of politeness, and as a way of ensuring that she knew she belonged to him and could not belong to anyone else, not that that was likely. The Widow was sturdy and uninviting, from that point of view, as was Marco himself. Sexual intercourse was a rite; a ceremony; a duty, but one carried out by a non-believer, as a matter of form. As he walked along, he felt his son's hand in his, he listened to the boy's chatter about how pleased he was to have Papà at home for a few days, and he knew that was what love really was: its object was not the woman, but the child.

They arrived at the house, and found the Widow in the kitchen, preparing something delicious. Marco liked her cooking almost as much as he liked his mother's. The two other boys, one seventeen, the other sixteen, entered soon afterwards; they had been minding the shop that their mother kept, which sold ceramics. They were pleased and slightly alarmed to see Marco. They bent over his hand and kissed it and then kissed his cheek. They were polite and very respectful, and they called him 'sir.' They knew that their entire financial position depended on him. Both boys were at school and helped in the shop in the holidays and on Saturdays. The shop did not sell much, but it provided an excuse for their income which came, they all knew, from Marco.

They sat down at the table, and the two boys answered his questions about their schoolwork, about what they had done in the holidays, the team games they played, their friends, the things they were reading, and how much they were both looking forward to going back to school in October. As they answered, they looked nervously to their mother who, they both knew, would rapidly rebut anything not strictly accurate. But they were both good boys; large, somewhat ungainly like their mother; they loved Marco and feared him as well; they knew they had to do their very best to please him, and what would happen if he were less than pleased. He was generous to them, and they owed him much.

The small boy, Bruno, the beloved son, spoke about all the things that had happened since Papà had been there last. Smaller than his brothers, naturally, though promising to grow to the same size, like them he was intelligent, but unlike them, in his father's presence, he was effervescent. His mother looked at him with satisfaction and adoration, and his father likewise. His two elder siblings also looked at him with devotion. The three of them were very close, very strongly united, which pleased Marco. His son, his beloved son, the person he loved most in the world, the one he strove to protect and whom he kept away from the corruption of Catania, was loved and happy.

The flat was not big, as it was thought best to keep a low profile, not to attract too much attention: there were two bedrooms, one for the elder two boys, and one for Bruno and his mother. They finished their supper – the cold pasta with cherry tomatoes and aubergine had been delicious – and then the Widow and the middle boy did the washing up while Marco discussed with the eldest his plans for university the autumn after next. He had promised to pay, but he wanted to know what he was paying for; he made it clear that hard work was expected. Then they all went to bed, first the boys, then the Widow, then Marco. He put on his pyjamas and got into the wide double bed; between himself and the widow lay their son, already asleep. It was at this moment that Marco gave thanks to God for this great gift he had received, that of a loving child. That of someone whom he could love and who loved him.

'Then everything is well?' he asked the Widow in a whisper, so as not to wake the sleeping boy.

'Everything,' she said, 'Everything. And you?'

'Everything,' he said, wondering if she believed this, but knowing that she did not really want to know. There was a distance between Catania and hilltop Caltagirone that should not be crossed. Well, he was allowed to cross it, once in a while, but no one else. Sometimes he wondered if he should send them further away, somewhere safer.

'You have been going to church?' he asked.

'Every Sunday,' she answered, knowing how particular he was on this subject. 'And the boys all go to confession at least once a month.'

He nodded, reassured.

'The parish is going to Lourdes in the last week of September,' she said.

She never asked for anything, he knew, and he thought of the four of them at the shrine in the foothills of the Pyrenees. He would never go himself. But it would be nice for them to go, his son, his son's mother, his son's half-brothers.

'Then you must go, even if it is expensive,' he said. 'All of you. I want you to go. Have you discussed it with them?'

'I didn't want to get their hopes up. Valerio,' this was the eldest boy, 'is getting more and more religious. And Mario is not far behind.'

'Well, that is good,' he said.

The Widow was silent, possibly asleep. He looked at her, then at his son. He whispered a prayer: 'Stretch out your hands to us, living and dying, Mary Immaculate, Mother of God.' He felt a sense of reassurance and comfort.

Outside, Caltagirone was at peace, except for the distant barking of a dog.

Printed in Dunstable, United Kingdom